Tonight, I will return to my Book Club.

It's been half a year since I've been to a meeting. The women will be kind, I know. Solicitous, perhaps even wary not to say anything that will bring to mind my tragedy. I hope I don't see pity in their eyes. It is not pity I need now, but understanding. Tender words and outstretched hands that will help me break my long isolation and rekindle the kinship with my friends.

And we are friends. Doris and I began the club out of desperation fifteen years ago. We were both new mothers living on the same block with a need for companionship, intellectual stimulation— and baby-sitters. The Book Club grew as our children did, new members joining, old members moving away, but always the core remained: Me, Doris, Midge and Gabriella. And now Annie.

I know my long absence has been a drain on the group. They're worried about me. And I miss my Book Club. I miss reading the books and discussing them. The books are key to the group, to what makes our discussions work. They provide a forum that is safe, so that during our meetings we can share our ideas, and later, our problems. And later still, our secrets. Mostly, however, I miss my friends. They are the true magic of the group. I see my life as a story, one I share with my Book Club. And though there are some surprises, there is no resolution. I am like you. My story could be yours.

"A heart-wrenching, sensitive tale that will delight readers...."
—*Painted Rock Reviews*
on *Girl in the Mirror*

MARY ALICE MONROE

THE BOOK CLUB

MIRA

Grateful acknowledgment is made to Rachel W. Jacobsohn for permission to print a passage from her book *The Reading Group Handbook*. Reprinted by permission of the author.

ISBN 1-55166-530-1

THE BOOK CLUB

Visit us at www.mirabooks.com

Printed in U.S.A.

To Markus
Grow old along with me!
The best is yet to be.

Acknowledgment

The Wednesday Night Book Club is more than a group of women who gather once a month to discuss books. It's a sisterhood. We are the best of friends, who have laughed and cried together. We have covered a great number of personal stories over the years.

None of which are included in this book! I know it will be tempting to scan the book to see if I've woven bits and pieces of these stories in these pages, but I haven't. I wouldn't dare! If anyone sees anything or anyone they recognize, it is because I have tried to portray glimpses of all women in Eve, Annie, Doris, Midge and Gabriella. Rather, it is a sense of camaraderie, support and friendship that I've shared within my book club that I've tried to convey in this story. And for that—and so much more—I'd like to thank:

Marguerite Abramson, Judy Beck, Paulette Collias, Ruth Ellen Cryns, Cindy Grotefeld, Anna Maria Kostecki, Jean Magee, Mary Lynn Owen, Susan Pagadala, Mary Pellegrini, Carmel Perrone Pearson, Diana Rasche, Roberta Scotto, Joan Slanina and Grace Weber

Prologue

Eve of Return

January 7, 1998

Tonight, I will return to my Book Club.

It's been half a year since I've been to a meeting. The women will be kind, I know. Solicitous, perhaps even wary not to say anything that will bring to mind my tragedy. I hope I don't see pity in their eyes. It is not pity I need now but understanding. Tender words and outstretched hands that will help me break my long isolation and re-kindle the kinship with my friends.

And we are friends. Doris and I began the club out of desperation fifteen years ago. We were both new mothers living on the same block with a need for companionship, intellectual stimulation—and baby-sitters. Back in 1983, the club was really a combination Book-LeLeche-Baby-sitting Club. The Book Club grew as our children did, new members joining, old members moving away, but always the core remained: me, Doris, Midge and Gabriella. And now Annie. We've gone through meetings where many of us had a child locked to our breasts, meetings where someone nodded, half-awake, on the sofa after a night up with a sick child, and meetings where, for no explicable reason, we drank too much wine and barely discussed the books at all. Today, most of our children are poised for leaving and once more we search for books to give this new phase of our lives meaning.

I know my long absence has been a drain on the group. They're worried about me. Annie phoned me twice already to see whether I was coming tonight. I read the previous month's book, a biography of Eleanor Roosevelt, but I had little to say on the topic of an intelligent, determined woman who triumphed in the face of personal adversity. I wonder if the group didn't choose the book especially for my benefit, perhaps to give me inspiration or as an effort to make my reentry positive. My life is not filled with triumphs. Whose is?

I grew up in a comfortable suburb outside of Chicago, and like most of the women in the Book Club, am a product of the Catholic school system of the 1950s. We can all laugh now when a book makes reference to the Baltimore catechism or flocks of nuns shrouded in starched wimples and jangling rosaries. We relish books that bring us back to that innocent time when we played without fear in the streets on summer nights till 10:00 p.m. How many books chronicled our era's passage from Motown to the Beatles and finally to acid rock? Or the painful choices of the Vietnam War years? All of us knew boys who wore either military uniforms or peace signs, or perhaps one who fled across the border, never to be heard from again. Now some of us know husbands—no longer young but aging without grace—who break family ties and flee. We devour stories about them, wondering, shivering.

I miss my Book Club. I miss reading the books and discussing them. The books are the key to the group, to what makes our discussions work. They provide a forum that is safe, so that during our meetings we can share our ideas, and later, our problems. And later still, our secrets. Mostly, however, I miss my friends. They are the true magic of the group. I see my life as a story, one I share with my Book Club. And though there are some surprises, there is no resolution. I am like you. My story could be yours.

One day, quite suddenly, my story changed. The setting shifted. The characters were rocked. If this were a plot diagram, my plummet was off the paper. The only constant was the point of view: first person, me, looking outward and inward, and seeing nothing.

I didn't see it coming. I guess that's what writers like to call "the element of surprise," that jolt from nowhere that catapults the hero into a new direction. The old gun-in-the-drawer trick. Whether the story is a mystery, a romance, an adventure, a comedy or a drama—in real life it's a combination of all of the above—you just don't know what's coming next.

For me, the change came on June 21, 1997. On that day, the corpse fell through the roof.

One

> All life is a story, and daily each of us collects stories.
>
> —Rachel Jacobsohn, *The Reading Group Handbook*

June 21, 1997

Eve Porter stepped out from her house into the brilliance of an early morning sun. She immediately raised her palm to shield her eyes; the piercing light was too strong.

Inside, her house was quiet and dark. Bronte and Finney were asleep in their rooms, the dog was whining, and she hadn't yet had a cup of coffee. Tom was prowling the rooms with nervous energy, gathering his work and packing last-minute items into his suitcase. Most mornings Eve liked to linger over her coffee, open the windows to the fresh morning breezes and relish her few moments of solitude before the family's demands pressed her into action. On this morning, Eve felt driven outdoors by her husband's prickly tension and a nagging guilt she resented. She needed some distance, just a bit of fresh air.

Eve remembered the days when she stayed one step behind Tom as he prepared to go on a business trip. "Here are your tickets. I found your beeper. Can I order you a cab? Don't you want anything for breakfast? Let me refresh your coffee." She was his trusty sidekick, or as Tom often put it, he was the captain and she the navigator.

Lately, however, she felt the ship was going down. For no one reason she could articulate, she'd begun looking for lifeboats. It wasn't so much that she doubted the competence of Tom, it was just that the buttons of his jacket didn't shine quite as bright anymore. Or perhaps the voyage was just too long.

Eve shook these mutinous thoughts out of her mind and stepped out into the morning air. "Today will be a good day," she said firmly, silencing her heart murmuring, "He will *not* ruin my day." She made her way toward the rustling breezes and birdsong in her garden, turning away from the closed, dark house. The early-morning air smelled sweet and the sun shone softly on the cheery colors of her perennial bed. She bent to admire droplets of dew cupped in the furry leaf of a lady's mantle.

Today was the first day of summer, she realized, her spirits lifting like a kite. She loved milestones of any sort: birthdays, anniversaries, holidays, checks on the calendar, notches on a growth chart. Today would be special, brand-new. She felt it deep inside. Summer was here with sunny days and balmy nights, the informality of barbecues and dips in the swimming pool. She was so relieved to have the grind of the school year finished. She missed playing with her children.

She really should wake them to say goodbye to their father, but they were so tired; she'd let them sleep a bit longer. Finney had a football game at noon and Bronte wanted a ride to the mall at two. With Tom gone for a few days, and the children out of school, she could relax a bit herself. Perhaps even squeeze in a little extra time in her garden this morning, she thought, noting that her to-bacco plants needed deadheading.

She slipped to her knees, relishing the coolness of the morning dew that soaked the thin cotton of her pajamas. She no longer expected anyone to help her with the weed-ing or the planting. The children had complained so bit-terly for so many years that she'd stopped demanding their time, and Tom, well, he never had the time or the interest. They had such busy lives and it was her job, as the mother and wife, to make certain all went smoothly in the home. But it was such a large home…and theirs was a large prop-erty, too, one of the largest in Riverton. The children were proud of their home and this she felt was her success. She'd decorated the twelve rooms herself, sewn countless yards of drapes and coordinated all the improvements. She'd even landscaped the entire lot, planting with her own delicate hands over fifty shrubs and countless perennials.

Gardening was her hobby after all, she told herself as she dug in the earth. No one asked her to plant these flow-ers that she adored. So why should she expect them to help? And wasn't it the mother's job, even duty, to make a home run smoothly? Wasn't she indispensable? Still, the thought that no one offered to help rankled as she reached to pull out the offending weeds, careful to get the roots.

The front door swung open and she lifted her gaze to see her husband hurry down the stone steps on his way to the garage. His coattails were flying, he was tripping over his luggage and he sent off sparks of irritation that she could feel clear across the garden. Though his dark suit was immaculate, his white shirt was gleaming and his tie had enough panache to be discreetly admired, her knowing eyes picked up the tight line of his lips that gave his chis-eled, tanned face a tautness too familiar of late. Tom wasn't a vain man. His hair might be thinning at the crown and his waist fuller, but Tom Porter still had movie-star good looks—looks that would have been a hindrance to his medical career except for the sharp intelligence and compassion in his dark eyes.

Eve didn't see his eyes this morning, however, because the light was too bright. She squinted and caught only the shadow of his passing.

"I'll phone you tonight," he called over his shoulder with a distracted air.

She didn't reply and instead rested her hands on her thighs and watched him raise the trunk of his sedan, then toss in his new garment bag. Next he gingerly rested his computer bag beside it. Eve knew exactly what was in that overnight bag she'd purchased for him for his fiftieth birthday. She'd laid in bed last night with her hands clenched in her lap silently watching as he packed it. The memory still irked.

"Why do you always wait until the last minute to pack?" she'd asked crossly. "It's almost midnight, Tom. I'm tired and we have to get up early. Your plane leaves at seven so you'll have to leave by six."

"I didn't have time to do it any earlier." His tone was sharp and he tossed a folded boxed shirt into the bag with an angry flip.

Eve bit her tongue, knowing this was true. She didn't wish to annoy him when he was so pressed for time. Still, she couldn't help the frustration boiling inside her. It didn't seem to concern him in the least that she would be kept awake for as long as it took him to pack.

"Why didn't you ask me to help? All I needed was your schedule. I'd have been happy to do it for you."

"I told you I was leaving."

"Yes," she replied in a tone that implied *How can you*

be so obtuse? "But I didn't know to where, or for what, until yesterday."

She used to always know where he was going, what topic he was speaking on, and made a game of packing for him. They'd laughed when she held ties up to his face and test-kissed him to make her selection. She took such pride in his appearance, as she did in her children's. Recently, however, the trips piled one on top of the other as his reputation grew. He'd sometimes forget to tell her when he was going out of town until he needed something, and then he'd inform her as an afterthought. Like yesterday's *"Oh, Eve, could you make sure I have enough shirts for San Diego?"* Whether she'd lost track of his schedule or he'd stopped sharing it with her, she couldn't remember anymore. All she knew was that somehow, she no longer packed for him. So she lay in bed, still and hard-limbed, watching.

"Look, just let me get it done," he said, rummaging through his closet, laying her aside. "Go on to sleep. I'll be a while yet."

She heard his dismissal, closed her mouth and folded her arms across her chest. In a cool silence that had grown over the past years, she watched him pack for the two-day trip, knowing exactly how he reasoned his choices. Three pairs of underwear, two fresh and an extra to change into should he go for a swim, two pairs of dark, cashmere wool socks and a spare polo shirt. He selected three Egyptian cotton shirts and a matching Hermés tie, a swimsuit, a flask of Scotch because he liked to work late in his room and, finally, the leather toiletries case. She'd meant to ask him why he still carried condoms in his bag now that she'd had her tubes tied, but never did.

She knew he wasn't fooling around and didn't want him to think that she didn't trust him. They'd been married for twenty-three years next month and a woman knew her husband well enough after all that time. She and Tom had an agreement, one forged on their wedding night and held sacred. They'd sworn that neither one of them would have an affair without first telling the other. Divorce or whatever might follow, but they'd vowed to have honor and respect in their marriage. They prided themselves on their honesty.

Kneeling in the garden with the sun's heat pressing on her back, Eve envisioned those condoms in that toiletry bag and her bare hands dug into the black soil as she forced out a deep dandelion root. A large worm clung to the soil around the weed, wriggling and coiling when she shook it off. She heard the car trunk slam shut and raised her eyes again.

"Honey, what hotel will you be at?" she called out.

"Oh, I don't remember."

He sounded winded and she cocked her head, her hands still in the soil. He stood looking at her with an odd expression on his face, as though he were waiting for her to say something more, or perhaps he was wrestling with what to say to her. Her breath stilled and her attention focused as she studied him for some signal, one hint that he wanted a kiss goodbye or a familiar pat on the rear as he hugged her. He used to love to hug her.

A new stubbornness kept her from leaping up and running into his arms as she always had before, a tenuous clinging to self-esteem after his rebuff in bed last night. She would not go to him first.

Keeping her silence, staying in place, she noticed his hair was damp with perspiration. He was a heavy sweater—all the Porters were—but it wasn't that hot this morning and he'd just come outdoors from the air-conditioning. He'd need a shower by the time he got to San Diego, she worried.

"I'll call you when I get there," he said, and her ears perked at the hint of sadness in his voice. "Give you my room number."

This was the usual modus operandi these days, unlike back when she carefully posted the hotel name and number on the kitchen bulletin board, up high beside the car pool schedule, the pizza lunch schedule and emergency telephone number. She nodded and opened her mouth to say goodbye, to wish him a good trip, maybe to say I love you, but he'd already turned his back.

She bent over her garden and dug her small, oval nails into the soil, squeezing it between her fingers. Her eyes swam in water, and through the white noise of pain in her ears, she heard the car door slam, the roar of an engine and the grind of tires along dry cement. When the sound of his car disappeared, she felt a tremendous sense of loss. They couldn't continue on like this, she thought, sniffing loudly. When he came home they'd have a long talk, maybe go out to dinner. Wiping her eyes with her elbow, she methodically tugged out scores of the tiny invasive clovers, ripping them out one by one, quick and neat.

By six o'clock that evening Tom was long out of her thoughts. Her day was busy and she didn't have time to dwell. In truth, Tom was gone so much of the time lately that she'd learned to cope without him. She was chief cook and bottle washer around here. The children depended on her. She knew she was the axis upon which their worlds spun. On this first day of summer, Finney had won the football game for his team with a score in the last quarter and Bronte had come home with a triumphant smile and bags of clothes she'd bought on sale at Nordstrom's with her birthday money. Eve wiped her hands at the sink, feeling especially pleased with herself because, despite all the chauffeuring, she'd found time to shop at the farmer's market and bake an angel food cake to serve with the fresh berries. She'd surprise the children and serve it with a cheery, "Happy first day of summer!"

"Children, dinner!" she called up the stairs. After hearing their mumbled replies from behind closed bedroom doors, she hurried out the door to her garden to pluck a few flowers for the table. So early in the season, it was slim pickings. Many of the flowers were just gaining ground. She stood with her chin in her palm, considering the selection.

"Mom! Telephone!" Finney's voice cracked on the final syllable.

She smiled, then checked her watch. "Is it a solicitation?" She couldn't abide those pesty calls at the dinner hour. She snipped off one rose, then two more, careful of the slant. After a moment, she heard Finney again.

"Mom! She says it's important."

Irritation tightened her lips. These telephone solicitors were getting so cagey. "Well, who is it?"

"She says she's from San…San…something hospital."

Eve felt a chill and a cloud passed overhead. For a moment, time seemed to stand still. As though she were a remote stranger looking through a lens, she turned her head and saw her world, sharpening the focus. She saw her lovely redbrick Prairie-style house with its imposing porte cochere lined in front by broad-leafed rhododendron, the shadow of her fourteen-year-old daughter in the windows on her way to the dining room for dinner with a telephone to her ear, her lanky twelve-year-old son leaning against the frame of the open front door awaiting her instructions with the impatience of youth. This was her perfect world and instinctively she knew she'd better take a good last look.

Her breath exhaled in a prayer. "You're just being ridiculous," she told herself. She had such a flair for the dramatic. Tom was on grand rounds at San Diego Hospital. It was a message from him. What was the matter with her lately?

"Tell them I'm coming!" she called to Finney. She gathered the roses, then ran up the front steps, surprised at how wobbly her knees felt. She ignored Finney's darkened gaze and went straight to the phone lying on the kitchen counter.

"Hello," she managed to get out through dry lips. "This is Mrs. Porter."

"Hello, Mrs. Porter," came the soft, even tones of the faceless woman. "This is Dr. Raphaelson at San Diego Medical Center."

"Yes, what can I do for you?"

"Are you married to a Dr. Thomas Porter? From Riverton, Illinois?"

"Yes…"

There was a brief pause. Eve felt the heaviness of the delay as an anvil on her own chest. Her breath stilled.

"Mrs. Porter, I'm very sorry to inform you that your husband had a heart attack this afternoon."

She clutched the telephone. "What? How? Where?"

"He was at the hospital when the attack occurred, but it was too severe. I'm sorry, Mrs. Porter. We did everything we could."

None of this made any sense to her. Tom was at the San Diego Hospital for grand rounds. He would be gone for two days and then he'd come home. They had things to talk about, to settle between them. What was this woman talking about?

"No, that's not possible."

"I'm very sorry, Mrs. Porter. Your husband died at two-thirty this afternoon, western time."

The woman's words were knocking on her brain but she wouldn't let them in. "I'm sorry." *Knock.* "Very sorry." *Knock.* If she opened up to the meaning, she knew she'd hear the toll, *He's dead, dead, dead.* She felt frozen. The phone dropped out from her splayed hands along with the three rose stems. Looking down, she saw pricks of blood trickling down her palm but she couldn't feel a thing.

Everything seemed to be moving in slow motion. In her ears was a relentless roar of waves. With halting breaths she slowly looked around the room, her eyes wide with shock. In front of her were the frightened faces of Finney and Bronte, who were instinctively moving closer to her. She held out her hand to ward them off, not wanting to be touched. She shook her head as her heart thumped loudly and her mouth worked soundlessly. Those cursed, painful words were forcing their way into her brain, their meaning scorching, cracking the ice and shattering her defenses. *Tom was dead.*

The searing words created a furnace in her chest, fueled by her pain, burning away her denial, creating a pressure in her chest until she couldn't hold it back any longer. She knew she was going to erupt. She slapped her palms against her mouth but the pain burst through, bellowing forth as a primeval scream at the top of her lungs.

Then she wrapped her arms around her children, pressed them close and felt them cling tight to her; Bronte's head beside hers, Finney's against her chest.

Two

The time is here for me to leave this life.
I have fought the good fight.
I have finished the race.
I have kept the faith.

—II Timothy, 4:6-8
The verse Eve chose for Tom's funeral Holy Card.

Saint Luke's Catholic Church, like the village of Riverton, was small but important. The gothic architecture, with its dark wood and beams, the blazing beauty of the stained glass and the intricate grillwork, was an impressive display of both artisan talent and the devotion of wealthy patrons. Riverton's Catholics fell to their knees in Saint Luke's in consistently steady numbers each Sunday. Yet, even by Riverton's standards, the turnout for Tom Porter's funeral service was impressive. Well-dressed people, their summer tans glowing, overflowed the narrow aisles and spilled outside the arched wooden doors.

Doris Bridges took her place at the front of the church. She held her hands firmly on the pew ahead of her, and with her chin held at a jaunty angle, she viewed the pro-

cession of people much in the manner of a general sur-
veying the troops. She was broad-boned and wide-hipped,
and her full chest heaved with a deep, personal satisfaction.
It was a good thing she'd stepped in at the last minute to
take charge of the funeral arrangements, she thought to
herself. She hated to think what a fiasco it could have been
without her. A travesty. Poor Eve, she was utterly despondent. Usually her friend was so organized and creative, but
Tom's death had shocked her into a comatose state. And
her in-laws... Useless. They were positively ancient! Certainly not up to the task of a large funeral. Doris mentally
patted herself on the back for doing what any good friend
would have done.

And she'd done well, she thought, looking over the altar
with a proprietary air. Dozens of tall, white lilies adorned
the snowy linen-draped altar. Beside it, near the commu-
nion rail, stood a table on which she'd placed a large,
recent photograph of Tom and a single, spectacular as-
sortment of white flowers. Eve adored flowers. Doris had
personally selected the unusual blooms, knowing Eve
would notice her touch. She couldn't trust a florist not to
fill in the arrangement with carnations.

Doris sat a pew behind the grieving family, far enough
to allow them privacy, but close enough that others would
know she was a close, personal friend. She tilted her head
and casually searched the crowd for familiar faces. Of
course, she knew many of the people, either through social
contacts, school or business. Her gaze was arrested by a
tall redhead sobbing uncontrollably in the side vestibule.
Doris didn't recognize her. Then again, how could anyone
get a look at her under that enormous floppy black hat?
Well, for pity's sake, Doris thought with indignation, such
a showy spectacle. You'd think she was the widow. Some
women had no self-control. It was her duty as a ranking

member of the community to set the tone, she supposed. When she made eye contact with the woman, she offered a careful, brief smile of acknowledgment with the message to rein it in. But the woman was oblivious and sobbed on.

She turned to look again at Tom's widow, who, in contrast, stood still and silent. She appeared little more than a faint shadow behind her black lace mantilla. Doris's heart seized with love for her friend. Here was a woman who deserved to sob. Eve was so utterly alone! Tom had been the pillar of her life. He had such vivacity and drive. He was well-known, liked and respected by everyone. Eve, however, was a private sort of person, very warm and friendly, but reserved. Tom and the children made up her world. And though she volunteered her time, she wasn't social. Doris recalled how once, over coffee, Eve had confided that the most important women in her life were the Book Club. Doris, who was extremely social, had understood and quietly agreed with her.

Where were the girls? she wondered, craning her neck to scan the crowd.

She spotted Gabriella across the aisle seated with her husband, Fernando, and their four children. They nearly filled the whole pew. *The apples certainly didn't fall far from the tree in that bunch,* she thought as she surveyed the long line of gleaming black hair on the bowed heads. They were a handsome family, devoted to each other. Gabby was loved by everyone who knew her, not only because her dazzling, wide smile and dancing, dark eyes cheered everyone simply by looking at her, but because her intrinsic goodness was obvious in her generous, caring gestures. It was typical of Gabby that in the past several days she had fretted over lackluster Eve and her poor, fatherless *bebes* and had brought truckloads of home-cooked meals to Eve's house. It was no wonder Gabby's shoulders drooped today.

Behind Gabriella sat Midge Kirsch, alone as usual. She wasn't an attractive woman physically, but even at a distance anyone could see the strength in the straightness of her lean shoulders, the steadiness of her dark-eyed gaze and the dramatic clash of a long, flowing black skirt and a military-blue shawl. Of course, you had to be tall to carry off such vintage clothing, Doris thought with a sniff. But she had to admit Midge delivered her own signature style to everything she did.

Annie Blake walked up the aisle, then paused just outside her own pew. Doris felt a flush of envy and sucked in her gut as she caught sight of Annie's willowy figure draped in an impeccably cut, dove-gray suit of a quality worthy of a successful lawyer. Everything about Annie smacked of sleek control. Her gray, sexy-high patent pumps shone, her itsy-bitsy black leather purse screamed order, and not one of her fine, perfectly blended gold hairs dared to slip from the chignon at the nape of her long neck. No matter how much money she spent, Doris knew she'd never look like that. Deep in her heart, Doris was convinced it was a cult secret that thin, attractive, successful women kept to themselves just to drive plump, dumpy women like herself crazy.

Annie's catlike gaze flicked expertly over those who sat nearby and Doris knew no detail escaped that radar sweep. When her gaze fell on Doris and their eyes met, Annie smiled in polite recognition, then with the quick decision typical of Annie, gracefully slipped in beside Midge.

Doris's hand smoothed the creases from her navy linen skirt that was straining at the buttons. It was several years old, not at all as stylish as Annie's, but a good suit was designed to last. Hadn't her mother worn Chanel suits that were decades old? Quality was always in style, her mother always told her. Still, the waistband pinched mercilessly and Doris promised herself as she sucked in her stomach that tomorrow she'd begin that protein diet she'd been reading about. And exercise, too. God only knew how many tomorrows we all have, she thought, looking again at the gleaming wood-and-brass casket that rested before the altar.

Who could have imagined Tom Porter would die so suddenly? She'd always thought he was full of life, so handsome with his quick smile and flashing dark eyes. More than once she'd envied Eve for the happiness and passion that was obvious in their marriage. So unlike her own. Doris brought her fingertips to her lips. It was always a shock when a vibrant man died, but when that person was as young as Tom Porter, everyone took the loss personally. Of course, everyone felt real sorrow and pity for the wife and children left without a husband and father. But an early death hit home because each survivor of a certain age felt the dark shadow pass over, reminding them that death was not reserved only for the old. That each day could be their last.

Feeling a sudden twinge of worry for her own husband, Doris turned her head and searched the entrance for the umpteenth time for sign of him. Her heart beat with hope when she saw Annie's husband, John, enter the church. His long, Swedish features and the perpetual tan that contrasted with his white-blond hair were easy to spot; he towered over those who clustered near the entrance. His piercing blue eyes scanned the crowd. Doris knew the moment he located Annie because his face broke into a smile at the very sight of her. He moved with the grace of an athlete toward the front of the church to meet his wife, unaware that the heads of women, young and old, turned as he passed. Doris's heart skipped a beat, wondering what it would be like to be so adored by a man....

Again she anxiously watched the door, expecting R.J. to follow John in. John worked for her husband and it seemed natural that they would arrive from the meeting together. After a few minutes, she checked her watch.

Her worry instantly altered to pique. He was inexcusably late! To think he'd had the audacity to imply that he might not be able to make the Porter funeral at all. Doris recalled how last night she'd put her foot down. Imagine, not show-ing up for a neighbor's—a friend's, a dear friend's—fu-neral service just because of a business meeting. It was beyond rude, it was unconscionable. Everyone would no-tice. She couldn't help the tsk that escaped from her lips. How could he do this to her? This sort of thing was hap-pening far too often lately, and was growing harder to make excuses for. And his hours... Impossible. She really had to talk to him again about his late nights. He wasn't a young man anymore. At fifty-four, he drank too much and did nothing but push, push, push with his construction company. That was the right formula for a heart attack. If he wasn't careful, *she'd* be the grieving widow. All alone, like Eve.

She shuddered at the thought and glanced warily at the casket, then over at Eve. Poor, poor Eve. The black suit dwarfed her delicate frame and the long, lace mantilla ac-centuated her face's wintry whiteness. From beneath the veil, Eve's watery blue eyes stared at the casket with stricken disbelief. She looked so fragile, paper-thin like the shell of a cicada left behind on the trunk of a tree. A sudden gust of air could blow her away. She was flanked on either side by her two children.

With a sudden rush of emotion, Doris reached out to clutch the hands of her own daughter, Sarah, and her son,

Bobby, standing at her sides. Teenagers, they tilted their heads to look at her quizzically, then with embarrassment. She saw bits of herself in their faces, and a lot of R.J., living, breathing proofs of their union. She squeezed their hands tightly. Family was everything, she thought. Poor Eve, to have lost Tom. The thought of losing R.J., of being alone, filled Doris with fear.

Annie couldn't wait to be alone. She stood at the base of the church's outside stairs tapping her foot, waiting for John to bring the car around. A final few stragglers chatted in small clusters in the open vestibule, but everyone else had left, either for the open house at Eve's, or home.

Annie felt consumed with an unusual despondency, a strange sense of floundering in rocky waters. Tom's death came as such a shock. Just a few weeks ago he was laughing as they chased him out of the living room for a Book Club meeting. She'd come home late from the office to hear the news on the phone from Gabriella. It hit so hard that she'd drank too much wine and clung to John all night long. She was an existentialist and didn't believe in an afterlife, so why his death shook her so deeply she didn't know. It's not like they were even close. *Eve* was her friend, not Tom, though she liked Tom well enough. The Book Club treated the husbands politely and twice a year they partied together. Nice fellows, but in truth, they barely knew them. The husbands were just sort of there, like window dressing. Still, Tom's death shook her, shook them all.

Someone she knew hailed her as he passed by and mumbled something about what a terrible shock this all was. She responded in kind and sighed in relief when she saw his back.

God, she hated these things. The somber faces, everyone

spewing out pat phrases, and Doris lording over them like a high priestess. And who was that redhead carrying on in the vestibule? She wanted to walk right up to her and slap her! *Get a life, lady. He wasn't your husband, for crying out loud.*

Eve hadn't cried; that's what troubled her. It pained her to see the stricken look on Eve's face as they wheeled the casket away. Her instincts told her Eve's feelings ran deeper than grief. Was it fear? Or perhaps guilt? Over what, Annie couldn't imagine. Eve and Tom had had one of those perfect marriages that gave the rest of them hope. People could always point to the Porters as living, breathing proof that good marriages still survived. Still, as a lawyer she'd handled many divorces, and over the years she'd learned that behind closed doors there were three sides to every story: his, hers and the truth.

Annie sighed sadly and shook her head, sure that the look of utter devastation on Eve's face as she stared at her husband's coffin was too raw for an easy acceptance and peace. She'd counseled far too many women over the years to miss that look now.

A brief beep from the curb was a welcome break from this train of thought. She looked up to see John's long fingers waving her toward their BMW.

"Are you ready to go home?" he asked when she climbed in.

Annie smiled up at John's solicitous face and nodded, her eyes expressing her gratitude that he could pick up on her needs so effortlessly. John was always there for her, watching out for her, caring for her. He really did spoil her.

"I'm more than ready," she replied, settling in and closing the door. She was relieved when the car swung away from the curb, leaving the church behind them. "Thank

God that's over. What an ordeal. Who knew Catholic masses could be so long? There wasn't a dry eye in the house.'' She began unbuttoning her suit jacket to the cool air-conditioning. While she did, she recalled the emotional eulogy and the message that one's time on earth was finite. While the priest implied that one should prepare for heaven, her personal credo was to live each day as if it were her last.

"How's Eve?" John wanted to know.

"I'm worried about her." She shrugged. "But there's nothing I can do for Eve now. Doris has everything under control at the moment. As usual." The latter, she muttered under her breath. "My turn to help will come later, when she needs legal advice. I hope Tom took care of her, that's all I can say. Otherwise, it'll be tough going for her."

She brought her fingers to her brow and closed her eyes against the sorrow she felt for her friend's suffering that pierced straight to the marrow. Eve appeared lost; it was clear she was going to need a lot of guidance. Annie knew what that felt like, knew how many hard knocks a woman could receive when she forged a new life of her own. She knew, too, that she'd be right by Eve's side, every step of the way.

"Let's get something to eat," John suggested.

"Right now, I could use a good, stiff drink."

John's eyes narrowed and his hands held the wheel tighter. "Isn't it a bit early for a drink? We haven't eaten a real meal yet today. How about we go out for a late lunch?" Then seeing her wrinkled nose, he said, "Okay, we'll call it an early dinner."

Annie waved away his suggestions, annoyed by his worry about her drinking. "I'm not the least hungry. My craw is crammed full with sadness and death and depression." She shook her hands in front of her, releasing the tension. "God, that funeral was just too, too sad. It's really staying with me. I'm sick of death and sympathy. Don't you feel the need to do something, oh, I don't know, something to reconfirm life?"

"Eating confirms life...."

"No. What I really want right now is to go to my own home, have a nice, cold drink from my own glass, then make hot, passionate love with my own husband—all afternoon."

John's frown turned upward. "Sounds good to me."

"I thought it might," she said, catching his smile. Her palms itched to rub over his smooth flesh, to feel the warmth of his life's blood. To rub skin against skin. He was a beautiful man, inside and out, and she loved him, needed him, more at this moment than ever before. This emotional tide had to be a result of the funeral, she decided. It wasn't usual for her to have these gushy feelings race through her, but today in church she'd had some kind of epiphany. Watching Eve walk down the aisle of the church behind Tom's casket, Annie was struck by how fiercely Eve had clasped the hands of her two children. In a flash Annie realized that Eve was gaining as much strength from Bronte and Finney as she was giving to them. There was a bond there, an energy, that was palpable.

For the first time in her life, Annie felt the desire to have a child of her own.

"You know," she said, leaning over and linking arms with him, "since we're talking about reconfirming life, and since we'll be making love...there's another idea I've been toying with." She waited till he glanced from the road to her. His gaze was at first curious. Then, the second time he glanced her way, he caught something in her expression. His face stilled and his eyes sparked with intense concentration, as though he anticipated her next comment.

She spoke slowly, wanting to be sure of her words. "John, I know you've wanted a child for a long time. While I was standing at the curb, waiting for you, I was thinking how life is so short, so precious. I don't think we should wait any longer."

A moment passed while a flush of color crept up John's cheeks. When he glanced her way a third time, she could tell from the excitement bubbling in his eyes that he was overjoyed, but trying his best not to appear overanxious, lest he spook her. She held back her smile, thinking that John would make a terrible lawyer. His eyes would give him away every time.

"Are you sure?" he asked, almost stuttering.

"Aren't you?" It was terrible to tease him.

He cleared his throat, utterly serious. "Sure, I'm sure. But I want to be certain that this isn't just some reaction to Tom's death. I mean, hell, Annie, this is so sudden. We've been married for five years and this is the first time you've ever agreed to so much as discuss having a baby. Every time I've brought it up you've stopped me cold. We aren't getting any younger. I sort of gave up on the idea of ever having a baby. And now suddenly you want one? What about your law practice? What about all that pro bono stuff you're so hot to do? How does a baby fit in with all that?"

Her eyes danced merrily as she poked at his arm. "So…you're saying we shouldn't have a baby?"

"No!" He almost shouted the word. He pulled to the side of the road and stopped the car. "No," he repeated after a deep breath, his shining eyes fixed on her. "I'm only trying to make sure you want one."

That was so like John, she thought, looking into his

clear, honest eyes. She stroked his arm lovingly. Her heart felt ready to burst. She wanted to give him the world, but she'd start with a baby.

"I'm sure," she replied, holding his gaze. Then, to deflect the intensity of the moment, she poked his arm one more time and winked, saying, "But I don't think I want to make one right here. Gearshifts and bucket seats can be pretty damn uncomfortable. So put the pedal to the metal, boyfriend, and take me home to bed!"

Midge drove home from the funeral to the far eastern side of Oakley, an area considered "risky" by the other women of the Book Club. The neighborhood bordered the western boundary of the city of Chicago, an area populated by low-income families, gangs and high crime statistics.

It was also an area where old buildings were being converted into fabulous lofts, an area where ethnic restaurants thrived, and where artists, bead makers, writers and eclectic religions could afford to rent large spaces. Pockets of creativity thrived in western Oakley and it was fast becoming "hot" property.

Back in the 1970s when Midge returned home after college and a failed marriage in Boston, the transient area fit her needs. She was searching for large, open space in which to paint that was affordable, architecturally beautiful and reasonably safe. This was usually synonymous with antichic—and that suited Midge fine. She was never one to worry about fashion. In fact, she made a point of living against the grain. She'd purchased a large loft in one of the area's first conversions, long before the current wave of lofts hit the country, and liked it so much that she bought the whole building for a good price during a period when the owner thought the area was going downhill.

Over the course of time she'd watched the area spiral

from a solid blue-collar neighborhood to an increasingly crime-ridden one, then later find rebirth under the loving care of a gay community. Gradually the neighborhood evolved into the charming blend of solid ethnic families, gay couples and artists that it currently was. In the process, she'd watched her investment go up, down, and back up again like an economic roller coaster, all because people were afraid their houses were worth less if minorities moved in. When people congratulated her on her investment, Midge always snorted and replied, "Hey, it pays not to be prejudiced. Why not try it sometime?"

Still, prejudice was an everyday fact of life for Midge. As an art therapist, she worked with young children and teenagers who were seething in anger against poverty and prejudice. She saw that anger as a powder keg waiting to explode. What made her job—her life—hard was that, when her work was done and she came home drained, there was no one to wrap arms around her and hold her, to tell her that she was loved and secure.

Midge well understood loneliness, and her heart broke for her friend, Eve, knowing what was in store for her. The transition from married to unmarried, from beloved to forsaken, was long and bitter. In time, a strong individual adapted and prospered, like any solid building. But, as any building needed loving tenants and a cohesive community to avoid crumbling, so Eve would need the love and support of her friends.

At least Eve had her family, Midge thought as she approached her building and pulled out a large metal ring of keys. The broad-based, redbrick building covered half a city block and housed several small studios and shops at street level. The top two floors had been converted into lofts, many rented by the shop owners. In the rear she'd created an enormous garden from what was once an old rubbish heap. Today, vegetables, flowers, a gazebo, chimes and birdbaths flourished in the haven for all to share. She was proud of the way she maintained this building and the relationships she'd forged with her tenants. They were her family.

Yet, they were not family. A realist, she didn't kid herself about that fact. As she made her way up the dark flight of stairs to her own door, the sound of her heels on the wood stairs echoed with a hollow loneliness. Yes, she knew this journey so well. She stood at the threshold of her loft, her arms hanging dejectedly at her sides, not ready to step inside and face her isolation.

It was an airy space, bold and modern, even masculine in the rugged disregard for feminine comfort or style. Much like herself. Usually she felt a tremendous release of pressure when she shut the door behind her. She'd throw her coat and purse over a chair and sigh with relief upon entering her own space. She might grab some cheese and crackers or a bowl of cereal—she never much cared what she ate—then head straight for a book or her paints.

Sometimes, however, the loneliness hit hard and unexpectedly. At times like these, there was a silence so intense she could hear herself breathe and she felt closed in, buried alive. Today, something about the funeral stirred the depths of a melancholy she strove to keep at bay. Was it witnessing the demise of a family? Or was it seeing the endurance of family ties even under the worst of adversity? The image of Eve clutching the hands of her children stayed with her. So beautiful…and for her, now so unattainable.

Midge closed the door behind her, mentally closing the door to those depressing thoughts. Tom Porter was her age when he died. At fifty, it was unlikely that she'd find that kind of security and joy in a marriage or with children.

She had to face the fact that when she was depressed or frightened, she'd have to dig deep and find her own security. When she wanted to watch a movie in bed on a cold night, she'd better get a cat for company. When she woke up alone on Christmas morning, well... Midge paused and took a deep breath. Well, she told herself with a stern voice, she'd just have to look around and see all that she had to be thankful for. She had a career, her art, good friends. This was her life; she'd made choices and now she must live them out.

She moved quickly to do something, anything, to divert the melancholy. Stretching out her arm, she punched the button on her answering machine and waited while the tape whirred. The nasal voice pierced the silence.

You have no messages.

Gabriella stepped into her modest, brick home in north Oakley and walked straight to her bedroom, not saying a word. She closed the door and quickly stripped off the confining navy linen dress and the sweaty, dark nylons, sighing mightily when her skin breathed openly again. She hated to wear constrictive clothing; it felt as though she were wrapped in a vise. But today especially, standing in the stifling, thick humidity of the crowded church, holding back her tears and agonizing for her friend, Eve, and those poor, fatherless, *bebes*... It was all she could do not to weep out loud, like that crazy redhead. After the mass she soundly kissed her husband and each one of her four children and made them promise never, ever, to die before her.

She pulled back her long, thick black hair with a clasp, then sat in the cool porcelain of her tub. As she sponged down her round, softening body, her pent-up sadness trickled down into the drain with the rivulets of cool water.

No, she sighed, closing her eyes as a worried frown creased her brow, she didn't need any bad thoughts to hover over her. She didn't want any of the sadness of the funeral to infiltrate her home. She wasn't superstitious...but things were going too good lately. Just too, too good.

Oh God, why did she even have the thought? It tempted fate to think of one's good fortune. Whenever things went too well, something always happened to clobber her. Gabriella abruptly turned off the water, wrapped herself in a soft cotton towel and quickly dressed in a flowing, bright-yellow sundress.

"Mami, I'm hungry." Her youngest was still dressed in his summer best, leaning against the kitchen counter watching television and nibbling Gummi Bears.

"First you change your clothes, eh? And hang them up, too," she said, rubbing his hair as he ducked away. "I'll make lunch. Go on now, put down that candy and no more TV."

Gabriella began pulling out the pots and pans to prepare a quick lunch for her family. Weekends were always hectic, but she loved being at the center of it all. The mother was the heart of the family, no? Her eldest two boys had soccer games at the high school and she never let them leave without a substantial meal in their bellies. Her sixteen-year-old daughter, however, was always dieting and it was a constant battle to get her to eat anything. What to make, she wondered, rummaging through the stuffed refrigerator. She turned to look over her shoulder when she heard her husband's step.

Fernando was a bear of a man, broad with dark hair all over his body and a soft rounded belly that protruded over his belt. He often scratched or patted it when he was lost in thought. He was scratching his belly now, Gabriella noticed as she followed his path into the kitchen, and her brow knitted when she caught sight of the pensive expression on his face. They'd been married for twenty-five years and she could pick up signs of a quake better than any Richter scale. And right now, her alarms were going off.

"Are you okay?" she asked him as he stepped beside her to grab a beer from the fridge. "Did the funeral get you down or something?"

Fernando flipped off the cap and took a long swallow. "Yeah, I guess so," he replied in a distracted manner. "Tom Porter was about my age, you know."

"Your heart is fine," she replied too quickly, dismissing the notion. Gabriella was a nurse and knew well that heart attacks struck men of Fernando's age with little warning. Her eyes narrowed as she studied his face, and when she saw the pallor there, blood rushed to her own. "You just saw the doctor for your physical. Your cholesterol was normal. Why?" she asked, feeling a sudden alarm. "Do you have chest pains or something?"

He shook his head and took another long draft from his bottle. Gabriella's hands stilled on the counter and she waited quietly for the quake. His lips pinched, the only movement on his face, but his eyes were restless.

"Remember I told you that there was a memo circulated around the office about a merger? They said there were going to be large-scale layoffs." He didn't look at her but spoke to the wall.

Gabriella did indeed remember that. They'd talked for hours about the possibility that Fernando's job as district manager of the electronics firm would be in jeopardy. Then Fernando had pointed out how he never missed a day of work, how he often stayed late to solve problems, and how he'd worked for the firm for over a decade. He'd seemed so confident and she slept easy at night believing he would be the last one any company would let go. But now, seeing the heartache in his eyes, she feared the worst. Her earlier premonition played in her mind and she silently cried out, *No, no, don't let him lose his job.* Madre de Dios, *please don't make us go through this.* Gabriella knew poverty and feared it.

She didn't say any of this to Fernando but took his large hand into her small one.

"They canned me," he said with brutal honesty. "Gave me my notice. In six weeks, I'll be out of a job."

He looked at her with both wariness and anger, as though he expected her to explode, to blame him for his failure as he surely blamed himself. For a moment she felt frozen by the shock of the words. This wasn't an it-could-happen scenario. This was the real thing. He was fired, let go, laid off, whatever words they used to stop his career— and his paycheck.

Her head lowered as she tried to make sense of it. "I…I don't understand," she ventured in a small voice. "You said you thought they'd keep you. That it wouldn't… How could they let you go?"

"Not just me. Fifteen hundred got the pink slip, most of them in middle management. It's happening all over." His hand plowed through his cropped black hair. "That's what worries me. There'll be a lot of competition out on the street for my level of position." His face creased and his hand left his hair to rub his brow, shielding his eyes.

She heard the worry in his voice, worry not for himself but for his family. As a young man he had worked his way through college while still managing to give his parents a portion of each paycheck. They'd married young, had children early and he'd never stopped working hard for his family. Gabriella looked at her husband's face and saw the

defeat that would kill him more surely than any cholesterol.

What did she have to be afraid of if he lost his job, she
wondered? She loved him. He was her husband, the father
of her children. She'd seen in Eve's eyes the depth of a
woman's desolation when her husband died. What did the
loss of a job matter when compared to that loss? She
moved to wrap her short, plump arms around him, her head
barely reaching his shoulders.

"We'll be fine," she said, and was relieved to feel his
arms wrap around her in a bear hug. Laying her cheek
against his chest, she relished his scent on his clothes and
the warmth of his arms. "You're alive and well and we
have four wonderful *bebes*. And I have a job, so we know
we'll make do until you find another one. And you will,
too. Soon. You just wait and see. We'll be fine," she repeated. "We just have to keep the faith."

Three

Between the dark and the daylight,
When the night is beginning to lower,
Comes a pause in the day's occupations,
That is known as the Children's Hour.

—Henry Wadsworth Longfellow, *The Children's Hour*

For mothers of school-age children, the first signs of fall are not the yellowing of leaves or a nip in the night air. They are the back-to-school sales, the purchase of book bags, binders and pens, and the mix of panic and excitement on the faces of their children.

Doris Bridges sat back on her heels on the floor of her library and fingered the old, worn copy of Dr. Seuss's children's book. She was feeling a wave of melancholy, having just said goodbye to her eldest son, Bobby Jr., on his way to college. He was the first to leave the nest and his absence left a gaping, empty space in her heart. Opening the book, she was flooded with memories of the countless times she'd read this story to Sarah and Bobby in this very room. They'd all loved Dr. Seuss's fantasy worlds—the children no more than her. How she used to enjoy watching their small tongues roll the strange sounding syllables in their mouths. Each child had a favorite. Sarah's was the faithful elephant who would not desert his friends in *Horton Hears A Who*. Bobby's was the rhythmic, marching beat of *Green Eggs and Ham*.

She'd secretly loved it when they tussled over who could climb into her ample lap, finally settling the dispute with one leaning over her left thigh and the other over her right. If she closed her eyes, she could almost feel the soft pressure of their heads resting against her breasts this very moment, feel the moistness of their foreheads after a bath and smell the sweetness of their wispy hair. Ah, such a perfume! Ambrosia. God must have created it just for mothers. The scent stirred primal instincts to love and protect the babies.

Her babies... Doris sighed heavily and opened her eyes, feeling a wave of weepiness. All that lay on her lap now was an open book, in hands that were so much older. Wide, freckled hands with large rings and painted nails. She remembered when she hadn't worn large rings for fear they'd scratch the babies.

The sound of her children's voices was still so clear in her memory; at times such as these their high-pitched singsong overwhelmed all other noise. So precious! As were the treasured images of her young family, with R.J. beside her, laughing his big, boisterous laugh. Where did the time go? Where did they all go? She sometimes felt that all she had left were these books. That like Horton, the big, clumsy elephant, she wanted to stand up in this huge, painstakingly decorated house that amounted to no more than a speck of dust in the real world and shout from the top of her lungs, "I am here! I am here!"

She lowered her head and sniffed, feeling a vast, dark cloud envelop her.

R.J. walked into the library with his usual bluster and stopped a few feet from her. From behind her lowered lids she saw that he stood with his feet wide apart and could envision his hands on his hips. She cringed, knowing without looking that he was frowning in disgust to find her once again wallowing, teary eyed, in her memories. She felt so sad, so often lately, and though she tried to hide it, sometimes the tears just spilled out. That lack of control frightened her—and it annoyed R.J. to no end.

"You've got to get out more," he said, frustration ringing in his voice.

"Oh, I'm all right," she replied with summoned cheer, forcing a tremulous smile and quickly wiping her eyes. "I just got a little emotional when I saw this book. Remember how I used to read it to the children? It was one of their favorites."

"Listen, I forgot to give these to John this afternoon," R.J. said, ignoring her question. "Could you run this over to him?"

She looked up over her shoulder to see R.J. dressed in a sporty linen trouser and blue jacket ensemble and smelling of aftershave. His thinning brown hair streaked handsomely with gray was slicked back and he had what her mother called "spit and polish." In his hands he held a large manila envelope out toward her.

"Are you going out?" She in turn ignored the envelope.

"I've got to be downtown in half an hour. I don't have time to drop these off myself. Just tell him I need his take on these blueprints asap."

It was more of a command than a request and Doris set the children's book in her lap with a heavy sigh that spoke clearly of her unwillingness. She'd looked forward to an hour of reading before she prepared dinner. Besides, she didn't like going over to John's house; she might run into

Annie. Lately, the quiet rivalry between them had escalated into a war. They still attended the Book Club together and the lunches and what-have-you. But underneath the polite smiles, both women recognized the teeth were bared.

''Why can't he come over and pick them up? He works for you, after all.''

''He's working on his house. Knee-deep in drywall.''

''He's always working on that house. It's like they're living in a camp. Nothing ever works, there's no place to sit, and the junk and materials are all over the place. You'd think he'd bring in some help and just get it done.'' Her exasperation knew no end when people couldn't get their living quarters in order. ''I don't know how they can live like that.''

''What do you care? He wants to do it himself.''

''But they've been remodeling that old house for over a year. I don't know how Annie puts up with it.''

''Annie's a good sport. And she's not hung up about stuff like that.''

The underlying criticism stung and made her resent Annie just that much more.

''Besides,'' R.J. continued, ''John's not just any carpenter, he's a goddamn artist. And that old house just happens to be a Frank Lloyd Wright.'' He shrugged. ''I don't blame him. He doesn't want anyone else mucking it up. He and Annie are taking their time, getting it done right.''

''Aren't you suddenly the artistic one?'' she replied acidly, wanting to return a small dig of her own. ''If I remember correctly, you're the one always grumbling about how long it takes John to get anything done.''

''It does. I hate for things to go slow when it's costing me money. But I'm smart enough to know John's the best and leave him alone, at least on his own projects. He can do what he wants in his spare time.'' He looked at his wristwatch and frowned. "Come on, I don't have time to yak about it. Just drop it off, will you? You've got nothing better to do."

That hurt—in so many ways.

"Here," he said, holding out the manila envelope in front of her and giving it a brisk shake. "You can always hang around and talk to Annie."

Doris heard the terseness in his voice that signaled an explosion if she didn't back off. So she accepted the envelope, and the task, with a testy grab. It was on the tip of her tongue to tell him that talking with Annie was precisely what she wanted to avoid, but he wouldn't understand or care. As far as R.J. was concerned, he and John were friends so Annie and she must be friends. It made things easier for him.

She recalled meeting Annie Blake five years earlier when R.J. hired John away from a rival Chicago building firm. John Svenson was their head carpenter, a well-respected craftsman, and R.J. had spotted his potential immediately. Doris had never understood why John took the job as design consultant for Bridges Building Company when his job description was, as far as she could tell, chief lackey. His pay was pitiful and it was only R.J.'s perversity that kept it low. John was loyal and worked like a dog for him. She knew R.J. liked to be in control, to have people beholden to him and thus emotionally chained to his side. So, instead of actual money, he preferred to give perks. And one of those perks was a great deal on a run-down Frank Lloyd Wright that R.J. had purchased for renovation. To a craftsman like John Svenson, the house was a once-in-a-lifetime dream. R.J. knew it and had used it as bait.

Fortunately, the two men clicked and within months became inseparable. R.J. was the front man, the architect with the plans and the deal. John was the quiet artist, adding style and focus to the designs. It was an award-winning combination. It was inevitable that the wives would meet and it was expected that they'd become equally good friends.

Well, she'd tried, Doris told herself. Didn't she invite her to join the Book Club? But Annie Blake was a renegade who didn't like to follow Doris's lead and there was a subtle struggle between them during book discussions as to who was the leader. There was no hope they'd ever become friends, Doris decided, dragging herself up to her feet. R.J. offered her his hand and she struggled not to lean too heavily lest he comment on her weight.

"I don't know why you two gals don't get along better," he said when she was on her feet. "You two are like oil and water."

"Baking soda and vinegar is more like it." She didn't mention that lately Annie's attachment to Eve was the last straw. It made Doris feel as if she were in seventh grade again and someone was trying to come between her and her best friend.

"Where are you going tonight?" she asked R.J. as he went to the desk to retrieve some papers.

"I'm meeting some clients at the club. I'll be late."

"I'll wait up."

"Don't bother. If it gets too late, I'll just stay at the club. I don't like to drink and drive."

"Then don't drink."

He merely snorted while he patted his pockets, locating his keys. He pulled them out and tossed them into the air, then caught them with a boyish flip of his wrist, smiling. Doris narrowed her eyes, noting a flashing on his baby finger; it was a narrow gold-and-black onyx ring with a single diamond in the center that she'd never seen before. It was a handsome ring, discreet, yet her nose crinkled as if she'd suddenly caught a foul scent. She knew R.J. never bought himself jewelry. And her father had always distrusted men who wore pinkie rings.

He bent at the waist to deliver a chaste, dry kiss on the top of her head and an affectionate pat on her shoulder.

"Thanks for dropping that off."

She held herself erect though her calves were killing her, watching as he strode from the room with a jaunty gait, without so much as a backward glance. R.J. always had such purpose and drive and it was clear he was a man with a mission tonight. Doris slowly replaced the Dr. Seuss book onto the library shelf, patting it into a neat line with the other books. Then she calmly, methodically, held out her left hand and with her right, twiddled the wide band of diamonds on her wedding ring, musing over the fact that in twenty-five years of marriage, she could never once recall R. J. Bridges worrying about drinking and driving.

Annie hung up the phone in her kitchen and smiled with satisfaction.

"You look like the cat that ate the canary."

She looked up at her husband perched on a ladder across the endless piles of dust, tools and wallboard that littered the floor between them. He wore his white overalls without a shirt underneath, exposing his long, lean, tan torso and sinewy muscles, still those of a man twenty years his junior. John's blond hair was tied back into a stubby ponytail making his prominent cheekbones all the more pronounced on his narrow face.

My, my, my, he was a handsome man, she thought, feeling a familiar surge. She caught his eye, and by the way his own gaze sparked and his smile widened, she knew he was picking up her thoughts. Or the gist of them, anyway. John had a highly tuned radar for sex. She saw him glance at the clock and chuckle, then turn his head to raise one brow suggestively. It was five o'clock on the button, her favorite time of the day for lovemaking. They called it The Children's Hour since they'd started trying to make a baby.

"That was Doris," Annie replied, slipping out of her sandals. "She's going to stop by later on to drop off some papers for you to look at. Apparently, R.J. is off to a dinner meeting somewhere."

John began wiping his hands with the towel hanging from the ladder. "That must be about the Delancey building. I thought I was going to be at that dinner. It's supposed to be very chummy, drinks-and-cigars kind of thing."

She pulled the elastic out from her hair. "I guess we're not chums."

He frowned, rolling up a ball of tape. "Sure we are. We're both friends with the Bridges."

"Correction. You work for R.J. and I'm in the Book Club with Doris." She stopped shaking out her hair and rested her hands on her hips. "We're neither of us their real friend."

John scowled. She knew it hurt him to imply that he wasn't equal to R. J. Bridges and his upper-crust friends. Not financially, certainly, but John considered himself an equal intellectually. That man-to-man kind of thing. And it hurt her that he was either too dumb or too stubborn to see that R.J. would never allow anyone equal footing in business, much less someone he preferred to keep under his foot. She'd known lots of men like that, especially in the legal field. It was as though her—a woman—winning a court case somehow emasculated the male lawyers. When it came to the sexes, Justice still wore a cloth over her eyes.

She'd understood this about R. J. Bridges from the first night she'd met him. From the heat in his palm when he took her hand, to the way he could undress a woman with his eyes and make her feel dirty. But John didn't. He didn't have the killer instinct—and she loved him for it. She sighed, seeing the hurt blaze in John's brilliant blue eyes. Her dear, innocent, trusting John. She'd be there to protect him from predators like R.J.

"I'll be your best friend," she said, sidling up to the ladder and tugging at the cuff of his overalls. "Wanna come down and play?"

The sulk vanished instantly as he caught wind of her playful mood. He cocked his head and offered a half smile. "What do you wanna play?"

"Well, I thought we'd take off all our clothes first," she said while very gently rotating her hips and unbuttoning her white cotton blouse with teasing slowness. "Then take a nice hot shower. Oooh, we'll let that hard, pulsating water beat down on our backs while we lather up the soap and spread it over every inch of our slicky wet bodies."

She cast a sloe-eyed glance his way and pursed her lips to disguise her smile of delight, his eyes had already glazed over and he had a stillness about him, like a cat coiling to pounce. Her own heart began to race at the thought of what she knew was coming.

"What then?" His voice was raspy.

She unbuttoned another button with agonizing slowness. She knew it drove him mad with desire when she stripped slowly to build the anticipation. It was a pleasure for both of them, actually—for her to tease and for him to make the final, decisive move. In their lovemaking, John was dominant. In this arena he asserted himself in ways that he did not in their everyday life.

She strolled over to the stereo and turned on blues music, then moved to the refrigerator where she pulled out a bottle of chilled white wine. All the while she played the classic stripper's game of hide-and-seek, offering him a flash of skin that he never quite saw. All the while, maintaining eye contact with him. Annie poured two glasses of wine, then took a long, slow sip, licking her lips when she was finished.

"I think I'd like a nice, fat, red, juicy strawberry in mine."

His eyes sparked, transmitting in his glance the message that he vividly recalled what they had done with strawberries a few nights earlier.

Annie slowly wriggled out of her blouse, letting the cotton slide off her arms to the floor. She wasn't wearing a bra and her small but round, firm breasts were mouthwateringly ripe, exposing rosy taut nipples the color of strawberries.

John licked his lips.

Next she slowly unzipped her jeans, undulating her hips free as she lifted one leg, then the other, and kicked the pants across the floor.

John practically threw himself from the ladder, leaping down to her side and grasping her against his torso. She loved it when he was wild like this, so hungry for sex that his body trembled with excitement. He was quick to arouse, ready whenever she was, and an insatiable lover. She'd fallen in lust with him first, but it was his skill and tenderness as a lover that broke down her defenses and made her fall in love with him.

With nimble fingers that could peel veneer he unfastened his overalls and removed both their underwear, his tongue never once leaving her mouth as he tasted and devoured the sweetness she'd promised.

"John, wait, wait..." she mumbled under his lips, laughing. "Dinner. I have to get the ham."

He pulled her down onto the drop cloth, spreading her out beneath him, fully intending to feast.

"Forget the ham," he said, dragging his lips down her throat. "I have a sudden craving for strawberries."

Doris parked her Lexus at the curb of John and Annie's house, anxious to deliver the envelope and get out as soon as possible. She harrumphed seeing that the front entryway of the house was under scaffolding. She'd have to make her way around the piles of brick and wood that lay like hulking beasts in the driveway to get to the rear entrance. She clucked her tongue in annoyance as she trudged around to the rear door of the low, spreading brown-brick house, careful not to step on any tools or trip in any holes.

She was panting with the effort by the time she climbed up the back porch and rang the doorbell. She tapped her foot after a moment and rang again. The button was soft to the touch. She cursed under her breath, realizing that it, like everything else in this house, probably wasn't working. Was anyone even home? She didn't hear anything.... Doris walked to one of the kitchen windows, and leaning far over the pair of wooden horses, peeked inside.

Her breath stilled in her throat as she caught sight of John and Annie slow dancing in the quiet room to the beat of some inner love song. His sinewy arms, bare under his overalls, held Annie's nude body against his long torso in a tight, possessive manner. His tanned hands cupped her alabaster hips while her slim arms clung around his shoulders so close her nose and lips were pressed against his neck. They swayed with hips joined and eyes closed. The passion between them was palpable and Doris gazed on with longing. When John pulled Annie's head back in a hungry, devouring kiss, Doris licked her own parched lips and sighed. She stepped back from the window, feeling an excruciating emptiness in her heart. A shiver of envy swept through her for that kind of tenderness in her own life.

She tucked the envelope securely between the back door and the screen, careful not to disturb the lovers, then quietly left the house unobserved. She walked away with a shaky gait across the uneven flagstone.

Doris wasn't ready to return to her empty house. On the way home, she stopped by Eve's place for some cheer and conversation. She hadn't seen much of her since Tom's funeral, though everyone had tried to call or just stop by frequently. But Eve was firm in her refusals, preferring her self-imposed exile.

Eve's house was an impressive redbrick structure well situated on a large property bordered by a black iron fence and ancient towering pines. Driving through the gates, Doris thought again how she'd always admired Eve's ability to soften hard edges in both her landscape designs and in her relationships with people. Just as the harsh, straight lines of the Prairie architecture were rounded by Eve's fabulous curved perennial beds and shrubs, so had her warm, womanly nature doused many flare-ups between obstinate opponents—both in committee meetings and on the playground. Doris missed Eve's presence in her life. She missed her friendship. Doris hadn't known that losing Tom would also mean losing her best friend. It wasn't fair! Eve was the friend who lugged over a bag full of perennials to share from her garden, or who picked up Sarah if Doris was ill. She was the one Doris would call if she was in a pinch or just needed to talk.

As she walked from her car to the front door, Doris was dismayed to see Eve's garden such a wilderness. Dried

leaves drooped under bent flower heads that appeared to
have given up the battle against choking weeds. The front
curtains were drawn against the daylight, adding to the
mood of neglect. All bad signs. Gathering her resolve,
Doris knocked on the door.

After a moment the door opened, revealing Eve's pale,
drawn face. She stood, blinking in the sunshine, then
forced a smile and exclaimed delight in seeing her. Her
eyes, however, were lifeless.

"I'm all alone tonight," Doris announced, stepping into
the soft floral foyer. The house was dimly lit, and as
gloomy as a tomb. "And I seem to remember your children are at camp, right?"

"Yes, and I miss them terribly," Eve replied, closing
the door. "Bronte and Finney have been there for a week
already and still have one more to go. They seem to like
it well enough. Their doctor thought it would be good for
them to get some fresh air and new scenery. But it seems
so quiet here without them. Without..." Her voice faded
and her eyes seemed to glaze over in pain.

Doris thought that it was a shame there was no camp
for Eve to go to. Her pallor and thinness was a tell-tale
sign that she wasn't going out or eating well. "So, we're
both alone. Do you want to go out to dinner?"

Eve rubbed her thin arms with her fingers and shook her
head. "No, not really. I feel so tired. Actually, I was going
to go to bed early tonight. Maybe watch a little TV." She
yawned and covered her mouth with her palm. "I'm
sorry," she said, shaking her head. "I just can't seem to
get enough sleep lately."

"Are you well?" Doris scanned Eve's face. "You look
so pale and you've lost weight."

Eve waved away her concern. "I'm fine. It's just being
inside and alone so much."

"I've tried to call you..." Doris interrupted.

"I know you have. Everyone has... And I'm grateful. But, it's not your company I'm lonely for. It's Tom's," she said with the air of a confession. "The sadness inside of me is so big it just sucks the energy straight from my bones." Then she smiled a bit too brightly, as though to dispel any doubt that anything was amiss. "Oh, don't worry, I hear it's normal. This is what the doctors call normal grieving. It's just a phase."

"It doesn't sound normal to me. You shouldn't be alone."

"I like being alone."

"But it's not good to be alone too much. Everything in moderation. Come out to dinner with me."

Eve shook her head. "I'm just not in the mood. I'm sorry, I don't mean to be rude. Think of this period as a kind of hibernation. I need to sleep for a while, okay? I'll be my old self in time."

Doris looked at Eve with doubt. She knew in her heart she shouldn't leave Eve alone, yet she couldn't think what to do to lure her out of her isolation. Doris was the type to fix things when they were broken. She couldn't abide a tear in a dress or serve coffee in a chipped cup, and it was obvious to her that Eve was somehow, well...broken. Then she thought of the garden and knew how to lure Eve outdoors. After all, a woman always felt better when her garden was in order.

"All right, you win. We won't go out to dinner. But your garden looks a little tired, don't you think? Let's take a few minutes to put your garden to bed, like we used to. It's a lovely evening. Come on, no laziness. It's got to get done. Go get your gloves and a pair for me. We can make a dent before the sun disappears completely."

Doris thought she caught a flicker of interest. Eve raised

one brow, shrugged, then a small smile of resignation eased across her slender face. Doris beamed with elation, for having succeeded, and gratitude, for not having to be alone this evening. Rolling up her sleeves she felt flush with relief that she wouldn't have time to recall the love and passion she'd witnessed in Annie's marriage, then compare it to her own. Eve wasn't the only one who needed care and mending tonight. Feeling a sudden surge of energy, Doris followed Eve into the kitchen, flicked on a light and called out, "Why don't I just make a quick call to North Star and order some Chinese for dinner?"

I will honor Christmas in my heart, and will try to keep it all the year. I will live in the Past, the Present, and the Future. The Spirits of all Three shall strive within me. I will not shut out the lessons that they teach.

— Charles Dickens, *A Christmas Carol*

Four

I will honor Christmas in my heart. I will live in the
Past, the Present, and the Future. The Spirits of all
Three shall strive within me. I will not shut out the
lessons that they teach.

—Charles Dickens, *A Christmas Carol*

The lights on the Christmas tree sparkled like distant stars
in the darkened living room. Eve's collection of Santa
Clauses were carefully placed on decorated tables around
the room and the delicate wooden crèche that she and Tom
had purchased for their first Christmas together nestled in
its place of honor atop the grand piano. Eve sat on one
end of the green velvet living room sofa cuddled under an
old afghan. She'd lost a lot of weight and the cold affected
her much more than it ever used to.

Opposite her on the other side, with her long legs
stretched out and one hand absently tugging at her shaggy
bangs, slouched Annie Blake. They were sipping coffee
spiked with brandy and listening to Frank Sinatra croon
"I'll Be Home for Christmas."

Eve's vision of the colored lights swam as the message

struck true: home for Christmas. That had been her single goal for the six months since Tom's death: to stay in her home until Christmas. But now it all seemed so pointless. Although the stage was set with the usual props, it felt as empty and cold as a deserted theater. Once this was a place of hospitality, merriment and revelry, a place where scores of friends and family came for a holiday visit and a cup of cheer. This year only Annie rang her doorbell.

"It doesn't feel like Christmas," Eve said softly over the rim of her cup.

"Aw, Eve," Annie replied with gentle exasperation. "What did you expect?" She rested her cup on her bent knee and pursed her lips. "It's your first Christmas without Tom. You have to face the fact that this Christmas isn't the same. Your life is different. No amount of creative decorating is going to change that immutable fact."

Eve shuddered, drawing the afghan closer around her shoulders and turning her head away. She didn't want to listen. "Bah, humbug."

"What am I going to do with you?" Annie asked with a sorry shake of her head. "I see you slipping deeper and deeper into this pit and I can't pull you out. You're so thin. So remote. So goddamn stubborn."

"I'm not stubborn," Eve retaliated, hurt. "I'm in mourning."

"No, you're way past mourning. You're dying. Fizzing out. Fading away before my very eyes. And it burns my butt."

"I'm sorry," Eve replied tightly, shifting her weight and retreating farther. "Then...just go if I make you so uncomfortable."

"Damn, you don't think I haven't thought about it?" she exploded. "It's hard watching this. It's hard for everyone who cares about you. You just won't listen to anything anyone has to say to you. You're deaf to all advice. It's driving your friends—the people who care about you—crazy." She paused, taking in the way Eve brought her knees up to her chest and tightened the afghan around her shoulders. "I'm sorry, Eve, but haven't you noticed that a whole lot of people don't come by anymore?"

Eve felt a burn on her cheeks. "Of course I have," she replied defensively. "I don't blame them. It's the holidays. I'm alone, depressed. I'm not exactly party material. Aside from making them feel awkward about tiptoeing around my feelings, I make for a difficult table placement. A single woman not yet social or socially acceptable to pair up with an unattached male so soon after..." Her voice trailed away.

"After Tom's death. Go ahead, say it."

Eve stuck her chin out and tightened her lips.

"Don't you see, sweetie, that's what I'm talking about. No more excuses. Tom's dead. Gone. You have to pick up the pieces and move forward. Not just for you, but for the children's sake. You're stagnant here. Going under."

"I'm doing okay...."

Annie slapped her forehead with her palm. "Hey, who are you talking to here? You can't keep up those false pretenses with me, sweetie. It might work with Doris and the rest of those Riverton matrons, but I'm not just your friend, I'm your lawyer. I do your books. I know your finances better than you do and I'm telling you, you're going under. Faster than the *Titanic* and," she said rolling her eyes, "this place you're carrying is about as big."

"It's not just some place. It's my home."

"Look, hon, I know you wanted, even needed, to stretch things out so you could be here for Christmas. It was a bad decision fiscally, I didn't like it, but hey, I didn't push you either, for the kids' sake. But the party's over. You have to move. Now.''

"I can hang on a little longer."

"No, you can't. In fact, I'm worried sick about what will happen to you if the house doesn't sell quickly. You should have sold last summer when the pool was open, gotten top dollar. But," she conceded, turning her head to take in the large room with the coved molding and high ceilings, "all this mahogany and balsam trim makes this a perfect holiday house and ought to push a lot of emotional buttons for buyers after Christmas. As your lawyer, I'm advising you to put this elephant on the market. And as your friend, I'm begging you to do it now."

Eve had heard this conversation before, knew where it was heading and felt the walls closing in on her. She set her cup on the glass coffee table with a shaky hand. "Where would I go?" she rasped, voicing the question for the first time. When she raised her eyes to Annie, they were wide with fear.

Annie slowly placed her cup on the table beside Eve's and said gently, "Where do you want to go?"

Eve shrugged her shoulders and shook her head. "It's not that I haven't thought about it. Bronte and Finney are happy here. Their friends are here. I can't pull them away from what they know, not after all they've been through."

"Hon," Annie said with her husky voice low and well modulated. "I'm not sure you can afford to stay in Riverton."

"There are some small houses...."

"You can't afford a small house here."

Eve sucked in her breath and brought her fist to her lips. "My God, what am I going to do?"

"Again, you have to answer that question for yourself."

"I can't. I can't..."

"Of course you can," Annie hurried to answer, moving closer to place her long hands over Eve's small ones. "And you're not alone. I'm here with you. Helping women in your situation is what I do for a living, remember? There's nothing to fear. You just have to see yourself in transition. Step by step, you'll get through this."

Eve nodded halfheartedly, knowing this was what was expected, accustomed to doing what was expected of her. She drew back. Annie sighed, released Eve's hand and did the same.

Eve chewed her lip and fingered the afghan. Annie's patience with her was wearing thin. She looked at Annie's long, slim body wrapped in cashmere and wool with diamond studs in her ears, short but polished nails and her blond hair loosely tied back with a clasp. Annie's self-confidence crackled in the air around her. She'd practically raised herself after running away at thirteen from her poor, "weird" hippie-commune home in Oregon to live with her grandparents in Chicago. There was nothing Annie felt she couldn't do if she tried hard enough. It was this sense of empowerment that led so many divorced, widowed, lost single women to her law firm, seeking her out, hoping a bit of her confidence would sprinkle on them, like fairy dust.

On the other end of the sofa, Eve felt all the more a thin, opaque shadow of women like Annie Blake, who faced the outside world on a daily basis, chin out, fists in the ready, making their own living. It wasn't envy she felt, but confusion. Who was this pitiful creature curled up on the sofa, cowering under a blanket? Where was the secure, attractive, competent woman she remembered Eve Porter to be? That woman seemed to have died with Tom.

"How did I let this happen to me, Annie?" she cried. "I'm not stupid or naive. I've always prided myself on my intellect. But for twenty-three years I let Tom make all the decisions about money. He liked to do it, and I..." She paused. "I didn't care. Sure, I handled the checkbooks, paid the bills, arranged for the lawn to be cut, the maid to clean twice a week and the shirts to be laundered. I mean, I'm not a moron. I raised my children. I supported my husband. I managed my family. I was good at my job."

She heard the defensiveness in her own voice and felt an overwhelming sadness that somehow, that job didn't matter much anymore. That her home was unimportant. She felt somehow less than Annie and other professional women working outside the home. And she resented it, deeply.

"Of course you were," Annie said, resting a hand over hers. "No one's saying you weren't, Eve."

"Don't use that tone with me," she snapped.

"What tone?"

"That placating 'Poor little Eve, poor helpless, mindless housewife' tone that working women like you are so good at dishing out."

"I see."

Eve looked up to see Annie draw her knees in tight. Guilt washed over her and she reached out to grab Annie's hand back. "I'm sorry. That wasn't fair."

Annie snorted and said, "I did sound kinda patronizing. I hate when people do that to me, too. To any woman. Hit me if I ever do it again."

"Ditto."

Both women laughed and squeezed hands. The tension eased.

"You know I'm on your side, pal."

"I know."

"I'm only telling you that you can't afford your old life-style any longer. I'm sorry, Eve, I wish it were different for you. But Tom... Well, you know.''

Eve knew. Tom had stretched everything to the limit, and like most baby boomers, expected to live to a ripe old age. He was a surgeon, raking in a healthy income and at the prime of his life. He'd thought he had plenty of time to start saving for the future. He didn't expect to die at fifty. But he did, leaving his family unprepared. They didn't have outstanding debts, but their life-style, as Annie put it, was titanic. His life insurance had carried them through the past six months but it was disappearing fast. In fact, they were broke, and at no time of the year was that fact more rudely apparent than at Christmas.

''Look at that,'' Eve said, indicating with a wave of her hand the sparse showing of gifts under the tree. ''The kids are going to be so disappointed this year. I couldn't afford to get them much of anything. They're used to mountains of gifts. It used to take us all day just to open them.''

''Yeah, well, I never had that many Christmas gifts so excuse me if I don't feel sorry for them. Well, I do, but not because of the number of gifts. Don't they have a clue what it took for you to keep them in this house through Christmas?''

''No, and I don't want them to know. Children shouldn't worry about money.''

''Bull cakes. I knew more about handling my money—what there was of it—at thirteen than my druggie parents did. Not making children worry about it and discussing it honestly with them are two different things entirely. What's wrong with letting them know money's tight? They're not stupid. They've probably figured it out already. You're going to have to tell them something. And soon.'' She craned her neck to peer through the arched entry. ''By the way, where are the little darlings?''

Eve didn't think Annie knew what she was talking about when it came to children. At forty-three, Annie had only married a few years earlier. Her big tribute to turning forty, and to a man three years her junior. She'd never opted to have children and often saw them in the same light one would see a mosquito at a picnic.

"They're at their friends' houses. They're always out these days. I don't think they like being here." She plucked at the afghan and remembered the years before when the house overflowed with their many friends. Now the house seemed like a mausoleum. "Perhaps too many memories."

Annie offered a bittersweet smile. "Maybe it isn't such a bad thing to move on after all."

Eve looked up sharply into Annie's eyes and saw flash in the pale-blue the icy truth about so many things. Annie was right. The children weren't that happy here anymore. Neither was she. Their life here was over and staying was like living in limbo. She'd been hanging on to this big house in the hope that somehow she'd get her old life back. The one where Tom carved out most of the decisions and she buffed and polished off the rough edges.

She'd been hanging on, when she ought to have been thinking, carefully planning her next step. She ought to have considered what job she could get, what schools her children could transfer to, where she could afford to move. Instead of dwelling in the past, she should have focused on the future. She ought to have dealt with her emotional upswings about having to leave her home, about having Tom leave her. Instead, she'd wasted months thinking.... No, that was the problem, she realized with sudden clarity. She didn't think. She'd merely wandered through the rooms of her house and stared blankly at her lovely things. Somehow she'd felt if she just held on a little longer...

What? A miracle would happen? Someone would magically come down the chimney on Christmas Eve and drop a bag full of money under the tree, just because she was being a good girl? Well, standing in the long line at the discount department store to purchase the one or two gifts she could afford only on sale had taught her that Santa Claus wasn't coming this year. Or next.

"I'll put the house on the market," she said. Usually, Eve was good at making quick, strong decisions and she felt a bolt of relief to find that part of herself once more. The dozen smiling, apple-cheeked, potbellied Santas suddenly seemed to be littering her room. She felt the urge to pack them all away, to clear the decks of dreamy clutter and sail on.

"That's my girl," exclaimed Annie. Then, "Oh God, did that sound patronizing? I'm sorry."

Eve shook her head and stared at her hands, clenching white in her lap while realization set in. When she spoke, it was like an avalanche, a bursting of a dam, the opening of a festering wound.

"Annie, I don't know how to do anything. Anything! Not my taxes, the mortgage, financial planning. I'm scared. I'm not prepared."

"You'll be fine."

"I don't know how to go out there and sign leases," she raged on, her voice getting higher and higher. "Or figure out insurance payments for the house, for the car, for our health. I don't even know what questions to ask. God, what job can I get? I haven't had a job in twenty years. I have to do something." She paused, stricken. "My children have only me."

"And you're more than enough."

Eve stopped, blinked.

"You *are*," Annie repeated.

Eve heard this. For a moment she felt her chest rise and fall heavily as the words sunk in. *You're more than enough.* Dear God, help me, she prayed. I have to be.

She leaned back on her side of the sofa, tucking her legs beneath her and tugging the afghan under her chin. Annie did the same. Judy Garland was singing "Have Yourself a Merry Little Christmas" and beside them, the fire crackled and sparked behind the iron grate. Eve felt the warmth of it slowly seep into her soul, gradually thawing the chill that had seized it in the past months and made her numb. An iciness that straightened her spine, stiffened her walk, paled her cheek and made her so very brittle that each time she'd suffered a smile at a sympathetic comment, each time she'd offered a pat reply to a holiday greeting, she felt sure she might shatter into a thousand shards of crystal.

In the quiet peace, however, in the company of her trusted friend, in the aftermath of a decision, Eve felt her wintry depression begin to melt. Deep inside she experienced her first gentle kindling of Christmas spirit.

After a while, Annie spoke again. "I see you have Dickens's *A Christmas Carol* on the table. That was this month's choice for the Book Club."

"Was it?" she replied vaguely.

Annie twitched her lips. Everyone knew that Eve loved books and reading with a passion and was unforgiving toward anyone who came to the Book Club meetings unprepared. It was the group's greatest concern that Eve had stopped reading.

"Why didn't you come to the meeting? We missed you."

Eve's toes curled under the afghan and bright-pink spots blossomed on her cheeks. "It was the Christmas party. It wouldn't have been much of a discussion."

"That's not what I meant. You need to be with us. We need you."

"I...I know. I just wasn't ready to share my own, personal story yet."

"The party was at Doris's house," Annie continued in a different vein, allowing Eve her space. "Again. As always, it was flawless, right down to the dripless candles and plum pudding."

"How is she?"

"You mean you don't know? I thought she was always hanging around here."

"No, not so much anymore. I like to think it's because she's busy. It's the holidays and R.J. likes to entertain."

Annie looked away with a harrumph, frowning, registering her doubt that that was the real reason. "Well, I say it'd do you good to come back to the group. Reading, discussing ideas, hell, just laughing it up with the girls. Drink a little wine, get a little silly. It's good for the heart and the soul." Her voice altered to reflect her worry. "You shouldn't be so isolated."

"Not yet."

"Okay, okay," Annie said on a long sigh. "I know that tone well enough after the past six months. But don't take too long. All the girls are anxious. They'll be knocking down your door pretty soon."

"I know. I won't." She paused. "You're all so sweet to be worrying about me."

"Yep, that's us all right. A bunch of sweet ol' ladies," Annie said in that rollicking manner of hers that threw caution to the wind, dishing it out and taking it back in full measure. At heart, she was a clown and couldn't stand too much gushy sentiment. Eve loved her for it, loved her tonight especially for taking off the gloves and speaking straight, for teasing her and treating her like a normal person again, not some fragile china doll that had to be handled carefully lest she break.

"I can see us in another ten or twenty years," Annie said, moving as she acted out the role, "sitting around the rest home table, reading books with large print, gumming our lips together and shouting our opinions at each other because we won't be able to hear."

Eve laughed until tears squeezed from her eyes at Annie's perfect pantomime. "Yes! I can see us now," she said, joining in. "We'll all wear large purple hats and clunky brown shoes."

"And we'll fart out loud and pretend we didn't notice. Hell, we probably won't even hear. 'Eh, what'd you say? Oops, pardon me! What?'"

Eve held her sides. It hurt so good to laugh again, mostly at herself. Annie could always do this to her; it was what cemented their friendship.

"Oh, Annie, stop!"

"What? You don't think the kids will be calling us 'old farts' behind our backs. Ha! Well, we might as well give it right back to them. Both barrels. But I'm givin' it to them right through my tight, sexy Calvin Klein jeans."

And she would, too, Eve thought chuckling. Annie Blake joined the Book Club five years earlier and right from the start everyone recognized that Annie was different from the usual Riverton matron. She was a little louder, a little brassier, a little more cool, and her opinions were always honest and on the money. And she had soul. It wasn't long before Eve discovered that Annie was a kindred spirit—a freer, blithe spirit.

"I'm curious about something," Annie said, wiping her eyes and settling back into the cushions. "I've been hammering at you for months to let go of this house and to get on with your life. And now, suddenly, you decide to do it.'' She snapped her fingers. ''Just like that. What happened? Am I a more persuasive lawyer than I thought or did I miss something here?''

The ghost of a smile crossed Eve's face as she gazed down at Dickens's book on the coffee table. How could she explain that all Annie's numbers on the ledgers, the sheets of meaningless papers that she'd signed, meant nothing to her? That inside the hard covers of that edition of *A Christmas Carol* lay the pressed petals of three yellow roses, picked six months earlier. That this tale by Charles Dickens, her old friend, was the first book she'd read since Tom's death. That tonight she felt as though she'd been visited by the ghosts of Christmas past, present and future and was shaken out of her complacency.

''Let's just say that, like Scrooge, I finally woke up and decided it was time to heed the spirits and change.''

''Well,'' Annie replied with brows raised. ''Whaddya know?'' She swooped over to pick up her coffee cup and raise it in a toast. ''Here's to change, sweetheart.''

Eve picked up her cup and raised it, smiling bravely despite the shivering inside at the prospect of what felt to her like jumping off a cliff.

''God bless us, everyone,'' she said, praying fervently.

Five

> Before she had married she thought she was in love.
> But the happiness that should have resulted from this
> love had not come; she must have deceived herself
> she thought. Emma sought to learn what was really
> meant in life by the words "happiness," "passion,"
> and "ecstasy"—words that had seemed so beautiful
> in books.
>
> —Gustave Flaubert, *Madame Bovary*

January 7, 1998

Doris stood in the foyer of her redbrick colonial home
and waited for the Book Club to arrive. A pure, sensual
pleasure embraced her as she glanced around her house,
making a last-minute check that all was in proper order. It
was the first Book Club meeting of the year and she
wanted everything to be perfect. The sparkling crystal
wineglasses were set out on the Sheraton side table beside
the bottles of wine: white, chilled, and red, opened to allow
time to breathe—something she'd learned from her father.
On the large dining table that had once been her mother's,

she'd draped snowy white linen and lined her grandmother's crisp damask napkins in an intricate pattern that
she'd admired once in a magazine. Someone could photograph this table and put *it* in a magazine, she thought
with a shiver of pride.

And the ladies would be sure to admire the clever arrangement of fresh flowers and greens, cut from her own
shrubs that very morning. She'd read somewhere how
women of culture and breeding always had their clippers
handy, and from that date on she'd hung a pair on a gros-
grain ribbon beside her back door.

Her pièce de résistance, however, were the French appetizers that she'd spent hours researching, shopping for
and preparing. She had to make something French, of
course, because this month's book was *Madame Bovary*,
a classic that she'd insisted they read after feigning astonishment that no one in the Book Club had actually read
the book.

In fact, she herself had never read it, but she'd go to the
grave with that secret—and her SAT scores. She'd heard
of it, of course, and seen the movie—the old version with
Jennifer Jones that everyone knew was the best. Now she'd
never have to pretend again because she'd read the novel
at last and enjoyed it thoroughly.

Even if she was furious at the character of Emma Bovary. How could she throw away a perfectly good life and
husband for the sake of her uncontrolled passion? Doris
could feel her heart rate zoom and her breath shorten just
thinking about it. What did it matter if Emma had "bliss"
or "passion" or "ecstasy"? These had little to do with
virtues that were the hallmarks of respectability. Indeed,
even womanhood. Virtues such as patience, self-discipline,
self-control, chastity, adaptability to others. Yes, especially
that. Qualities that her mother had, that her grandmother

had, that were instilled in her as a child by example not by name. Emma was, in her opinion, selfish and immoral. She deserved to die.

Well, she thought, stroking her neck, that might be a bit harsh. It was easy to sympathize with Emma's romantic nature, especially at first. All new brides dream of a perfect marriage with love and passion in the moonlight, husbands on pedestals, pretty curtains on the windows, fringed lampshades, no other bride's bouquet before hers. She certainly had.

But Emma went too far when she grew bored and forsake her duty, especially to her child. What mother could forgive Emma the desertion of her child! And though her husband may have been a bit dull and plodding, he wasn't all that bad. Men were men, Doris decided, brushing away the uncomfortable image of her own husband with that phrase.

Emma Bovary should have settled with what she had. *She'd* settled, hadn't she? Why, most women settled, dug in, called upon those womanly virtues, and made it work. And Doris was champing at the bit to make that statement tonight.

The Pennsylvania tall clock chimed seven times. Doris shook away her musings and glanced in the magnificent Viennese mirror in the foyer, smoothing her strawberry-blond hair that fell neatly to her double chin, but not too stiffly. That was one of her mother's cardinal rules: *Always make it look effortless.* And, *Treat your family like guests and your guests like family.*

She thought of the Book Club as family—an extended family. With them she wasn't the wife of the flamboyant builder and architect, R. J. Bridges, or the mother of eighteen-year-old Bob Jr. and fourteen-year-old Sarah. She wasn't the PTA president or the chairwoman of the Children's Welfare League. With these four women, some of whom she'd known for over twenty-five years, she was just Doris. With them, especially after a few glasses of wine, Doris might surprise even herself with comments on a book or an issue or a secret that just popped out like a bubble. With the Book Club, Doris always felt uncensored. They weren't her judge and jury, they were her peers. Her friends.

Friends. A stab of disappointment coursed through her as she recalled that Eve Porter had sent her regrets and would not be coming tonight. How could Eve do that to her, she wondered, hurt? She could understand Eve's not attending meetings at other women's houses the past few months; she even forgave her for skipping the Christmas party. After all, hadn't her mother said, *Never bring your problems to a party?* It was unforgivable to make things awkward for the hostess and Doris knew Eve was only being sensitive. But not to come to *her* Book Club meeting? You just didn't do that to a friend. Ever since Tom's passing, the only person Eve had depended on was Annie Blake. It was as though all the years of close friendship the two of them had shared—their children playing together, shopping, hair appointments, taking turns for twelve years being room mothers for the girls—had been tossed aside.

The doorbell rang, and like Pavlov's dog, a smile sprang to her face. She took measured, graceful steps to the front door.

It was Annie Blake. Lately she had a physical reaction to Annie, usually a sucking in of the stomach. Annie seemed to be everything she was not, to have all she did not. Doris held her smile in place by force of the virtue of self-discipline.

"Annie, how nice to see you. Won't you come in?"

She heard the tension in her own voice, saw Annie's eyes search the room beyond her shoulders, then glaze over when Annie realized that she was the first one here and thus compelled to make polite chitchat. Doris bristled, feeling somehow dismissed in her own home.

"Let me pour you a glass of wine."

"Thanks," Annie replied, shaking off her coat. "I could really use one."

"Oh?" Doris took Annie's coat, fingering the cashmere wool with quiet envy. "Why is that?"

"It's been a hell of a day. What is it about the New Year that makes women want to change their lives—and be in a hurry to do it? Is it the New Year's resolutions? My phone's been ringing off the hook and poor Lisa is at her wit's end."

Lisa, Doris knew, was Annie's secretary. Again, she felt a slight shudder of insecurity in the presence of this dynamic woman who had such things as her own secretary. That was inconceivable to Doris. She herself had never wanted to work "outside the home," as she put it. In fact, she thanked God daily that she was wealthy enough not to have to. Yet, there was a worldliness about professional women that intrigued her.

"Red or white?"

"White. Hope it's cold. I'm parched."

"But of course." She made it sound like the French, *mais oui!*

Following Annie's long strides into the dining room, Doris surveyed her sleek crepe wool pantsuit in a rich chocolate-brown that slid along her toned, well-exercised body. Her cream-colored silk blouse had the top three buttons left open against her long, slim chest in a sexy insolence that irritated Doris. She thought Annie looked foolish—at her age.

No one could ever say that *she* didn't dress her age, or know what was appropriate, in dress, style and manner. Her figure might not be as slender as it once was, but she wasn't a girl anymore, was she? And she didn't dress like one, not like Annie who wore the same clothes as Doris's college-aged daughter. Everyone knew children were embarrassed to see their mothers dress too young or sexy.

Still, a frown deepened in her plump, pinkened cheeks as she caught sight in the mirror of the rounding bulges at her own hips and belly that the belt of her expensive ice-blue silk dress seemed to accentuate. Her heart withered knowing instinctively that Annie wouldn't be caught dead in a dress like this. Her daughter would call it an "old lady" dress.

"Oh, these are real cute," Annie exclaimed with enthusiasm at seeing the several elegant trays filled with the appetizers Doris had slaved over. "What are they?"

Doris approached the table with a proprietary air. "They're canapés," she replied, enunciating carefully and establishing her superiority at knowing such things.

Annie's eyes flashed with amusement and something else that Doris refused to acknowledge as pity. "No, I mean, what's in them? Is that shrimp or crab? I'm allergic to crab."

Doris blanched but smiled again and replied through thin lips, "Crab."

Doris watched as Annie reached for a spinach quiche and nibbled it in mincing bites while looking around the room with thinly disguised boredom.

"Have you seen Eve?" began Doris. "She's not coming tonight, you know."

"I know," Annie confirmed, dabbing her mouth with one of Doris's grandmother's damask napkins as though it were paper. "I tried to drag her over, but you know Eve when she's got her back up."

"Well, I hardly think she'd need to be dragged over to *my* house. She's been here many times, for many years."

"Oh, it's not that," Annie replied quickly.

Doris was pleased to see her retreat. Eve was *her* friend, after all.

"She has to be dragged anywhere," Annie continued. "You know how she's been lately—isolated. She's got to snap out of it."

Doris raised one brow. "That's an interesting way to describe a woman's period of mourning. I'd always assumed a year was appropriate."

Annie skipped a beat and when she spoke again, her normally low voice dropped an octave. "I wasn't referring to mourning. Perhaps you haven't noticed that Eve's been having a hard time of it. She's not herself and I'm worried about her."

"Depressed? Our Eve?" Doris tsked. "She's just going through a bad spell. She'll be fine." She reached out to pat Annie's arm in a condescending manner.

Annie held herself erect. "I know she will. I'll see to it."

"Is that part of your job description, too?" Doris asked with a steady smile.

Annie's eyes narrowed as she studied Doris's face with the focus of a cat eyeing a plump canary. Silent and still, but lethal. Doris returned a rigidly polite smile.

The doorbell rang again, sounding to Doris like the bell of a boxing ring. She promptly excused herself, feeling breathless and numb, as though she'd just received a solid right hook but hadn't yet hit the mat. It was only the first round. She was relieved beyond words to find Gabriella and Midge at her threshold, almost hauling them into the house with shrill welcome.

They entered laughing, shaking off snow, explaining as they removed their winter coats how they'd managed to "chow down" some pasta in Little Italy before heading out to the Book Club, which worried Doris tremendously. "I hope you're still hungry."

They hurried to assure her they were as they each flopped large leather bags crammed full with manila folders and type-filled papers onto the floor. They each pulled out well-worn paperback copies of *Madame Bovary*. Gabriella's had dozens of yellow sticky slips poking out and Doris smiled, knowing that when Gabriella prepared, the discussions were always lively.

As they moaned about their harried day, Doris listened quietly with her hands folded thinking to herself, *Two more working women.* She knew this, of course, but tonight, on the verge of her fiftieth birthday, it hit her differently, like another punch from another angle. They seemed so very busy, so very alive. They seemed to have such purpose.

Midge was a therapist and an artist. Gabriella was a nurse and a mother. That's how they described themselves, each giving emphasis to the conjunction *and.* Both worked at the University of Illinois which fostered the close friendship they shared. The Odd Couple, Doris always called them because they couldn't be more different.

Midge was unmarried, a feminist who wore her long, dark skirts and artsy sweaters like a uniform. She was boldly antifashion, or as Doris once whispered behind her palm to Eve, a reverse snob. Secretly everyone in the Book Club admired Midge's scrubbed, handsome looks, her unmade-up face and nails and her long, striking mane of natural pepper-and-salt that she defied dying and wore as proudly as a flag flapping loose around her straight shoulders. Not that any of them would choose that style for themselves, but they all agreed it worked for Midge with her tall, willowy, flat-tummied body and her complicated, fierce intensity.

Gabriella, in contrast, was all accommodation and smiles. This amused Doris, who couldn't imagine how anyone could be so cheerful working a part-time job with four children at home. Gabby's flat, round face was carved in half by the smile that always dominated it. Her smile revealed a mouthful of large white teeth and squeezed her dark-brown eyes into small half-moons over enormous round cheeks. Gabriella wore little makeup either, but she loved color and swathed her plump, short body in bright oranges, shocking pinks and sunny yellows in swirling patterns. With her golden skin she resembled a soft, ripe pear.

Now that everyone had arrived, the group slipped into the comfortable pattern of prediscussion chitchat. First they complimented Doris on her clever French menu while she preened and pressed them each into making the most critical decision of the evening: red or white wine. While they nibbled and drank, they poured out good feelings and mutual affection as liberally as the wine. This phase finished, they eased into catching up with what had happened in each of their lives during the past month.

Doris was boasting shamelessly about Bob Jr.'s exploits at Georgetown. "He made the crew team. Just think how much fun it will be to visit him in Washington D.C. this spring, when the cherry trees are in bloom! Can't you just see my Bobby on one of those cute little rowboats on the Potomac?"

"A scull," corrected Midge dryly. She'd lived and studied in Boston, and delighted in pricking pomposity.

Doris flushed furiously, feeling another punch.

Gabriella's husband still hadn't found another job. Each month that passed, Gabriella had added more hours to her schedule at the hospital. Now she was working at least thirty hours a week. Fernando was growing increasingly depressed and anxious, so it fell to Gabriella to not only work harder, but to be cheerful and make everyone in the family happy and relaxed.

"Fernando is looking for just the right position," she said with a wide smile that assured everyone it was just a matter of time and not to worry—she wasn't! Only Midge knew the truth and she met Gabriella's gaze with a reassuring nod.

Midge's mother was coming for a visit from Florida next week and she didn't know how she was going to stand it. "The woman drives me crazy," she moaned, shaking her head. "She thinks she has to make this maternal pilgrimage every year to visit her single daughter. All she wants to know is when I'm going to get married again." She reached one of her long arms over to grab a canapé. Waving in the air to make a point, she added, "You'd think she'd get it into her head she's not going to be a grandmother."

"Why not? Just because you're not married doesn't mean you can't be a mother," said Annie.

Midge held the canapé still in the air and looked at her like she was nuts. "For God's sake, Annie, I'm fifty years old!"

"So what? You're fit, you eat well, you're in prime physical condition. Who says you can't have a baby? There are lots of older women having babies today."

"*I* say I can't have a baby. I'm not the nurturing type." She popped the appetizer into her mouth. "Besides, why would I want to breastfeed and change diapers at this point in my life? I've worked hard to find out who I am and I don't want to look back. Hooray for fifty, I say."

Doris leaned closer to catch every word of this conversation.

"I don't think being fifty has anything to do with it," Annie argued back.

"Yeah, well, it has a lot to do with your eggs," chirped in Gabriella. "She might look young but her eggs are dried up. I've seen those old eggs under the microscope and I know."

Annie's face darkened, then she stuck out her chin and said, "I don't believe that's true for every woman. What about those older women having babies you read about in the paper? Some of those women are in their sixties. They look like grandmas, but they had the babies."

"Those are surrogate eggs."

"Not all," Annie said resolutely. "There are lots of women in their forties having babies. What about Susan Sarandon?" When Annie got that tone, no one could convince her otherwise; she had her mind made up.

Gabriella, having heard this sad argument many times in the Women's Health Center, sighed and shook her head, knowing the futility of listing facts and data.

"In fact," Annie said clinking her glass, "I've got some news myself."

Everyone quieted and leaned forward.

"John and I've decided to have a baby. Actually, we've been trying for months now."

There was a long, strained silence.

"Well, don't everyone shout at once," Annie quipped, a blush betraying her.

Gabriella rushed to hug her. "I was busy biting my tongue for what I'd just said about old eggs. Of course I'm happy for you, if this is what you want."

"*Is* it what you want?" Midge asked, cocking her head.
"Or is it what John wants?"

"Both of us. He's wanted a baby since we got married
but after Tom's funeral I finally decided that hey, it's now
or never, right? The ol' biological clock is ticking away."

That old clock has run down, Doris thought to herself.
Annie was forty-three years old! Who did she think she
was kidding? She should be worrying about menopause,
not having a baby.

"Are you sure you want to be making lunches and driving carpool when you're fifty-three? Sixty?" she asked.
"And won't it interfere with your work?"

"It'll all work out," Annie said in her typical bravado.
"I don't intend to let it interfere with my job. I'll get lots
of help, and as for being sixty, what's sixty? *I think young
therefore I am.* That's my motto. It's how you feel inside
that counts."

"Well, your insides are going to feel tired," Doris replied dryly. "Trust me."

There was a chorus of agreement, yet they did not give
voice to the arguments uppermost in their minds: how, at
her age, the odds of getting pregnant were slim and the
odds of Down's Syndrome high.

Annie's shoulders slumped and she crossed her arms
tightly across her chest.

"Well, I think it's terrific," Midge surprised everyone
by announcing in a loud, authoritative voice. "The rest of
us are moping around worrying about wrinkles, and moan-
ing about hot flashes, gray hair and sagging boobs, and
you're out there getting pregnant." She raised her glass
high in a toast. "You go, girl!"

Suddenly it was a rallying call. The mood shift was
electric and everyone was raising their glasses, laughing
loudly. Relief and victory was visible on their faces as they

made jokes about menopause and aging and all the horrors of the inevitable change that they were marching toward like soldiers. Good soldiers facing certain doom. Now they had Annie to hold up as a symbol of defiance. They gloried in her fertility. It was a shared fertility.

In all the excitement and laughter, no one heard the doorbell ring, or the front door open. No one saw a small, slim woman in the long black wool coat enter the foyer, her library, hardcover copy of *Madame Bovary* clutched in her leather-gloved hand, her dark-brown hair tucked into a beret. She stood quietly on the outside of the tight circle, looking in, her pale-green eyes guarded. She stood and waited, her face a closed book.

Doris sensed a new presence in her home and turned her head. Her heart beat furiously with pleasure as she caught sight of the woman at the threshold. She felt a gush of triumph. Doris just knew she'd come to *her* house!

"Eve!" she called out in a high-pitched voice and ran toward her, open-armed.

Heads turned, sounds of delight pierced the air, and in a blur of color and motion, Eve Porter was kissed and hugged and loudly welcomed back, again and again. In return, Eve smiled and wept and told them all how she missed them, too, and could they forgive her for staying away so long, and yes of course, she'd read the book! With words and movements they gathered her carefully, firmly, lovingly back into the circle of the Book Club, each feeling a joy, a deep satisfaction that the circle was complete again, stronger, now that the missing link had returned.

Later that night Doris was floating on air, feeling that the whole evening had been a complete and utter success. Everyone had exclaimed how this was one of the best meetings ever as they left, and it was true. She did know how to throw a good party. *Treat your family as guests and your guests as family.* The crystal clinked in her hands like bells as she cleared away the last of the wineglasses from the library where the Book Club had completed one of their best book discussions. Annie had vehemently defended Emma's passion and rung Emma's husband, poor dull Charles, through the ringer. But Doris was smug with the satisfaction of the group's ultimate support of her own position that, to put it crudely, Emma was a slut.

"Thank God they're gone," R.J. said with a grunt as he strode into the library. Her husband always made a powerful entrance; it was ingrained in him like a whorl in a slab of hardwood. "Couldn't stand another moment of that damn squealing."

Doris bristled. "We do not squeal. We were simply laughing and talking." She picked up the tray of appetizers in a huff.

"Leave that. I'm hungry." When she put the tray back onto the coffee table, he poked around them with his index finger, then pointing to the canapés he asked, "What are they?"

Doris narrowed her eyes and thought suddenly of Annie Blake. She and R.J. were a lot alike. Blunt, bold, beloved by all—and shrewd.

"Crab."

He frowned in distaste and reached for the quiche, picked one up and tossed it in his mouth like a peanut. "These are pretty good," he said with his mouth full. "What was all that caterwauling about?"

"Oh, R.J.," she exclaimed, deaf to the insult, "it's wonderful. Eve's back in the group. I knew she wouldn't miss a meeting at my house. She's too good a friend. You should've seen Annie's face," she said smugly. "I could tell she didn't know she was coming. What did she think?

Eve and I've been friends for years. We live only a few blocks apart. We raised our children together, for heaven's sake. Remember how Sarah and Bronte liked to wear the same thing every day? And how they got braces at the same time? One just doesn't forget that kind of friendship. I'll never understand women like Annie Blake. She thinks she's so superior just because she's a lawyer.''

''She's a damn good lawyer.''

''Well, she should know enough to dress her age.''

R.J. glanced at her, smirked and swirled the ice in his glass of Scotch. ''She looks pretty good, if you ask me.''

Doris knew that look in his eye and suddenly felt as if she'd absorbed a wallop in the solar plexus, the KO punch that dropped her to her knees. All the success she'd felt earlier drained like blood, leaving her pale and shriveled.

''You should do some exercise,'' he continued, popping another quiche into his mouth. ''Join the club. Now, don't get huffy. You want to look good too, don't you?''

She looked at his tall, muscular trim body that had survived years of football, then handball and now golf. ''I wasn't aware that I didn't look good.''

''Come on, you've put on twenty pounds at least.''

It was thirty. Doris sucked in her stomach and hunched her shoulders. ''Who would I be losing weight for? I like the way I am. I'm not pretending to be twenty any longer.'' Then, seeing something in his eyes that was somewhere between disgust and resignation, she hastened to add, ''But I'll think about it. It'd be good for my health to walk more. And now that the holidays are over, I suppose I should start a diet. To lose these few extra pounds.''

He'd already stopped listening to her and was walking toward the television.

Doris tightened her lips against the banshee's howl in her chest, fought for control, then turned her back and left the room in a silent fury. He hadn't really listened to her in years. He hadn't paid a compliment to her like he'd just paid to Annie in years. He hadn't approached her in years, not sexually, not the way a man approached a woman he was attracted to. Not the way a man should feel about his wife. Certainly not the way she'd read about in books.

Turning her head before climbing the stairs, she saw him bend over to insert one of *those* movies into the VCR. A lump formed in her throat that she couldn't swallow down, a craw full of anger and hurt and shame that he sought pleasure alone, with a movie, rather than in her own, lonely bed. She'd assumed it was impotence; she'd read that about men his age but didn't dream of ever asking him about it, even though the magazines always said that she should *keep open the lines of communication*. It was just too embarrassing, even to say the words: *impotence, sex, orgasm*. She felt a shudder of revulsion at the thought of saying, even whispering, those words to him. She didn't even know what a G-spot was much less where to find it.

But she was curious…oh so curious.

Grasping the railing until her knuckles whitened, she watched as her husband, her lover, stretched out to grab another handful of her artful French canapés, then ease his broad fifty-four-year-old backside into his favorite leather chair, swinging the library door shut with his free hand.

Doris's head slumped and she felt very old as she slowly climbed the broad staircase to her room. As she brought one foot over the next, she recalled the arguments Annie and the rest of the group had raised in defense of Emma Bovary. Annie was passionate, as usual, in her defense of Emma, claiming she had remained true to her dreams until the end, even if those dreams were unrealistic, superficial. Midge had said how sad it was that women were so often betrayed by their dreams.

"And the men they loved," Gabriella had added.

It was Eve's heartfelt statement, however, that rang true with the Club, eliciting nods of agreement and sighs of sympathy—even from Doris.

"We shouldn't be so quick to judge or condemn. If Emma had had one true friend, someone who could steer her straight, and who she could pour her heart out to, then I really believe she'd have pulled through."

"She should've been in a Book Club," Gabriella said to a chorus of agreement. "She needed to talk to women."

"Yeah," added Midge, nodding. "But instead she depended on men for all her happiness and look what happened to her."

Everyone had laughed, except Doris. Now, however, as she entered her bedroom and stood before the immense California king-size bed that was big enough for even large R.J. and plump Doris to sleep in and still not touch all night long, Doris started to laugh. It came out as high, choking sounds in her throat, then altered to a low keening wail that would not be controlled.

Eve sat down at her kitchen table and slowly sipped the hot milk she'd prepared. She didn't know if it was an old wives' tale that hot milk helped you to sleep but she thought it was worth the try. Since Tom's death, she'd hardly had a decent night's sleep, waking up several times a night in a sweat of panic. If this didn't work she was going to try Prozac. She took another long sip when the phone rang.

"Just wanted to make sure you got home okay." It was Annie, and Eve knew she was really asking how she'd handled her reentry to the club.

"Sure, thanks. But really, Annie, it's only a few blocks."

"So, what'd you think?"

"I thought you and Doris were going to duke it out on the Oriental rug."

"I wish. I love a good fight. Besides, she's such a know-it-all. She likes to ram her opinions down our throats."

"Doris feels things very intensely. She has strong opinions about everything."

"So does R.J. It's beyond me how she and that husband of hers can live together."

"It's a big house."

Annie laughed.

"It was great to be back."

"It was great to have you back. Everyone was saying so."

Eve smiled, knowing it was true. "Annie? You know when I was talking about how great it was to have a friend to pour one's heart out to? How it saves one's sanity?" She paused, her eyes crinkling at the thought. "Well, I was talking about you."

There was a pause. Then came Annie's voice, much subdued. "Ditto."

Six

> When a condition or a problem becomes too great,
> humans have the protection of not thinking about it.
> But it goes inward and minces up with a lot of other
> things already there and what comes out is discontent
> and uneasiness, guilt and a compulsion to get some-
> thing—anything—before it is all gone.

> —John Steinbeck, *The Winter of Our Discontent*

The alarm clock went off at 7:00 a.m., clicking on Annie's favorite easy rock station. She grumbled, rubbed her
eyes and automatically reached over to grab for the thermometer and stick it in her mouth. The house was veiled
in a damp, chilled gray, prompting her to tug the comforter
higher over her shoulders while she lay on her back and
waited. Annie hated February and she didn't need a weath-
erman to tell her a storm was blowing in. It was the kind
of morning that made Annie want to cuddle up and stay
in bed with a good book.

John yawned loudly beside her, sleepily patted her bare
thigh with his long fingers, then rose in a swoop in a beeline for the bathroom. Every morning it was the same;

while she lay in bed with a thermometer stuck in her mouth, he'd shower, shave, then make coffee. When did their lives become so routine, she wondered? She knew the answer—since she'd started her campaign to have a baby.

She pulled the thermometer out of her mouth and squinted her eyes at the itsy-bitsy numbers that seemed to be getting harder to read these days. Surprise shifted her mood and her mouth eased to a grin as she brought the thermometer close to her nose.

This morning they'd break the damn routine! There was a definite rise. Sitting up, she reached over to the bedside table and grabbed the pad of paper that charted her ovulation for the past six months. She had a dozen books that showed graphs and charts of what ovulation should look like. No definite pattern had become apparent, which was driving her crazy, but this month even a dummy in science like herself could see a clear dip-rise of her body temperature.

"John!" she called out, thrilled at the first clear sign of ovulation she'd had so far in this grueling ordeal. "Get your butt back in this bed. Look! I'm ovulating!"

John ducked his head out from the bathroom. Half his face was covered with shaving cream but over the white his brows scowled. "Now?"

She heard the irritation in his voice and it nettled her. "Hey, I don't plan these things. But take a look. It's a beauty. I'm talking textbook case here. We've got to do it."

He sighed and rolled his eyes. "Look, I'm running late as it is. I've got to be on time for the building inspection."

"It'll only take a minute."

He gave a short laugh and muttered something under his

breath about how she'd got that right. Annie could feel her temper rise.

"You know what I mean…"

"How about tonight? I don't have the time right now, and frankly, I'm not in the mood. I'm sure your egg won't dissolve in a few hours."

"I can't tonight. I'm booked with pro bono appointments, remember?"

He put his hands on his hips and thought. "Okay then, lunch. I'll find a way to meet you here at, what, twelve-thirty?"

Annie frowned and shook her head. "I can't. I'm in trial this morning. Damn, this is harder than arranging a business meeting."

"That's what our sex life is beginning to feel like."

"Well, whose fault is that?" she retorted, flipping back the covers and rising in a huff. "Every time we make love lately it's wham, bam, thank you ma'am."

John's face colored red against the white shaving cream. "That's because that's how I feel. I get called to service you on a minute's notice. You lie there like a rock and afterwards you don't say anything, just prop a bunch of pillows under your hips and watch the clock."

"Thanks a lot. You know damn well that's to increase the chances of fertilization."

"Knowing it doesn't change the fact that it cuts out any of the cuddling and talk we used to do after sex. I'm getting really sick of this routine, Annie. Sick and tired."

"You're the one who wanted a baby!"

"Not just me. Don't throw that on me now." He paused and she could see him visibly collect back his anger and calm himself. "And I do want one," he said, his voice conciliatory. "But why can't we make a baby like other couples? Why does it always have to be so manipulated and controlled?''

''Because frankly we haven't been so lucky in the conception department, have we? It's been eight months, so this isn't exactly as easy as we thought it'd be. We need to increase our odds. I've done the research.''

''Research…'' He shook his head, then faced her. ''So it's been eight months. So what? You do this with everything, Annie. When you want something you want it now. You forge ahead and leave no room for error. It's do this, do that. Just look at the way you're eating nothing but sausages and bananas!''

She stuck out her chin and her eyes flashed. ''It raises the sodium and potassium levels in my body. You said you wanted a boy.''

''No, *I said* I didn't care. *You* want the boy, Annie, and that's what I'm talking about. Just having a baby isn't good enough. You're even trying to control the sex of the child!''

''You make it sound like I'm some sort of sex Nazi!''

''You are!''

''Well, I quit!'' she shouted back, furious now. Reaching over, she grabbed the chart and tossed it in the air. The pages covered with little penciled squiggles fluttered in the air between them. ''I quit, do you hear me? You can take this damn thermometer—'' she picked it up and threw it at him ''—and this whole damn project—'' in a blind fury she grabbed the alarm clock ''—and shove it!'' She hurled the clock. John ducked and it crashed against the wall behind him, falling to the floor in a dozen pieces.

When John straightened, his shock and fury were evident in the tautness of his shoulders and the clenched fist around the razor.

Annie stood on the other side of the bed staring back,

panting, arms at her side. A glob of shaving cream was hanging from his chin by a slim thread of soap. It thinned and fell soundlessly to his chest. He looked so shocked, so...funny standing there naked with a half-shaved face amid the rubble of an alarm clock, that she started to laugh. Now that her anger and frustration were spent, her mind cleared. It was always this way with her. When her anger flared she was blinded by a red smoke of fury. Once she exploded, however, the anger was gone and she let it go without a grudge.

Now, Annie was sorry for her explosion of temper, sorry that she'd goaded him, sorry that she'd thrown the clock. Sorry, too, that their love life was in shambles.

"You think this is funny?" he asked.

"Yes," she replied honestly. Then, with the smile disappearing, she said more soberly, "In a pitiful kind of way."

"Well, I'm not laughing." He turned to go back into the bathroom.

"What are we yelling at each other about?" she called after him. "I want to make love to you, John. Most husbands would be grateful to wake up to a horny wife."

He paused and turned his head over his shoulder. It was sadness, not humor, she saw in his eyes. "Yeah, so would I."

That stung. She felt the desire to fight flare up again, but she controlled it, instead flopping on the bed and pinching her lips tight. The rigidity of her shoulders and the tilt of her head as she stared at the wall spoke very clearly of her pique. Not just at the fact that he was being obstinate, but at the fact that she wasn't yet pregnant. And more, at his seeming willingness to dump the whole responsibility for getting pregnant at her feet.

All that was left unsaid between them she understood

clearly. It was her job to conceive, because she was a woman. And it was her failure if she didn't conceive. Annie didn't like failure.

"Just forget it," she said, her voice low and dangerous. She was half serious, half testing. "Just forget the whole damn thing."

There was a tense silence during which Annie sat seething, extremely aware, without seeing him, that John was still standing in the doorway of the bathroom, staring at her. She waited for what seemed an eternity, knowing that he was warring within himself whether or not Annie would really dump the baby project. She was taking a calculated risk: John excelled at long silences. If he went into one of his grand sulks, it could go on for days. But she didn't have days. Her body—her egg—needed him and his sperm—today.

"Annie," he said at last, his voice conciliatory. "This has got to stop."

She knew instantly that he didn't want to give up the effort to have a baby, no matter what he said, and felt a profound relief.

"We're fighting more than ever," he continued, walking near. "And it's because we're getting all freaked out about this baby thing. I hate charting our lovemaking. It's so clinical, so perfunctory, so routine. It's everything I'm against."

"You think I like it?"

"No, I don't." He put his hand on her shoulder—a first step. She leaned into his body. "I miss making love to you, Annie. The way we used to. Spontaneously."

"I do, too," she said softly.

"These matings..." He almost spat out the word. "I don't like what they're doing to us and I've been thinking. Maybe it's just not worth it."

She turned to face him, uneasy that he'd even consider stopping the effort, realizing the depth of his despair to even suggest it. She wanted a baby. Badly. More than anything else. She just had to have one.

"Sure it is, John," she replied persuasively. He needed encouragement now. Gentle cajoling. "I know you want a baby. I know I can give you one. Hey," she said, venturing a smile. "You know my motto. Nothing worthwhile comes easily. I'd say a baby was worthwhile, wouldn't you? So we just have to work a little harder for it. Right? And you know what?" she asked, her voice teasing, "I can't think of a job I'd rather have than this one. Come on, John," she said, tugging off his towel. With a half smile, she reached up to playfully wipe the remaining shaving cream off his face. Then, dropping the towel and her gaze, she leaned forward to kiss his body seductively.

"Let's try again," she whispered, turned on by his erection.

She opened her arms, and when he slipped into them, she smiled exultantly. The timing was ripe for this, she thought as she returned his kisses and maneuvered him into her body. "Oh yes, John, I love you," she whispered by his ear. She did love him.

And she was sure she would make him a wonderful baby this morning.

The following week, Midge peered out her window and frowned at the thick layer of snow covering the streets. Her mother was due for a visit soon and even a Chicago native like Edith could have trouble after several years in balmy weather. Midge had not worried about her mother since she'd moved to Florida ten years earlier. Her brother in Atlanta visited Edith in Vero Beach frequently and often brought his wife and children with him. It was a happy arrangement, one that freed Midge from feeling any guilt over the few times she'd traveled south herself. Years of therapy had taught her to relish the breathing space.

She stepped away from the window to finish the dread job of cleaning up her loft. Midge put cleaning house right up there with cooking and ironing on her hate-to-do list. Domestic chores bored her and what was the point? She lived alone and food didn't particularly interest her. Most mornings she'd pour cereal into her empty coffee cup to avoid dirtying another dish, and dinner was a frozen low-fat entree cooked in the box. The scent of the turkey breast currently roasting in the oven beside two baked potatoes was foreign in this loft.

Midge scooped up a pile of discarded towels from the bathroom floor, looked at them a minute, then threw them in the bathtub and drew the plastic shower curtain. Next she shot sprigs of Windex on the sink and mirror, then gave them a quick once-over. A little sparkle and shine worked wonders, she thought as she scanned her bathroom. It was a functional room with visible plumbing, a basket full of newspapers and magazines beside the toilet, and her toiletries scattered on a dusty wrought-iron table.

Her mother would hate it. There were none of the feminine touches Edith deemed essential. No wide, well-lit mirrors, or matching towels, not even a scale—and God knew her mother never started a day without a pee and a weight check.

Well, it suited her, she thought, feeling the familiar stirrings of resentment that nothing she did was ever good enough for her mother. Why did she care, she asked herself? It was just her mother.

Midge paused and took a deep, relaxing breath, the kind that belled the belly and lowered the tense shoulders. "Mother..." she sighed aloud, gripping the edge of the sink for support. Edith Kirsch was the one woman on earth who could intimidate Midge. She'd spent a lifetime escaping the clutches of that woman's expectations, and every time she thought she'd finally grown up and gone far enough away to form a separate identity, bam! One visit from her mother sent her reeling back into the nursery.

Stop! she scolded herself, warding off the furies. She didn't have time to deal with old issues now. She glanced up at the clock. Her mother was due in ten minutes, and Edith was never late. Besides, her therapist told her to take deep breaths and let go of all that old anger. In and out... Breathing deep and exhaling long, Midge told herself it would be a fine visit—just peachy—if she could stay out of her mother's way for the few days she would be in town and steer clear of anything having to do with men, marriage or sex.

Midge looked at the bottle of cleaner in her hand, her mind grinding away like a tire stuck in the snow, then pulled back the shower curtain with a jerk and tossed the bottle and the rag into the tub, too. She made a quick check in the mirror and smoothed back a few tendrils from the long braid that fell down her back. Perhaps it was the anticipation of her mother's perusal, but she paused before the mirror to study the face that stared back at her.

It sometimes stunned her that she barely recognized the face she'd lived with for fifty years. She'd never been one to gaze at her reflection, to try on different makeups or expressions, not even as a teenager. Tilting her head, she studied her bone structure as an artist would a sculpture. She had bold bones that produced good strong lines at the cheeks and jaw, and angled her prominent nose in a Picasso-like manner. An interesting face, from an artistic viewpoint—but not, by any viewpoint, a pretty one. If she were a man, she'd be considered ruggedly handsome. Being a woman, she was unattractive. Not at all the vision of femininity her mother was.

The doorbell rang and Midge felt a surge of excitement flood her, despite her misgivings. She hadn't seen her mother in over a year.

Opening the door, it was as though she'd seen her mother just yesterday. Her smile widened as her gaze devoured the petite woman at the threshold. Edith never changed. She looked as radiant as ever. In contrast to herself, Edith was a tiny woman, just five foot two, with the bones of a sparrow. In fact, that's how Midge always saw her mother, as a small, delicate songbird with brilliant plumage, bright, dark eyes and movements that were quick yet graceful. She always dressed to the nines, as she put it, coordinating her shoes and bag to her outfit.

Edith's bright eyes appraised every inch of her daughter with a mother's clipped efficiency. Then stepping back, she tilted her head, pursed her lips, raised one perfectly plucked brow and gave Midge a sweeping perusal referred to as *the look*. Without a word spoken, Midge understood that her own artsy-chic choice of clothes, her graying hair, her unmade-up face, did not win her mother's approval. It was all so quick, and so devastating. Midge felt the heat of shame but kept her smile rigidly in place.

"Well, aren't you going to give me a kiss?" Edith's flippancy was a buffer.

"Of course!" Midge bent low to wrap her arms around her mother, feeling as always like a giant beside her. Yet, close up, she relished the feel of her mother's arms around her, the scent of her familiar perfume.

"Come in, Edith," she said, swinging wide her arm.

"One moment, dear. I have to collect my luggage from the limo." Her mother had insisted she come by limousine ever since her friends in Florida regaled her with stories about how it was the only way to get to and from the airport. "No fuss, no muss!" she'd told Midge after Midge had argued how she would be happy to pick up her own mother, for heaven's sake.

"Let me help," Midge said.

"No, no," Edith replied too quickly, her gaze darting back and forth with anxiety. "The driver brings up the luggage. It's part of the service, you see." The way she said it implied, *What did I tell you?* "You just stay put."

Midge waited by the door, craving a cigarette for the first time since giving them up over a year ago. A few minutes later she heard the measured footfall of a man carrying a heavy weight. Sure enough, the tall, muscular driver in a cheap, black suit labored up the stairs loaded down with two immense suitcases. Midge's mouth slipped open as she gasped with the sinking realization that this was enough luggage to last a whole heck of a lot longer than a week.

"I'll be right back with the others," the driver said, turning the corner of the stairwell.

"Others?"

Edith just waved her hand and disappeared back down the stairs. Midge didn't move a muscle as she waited, then watched the gentleman carry up a dainty hat box tilting precariously atop a taped, brown mailing box big enough to carry an entire wardrobe. A few minutes after he'd disappeared again, Midge heard the gentle tapping of high heels on the stairs. She opened her mouth to ask why on earth Edith needed so much luggage when her throat seized, her eyes bugged and her breath stilled.

Edith turned the corner and advanced the final two steps in a mincing motion, with a coy expression on her face. But all Midge could see was the small, smudgy ball of white fur and buggy black eyes in her arms.

"You brought your dog?" she croaked, incredulous that even her mother could be so callous of her feelings that she'd bring her dog along for a visit without asking.

"I just couldn't leave Prince," Edith replied, her voice too high. She was stroking the wiry white curls of her toy poodle's head so hard she pulled the eyelids back, causing Prince's eyes to bug out all the more. "He got a terrible case of diarrhea the last time I left him at that horrid Dog's Day Inn. I swear I thought my baby would perish if I submitted him to that torture again. Honey, *I'd* perish of loneliness without him. Oh, please don't be angry at me. He's such a good boy and I promise I'll keep him out of your way. Why, Prince is such a little thing, you won't even know he's here. Just like me!"

Midge was choking back her fury, swallowing so hard she couldn't speak. It's only for a few days, she told herself over and over again, breathing deep. In and out... She stepped aside, swinging her arm open, allowing her mother to pass.

She followed the sparrow's flight path throughout the open, airy loft, seeing her home as her mother might. The upholstered sofa and chairs clustered before a brick fireplace were mismatched and tossed casually with oversize kilim pillows. The long, curved bar that surrounded the kitchen was littered with corked wine bottles, piles of books and assorted sculptures. In the far corner, before a spread of tall windows, two heavy wooden easels stood empty beside paint-splattered tables topped with neatly organized brushes. Against the wall were stacks of completed canvasses.

Midge liked to think her place was a statement of her dedication to talent, not fashion. But she could tell by the expression on her mother's face that she saw it as a decorator's worst nightmare. Her breath held, however, when her mother's gaze alighted on the wall-size paintings that filled the west wall of the loft. Midge felt about her work as any mother would when someone inspected her children. Or for some people, their dog. She waited in a tense silence.

"Could you get Prince a bowl of water, dear?" Edith asked, turning to face her with a starched smile on her face.

Midge's breath hitched. Edith had nothing to say about her paintings. They were dismissed without notice or a word.

"Sure," she forced out, turning away so her mother wouldn't see her disappointment. "How about some wine for you? I've uncorked a nice bottle of Margaux."

"Oh no, dear, I never drink red wine anymore. Those sulfites give me a headache. Please say you have a martini? Vodka? With a lemon peel?"

Midge closed her eyes against the headache that was already forming in her temples. "No lemons, but I've got olives."

Edith sighed with disappointment. "That'll do, I suppose."

Midge gritted her teeth and plopped an olive in Prince's water, too. She hoped the little bugger would choke on it.

After the martini was served and she was fortified with a glass of the Margaux, Midge felt her equilibrium slowly return. They briefly discussed Edith's flight to Chicago, the books she'd been reading, her bridge game, the nasty change in weather—safe topics that broke the ice. The conversation moved up a notch when her mother complained about how her grandchildren's manners were shocking. "It's like eating a meal with animals!" she said, slipping Prince a dog treat. The dog chewed the biscuit with noisy relish, dropping crumbs all over Midge's sofa with fearless abandon.

As the sky darkened and a second drink was poured, Edith relaxed by slipping off her jacket, easing back into the sofa's cushions and announcing that she found her condo in southern Florida utterly confining and the life-style boring.

"There's no culture," Edith said, plucking out the olive with a wrinkled nose. "There's no *there* there. Florida's great if you like to walk on the beach every morning and pick thousands of shells. But after you've done that..." She rolled her eyes. "*C'est tout!* Besides, I miss my old friends."

"You've made new ones." Midge wasn't feeling sympathetic. Her mother had been hell-bent to move to Florida years back, dragging her back and forth to help find the condo, all the while professing that she couldn't endure another Chicago winter.

"Everyone's too old down there," Edith continued. "One foot in the grave. And there's not a decent man to be found. They're all either hobbling around or married. I'm lonely for some male companionship. And I'll tell you," she added, perking up, "the man I saw in the airport bar..." She rolled her eyes suggestively, then sipped daintily from her martini, closing her eyes and almost purring. "Oh là là."

Midge shifted in her seat, uncomfortable with the notion of her mother scouting out babes in the bar. There was something smarmy about listening to one's own mother's love stories—especially when she herself didn't have any.

"Please tell me you didn't try to pick him up...."

"No," she replied with an incredulous expression, "another woman met him there, probably his wife." She tsked, then leaned farther back into the sofa's cushions and looked long and hard through a drunken haze at her daughter. "But what if I had? What would be so wrong with that? Do you think because I'm of a certain age I can't attract a man any longer? Or, God forbid, that I don't want one?"

"No, Mother, but there's such a thing as dignity."

Edith threw back her head and laughed a throaty laugh. "I think we have more than enough of that in you for one family. You'd do well to drop a little of yours, darling, and go out and mingle more. Shake it up. It's no wonder you haven't met a decent man. You'll never find anyone if you don't hunt."

"Maybe I don't want to hunt for anyone."

Edith waved her hand dismissively. "Of course you do, honey. You're just too shy. You keep your nose stuck in your paints. Stick by your mama, I'll show you a few tricks of the trade."

She clicked her tongue and ran her palm along her hips in what she clearly thought was a sexy move. Midge thought she was going to be sick. In a flash she remembered the first time she'd come home from Boston College. It was parents' weekend and her mother didn't want to come out East just to hang around a bunch of rah-rah-rahing freshman parents. So Midge decided to fly home to surprise her. And, too, because she didn't want to hang around the dorms while all the other freshmen's parents were getting tours, participating in events and taking their kids out to dinner. When her mother had opened the front door, however, she was not happy to see her. Why are you here? she'd asked in a heated whisper, then looked over her shoulder into the house. Grabbing her purse, she'd closed the door behind her and, stuffing a few twenties into her hand, told Midge to go to the Carlyle Hotel in town. She had a houseguest. When Midge moaned and asked why she couldn't just sleep in her own room, Edith merely rolled her eyes, clicked her tongue, and said with that same coy expression how her *friend* didn't know she had a college-age daughter and she didn't want him to know, either.

"I'm homesick," Edith was saying, still stroking Prince's head. "I miss the Midwest. The smells, the accent, the life-style. I miss the city."

Midge prickled that her mother didn't mention her own name in that lineup. "But what about your life in Florida? Your friends there? The condo?"

She shrugged her slim shoulders as though to say, *What about them?*

Midge glanced quickly at the mountain of luggage and swallowed hard, sensing with thinly disguised dread where this conversation was headed. She could feel the migraine building power like thunderclouds.

"What about Atlanta?" she offered eagerly as a detour. "It's a great city, nice climate, and Joe and Liz would love to have you nearby." Her brother and his family would kill her if they'd heard what she'd just said. Edith drove Liz crazy with her less than subtle suggestions on how to raise the boys.

"I suppose," she said with a sigh.

Midge's blood went cold and she set her wineglass down on the wood table. Drawing herself up, she met her mother's gaze and asked directly, "Mother, how long are you planning to stay?"

Midge held her breath as her mother's face turned impish.

"Indefinitely," she said, brows up and eyes bright.

Midge must have screeched or jolted, she didn't know, but Prince leaped to his tiny paws and jumped from Edith's lap. He scurried across the wood floor with his long nails clicking to stand at Midge's feet, and yelped so hard his whole body left the ground. Midge heard the barks as explosions in her already aching head and raised her hands to her ears.

"Hush, Prince," Edith called out, clapping her hands. "We must be good guests. Stop that. Come here right this minute. Prince!"

Midge stared down into the bulging black eyes of the little dog who, it was quite obvious, obeyed no one but himself. She lowered her head to within inches of the bouncing ball of white fur, took a deep breath, then bellowed, "No!"

Instantly the poodle stopped barking and lowered itself belly-down on the carpet, eyes quivering in submission. Across the carpet, her mother sat upright with her hands flopped in her lap and her mouth agape, as though she'd lost all her wind. Midge felt a soaring triumph that she'd managed not only to silence a runt of a dog, but for once, her mother.

March comes in like a lion and goes out like a lamb. Eve had always liked this expression, though she didn't know why exactly. Probably because it implied: Let the worst blow in, let the cold winds howl.... We can endure because we know in our hearts that kinder, gentler times are ahead.

She said this phrase to herself often in early March. There were still a good two months of cold, iffy weather coming. She always wanted to slap the person who felt compelled to remind everyone in March that, "It can always snow in Chicago in May!" She was so ready for the warmth of sunshine on her face again after this long, hard winter—for some joy in her life after so much sadness. Putting the house on the market was hard enough, but

waiting in limbo for someone to buy it was even harder.
The torturous waiting had accomplished one feat, however.
It made her eager to clean out her closets and rid herself
of mountains of clutter that she'd accumulated over the
years. How could she have collected so much stuff?
Stuffed animals, baby clothes and paraphernalia, half-
finished craft and sewing projects, piles of children's art-
works, old books... It was endless.

The Goodwill truck had been a regular at her house over
the past few months. The last things to go were Tom's
personal items. Clearing out these tangible memories were
the toughest, not only for her but for the children. So, on
this first day of March, while the children were away at
school, Eve tied an apron around her waist, took a deep
breath, then opened his bedroom closet. The sight of the
row of dark suits and trousers, the line of laundered shirts
and an array of colorful ties hit her like a blast of winter
air. She gasped and let her gaze wander over the three
upper shelves crammed with hats, gloves and who knew
what else. Below the suits lay Tom's shoes: plain leather
tie, tennis and sandals. Eve squared her shoulders and entered the closet. It was time for this first letting go.

Annie had already tidied up the banking, investments
and retirement plans. Her friend couldn't have been more
patient, teaching her reluctant pupil what she needed to
learn to take over her own finances.

Now it was her turn to finish putting her house in order.
She was resolved to get through this task quickly, but
when she pulled out the first suit, the moment her hand
touched the fine wool, her heart lurched. She brought the
jacket to her nose and inhaled the faint scent of his body,
still lingering in the fibers. She'd heard that scent was a
great trigger of memories, and oh, it was true. They hit
like a tidal wave, flooding her.

But she was better at navigating her emotions now. She wiped her eyes, sniffed, and carried on. One by one the beautiful suits were neatly folded and placed in one of the three large boxes destined to go to charity. As she packed, she recalled with sweet nostalgia the last time she'd seen Tom wearing the navy double-breasted suit, or the brown suede jacket, or his dinner jacket and cummerbund. He looked so handsome in formal wear....

The boxes filled quickly, and as she closed them up and taped them tight, she felt as though she were sealing away a part of her own history with them. She saved the military uniform from his Vietnam days, as well as personal pieces of jewelry and accessories—things the children would want to keep. Next she went through his toiletries, selecting those items that could be donated and those that had to be tossed out. It pained her to discard even a half bottle of used cologne or leftover medications that littered the bathroom shelves. It was hard to think that anything that Tom had once held in his hands was garbage.

By early afternoon, she'd completed a clean sweep. All that remained was the no-man's-land of his upper closet—"the pit," Tom had called it as he tossed anything and everything into it. Pushing back a fallen lock of hair, she climbed up the step stool and began sorting through the miscellaneous junk: flashlights, an old stethoscope, a blood pressure cuff, a few firecrackers, leather gloves and a dusty felt hat. High on the top shelf, behind a blanket, she found an old metal file box. Pulling it down she smiled with surprise. Why, she hadn't seen this old thing in years! It was one of the few items he'd brought to their first apartment, that and an old brown leather recliner that was an eyesore. Her hand glided over the cool metal as memories of those early years of their marriage flitted across her mind. How young they were! They thought they'd known everything.... He used to store his important papers in here, treasured items that he held very dear and very private.

Curious to discover what was still inside, she tried opening it, but it was locked. She climbed down the ladder and carried the box to the kitchen. After a few crude tries with a knife, the old lock popped open. She felt a tremor of excitement as she carried it to the table, sat in a chair and slowly opened the lid.

Only a few items lay inside. She pulled out an old pocket watch, the glass of which was shattered. She recognized it as belonging to Tom's grandfather, a keepsake from a man he didn't remember. Next she discovered an old Roman gold coin that he'd received from his favorite uncle when he graduated from high school. Her heart beat faster, realizing that these were very special treasures. There was his first set of surgical tools, a ring of keys of no known significance and an old, canceled bank book that dated back to the year of their wedding. Inside the book was a photograph of the two of them looking very much in love on the beach in Cancun. Oh, and they were, she thought fondly, eyes misting. This was a photo from their honeymoon, and this was his canceled savings account for that trip. He'd saved for a year to take her away somewhere special. She pressed the book to her heart, then looked again into the box. She found a few Father's Day cards from the children and her heartstrings tugged, grateful that he was so sentimental he'd kept these sweet mementos. He'd never told her.

On the bottom was an envelope that was newer, crisper than the others. She tore it open, expecting a child's drawing or perhaps a letter. All that fell out was a Polaroid photograph of a woman. She was lovely; a willowy redhead with soulful eyes and full pouting lips turned up in a sultry smile. She was attractively dressed in a well-cut dark suit, as though on her way to an important meeting. Her clothing, her stance of confidence, spoke of her being a professional, bright, savvy.

There was something about her that rang a bell with Eve. She couldn't quite place her, but she knew she'd seen her somewhere before. But where?

She'd have to come back to it later, she decided, placing all the treasures back into the box for safekeeping. The children would be home from school soon and she needed to get all of Tom's clothing out of sight before they arrived. They might be upset that she was getting rid of them.

Still, as she worked, the image of the mysterious woman niggled at her, rousing her dormant suspicions. Sliding the file box onto the shelf, her hand lingered while her fingers tapped the metal. Who was that redheaded woman?

Seven

> Gather ye rosebuds while ye may,
> Old Time is still a-flying:
> And this same flower that smiles today,
> Tomorrow will be dying.

—Robert Herrick, *To Virgins, to Make Much of Time*

It was spring at last! The earth was full of hope and promise, even if in Chicago there were still patches of muddy snow on the front lawn. Shoots of brave crocus broke through the soil in cheery yellow and purple to open in the warm sun. Eve felt inspired as she loaded the last of her personal possessions into her car, a boxy green Volvo wagon that was old enough she could afford to keep it. She'd sold Tom's new black sedan. And most of her antiques. And her Japanese porcelains, her Oriental carpets, her gold coins, and at long, blessed relief last, the house. Annie had been right, damn her, but she should have sold the house last summer. As it was, Eve limped through the winter months, lowering the price bit by bit, watching the mortgage gouge into her nest egg, until a doctor who was moving to the University of Illinois heard about the house from a colleague and stopped by during a visit. In one whirlwind weekend his wife flew in, fell in love, and they bought it on the spot. Annie was stunned but crowed, "Coming from New York, they're probably popping the bubbly thinking they stole the house from you!"

Nonetheless, it broke Eve's heart to sign the sale contract. So many years, hours, precious minutes she'd spent in this house.

But that was last month. This month, she was glad to be rid of the burden and eager to get settled into her new home. Gabriella had rushed over the afternoon after the sale, her nut-brown eyes sparkling and her large mouth cooing about fortune and fate and lucky stars and how she wouldn't believe it but the glorious, funky, positively ancient apartment complex in Old Town Oakley that Eve'd always admired was going condo. Together they hurried over as fast as Gabriella's gold Saturn could get them there to inspect the gothic, brick and stone complex of apartments.

The Santa Maria wasn't secluded or elite. Rather, it was located in the heart of the town near shops and across the street from a large park that was a favorite gathering place of high school boys playing Frisbee, Sunday morning dog groups and countless art fairs. There was no doubt that a move here would be a definite step down for the Porters. The largest unit was a two bedroom plus study. She'd have to squeeze Finney into the small room without a closet. But Eve loved it the moment she stepped inside. Each condo housed an enormous stone fireplace, ten-foot ceilings, tall bay windows overlooking the park and nooks and crannies that were only found in old buildings. Plus, it positively reeked of old-world charm. She'd just known it would be like this.

Like a bird-dog with a keen nose, Eve was blessed with

a sharp sense for discovering the unique. Whether it was an antique in somebody's attic, a first edition lying in a box of paperbacks, scouting out the best view while hiking, or discovering the crustiest bread in town, Eve found it. She held her breath and, acting on instinct, purchased one of the larger units that very day, clobbering her bank account and assuming debt in one fell swoop. But later, over chardonnay, Annie had assured her there was nothing like a mortgage to develop her credit rating.

All that was left now was to close the door on her old house—and all the tenacious feelings still clinging to it like the vines of the grape ivy on the west wall—lock it securely and drive away. Eve hefted her two bulging suitcases into the rear of the station wagon, feeling as if she were twenty years old all over again, leaving her parents' house and getting her first apartment.

Except she was forty-five.

She didn't feel forty-five today; she didn't *want to be* forty-five. She'd never had her own apartment, she realized with surprise. She hadn't planned it that way, it just happened. She went from home, to college, to marriage in rapid-fire order, a natural transition that so many other women of her generation went through. Resting against the dusty Volvo, she thought how she'd never really had any time alone. Just for herself. Not like Annie, who'd traveled across the United States and Europe with a backpack like a vagabond. Not even like her own daughter, Bronte, who'd spent a summer testing her limits in the Colorado Rockies at camp. She was jealous of that kind of self-exploration, that kind of freedom. Eve Brown Porter had always been somebody's daughter, or wife or mother. She'd moved from being taken care of to taking care of others as easily as slipping into a warm pool. One step, hold your breath, and you're immersed. But don't stop stroking or you'll drown. She wondered what it would be like having no one to take care of but yourself, to stop stroking and just let go? It seemed unfathomable.

Well, someday she'd take a trip all on her own, she vowed, slamming the trunk and slapping the dust off from the seat of her jeans. But not yet. She had many miles to go before she slept, as Robert Frost put so eloquently, starting with convincing two sullen children that moving the few miles from Riverton to Oakley was not the end of the world.

She entered what was once her house and walked through the first floor, her footsteps echoing in the large empty rooms. It was a fine house, a handsome house. A happy house. She hoped the next family would be happy in it, too, and made a mental note to send them flowers on their moving day.

Her hands slid along the banister as she hurried up the stairs to the children's rooms, remembering all the times she'd climbed these steps in the past. Rushing at the sound of gagging and throwing up in the bathroom, storming when she heard talking on the telephone after 11:00 p.m., sleepily to kiss warm, sweet-smelling foreheads goodnight, stomping to lay down the law, tiptoeing to wake a yawning, smiling child with a birthday breakfast in bed.

She found Bronte and Finney on the floor of the landing sitting close together and hunched over in whispered conversation. Their faces were thunderous, sucking the sun right out of Eve's warm spring day. Finney bent to wipe his eyes with his sleeve. Eve paused at the top of the stairs, physically hurting to see them in such pain, wishing she could gather them up like flowers close to her chest and reassure them with all the right words. But she knew there were no words that would make them feel better; she prayed that time would. And she also knew better than to touch them when they were in this mood. They'd shrug her off, hate her all the more for forcing them to forgive her what they perceived a horrible injustice. So she opted to be practical.

"Okay, kiddos," she said, clapping her hands, forcing a ray of brightness into the gloom. "Rise and shine! It's time to go."

"I...don't...want...to...go." Bronte's eyes, so much like her own, were two green flames in her pale face and her pointed chin jutted out angrily.

Oh boy, here we go, sighed Eve to herself. "We've been through this a million times. This isn't our house anymore."

"And whose fault is that?"

"It's nobody's fault."

"Why'd you sell it? Why couldn't you keep it? Dad would've kept it. He'd have found a way. You always do everything wrong."

Eve let this go. "Honey, I had no choice. I... We can't afford to stay here anymore. End of story."

"I'll get a job. So will Finney."

"Yeah," he mumbled, still not looking at her. It was the first word she'd heard him speak all day. Of the two of them, Eve was most worried about Finney. In the past months her gentle-hearted, spontaneous, free-natured boy had changed into a sullen, guarded preteen, uttering only slurred, monosyllabic phrases.

"Be realistic," she said gently. "Besides, it's all done. The house is sold. We're moving into our new home today. Let's go."

"You're ruining my life!" screamed Bronte, climbing to her feet, her face flushed, her fists bunched and bobbing like a bantam. At only fourteen, already she was two inches taller than Eve. When she bore down on her mother with teenage frustration and anger pouring out like lava from a volcano it might have been intimidating to some women. But not Eve.

"How am I ruining your life?" Eve screamed right back at her, chin up, taking one step closer. "I'm doing the best I can."

"You're tearing me away from this house. My neighborhood. All my friends."

"I am not! You and Finney get to finish out the year in Riverton and then you're going to the same high school with all your friends. So don't give me that. It's Finney who's having the toughest time. He's got to go to a new school next year. He'll be the new kid, not you. But I don't hear him complaining about how I'm ruining his life."

"That's because he's not telling you. Go on, Finney, tell her."

Finney kept his head down low and began pinching the skin on his arm.

"He just won't tell you," Bronte ground out.

"Come on, kids, give me a break," Eve said fighting back tears. "I'm not trying to make you miserable. I love you. I wish we didn't have to move. I wish I could find a way to stay here for your sakes. I wish we had loads of money." Her voice hitched. "I wish your dad was alive." She stopped to swallow hard. She would not cry in front of her children.

Bronte quieted, quickly deflated at seeing her mother on the verge of tears. Her contorted face expressed remorse. "I'm sorry, Mom."

Eve sniffed and offered a weak smile. "I am, too." She opened her arms and Bronte bent low to somehow shrink herself and squeeze into them while Eve thought, My poor half child-half woman. Finney rose clumsily to his feet and clung tight, his thin body a bag of bones.

"We'll be okay," Eve said, her voice cracking but strong as she squeezed them tight. "We're the Three Musketeers. One for all and all for one."

Bronte and Finney sniffed and nodded, then released her and stepped back, embarrassed by either the sentiment or the cornball phrase. She'd never know and it didn't matter. What mattered was that the storm had passed.

Eve took a deep breath, then mussed the thick brown hair on top of Finney's head and gently tucked a wayward tendril behind Bronte's ear. The plains and valleys of their tearstained faces loomed soft and achingly beautiful on Eve's horizon.

"Let's go home."

"Here they are! Over here, Eve. Park here!"

Eve spotted Gabriella arching on her tiptoes and waving her plump arms in wide arcs over her head, barely visible over the row of parked cars in front of the Santa Maria complex. Annie and Midge stood militantly in a parking space blessedly close to the front entrance of her building. Doris was stuffing quarters into the meter. Eve's heart skipped gaily on seeing each of them, like a pebble bouncing across a span of water—one, two, three, four, Gabriella, Midge, Annie, Doris.

"Thank God you got here!" exclaimed Gabriella, grinning into the open window after Eve finished an ace parking job into the tight spot. Parallel parking was a new fact of life for her; there would be no more rolling into her driveway, punching the automatic garage door opener and slipping to a secure parking spot. There would be no more garages.

"What the hell took you so long?" asked Annie, opening her door. "We've been duking it out with the natives, defending your parking space. I thought someone was going to call the cops!''

''What are you guys doing here!'' Eve couldn't help squealing—had to do it.

''We heard someone was moving in!'' exclaimed Midge, moving in for her turn at a hug. ''We finally lured you out of Riverton to our neighborhood. Welcome to Oakley, sweetie.''

''Yeah, to the real world.'' Gabriella winked, acknowledging the silent feud between large, progressive, more cosmopolitan Oakley and small, conservative, slightly snobby Riverton. Both communities had their share of drop-jaw houses and wealth, but where Riverton's population was predominately white, upper class, Oakley celebrated its diversity.

''Bronte, come out of that hot car and say hello,'' called Doris, leaning into the window. ''Finney, you too!''

Bronte responded to the iron in Doris's velvet voice, as she had so many times growing up, and climbed from the car with Finney right behind her.

As if on cue, the women ignored the sour expressions and humped-shoulder stances of the children, instinctively giving them their space. All were well acquainted with the power and duration of a teenage sulk.

Eve, however, was beaming as she took in the smiling faces of her friends, weak-kneed with gratitude at seeing them here to help, taking care of her, making sure she wasn't alone. Stepping inside her condo she was speechless to find they'd already washed the windows until they sparkled and the hardwood floors until they gleamed. They'd scrubbed the single bathroom, thinking ahead to add rolls of toilet paper, a fancy bottle of liquid soap and even expensive, decorated paper towels, that she knew had to come from Doris.

It was typical of Doris to place a flower beside a kitchen sink, or spritz scent in a dark, musty back stairwell, knowing a woman needed such things at such times. She'd already placed a book of poems by Gwendolyn Brooks on the toilet lid. Eve always had books and magazines stacked in her Riverton bathroom. Dabbing her fingers on the thick paper that felt like cotton, Eve felt luxurious in her cramped black-and-white bathroom with the leaky toilet and the chipped porcelain sink.

The afternoon sped by in a blur. She dispensed Bronte and Finney to the park across the street with ten dollars in their pockets and a kiss, instructing them to come back at six for dinner. The movers arrived a few minutes later, and rolling up her sleeves, Eve began setting up house. With the help of four sharp-eyed, wily generals, the furniture was set in place with the efficiency and speed of a military formation drill. There wasn't a slacker in the bunch, one outdoing the other in generosity and talent. Except, by decree, Annie.

"Annie, you get out of here," Gabriella exclaimed, tying a sunflower-yellow apron around her waist. "You have no business lifting those boxes. *Madre de Dios,* you brainy types don't have any common sense. Now go on, get out of here and find something easy to do. Better yet, put your feet up."

Eve, unloading a box of glasses, froze, her hand in midair. She'd never heard Gabriella order Annie around like that. She was even more amazed to watch Annie meekly obey. Annie had missed her period and nurse Gabriella was watching her like a mother hen. They were a group of mother hens, actually. For the rest of the afternoon, the women had an unspoken agreement to take care of Annie, who didn't know the first thing about being pregnant, and as far as they could tell, didn't have good instincts, either.

They chased Annie away from any lifting or hard labor, brought her cool water to drink and ordered her to "just sit down and take a load off." Annie protested and argued, but everyone could tell she was secretly delighted with the obvious care and love of the group. In the end, Annie managed to accomplish little more than inserting new lightbulbs into the sockets.

"Have you read this month's book?" called Midge from under the kitchen sink. She'd brought along her tool chest and was installing a rollaway garbage basket. She'd already added an extra deadbolt on the front door. "Fabulous. I couldn't put it down."

"You're kidding? I couldn't pick it up. Boring, boring, boring," Doris replied as she unpacked the kitchen dishes and utensils onto the myriad new Rubbermaid items she'd placed in every cabinet. "Mysteries are all the same. Someone gets killed, someone hunts the killer down, killer gets punished. The end. It's such a waste of time."

"I could say the same thing about your romances."

"You've never even read a romance, so how would you know?"

"How many mysteries have you read?"

"I think you two are missing the point," Gabriella chimed in, sticking her head out from the oven. "It's not about choosing just a good read. We all have our favorites. We need to pick books that promote a good discussion. I mean, I love it when we all get fired up about some topic."

"Remember Doris with *Madame Bovary?*" asked Eve, walking in with another box in her arms. "I thought she was gonna scratch Annie's eyes out."

"I was not!" Doris exclaimed, but she was laughing.

"I loved that you got so hot and bothered," Gabriella said, flapping her towel in the air. "Hearing all that helps me to pick apart my own feelings, you know?"

"But we don't always know what will get us going," Midge argued from under the sink. "Some books just don't have enough complexity to generate a discussion, so we at least have to try and pick ones that do."

"Sure," persisted Gabriella. "But we still have to read all kinds of books, books we might never pick up on our own. And there's no way I'd dissect and study a book on my own as much as we do in the group. So sometimes a book I think I'll hate turns out to be wonderful after all. Remember that book on civil rights?" She shrugged. "So maybe you don't like mysteries, Doris, and maybe you don't like romance, Midge, but at least you know that about yourself."

"And maybe you've only read one," added Doris wryly. "How can you judge a genre by one book?"

"You're right," said Gabriella. "I think it's a mistake to only read literary books, or nonfiction, or classics. Or any one genre. Then we'd be stuck. I'm curious about those books that get the buzz, or make the *Times* list."

"And paperbacks. Can't afford those hardcovers every month."

"That's for sure. Do you know how much they…" Eve stopped short, catching sight of Annie's pale, drawn face as she walked into the kitchen from the hall. Their eyes met and Eve read a cry of worry in them.

"I'm spotting," Annie whispered.

The work was instantly abandoned as the women gathered around Annie, getting her to lie down on the couch, feet up, while they plied her with questions. Gabriella was furious when she heard Annie hadn't yet been to her doctor.

"I'm only a few weeks late. What's all the excitement about? Women have babies every day. I'll get there."

"But you've been trying to get pregnant for months,"

Gabriella sputtered. Her face was red with indignation. "Do you mean you haven't talked to her yet?"

"No! I wasn't pregnant yet! What's to talk about? I've been taking my vitamins, drinking my milk and not drinking alcohol. I've read tons of books. So what else is there?"

"A physical, for one," snapped Gabriella, placing pillows under Annie's feet. "Blood tests. Oh, why am I even explaining any of this to you? You don't listen."

"Yes I will, Gabby." Her soft voice, so uncharacteristic for Annie, was a testament to her fear. "But what should I do now?"

"Well, there are a lot of reasons why you might be spotting. Hormones are all crazy in the first trimester."

"That's true," added Eve, placing a hand on Annie's shoulder and offering a reassuring squeeze. "I spotted in my first pregnancy."

"Did you?" Annie's eyes were hopeful, relieved.

"You should call your doctor. Now." Midge's face was set. "Tell her it's urgent."

"Okay, okay. Where's the phone?"

The women clustered in silent support as Annie called the doctor. Her brief hushed conversation ended with an appointment for the following morning and strict orders to go home, go to bed and stay there. They hung around her, chatting, but no one wanted to mention what was upmost on their minds: Annie's pregnancy. It was as though their collective silence on the topic was a protective wall.

After John came to take her home, however, it was all they could talk about. Their worry rang in their criticisms. "How could she not have seen her doctor?"

"She didn't even take one of those home pregnancy tests!"

"She works too hard."

"You've got to sit down when you're pregnant or you'll get all kinds of problems. Especially for a first baby at her age."

"Everyone knows that. Why, I had..."

And the war stories began, one after the other, about their swollen ankles, a month of bed rest, the odd cravings and the long, longer, longest deliveries, keeping them going as they toiled through the rest of the afternoon.

By the time the sun set, the condo was comfortably settled and the women began unwrapping the mountains of food they'd all contributed, smacking their lips. Pans and bowls filled with lasagna, marinated vegetables, cold grilled chicken and shrimp, brownies and chocolate chip cookies, tiramisu, loaves of freshly baked bread from the bakery next door, and bottles of champagne. The mood rose like the bubbles after Annie called.

"Relax girls, false alarm!" she reported. "The spotting's stopped and John's serving me in bed like I'm the Queen of Sheba."

Finney and Bronte returned home on time, each carrying small brown bags of minor purchases in their hands, weary frowns on their faces. Finney loaded his plate with food while Bronte picked a few nonmeat portions, then they both sneaked off to their new bedrooms and closed the doors. Eve could hear their favorite music gently playing through the walls—Bronte's rhythmic, Finney's rap—and stared at the closed doors clutching her towel, feeling very shut off from their worlds.

Later, while Midge, Doris and Gabriella were in the kitchen chatting and wrapping up the leftovers that would carry her for days, Eve stole a moment alone to walk through the five rooms of her new home. Flicking on lights one by one, she regarded the altered effect in each as the day's light dimmed. The hall seemed so long and dark, the rooms so small. She collapsed onto her sofa that fit so well before the fireplace and laid her chin on the soft green velvet. She was feeling moody and introspective. There was something unique about the first night in a new home, not filled with anticipation like Christmas Eve, or fraught with worry, like before an exam or an interview. She couldn't put her finger on it, but everything was so foreign, so different and new. Everything held promise.

The lights from her favorite antique Japanese porcelain lamps made soft yellow halos in the corners of the room. Despite the warm night, Midge had lit a fire with good, dry cedar, filling the condo with a heady fragrance. All around her were her favorite things, her favorite people, each specially chosen to go the distance.

As the night deepened, her friends tossed in the towels and came to join her in the living room. The heat rose as the fire grew so they opened the large bay windows. Outside, waiting for them, was a symphony of music from the streets below. The women sat together in a comfortable silence; there was nothing more to say. They yawned, closed their eyes, stretched their legs and listened in a companionable mood to a different music, the music made by the low laughter in the next condo, the shouts of strangers in the park, the atonal horns of traffic and the high soprano of a mother calling a child indoors, all against the rhythmic backbeat of pulsing life and movement. This magical song took them all far from the muted peace of the suburban blocks they were familiar with, far, farther back to their youth, when they were smooth skinned, slim and sassy, when they walked the city streets with swinging hips, when their worlds delivered pearls.

On that balmy spring night that smelled of rain and new promise, each of the women who came from her large home, with comfortable furnishings and extra rooms to

store all her many things, felt a disquiet in her breast that
she could not put into words. It would take time to sort
out, but it felt at the moment a little like envy. Not jealousy. They only wished the best for Eve. But in some as
yet unvisited place in their hearts, in varying degrees, each
woman settled back into a chair or leaned against the wall
and listened, wondering what it must be like to embrace
change and start fresh.

Much later, when the Book Club left for their own
homes, when the night music ended and it seemed the
whole world was in a deep sleep, Eve lay on her back in
her room staring at the ceiling, terrified of the changes in
her life. Her breaths came short, her heart was palpitating
wildly, she couldn't seem to get a chest full of air. Worst
of all was an overwhelming sense of panic that held her
in its monstrous grip.

It wasn't the first time. These attacks began soon after
Tom's death, waking her from her sleep or sometimes, like
tonight, not allowing her to fall asleep at all. This fore-
boding fear struck out of the blue but she'd thought, hoped,
they'd dissipated in the past months. He'd been dead ten
months next week. Tonight, however, the fear returned full
force when she'd turned off the lights, locked the door of
this unknown place, climbed into the cool, cotton sheets
of the double bed and reached out automatically to Tom's
side of the bed.

She still couldn't lie down in bed without expecting to
be scooped up in his arms, to feel his smooth, cool hand
caress her breasts with comforting possessiveness before
tucking her bottom slap back against his groin, sometimes
hard, sometimes soft, like spoons, each matching one's
breathing pace to the other's before drifting asleep. It was
that ingrained pattern, those tender, nonpassionate, ach-

ingly familiar gestures that she missed more than the tumultuous passion of sex—feeling Tom beside her, the bone of his chin in her neck and the fine hairs of his arm against hers, hearing him snore, smelling his skin. It was as natural to her as breathing. She sometimes still wriggled her bottom, jutting it back inches, expecting to feel him there. Instead, feeling the emptiness broke her heart.

Tonight especially, in this dark, strange apartment that smelled, sounded, felt different, she was smacked with the reality that Tom was really gone. That her skin would be cold that night. That the only smell in these sheets was her own. That she didn't have him to cover her with his strength any longer.

She reached over and placed one of the pillows longside down on Tom's side of the bed under the blanket, then another, to form a mass beside her. It was silly, she knew, but in the wee hours, when she closed her eyes, she could butt back against the pillows and fool herself, just for a while, that Tom was still there beside her.

Eve didn't want change. She wanted Tom back.

Eight

> "All you need is confidence in yourself. There is no
> living thing that is not afraid when it faces danger.
> True courage is in facing danger when you are
> afraid..."
>
> —L. Frank Baum, *The Wonderful Wizard of Oz*

"**W**hat do you mean, I'm not pregnant?"

"Annie," said Dr. Maureen Gibson folding her hands
and looking Annie straight in the eye. "Your HCG results
are negative. The tests don't lie. I'm sorry, but you're not
pregnant. You never were."

"But—" she sputtered, feeling the injustice of this ver-
dict and a tremendous sense of loss over what was apparently nothing more than a dream. Emma Bovary running
after Rudolphe flashed unbidden in her mind. "But I
should be! John and I are screwing like rabbits. I've been
off the pill for months. I don't understand."

"We've talked about this. At your age, you can't assume you'll just get pregnant."

"I'm not typical," she replied, feeling a flush of frustration at the mention of that *age thing* again. "I eat

healthy foods. I'm a runner, I ride my bike, exercise. Look at these thighs," she cried, pointing to her long, sinewy, tanned legs that John compared to those of a racehorse. "And my biceps. Go ahead, feel them. They're like iron. I've got the body of someone ten years younger."

Dr. Gibson refrained, holding the chart close to her chest. "Your insides are forty-three years old. Your uterus, your eggs…you can't change that."

"Oh, no," she said, shaking the image of Gabriella pointing her finger from her mind. She didn't want any negative thinking now. She needed to rally. "It's too soon to throw in the towel. We haven't even begun to check out my options here. I can afford to play this game."

Dr. Gibson pursed her lips, her knitted brows giving away her worry. Or was it frustration? Still, she calmly leaned against the table and replied, "Yes, that's true. We can begin to explore fertilization procedures. Some of them are expensive."

"That's no problem."

The doctor paused a second, registering, then continued in the same tone, "And some of them take time, which *is* a problem." She looked up into Annie's eyes, letting her know in no uncertain terms that she was not going to allow Annie to "play a game." Annie swallowed and nodded, respect sparking in her chest. She knew Maureen Gibson was no-nonsense, but she was fair and had a big heart. Annie came to her six years earlier on Gabriella's recommendation—she worked in the same women's health clinic. Annie hadn't seen a gynecologist in three years—she was always too busy and put it off—but when Gabriella had heard that juicy fact at a Book Club meeting, she went nuclear as only Gabby can when it came to health issues. Annie was sent to Dr. Gibson, a woman—which Annie had insisted on—of about the same age—which Annie liked—who ran every test in the book and had Annie toeing the line ever since.

"There's a procedure where we can harvest your eggs by laparoscopy, then fertilize them with your husband's sperm. Of course, we'll have to test those critters, too."

"No problem. He wants a baby as much as I do. More. As soon as possible."

"Good. We could also consider in vitro. It's eight thousand dollars a pop, with no guarantees."

"Sign me up." She started wagging her foot. "Let's get started."

The doctor scratched her head wearily. "Annie, slow down. Don't set such high expectations."

"I always set high expectations. That's how I've achieved as much as I have. Raising the bar and kicking higher."

"I admire that, as long as it's realistic. But the fact is, we're pushing it at your age, battling against time."

Annie shifted her weight. She could handle most things in life, but not this trampling of time. It made her edgy, it was so out of her control.

Dr. Gibson paused to remove her glasses and chew at the end of one side in thought. "There's something else we need to consider here," she began slowly. "Why you're skipping periods. There's always the possibility that you could be entering early menopause."

Annie felt the blood drain from her face and her limbs hung loose like noodles. Menopause? That was for old women. Not her. She was young. Vibrant. Attractive. Her boobs were still perky. There wasn't a goddamn wrinkle on her face.

"Menopause?" she blurted out. "What, are you crazy? I'm still young. I'm still fertile. I'm only forty-three, not fifty. And John just hit forty."

"It's a common misperception that menopause only happens after fifty, that your periods suddenly end. In fact, it's a long, slow process that can take months, even years, before the actual cessation of menses. Premenopausal symptoms can start in the late thirties to early forties."

"Well, it's not happening to me."

"Maybe not. Have you had any hot flashes, palpitations?" Dr. Gibson pushed on.

Annie could have killed her for the calm she'd admired moments ago, especially now that she did feel palpitations of anxiety racing through her. And any sweats now were because they were even discussing the dread *M* word. She shook her head vehemently.

"Any vaginal dryness during sexual intercourse?"

"No, no, none of that."

"How about your periods? Would you say they were regular in the past?"

She shrugged. "To be honest, I've never been all that regular."

"Okay. We already know you've only had spotting this cycle, and you missed the last one. Something's going on in there. Any excessive bleeding?"

"Oh, yeah. Very heavy, but lots of women have that from time to time. It doesn't mean anything."

"It might. Take it easy, Annie, you look like you're facing a firing squad."

"I feel like it."

"There's nothing to be afraid of. Menopause is a natural phase of life."

"Not for me it isn't. I'm not ready!" She swallowed down the panic that was rising. She didn't feel different, why did her body have to change? "Dr. Gibson, be honest. Do you think that's what's going on with me?"

Dr. Gibson smiled and shrugged her slim shoulders,

"No, probably not. You're getting a reprieve. I'm going to run a few tests and I want to take a Pap smear. Says here," she said, putting on her glasses and studying her chart, "that you missed your last one." Her tone was censorial. "We sent you reminders."

"God, I forgot to reschedule. I'm sorry. I had a case that went to trial and, well..."

"It's not a good idea to let these things slip."

"Wait, wait, I can hear it coming. *Not at my age.*"

"Precisely."

"Well, *at my age,* Dr. Gibson, I want to have a baby." She said the words, needed to say them, to hear them spoken aloud in order to focus the goal in her mind and dispel the cloud of gloom. Her face set in an expression of rock determination that John would have recognized and which would have immediately sent him stepping out of her way. "And I intend to have one."

Alone, Annie finished dressing in slow motion, feeling as if she'd just stepped out of a dream, a nightmare. As she buttoned the small pearl buttons on her blouse, tucked it in her suit skirt and smoothed away the wrinkles from her flat, unpregnant belly, she couldn't think beyond these simple movements. Her mind was dazed, taking a break. But her body, her crotch, felt as if it had been pinched, poked and probed. She wanted nothing more than to slip on her shoes and get far from the smell of antiseptic and the cold tile walls.

It wasn't until she entered the waiting room and saw John nervously tapping his foot that it really hit her. *She wasn't pregnant.* There was no baby inside her, no little bun in the oven. The sense of loss rose up to hit her, shaking her equilibrium, causing her to sway and grip the door. And now she'd have to tell John. She'd have to be strong, for him.

He looked over her way, his long face and his large blue eyes as sweet and trusting as a puppy's. His face blossomed into a smile of such relief and love at seeing her, she almost expected him to wag his tail. She wanted to weep. In one fluid movement of his long, lanky body he was on his feet, crossing the room and holding her hands. His face was lit like a boy's at Christmas.

"Well? How'd it go? How far along are you?"

"Let's go home," she said in a tight voice.

The light in his eyes dimmed in a blink. It killed her to know that, in a few minutes more, she'd extinguish it completely.

On a sunny afternoon in April, Midge found herself standing before her easel dressed in paint-splattered jeans and a long-sleeved shirt, painting behind a makeshift barricade of boxes, chairs and canvases designed as a fortress against one small poodle. Ever since that first commanding outburst, Prince had taken Midge on as his new master. He was mad in love with her, following her around the loft, waiting for her at the door when she left, whining. Prince's slavish devotion to Midge was driving Edith crazy, as well as Midge.

"You own this whole building, don't you, dear?" Edith asked Midge.

"You know I do, Mother. Why?"

"Oh, I was just thinking. I've been here for quite a while and I'm sure I must be overstaying my welcome."

Midge glanced over her shoulder. Edith was sitting at the counter polishing her fingernails. The ever present cup of coffee was but an arm's length away. Edith was wrapped in a fluffy, pink, quilted bathrobe and the most ridiculous pink terry slippers that had enormous bows on the front.

"What could possibly make you think that? It's only been, what, five, six weeks?"

"Don't be a smart aleck. You know I'm grateful, darling. But as I was saying, I like it here, and as I'm in no hurry to get back and I don't want to be a burden, I was wondering... Isn't there a nice little apartment available in your building? I don't need anything too big. It's just little ol' me. And Prince, of course. And think! Won't it be fun living close together again? Just like old times!"

Old times were exactly what she wanted to avoid and felt sure her face expressed this. Midge could feel the walls of her big, spacious loft closing in on her. There wasn't enough room in this *city* for the two of them, let alone the same building. And *her* building! My God, that would make her her own mother's landlord! That would mean contracts between them. Demands. Money would cross hands. The other tenants would lump them together. She shuddered with the thought that Edith would make a pass at handsome Mr. Lyon, the gay French tailor. No, no, no, she groaned inwardly, this would never work out. It was suicide. Or murder... She'd end up killing her mother for sure—or her little dog.

She set her jaw and dug in. This was a familiar impasse between them, sadly enough. Midge had always, even as a young girl, had to stand up in her own way to this tiny powerhouse, to match her will against Edith's like two iron fists wrapped in velvet gloves.

"How can you? What about your condo in Florida?"

"I've been meaning to talk to you about that," she said, her voice hedging. "You see, expenses were getting very tight and I'm living on a fixed income. It doesn't amount to much, certainly not enough for me to keep up two places."

Midge set down her paintbrush and faced her mother squarely. "You sold it."

Her mother licked her lips, set down her nail polish brush and nodded. "I've only just heard from my broker that he's found a buyer. I'd like to sell it, but it's all a bit nerve-racking, moving about at my age. I can't just bounce back and forth. I'd like to stay in Chicago if I could, but I wanted to talk to you first, of course."

Midge stared, speechless, across the room at Edith. All her life, her mother had never wanted to talk about her decisions, much less ask Midge's permission. It was far more likely the condo was already long sold. Midge squinted, expecting to see the familiar flash of determination in her mother's eyes.

So she was surprised to see instead that Edith's eyes were soft and vulnerable. The afternoon sun was not kind to her face. Her skin was soft and sagging, and her wrinkles carved deep lines in her makeup. Midge caught a fragility about her mother that she hadn't noticed before. Those tiny hands were trembling, her legs looked like matchsticks and her auburn hair was thin and gray at the roots.

Midge saw with a bolt of shock that her mother was *old*. Really old. She felt dizzy with the realization that, sometime during the past year or so, her vibrant mother had become frail.

"I'd really like to live near you," Edith continued in an uncertain tone of voice. "And if I had my own little place, I wouldn't be such a bother with all my stuff. And with Prince." Her eyes shone a little too bright, as though nervous, perhaps afraid that Midge might say the *No* forming on her lips.

In a mind-bending turnaround, Midge knew that she was the strong one now. The roles had reversed. And her mother knew it.

Midge's shoulders lowered as all fight fled. Looking at her crazy mother who she loved despite everything, her lips eased into a hesitant smile and the word *Yes* slipped from her mouth.

Eve's next few weeks were filled with the kinds of busy chores that she excelled at and she felt the stirrings of her old confidence returning. She acquired a new phone number, notified friends and relatives of her new address, shopped for necessities for the condo and generally fussed over everyday details. All small steps, she knew, but in the right direction. With the children, she was meticulous in her care, driving them to and from school, packing special lunches with cheery notes tucked in the brown paper bags, driving them to and from their friends' houses that they could no longer walk or ride bikes to. She hated driving and felt glued to the car, scrambling to get work done between chauffeuring, but prided herself on never once complaining. Once again, she was supermom.

In her heart, however, she knew that it was just a matter of time before the anvil hanging overhead fell. It did on the first of May. Annie called to invite her to lunch.

They met at La Bella, Annie's favorite Italian restaurant, which served the fresh porcini risotto she claimed she'd kill for. When Eve arrived, Annie was already seated and looking at the menu. A bottle of white wine waited on ice. Eve kissed her cheek, thinking that Annie looked thinner, more pale than usual.

"Are you feeling all right?" she asked when she took her seat.

"Is that a social pat phrase that I should reply to with,

'Yes, dahling, I feel wonderful!' or are you really interested in the sordid, boring details?''

Eve unfolded her napkin and dabbed at her lips. ''What do you think?''

''Okay, then, I feel lousy.''

''Lousy in the body or lousy in the spirit?''

''Both.'' Annie rested her forehead against her long fingers for a moment, then made a quick, brushing movement with her hand, as though to sweep away the pesky malaise. Eve watched her closely, her ears perked.

''I'm anemic,'' she announced with an inappropriate brightness. ''It's the new chic problem, don't you know. And I'm taking all these horrid green iron pills that make me ill to my stomach and cranked-off. What kind of justice is it to have morning sickness and not be pregnant? And John...'' she said with a tone clearly indicating her frustration. ''He's the very picture of health and robustness. Apparently he's got loads of strong, healthy uber-sperm in search of an egg. Which apparently I can't provide.'' Her face twisted and she quickly looked down at her hands. ''Which explains the lousy spirit part. So, there it is.'' She raised her chin in a staccato movement, ending the conversation with a clipped nod to the waiter, who promptly approached to pour out two glasses of the chilled Vouvray.

Annie tasted the wine, muttered, ''That's fine,'' to the waiter and immediately studied the menu, effectively cutting off any more discussion of babies.

Eve understood the signal and reluctantly let the topic slip by. She knew Annie never liked to dwell on her private life, preferring to discuss others' lives, business or some juicy gossip and a good laugh. She was a hard worker, reliable and respected by all. Yet she allowed very few people close. Eve knew that she was probably Annie's best friend, next to John, yet even to her she rarely opened up about her problems. Annie considered it whining, and as she once told Eve with a shudder, she had enough of that in her practice to ever indulge in it herself.

Eve admired the confidence with which Annie did everything, even ordering wine. Eve knew a lot about wine but Tom had always ordered for them. He studied the list and took great pleasure in selecting the correct wine to go with a particular food. It was never discussed, but the man's role was always understood. Annie just naturally assumed the role, and Eve let her. Annie was a woman comfortable in a man's world. Eve sometimes wondered how John endured his wife being the dominant one in their marriage. Tom never could have tolerated it. But who was to say which was better? Each couple worked out their own arrangements. Still, she suspected John had his own iron strength somewhere, deep and quiet, or Annie wouldn't have been able to stick with him.

Eve sipped her wine slowly, watching with worry while Annie helped herself to another glass. There was a new recklessness to Annie's behavior, a come-what-may attitude that she suspected hid some deep hurt.

"This isn't what I wanted to talk to you about," Annie said after they received their orders. "At least not before I down this bottle of wine. I've been waiting for that phone call telling me you found a job...."

"Bronte's graduation is around the corner," Eve replied, suddenly losing her appetite and pushing the risotto around the plate. At some level, she knew that the search for a job was going to be pure torture, that she would have to face her demons. "Surely there's more time. There's so much to do and Bronte needs me now. And I'm on so many committees for graduation."

Annie would have none of it and spoke bluntly. "Cut the crap, Eve. That delay tactic won't work again. You've lost your cushion. Go get your skinny butt out there. It doesn't matter if you go back to teaching or be a checkout girl at the grocer's but you need the money. Unless, of course, you plan to rope yourself some old millionaire.''

Eve paled at the thought of dating again, much less marrying. "Don't be ridiculous. I'm still married in my mind to Tom. And in my heart. One doesn't just toss over twenty-three years of monogamy."

Annie's face clouded and she looked off. "Yeah, well...whatever, Eve. The well is dry, sweetheart. I've done my best to boost you along bit by bit, but I wouldn't be a good friend, or a good advisor, if I didn't warn you now. And that's what I'm doing, Eve, in the firmest, strongest way I know how. Get a job. Any job. I mean now. Not after Bronte's graduation. Or you'll end up on skid row."

Eve clenched her hands in her lap and thought how it was easy for Annie to tell her to hurry up and go get a job. It was no big deal for her. She was a professional, used to dealing with people—strangers—every day. To Eve, that part of the world was "out there" somewhere, far beyond the gates of her garden. It was a very big deal.

"Bronte's had a tough semester. She's fallen off the honor roll to barely pass. She came home with a warning last week. She's getting an F in math. An F! The counselors said it was to be expected after the trauma of her father's death and that she needs time to heal. But Porters don't get Fs!''

"In an ideal world you could stay home and hold her hand, except that this isn't an ideal situation. There isn't any more time. Just as there isn't any more money. Here, let me show you a few classifieds I pulled for you. They're legitimate, close to home, and they draw on your background.'' She spread the ads on the table between them. ''Go on, don't pull that face on me. Just take a look.''

One ad was for a receptionist in a doctor's office, another was for a secretary in the English department at a local college.

''Thank God you have computer skills or you'd be compelled to do retail.''

Eve read the ads slowly. As the words swam before her eyes, she felt her back stiffen.

''Annie,'' she said, slowly raising her gaze from the ads to her friend's eyes, ''Why would I want these jobs? I'm a teacher.''

''No offense, Eve, but is your certification up-to-date? I didn't think so. Honey, you haven't been inside a classroom in over twenty years. No one is going to hire you as a teacher without updated skills and experience.''

''But I have a master's degree in English.''

Annie snorted and shook her head. ''That and a buck will get you a cup of coffee.''

Eve felt something harden in her gut even while her body quivered with waves of anger. She had long since taken over her own finances, such as they were, but she still relied heavily on Annie's advice and guidance. As grateful as she was—and she really and truly was—she sensed that the balance between them had tilted. Independence had changed her. She was feeling chafed that Annie somehow had gained the upper hand in their relationship and was becoming a bit of a bully.

''Look, don't get me wrong,'' Annie continued in a pressing tone. ''I respect your skills and more, I respect your intelligence, your work ethic, your compassion. Whoever gets you will get a gem. *I* know that. But *they* won't know that. They'll just see…'' She paused, twiddled the stem of her glass and pursed her lips. ''I'm sorry, Eve, there's no nice or easy way to say this. I'm just going to be blunt. They'll see an attractive, middle-aged woman who played house for years. It's cruel, I know," she said quickly, holding up her palm against the flame in Eve's eyes. "Unjust, unfair, un-everything, but that's the way it is. You can build on your background in time," she said softly now, sympathy entering her voice. "Take courses at night and get what you want. In time. Consider these as transition jobs."

"I'm going to get a teaching job." Eve sat in a stubborn silence and saw the frustration Annie barely kept back, a look she felt sure she wore herself. There followed a tense impasse.

"So, now I'm the evil friend, am I?" Annie said dryly, attempting to deflate the tension with sarcastic humor.

"No," Eve replied, relieved but holding firm. "You're my dear friend. But this is my life, not yours. My decision. I've got to try."

Annie nodded, more with resignation than conviction. "At least let me help pad your résumé a bit."

"No." There was no compromise in her voice.

Annie surprised Eve by laughing then. Laughing lightly, without scorn or derision. Eve felt buoyed by the sound, carried away by it in a wave of helium delight.

"I love it," Annie said, reaching across the table and taking Eve's hand. "Love the attitude, love the grit, love the dream." She squeezed the hand. "Love you, babe." Their eyes met and the gaze cemented their friendship. "It's tough out there, as I fear you're going to find out. But go for it if you must. Just know I'll be here for you one way or the other. You do know that, don't you?"

"Yep," Eve replied, squeezing back. "Me, too. Whenever." She meant it, hoping someday she'd be called on to be strong for Annie.

Annie shifted back in her chair and picked up her tableware, attacking her risotto with gusto. "But since you're going for broke here, literally, I'm picking up the tab for lunch. No discussion."

"Okay," replied Eve cheerfully, gratefully. Then, readjusting the balance between them again she added, "But I'll get the next one."

The next day while the kids were in school, Eve polished up her résumé, dug out her credentials, dry cleaned her old navy Armani suit, pulled out her classic Ferragamo pumps and telephoned the two small colleges located in town for appointments. She didn't want to travel too far from home, she reasoned.

Her first wake-up call came when Saint Benedict's College wouldn't even make an appointment. The secretary coolly informed her over the phone that an application would be sent to her address, which she should complete and return.

"We'll notify you if an interview is requested," the secretary said with dismissal, hanging up before Eve had the opportunity to utter a polite goodbye, much less a thank-you. Eve's hand shook on the receiver after she'd slammed it down. No one had ever talked to her that way before! It knocked her self-confidence a few rungs down the ladder.

Lincoln College granted her an appointment, but only for the position of substitute teacher. The pay was minimal, but after Saint Benedict's rejection, Eve was eager to get anything in hand.

As she walked through the halls of the small, private college, clutching her fine leather briefcase, her heels clicking on the polished tile, she felt surrounded by youth. *Babies, they're just babies,* her mind screamed out!

Girls and boys, not much older in appearance than her own Bronte, brushed by her at a clipped pace. Some gathered in groups, books tucked under their arms, laughing with that loud, carefree boisterousness she could no longer bring herself to do. Here and there, standing alone or slumped in a chair, an individual was engrossed in a book, oblivious.

Eve was universally ignored.

She caught a glimpse of herself in the window as she passed. The reflection was that of a small, trim woman, smaller than many of the girls around her. Her long dark-brown hair was upswept in a smooth twist and clasped with a tortoise clip she'd borrowed from Bronte. If she glanced quickly at the reflection as she passed, she saw an attractive, stylish woman. A professional woman. Perhaps even a young woman. But in the eyes of the truly young around her, she was old. She'd crossed some line. She'd become invisible.

What was it, she wondered, pained? Her clothes? Certainly her suit, pumps and pearls marked her; she was one of "them." But if she removed the pearls, kicked off the pumps, slung her jacket over her shoulder, swung her hips and smiled... What then?

She knew what would happen; it'd happened so many times before. She might get a turned head, a discreet glance beneath a raised brow, enough to give her a momentary thrill that she was still being admired, that she still "had it." Then the dewy-faced looker would catch on to some undefinable cue, the searchlight would switch off and he'd turn his head and move on. What was it? Some pheromone that the young and available gave off? A subtle movement or a tilt of the head? Something in the eyes?

Whatever it was, it had slipped through her fingers, slowly, soundlessly, like sand. She didn't even realize it was happening, but suddenly all she had left were a few grains, and she was holding on to them, tight.

And yet, it wasn't that sexy aspect of youth she coveted now. Perhaps a year ago, when she was secure in her marriage and it was all an amusing game. But no longer. What had her quaking in her pumps as she sat in the waiting room of the personnel office and perused the three twenty-something-year-old women seated across from her was the confidence that shone like a beacon from their eager, fresh, oh so damnably energetic eyes. They were sharp, prepared, hungry. This wasn't about being attractive or finding a mate. This was about survival. This was her competition.

Her toes curled as she fingered her résumé, seeing in her mind's eye the date of her college graduation: 1974. Were these women even born then? Why hadn't she taken courses to brush up? Why hadn't she taken Annie's advice to pad her résumé a bit?

When her name was called, Eve marshaled her wits along with her briefcase and strode straight-shouldered across the waiting room, ignoring the sharp surveillance by the other three women, telling herself that was not derision she saw in their fresh eyes. Stepping into the cramped, gray, unadorned office, however, she knew she was doomed when the woman behind the desk stood up to shake her hand.

The large-boned, blunt-faced woman appeared much younger but it was impossible to guess her age. Ms. Kovac was a mountain of a woman with lifeless, cold eyes behind heavy, dark-rimmed glasses. She wore no wedding ring on her hand and had no personal photographs on her desk. In fact, there was nothing in the gray square of space to indicate any personal preferences or style or personality at all.

"Take a seat, please," she said with a brisk wave of

her hand indicating the steel chair. She offered no name, no eye contact.

Eve sat and crossed her ankles instead of her legs, a reflex after a lifetime of training. The silence was oppressive. Eve felt the last shreds of her confidence shrivel as Ms. Kovac read her résumé with her mouth set in a grim line. At last she cleared her throat, flattened the résumé on her desk, then folded her hands over it. She studied Eve with the same cold perusal a judge would survey a convict who'd just been found guilty—guilty of wasting her time.

"You have no teaching experience?"

"Well, I've volunteered at the Literacy Center for the past five years. And there was my student teaching, of course."

"Are you familiar with current methods of pedagogy?"

Eve ventured a smile that was not returned. "I can't imagine teaching has changed all that much in the past—" she paused, not willing to offer the number "—years."

"Yes, well...I don't think the chairman of the English department would agree."

It went downhill from there. For the next twenty minutes Eve answered question after question in halting sentences, while thinking in a blind fury that this underpaid, bitter personnel employee of a mediocre college delighted in making it painfully clear to an attractive, seemingly well-to-do suburban housewife how out of touch with the world of academics she was. Unspoken was the message that she was naive to think a master's degree in English would qualify her to teach that subject. It was clear to Eve from Ms. Kovac's repeated, pointed questions on teaching methodology that she didn't care a whit how well Eve understood the cadence and power of Keats, Coleridge, Burns and the other Romantic poets, or wished to hear her discuss her thesis on *The Visionary Company of William Blake.*

That twenty-five years of extensive reading, writing newsletters and volunteering at literacy clinics had no bearing whatsoever on the teaching of literature, even as a substitute.

This she pounded into Eve's head mercilessly, causing her shoulders to slump and her chin to inch closer to her chest. Eve was made to feel guilty for not having updated her résumé, guilty for wasting time on things like motherhood and family and volunteering, guilty for being forty-five and unemployable.

When Ms. Kovac looked at her wristwatch, then leaned back in her chair and said, "You do realize, Mrs. Porter, that there are many applicants for this position?" Eve had had enough. She rose and shook the woman's hand.

"Thank you for your time, Ms. Kovac. It's clear Lincoln College is not the place for me," she said in her best clipped tone, leaving the stunned woman to figure out whatever she pleased from the statement.

As she strolled out the door, past the three young women who watched her sloe-eyed, she slipped off her jacket and slung it over her arm. Walking through the halls she pulled the pins from her hair, shaking it loose like a filly would her mane and swung her hips to the left and right in tempo with her arms. She ignored the curious, searching gazes from the boys as she passed—they were children! Her eyes were straight ahead.

Pushing open the heavy wood door, she stepped out into a beautiful spring day and felt the sunshine kiss her cheeks and smelled the faint scent of apple blossoms in the air. She breathed in great gulps of the fresh air, feeling as though she'd barely escaped with her identity. But she had escaped and was free; this was her life. Instead of being beaten into the earth by the heel of conceit, she felt like a young shoot bursting through the soil.

Damn Ms. Kovac and all the women like her who found pleasure in plucking out the joy and success of other women. She would not let them get in her way or trivialize her intelligence and experience just because it didn't fit the mold. She strode through the countless pale-yellow tree seedlings whirling through the rarefied spring air like cheery helicopters. She should be grateful to that poor, plodding woman who existed only in that fluorescent-lit, gray cubicle. That dog had pulled back the curtain, forcing Eve to see the man pulling the levers and pushing the buttons. The man was the reality. Her degrees were all an illusion. She'd been waltzing in Oz.

As she made her way home, Eve decided it was high time to click her Ferragamo heels and wake up to the way it was.

Nine

And closely akin to the visions…was the call still
sounding in the depths of the forest. It filled him with
a great unrest and strange desires. It caused him to
feel a vague, sweet gladness, and he was aware of
wild yearnings and stirrings for he knew not what.

—Jack London, *The Call of the Wild*

It was a quiet night. Outside her window a neighbor's dog
howled at the quarter moon. Eve sat at the secretary in her
living room listening to the throaty call and felt a strange
stirring in her breast that quickened her breath and caused
her to tighten her fingers around the pen in her hand. She'd
been sitting for the better part of an hour, staring in turns
at the moon and at the application for a position as an
administrative assistant in the English department at Saint
Benedict's College. Her first job application in twenty-five
years.

Outside the dog cried again. Deep inside she felt the
rustlings of change in the scented air. Like Buck in this
month's Book Club selection, *The Call of the Wild,* she
sat rigid, ears cocked, nose high in the air, sensing an

approaching message, sniffing at what was as yet only a distant scent.

Yet, while excitement quivered, she was hesitant, knowing she stood alone in the wide-open space of uncertainty. The winds of anxiety and fear engendered by more than a quarter of a century of experience buffeted her. She'd learned the rules of fang and club, been kept in line by the tethers of social mores and tradition, whipped by the lash of women's tongues and men's criticisms. Despite her eagerness to move forward, her paw lingered in the air. She crouched back.

Why did she hold back? What was she afraid of? What expectations were there to meet? She wasn't the doctor's wife anymore. Or the Riverton matron who served on committees, drove carpool and rallied at sports events. Nor was she any longer the naive child seeking approval. She felt young again, despite the softening of her skin and the graying of her hair. She felt young deep in her heart. She wanted to laugh out loud like she saw the students at Lincoln College do, with their heads back and their mouths wide-open.

She had the urge to test her limits rappelling high on a mountaintop or traversing snowy fields with a dog team. Most of all, she wanted to go back to school, to update old skills and learn new ones. She wanted to grow. Never again would she allow someone like Ms. Kovac to put her paws on her back. This Eve Porter was showing her teeth and fighting back.

Jack London had put it succinctly when Ol' Buck stirred in his sleep, his paws running in the air, hearing the call of the wild. It was an ancient howling that awoke all beasts from their stupor and awakened them to survival.

She heard the calling in her heart, in her soul, in every fiber of her being. She would survive, Eve decided, sitting up straight in her chair. Her period of mourning was over. It was time to live. Each day was precious and she would embrace each one, be grateful for each one.

Taking a deep breath, she leaned forward and, in her finest Palmer Method script, wrote her name: *Eve Porter*.

Not Mrs. Thomas Porter. Nor Miss Eve Brown. She was Ms. Eve Porter, a blending of both the energetic, curious, outgoing girl she once was and the sedate, respectable wife and mother she'd become. She stared at the name, wondering who this new, unknown Eve was. She was sure she was someone she wanted to get to know better. Or perhaps, rediscover.

Eve smoothed out the application with her palms, feeling the crisp cool paper on her skin as she quieted the stirrings of doubt in her breast. Then with quick, decisive movements, she folded the application into thirds, stuffed the envelope and affixed a stamp.

"There, it is done," she said aloud, then released a long sigh, nodding. She'd get this job, she felt it in her bones. It may not be the teaching job she'd hoped for, but it was a first step. Then she'd take another, then another, on her way toward her goals.

Eve heard the call of the dog again and, turning her face to the moon, smiled, answering the cry in her heart. She'd stuck out her paw into the path. She was running with the pack.

Two weeks later, at the same desk, Eve opened her purse for a last-minute check that she had everything she needed before leaving for her first day at work. Her wallet, her lipstick, her car keys—everything was in order. Her hands shook as she closed her purse and clasped it tight.

"It's gonna be okay, Mom."

Bronte stepped forward to wrap her long arms around

her mother and give her a reassuring hug. "I'll take care of Finney so don't you worry about a thing."

Eve's heart melted. "I have cheese and sandwich meat in the fridge for lunch. And salad. Make sure Finney eats his veggies. Oh, and Nello's brother is going to drive them to the baseball game at three. That's the schedule for today. Later this week I thought you and Finney might want to go to the movies so there's money in an envelope up on the bulletin board. But don't spend it all in one day. There's enough there for treats during the week, you know, like ice cream or something."

"Mom, we've gone over this a million times. I've been a baby-sitter for years. Trust me, I can handle one creepy brother."

Eve sighed and tucked Bronte's hair behind her ear, then cupped her slender cheek in her palm. Her daughter looked so old, and she looked so young.

"I wish it didn't have to be this way. It's not the way I'd like for you to spend the summer before high school."

"It's cool. Summer school starts next week and there're some really good courses I want to take. I think it's Finney who's bummed. He doesn't want to go to summer school."

"School? He's taking video production and football, for heaven's sake. That's not school, that's fun."

"You know Finney."

Eve chewed her lip. No, she didn't know Finney, she thought with worry. She couldn't find the cheerful little boy she used to know beneath the facade of the remote, distanced young man she lived with now. He spent most of his time either on the phone with his friends or at their homes. He never invited anyone here. He never invited her in.

"Oh, that reminds me. If you want to have some friends over, that's fine, but no more than two. And no boys."

"Duh." Bronte's lips twisted with annoyance.

"Why don't you invite Sarah Bridges over? I haven't seen her in a while."

Bronte's face darkened and she shrugged.

There was a story there, but Eve knew better than to broach the topic now. Maybe later, when she came home.

"My number at Saint Benedict's is on the bulletin board. And the emergency numbers. Let's see, what have I forgotten?"

"Go already, Mom. We'll be fine."

"Really?"

"Goodbye!" Bronte offered another hug. "Good luck on the new job, Mom. You'll be great." She turned her head and called over her shoulder, "Finney! Mom's leaving!"

"Oh, he doesn't have to say goodbye. Let him be."

Bronte's face was mutinous. "He does, too. You let him get away with murder."

"Be easy on him."

Bronte was about to retort when Finney appeared in the hallway. He walked toward them, head down, shoulders up and hands in his baggy pants pockets. His soft brown hair was parted in the middle and was growing long, fringing the base of his neck. When he looked up it was with a jerk of his head that shifted the shock of hair back from his eyes.

Eve reached out to smooth it back. Finney ducked away from her reach. She laughed a bit but only to disguise how much it hurt that he no longer let her touch him.

"Be good," she said, "and mind your sister. She's in charge."

Finney nodded and shrugged, then turned to walk away.

"What? No hug goodbye? It's my first day of work and

I could use all the moral support I can get. You're my only guy, don't forget.''

She caught a glimmer of affection in his eyes as he stepped forward to deliver a lackluster hug. But she hung on tight, squeezing him, and for a magical second she felt him squeeze her, too, and pat her back. Then he stepped away, seemingly embarrassed by the moment.

She looked in the faces of her children and physically ached with her love for them, was loath to leave them. It seemed only yesterday that they were underfoot, needing constant supervision. When did they grow up? Could she really leave them on their own while she went to work?

She'd never once before considered what it might've been like all those years for Tom when he said goodbye every morning on his way to the office, or before leaving on one of his many trips. When he bent over to receive a warm milky kiss from his children, did he feel a twinge of regret at leaving them, such as she did now? At what point, if ever, did it become perfunctory, like brushing one's teeth or saying a pat ''Good morning'' without bothering to look up from the morning paper and meet their eyes.

How did she and Tom ever reach the point where they took their relationship so for granted that he could leave on a business trip that took him away forever and not even say goodbye?

The pain was still so raw that she winced. *She didn't even say goodbye.*

''Mom, it's okay,'' repeated Bronte, misunderstanding her anguish. ''We'll be fine. I'll take care of everything.''

Bronte was trying so hard to be competent. It shamed her that her mother doubted her ability.

''I know you will,'' Eve replied, sounding as though she meant it even as she worried. ''Well,'' she said, grasping hold of her purse and straightening her shoulders. "I guess this is it." She looked her children in the eyes, vowing never to leave or allow anyone she loved to leave her again without saying goodbye.

"Goodbye," she said through a tight smile that held back too much emotion. "I love you!"

They closed the door behind her. She stood quietly in the hall and listened if they locked the dead bolts, smiling when they did. Wiping her eyes, she walked forward, packing in her heart the echo of their "I love you, too!" as neatly as she'd packed a tuna sandwich for her lunch.

The immersion process into the working world was much less painful than she'd expected. The small, crowded office of Saint Benedict's English department was located in Saint Augustine Hall, at the rear of the second floor overlooking the commons. Overflowing from the entrance was a throng of students that pressed into the anteroom, each of them waving a registration form with a forlorn expression on his or her face. At the other end of the room, seemingly barricaded by a long metal table, stood a trio of women hunched over stacks of forms.

If she'd expected a cordial welcome, a tour of the facilities and perhaps a cup of coffee, she was mistaken. She hadn't been in the office for more than a few minutes when she was accosted by a thin, nimble, elderly woman with the bright-blue eyes and short haircut of a pixie. She must've had a streak of magic in her to pick Eve out from the crowd.

"You must be Mrs. Porter! At last! Come right this way, far from the madding crowd. You're an absolute godsend. Wish you could've been here last week but you're here now, that's all that matters. It'll be a baptism by fire, I'm afraid, but you look up to it. Let's sneak around to the other side of this table, careful now! Watch that stack of books on the floor.''

The elderly woman with snowy-white hair slipped around the piles of clutter like a sprite. When they reached the safe island of peace behind the dividing tables, she handed Eve a stack of forms in triplicate and said, ''I'm Pat Crawford. Welcome to your first registration.''

That was how it began. At first she felt as though her mind were a sieve and she'd never digest all the instructions that were tossed at her from three directions in rapid-fire order. In short time, the words coalesced to make sense and she quickly learned how to fill in the registration forms, schedule appointments with teachers and, when the case merited it, an appointment with the mysterious chairman who never emerged from behind his office door. It was her skill in maneuvering grumpy, complaining children, however, that endeared her to Pat Crawford and the rest of the staff of the department. Eve worked right through lunch, pausing only to unwrap the ''I love you'' messages in her mind from time to time as fortification when the lines of students seemed endless or their complaints too strident.

By three o'clock the lines had dissipated and a peace settled over the office. Eve's hand ached from holding a pencil and filling in circles with graphite. She stretched her fingers while massaging them.

''This is the eye of the hurricane, so enjoy,'' Pat Crawford said, pouring out freshly brewed coffee into three cups. ''Another load will be coming in at about five o'clock.''

Eve's eyes widened with alarm. ''Five o'clock? I have to leave promptly at five, I'm afraid. I—I know it's my first day,'' she stammered, ''but my children are alone. I have to make dinner and…''

"Oh, don't worry about that. We have someone on loan from Accounting who'll be coming in after you leave. They never have the push we do in English and no one expects you to kill yourself on your first day. Here," she said, passing her a cup of coffee. "You've earned a break, don't you think?"

Eve greedily sipped the coffee, not caring if the surge she felt humming in her veins was a result of the caffeine punch or purely psychological. For her, coffee was comfort food. The warm cup soothed her aching hand muscles as she breathed in the heady aroma.

"You haven't met the chairman yet, have you? He's a doll. We all love him. If he seems rather gruff, well, just ignore that. He's a perfectionist and doesn't mean it. He's really very nice." Pat's eyes sparkled just speaking of him. "Well, I suppose now's as good a time as any," she said, approaching with steaming coffee in a dark-blue ceramic mug that had the word Read emblazoned across it.

"You mean, there's actually someone behind that door? I thought it was just a facade."

Pat laughed. "He hates registration and hides out. We try to protect him as best we can." The other two women nodded in agreement. "But he's very accessible, really, when he doesn't have his nose in a book. Then he roars if he's interrupted. Come on. Let's enter the lion's den."

Interesting analogy, Eve thought to herself. The lionesses protecting the king. She set down her coffee with a reluctant sigh and trotted after Pat Crawford toward the mysterious chairman's office. Pat knocked almost coyly three times on the door. Eve's hand darted up to smooth back her French twist. When a deep voice called for them to enter, Pat turned her head and winked at Eve, then pushed open the oak door.

Eve lingered at the threshold, ears cocked, eyes wide,

hesitant to proceed. Pat looked over her shoulder and moved her fingers rapidly, indicating that she should follow. Eve's intuition was tingling and she stepped slowly, cautiously into the open space.

The late-afternoon sun poured in through the enormous gothic windows and spread its light over a wide walnut desk overflowing with papers, books, pens, exam pamphlets and paraphernalia carelessly strewn over every spare inch. Behind the desk a man slouched in a leather chair with his back to them, one ankle crossing the knee, his silver and dark, longish hair tousled and his chin cupped in his palm. He was reading a thick book, oblivious, basking in the afternoon light much like a lion king resting on a high rock overlooking the savanna.

Eve's gaze darted about the room, picking up clues. His tastes leaned toward the classic, she mused, sighting a worn, muted Oriental rug spread over the floor, the two gothic wood chairs upholstered in tapestry fabric and an imposing gargoyle perched on the windowsill. A graduation gown was draped across the back of one of the chairs, a wilting arrangement of flowers sat neglected on a side table and more registration forms were piled up in a corner beside a dusty slide carousel. The overwhelming influence in the cozy lair, however, was the presence of books. One entire wall was bookshelves, crammed full of leatherbound volumes in muted colors. Books were stacked on the floor in the corners, under tables and on tops of tables. Eve sniffed the air, catching the heady scent of knowledge. It drew her in. She let down her guard.

"Dr. Hammond?" called Pat in a gratingly cheery, friendly voice. "Coffee! And there's someone you should meet."

Eve took a cautious step forward into the light.

The chairman raised his head from his hand as though

startled, slipped his glasses off, then turned to look over his shoulder. His blue eyes were as piercing as lasers and made a dramatic contrast to the glowering, dark expression of his face. He obviously was annoyed at the interruption.

Eve pulled up short, unprepared. She'd expected some crusty old vulture or a soft-fleshed, benign professor. Dr. Hammond fit neither stereotype. He was clearly a lion of a man, all large, chiseled bones and majestic bearing. He was elegantly appointed and outwardly poised, but she could sense a wild fury within held taut by a will of iron. Intelligence shone in his large, deep-set eyes and sensuality teased in his full lips, pursed now in inspection. Streaks of silver at the temples and deep lines carved at the corners of his large eyes placed him somewhere in his mid-fifties, and he had that grace of movement and reserve that was a blessing in men as they aged.

His chair squeaked and he brought his long fingers together to steeple under his chin. He had enormous hands, she noted, and strong, heavy bones, unexpected in an English professor. He did not wear a wedding ring. His eyes grew smoky with curiosity, then appreciation. She might have felt unnerved by the perusal, but instead, quite to her surprise, she felt a resounding punch of attraction. Unexpected—and all the more powerful.

"I'm Dr. Paul Hammond," he said, his voice articulate in a mild British accent. He offered his hand.

She hesitantly took it. His long, strong fingers closed over hers, engulfing her hand, and with a searing flash her whole mind and being focused on that small expanse of skin making contact with his. She ordered her foolish body to relax and breathe normally. Her response was silly, ridiculous, she scolded herself, feeling the torch of a blush touch her cheeks. This was precisely what she thought might happen if she touched him.

"Welcome to the department, Eve Porter," he said with enviable calm, holding her hand for a fraction of a second too long. He offered her a smile so deliberately ravishing she felt her knees turn to jelly.

"Thank you, Dr. Hammond," she replied quietly. They were both, it seemed, being exceedingly polite. Then, as though turning off a switch, the gleam in his eye went out. He released her hand suddenly, looked away, then leaned back in his chair and picked up his book. "I'm sure Pat will get you anything you need, won't you, Pat?"

Pat, seemingly disappointed at having her *petite fête* cut short, set the cup of coffee down on the desk before the chairman and picked up a few papers from his desk in a delay tactic. "Of course I will! We've had a fine start already. Eve caught right on."

"Very good then." Slipping his glasses back on, he looked down at the pages, instantly engrossed. He dismissed them with a swivel of his chair.

Pat accepted the humiliation with a hum of acceptance and turned to leave. Eve, however, felt slapped. She raised a brow and straightened her shoulders, then after missing a beat, followed Pat from the room with cheeks aflame. As she concluded the final hour of her first day's work, Eve stubbornly refused to even entertain in her mind the dangerous thoughts that were bubbling beneath her calm facade. As she filed the student registration forms in alphabetical order, she reminded herself that Dr. Hammond was not her neighbor, or her colleague, or her friend. He was her boss. This was a new type of relationship for her and she couldn't react emotionally. She might want to harrumph, announce to the world that the chairman of Saint Benedict's English department was an insufferable boor and kick up her heels and quit. But she had to face the fact that he didn't care if he was rude—at least not to her—

and if she wanted to keep the job she'd have to set up a new strategy for dealing with her injured pride. Tom wasn't here to make it better anymore. She couldn't just quit. At this point, she needed Dr. Hammond more than he needed her.

A short while later, the chairman's door swung open and he rushed out, coattails flying and briefcase in his hand, reminding her so much of Tom that her heart leaped to her throat. Pat and the two temps fluttered around him, wishing him goodbye, accommodating his every need, giggling. His very presence turned them on like lightbulbs. Eve remained seated in the dark corner bent over an open file drawer, watching the display from under half lids. She noted that his gaze searched the room for her, and once finding her, he offered the slightest nod of his head.

She reciprocated in kind.

He left without a word.

It was character building, she decided with a sigh. She finished the tedious filing, washed out the coffeepot in the ladies' room down the hall and collected the trash from the office. Then, having completed the most menial chores, she gathered her belongings. It was five o'clock on the button. Eve was uneasy that she appear to the others to be a clock-watcher. Nonetheless, she was determined not to shortchange her time with her children. As it turned out, no one expected her to. Pat stepped forward to warmly thank her for a wonderful first day and they all waved a cheery goodbye, calling out a heartfelt chorus of, "See you tomorrow!"

"There's no rest for the weary," Eve muttered with a yawn as she stopped at the local grocery store to pick up some last-minute supplies for dinner. Thunder rolled in the sky, promising a much needed rain. The humidity was oppressive, hitting her like a wall as she stepped from the air-conditioning of her car into the street. She could barely put one foot in front of the other she was so tired, yet now she had to rally to prepare a meal. Her children were hungry and there was no one else.

Pushing her cart down the aisles, Eve carefully checked the prices, selecting in most cases the generic brands instead of her usual favorites. How cavalier she'd been in her old life-style about money! Back then her biggest concern was time. She was always in a hurry and it didn't matter how much something cost. If she needed it, she bought it. No worries. Such a luxury was unthinkable now. Ironically, she was much more pressed for time but now she had to be frugal. Each dollar counted. Money was tight until her first paycheck. As she waited in line at the cashier she mentally calculated the cost of her groceries. When she was finished ringing up and laid out dollar after dollar into the cashier's palm, her hands trembled slightly. For the first time in her life she didn't know if there'd be enough in her purse or whether one can of peas or a box of cereal would have to be set aside.

She sighed in relief when she had enough...but barely. All the euphoria of her first day at work dwindled as she counted the four dollars left in her wallet. When did groceries start costing so much? My God, she thought, closing her wallet as a numbness spread through her body. Would she make it until payday? There were no cushions to fall back on if she made an error. No one to step forward with a few extra dollars if she ran short.

The rain came with a sudden swelling of wind that brought angry streaks against her windshield. As she drove the final few blocks to her home through rush hour traffic, she counted her worries in time with the clicking of her wipers. While driving around her block three times hunting for a parking space, it hit her how every aspect of her life was a struggle now. She finally found a spot three blocks away from her building, which meant she'd be soaked by the time she ran inside. After squeezing her Volvo in, she yanked up the parking brake, then pounded the steering wheel to vent her anger against the fates that had forced her into such a position—at this point in her life.

She'd worked hard for years, being the good wife and the good mother. She'd had her turn counting pennies and saving toward a better future. Now should have been her time to sit back and reap the rewards. Instead, she was thrust back out onto the streets to start all over again. To get her nose rubbed into it again by proud, arrogant men like Dr. Hammond and unsympathetic clerks. Only now it was worse. She wasn't young anymore. She didn't have the same energy. She expected more respect. And now she also had her children to care for. Lightning flashed outdoors and thunder rumbled as the rain came down in torrents.

Tears began to pool, the first tears since she'd sold her house. She let them flow down her cheeks unashamedly. It wasn't Dr. Hammond she was angry at. It wasn't the high cost of groceries that brought tears. In her heart, she knew the pain that had been growing inside her since early that morning when she'd said goodbye to her children. All day the kernel had burrowed deep like a thorn under the skin. Eve knew who she was really angry at: Tom.

"How could you die and leave me like this?" she cried, clenching her fists and pounding the wheel again. "How could you die before I said goodbye?" Her heart felt torn in two, one part lonely for him and one part angry, oh so angry, at him. Guilt tumbled with regret and anguish that he hadn't said goodbye, either.

"God, it was cruel of you to take him like that!" she

cried. "At such a time... We'd had so many good times. We had things to settle. Words to say. Didn't you know? You must've known." She held her forehead in her palm. Remorse was the greatest burden, greater than the burden of making ends meet. If only she'd had five more minutes with Tom, she wept, wiping her eyes. Just five more minutes to tell him that she loved him.

She lowered her head, and in the solitude of her car, released a maelstrom of tears that shook her slim body like a willow in the roaring wind and washed away a year of pent-up sorrow from her soul.

A short while later Eve collected herself and ran the few blocks to her condo, grateful at least that the rain would mask all signs of her tears. She could not yet bring herself to cry in front of the children. They needed her strength now, not her hysteria.

"Yum, what's that I smell?" she called out in forced cheer, stepping into her condo and sniffing the scent of garlic in the air.

"Dinner," called Bronte, coming down the long hall from the kitchen to greet her. She was wiping her hands on the apron tied around her waist and her face was beaming with pride. "You're just in time. I'm ready to take the noodles off." Then, seeing her mother shake off the rain from her coat, she handed her a towel. "Hey, you're soaked."

Children loved to state the obvious. "You made dinner?" Eve was hesitant, conjuring up macaroni and cheese. "But I bought..."

"What?" Bronte asked, snooping inside the grocery bag. "Chicken? Good. I'll cook it tomorrow. Those cookies look good, too. But tonight it's spaghetti. It's all we had in the cabinets but I added extra veggies and I thought we could pile on lots of cheese. Oh yeah, and salad. And I bought this great loaf of bread with that money you left us.''

''You made all that?'' Eve felt as though her daughter had just removed a heavy burden from her shoulders. To think, Bronte could prepare dinner.... In fact, Bronte could do so much more. As she walked toward the kitchen, she saw that the condo had been tidied, laundry had been washed and folded into neat stacks, fresh flowers decorated the table and Finney slouched in his usual position in front of the television. All was in order. Finney and Bronte were getting along just fine without her.

''Go wash your hands for dinner,'' Bronte ordered Finney in a tone that Eve recognized as her own.

Then, in a sweeter tone, Eve too was ordered to take her seat. She complied, feeling as though she were eating in a restaurant rather than her own kitchen. During the meal she shared stories of her first day at work in between compliments and exclamations of astonishment at Bronte's talents. So grown-up! So dependable! Even as she spoke these truths, she felt a wrenching tear in her soul's fabric, realizing that she indeed was *not* indispensable to her children. She felt as if she were floating between two worlds, somewhere in limbo.

''Aren't you eating, too?'' Eve asked as Bronte hustled between table and kitchen. Now she was serving a cake that she'd baked from a box.

''Oh, I've been eating all day. Tasting and nibbling. I couldn't eat another bite.''

Eve understood that feeling and smiled, amazed once again at how very grown-up her little girl was becoming. So very much a woman.

* * *

After the dishes were done and they all collapsed on the sofa to watch television, the telephone rang. It was Doris.

"How'd it go today?"

"Oh boy, I'm pooped."

"I can only imagine. No, maybe I can't. Going back to work... Honestly, I'm so proud of you."

"I'm just muddling my way through. I'll tell you who I'm proud of, though. Bronte. When I came home she had the house all cleaned up and dinner on the table. She even baked a cake."

"You're kidding." There was a note in Doris's voice that Eve recognized as squelched jealousy. Doris was always competitive when it came to their girls. "I'm not even sure Sarah knows how to turn the oven on."

"I didn't know Bronte could either, but apparently she can—and a whole lot more. We shouldn't underestimate them. I feel I can really depend on her now."

"Well," Doris said with a small huff. "She's not going to cook and clean all summer, is she?"

Eve chafed under Doris's censorial tone. "Of course not. She's taking classes this summer, too. I'm not Simon Legree."

"Oh, I know," Doris rushed to say, squelching the flare of temper in Eve's reply. "I just meant that she's still so young and needs free time to play with her friends."

"Speaking of which, we haven't seen Sarah in a while."

There was a pause. "Oh, she's been so busy. And Bronte's not next door anymore."

"No, but we're not at the other end of the earth, you know. We'd love to have her over."

"Of course." She paused again, longer this time. "But to be honest, without you home, we can't trust that word won't get out and boys won't start to flock over. You know how that happens. It's not a good idea to leave them alone too often or too long. Why doesn't Bronte come over here?"

Eve ordinarily would have agreed instantly that leaving girls this age unattended was an invitation to trouble. But these weren't ordinary times. And there was something else that wasn't being spoken aloud. Eve felt that, somehow, her new place might not be thought of as quite up to snuff.

"It'd be wonderful if you could swing by and pick Bronte up once in a while and bring her over to your place. Maybe take them all to the pool. She doesn't see her old friends much anymore. I'm sure it's just a matter of getting them together. But we'll have to arrange it on days that Finney goes to a friend's house, too." She sighed. "It's all so complicated now."

"I'll be glad to drop him off wherever. Just let me know."

It was a welcome offer and Eve was grateful. "I'd appreciate that."

"So tell me, how was your first day at work?"

"Oh, all right, I guess."

"You guess? What happened?"

"Nothing. It went well. The ladies I work with are nice enough. I walked into a wall of students clamoring for help. It was wild. But I caught on pretty quickly. Really, it was no different than when you and I used to be room mothers for the first grade."

"Don't tell me they all wanted to go to the bathroom at the same time?"

Eve laughed, thinking that in so many ways it was just like that.

"It was more the chairman that was the problem. A detestable man."

"Rude?"

"Worse. He was perfectly polite and said all the right words but then he just turned his head and ignored me, as though I wasn't even there. I was mortified."

"Eve, he probably didn't even realize that he did it. Men in power have tunnel vision. R.J. does that sort of thing all the time. Runs over people every day and doesn't look back because he doesn't even see them. Don't take it personally."

"I know how I'm going to handle it. I'm taking lessons from Buck in *Call of the Wild*. First, I'm going to watch and learn every facet of that organization, from the filing to the name of every faculty member. Next, I'll work harder and better than anyone else. I'm going to make myself indispensable. Then we'll see if he ever dares dismiss me again."

"Forget it. He's the leader of the pack, Eve, if you're going to use that analogy."

"No, the women are in the pack. He's the driver of the team. The master. The man with the whip and club."

"Be careful, Eve. That's all fine and good for dogs and wolves, but we live in the man's world."

"Well, I'll be damned if I'm going to mince around him and bring him coffee like he was my master. And if he expects me to lick his hand I'll snarl and bite it!"

Doris paused. "Honestly, Eve, I hardly recognize you when you talk like this. First of all, even the dogs in London's books recognized their masters and obeyed them. Don't forget that elemental law of nature. Besides, there's nothing wrong with bringing him a little coffee once in a while. Play it smart. You shouldn't be so confrontational. Smile a bit and make nice-nice. Keep the men happy. It makes them feel important."

Eve swallowed. "I just can't. I won't."

"Eve, you need this job to survive. Don't do anything

to get him too mad. I know about men like this. Trust me. You'll get yourself fired. Or, at the very least, he'll make your job miserable.''

Eve pursed her lips and twisted the phone cord in her fingers. There was a time not so long ago when she would have listened to Doris, perhaps even agreed with her. This was the way she, a woman, was brought up. To build up the man's ego at the sacrifice of your own. To accommodate his needs, and the needs of others. Your own needs could wait.

Now, Eve wasn't so sure Doris was right.

A faint howl rose up outside her windows. It was her neighbor's dog again. Her ears perked to the sound and she rose to follow it, stretching the telephone cord as she moved toward the windows and opened them wide. As Doris continued her diatribe about how she should, as it were, submit to the harness, the neighbor's dog cried again. It was a full throaty song this time that rose high up to the moon hanging full in the sky. Eve thought of Buck at the edge of the forest. She felt her hackles rise and was filled with a deep hunger and disquiet. She hadn't felt this stirring this strongly since she was young and full of her own dreams—a time long before Tom and the children.

In the other ear Doris's words of *shoulds* and *ought tos* sounded like the wailing of a lost soul, the cry of a banshee in a castle's keep. Eve lowered the telephone receiver and tilted her head toward the open window. If ever there was a chance that she would listen to Doris and be strapped into the harness, that time had passed. Eve stood at the window, faceup to the warm light, and felt the pull of the moon.

Ten

> Oh man! admire and model thyself after the whale!
> Do thou, too, remain warm among the ice. Do thou,
> too, live in this world without being of it. Be cool at
> the equator; keep thy blood fluid at the Pole. Like
> the great dome of St. Peter's, and like the great
> whale, retain, O man! in all seasons a temperature of
> thine own!
>
> —Herman Melville, *Moby Dick*

The Oakley Bath and Tennis Club was housed in an old Tudor-style postwar building that was crisscrossed with lines of ivy, was crumbling at the base and needed a good face-lift. Most of its patrons felt right at home there.

A newer, sleeker health club had opened up down the block and had a growing membership, mostly of the younger, new-mother-trying-to-get-her-size-six-figure-back set. The ladies of the Book Club, however, had decided to be faithful to the Oakley Bath and Tennis Club, preferring its old-world classy comfort with all of its aging flaws to the high-tech glare and blare of the new club. Not to mention the annoying sight of those high-perched bosoms and taut tummies of its younger clients. As Midge often said, "Who needs that?"

Eve closed her locker door and turned the key, thinking as she did so that she was closing this part of her life as well. Her membership would end this week and she couldn't afford to renew it. Not that she'd used it much since Tom's death anyway. She was thin now; her clothes hung shapelessly from her like from a wire hanger and food held little interest for her. It was too bad that she couldn't afford the club dues any longer. But in the scheme of things, she thought, tossing the towel around her neck and moving forward, it was a small loss. She still had her feet, a pair of jogging shoes and nature outside her door.

"Let go. Go on," she murmured to herself, a mantra that she'd adopted over the past few weeks. That, and the prayer to Saint Francis of Assisi she'd learned as a child, helped her keep her equilibrium through the rough moments.

Passing through the women's lovely, gardenlike locker room, her gaze traveled across the lattice-covered walls, the coolers of chilled water dripping with condensation, the stacks of neatly folded white towels. There were Italian wooden trays filled with artfully arranged brushes, combs, soaps, lotions, sanitary napkins, breath mints and a myriad of sundries that a woman might need. This club had a European charm that was as comforting to the soul as it was uncomfortable to her new spirit. Its very attentiveness to feminine luxury represented a life-style for women that she no longer felt akin to, that in fact, few women she knew today still were.

Her mother would have loved this place, would have approved of her membership. And would have been appalled that she was giving it up. She, a doctor's wife. She always suspected that her mother wanted her to follow in her footsteps. But the shoes didn't fit. The older women here, those like her mother who remembered World War II and raised children in the 1950s era, sat and read or chatted comfortably in the lounge or the restaurant, or kept a steady, but easy, pace on the treadmill. The club, for them, was a safe place to come to and feel they belonged. They didn't see the curled edges of the wallpaper.

She, too, was once dazzled by the elegant trappings. Now she saw them as inconsequential backdrops for the real reason she and other younger, Vietnam War era women came to clubs today. They came not for lunches and gossip but for quick exercise routines and personal trainers. They were not facing menopause with whispers and resignation. They were crunching and sweating, pushing back time's boundaries, year by year, inch by inch.

But today was Eve's last day here. Resigned, she reminded herself that she was more keenly interested in building up her mind than her body right now. And so far, her inner self was firming up. She had a new condo, she was getting a grip on her finances, and most importantly, she finally had a job. Her future was now.

She pushed open the door and stepped into the glare of mirrors, shiny chrome and black metal of the newly renovated gym. The scent of sweat mingled with air freshener assailed her nose and she readily spotted Midge furiously pedaling away at a stationary bicycle. Her long hair was pulled back into a thick braid and a halo of soft gray frizzed along her scalp. Her face, not pretty in normal situations, was almost comical in her fierce determination. Midge's defined muscles were slick with sweat, dampening her gray University of Illinois T-shirt in patches across her flat chest.

"Whoa there," Eve said approaching. "What's got you working up such a lather?"

Midge caught her eye, nodded in mute acknowledgment, then held up one finger indicating that Eve should wait a minute. She ducked her head and pedaled like a demon was chasing her for a few more minutes, completing her cycle, then gradually slowed down while she gathered her breath. Around them, three other women Eve didn't recognize worked the machines at a slower pace while watching the overhead television.

Eve handed Midge a towel. "Where is everyone else today?"

Midge patted her face with the towel, emerging from behind the white cotton with a weary grin on her bright-pink face. "They all pooped out. Gabby had to take her youngest to the dentist but she'll catch up with us. Annie says she's flooding again and doesn't dare get on a machine until she checks with her doctor. She and Doris are meeting us for lunch. And *you're* late." Midge feigned sternness but her eyes glowed with affection. "So get yourself up and at 'em on the machines."

"They say misery loves company," Eve said in singsong, climbing up on a tread machine. When Midge took the one beside hers, however, Eve raised her brows and exclaimed, "Don't tell me you're not done? You look exhausted."

"I need to work out. I'm so tense lately I'm getting headaches and I feel like I'm going to burst."

"What's up?" Eve asked.

"My mother. She's decided she likes it here and is renting an apartment." She rolled her eyes. "To be near me."

"I think that's sweet."

Midge replied with an unladylike snort, "That's hardly the word I'd use to describe that petite, fireball of a woman who likes her steaks rare, her martinis dry and her men virile."

"You're lucky you have a mother. I really miss mine," Eve said wistfully. "We were close even though we didn't live near each other. Used to talk on the phone every week. It's not so much that I needed her advice. We were quite different, really. I just enjoyed hearing her voice." She sighed and looked out the window. "We talked about everything—and nothing."

"Edith's been in Chicago for a couple of months now, and though we talk, I can't say we've yet had a heart-to-heart. I've tried every trick I know, and as a therapist I know quite a few. And I caught that poodle peeing on a canvas in the corner yesterday. Thank God it was a blank or I'd have tossed that puffball out the window. What kind of person comes for a week's visit, stays a couple of months and brings her dog along, too?"

"A relative?"

Midge laughed and increased the speed of her treadmill.

"I adore your mother, Midge. She's a gas. Always was."

"Sure you do. Everybody loves Mom. Fun Edith, the wild-and-crazy gal. The life of the party. But you don't know her. Shoot, I don't really know her. Part of me adores her, too. She's my mom. And part of me wants to kill her...and that mangy dog," she muttered under her breath. "She's secretive about things that matter. Her deep inside feelings, her true history, and not the smoke screen she tells me. I don't know the realities of who she is, really. There's this wall she refuses to let me pass."

Eve thought that Midge had just described herself. The pace picked up and Eve adjusted, her heart rate quickening.

"Midge," she said with a choppy cadence as she hustled. "You still have time to try. My time is over. For both my mom and my dad. But I don't have any regrets. They both were ill and I had time to say what I had to before they died.'' She paused, thinking of Tom, feeling an old dagger strike. ''Make the most of your time.''

Midge shrugged and picked up her pace.

Eve, wiser by her many experiences with death and loss, shook her head with resignation. Even a therapist like Midge who had studied grief and consolation in textbooks had no real clue how powerful the loss of a parent could be.

''I wish my mother lived next door to me,'' Eve added with a whimsical note. ''Just so we could chat. Shop. I'd like to show her how well I'm doing, show her my condo.'' She chuckled. ''Let her tell me how wonderful I'm doing. Mom's are our best cheerleaders. No one else ever cares quite the same. Who else is going to be as angry at you when you do something wrong, or be as proud of you when you do something right?''

Midge closed her eyes. She recalled the bitter fight she'd had with Edith on her sixteenth birthday when she'd refused her mother's gift—a nose job.

''Did you ever stop to think that maybe this wasn't just a gift for you? Maybe it was a gift for me, too,'' Edith had demanded.

Midge took a deep breath and opened her eyes to look at Eve. How could she explain it to her? Eve had no clue what it was like to grow up never once feeling the glow of her mother's approval.

''You don't know Edith,'' she said. ''As far as she's concerned, everything I do is wrong. She doesn't want to talk, she wants to tell. She doesn't want to just shop, she wants to dictate what I buy. Who I see. What I do. God, that woman is so controlling. I moved out of her house at eighteen because I couldn't stand it then. What makes her think I can stand it now? Why does she think I live alone?''

"She probably thinks you're lonely. And...you're her child."

"Damn," Midge muttered through pants. Her face was bright-pink again. "But I'm not a child."

"But you are. *Her* child, anyway. I hate to say it, but I can't imagine ever really seeing my children as grown-up. At least so much so that they won't need my advice."

"Eve," Midge said, her eyes wide with frustration. "Listen to yourself. Do you have any idea how smothering that is?"

Eve caught her breath, stunned by the question. She'd never thought of herself as the smothering type. "I'm...I'm not!" she blurted in reply. Yet, how many times had she heard her children groan, *Come on, Mom,* when she questioned—grilled—them on their whereabouts or homework or choice of movie? How many times had Tom looked up from his work and said in a cajoling voice, "Aw, let 'em go. They'll have a good time."

She puffed up her cheeks and exhaled a big chunk of her parental confidence, recalling, too, how capable Bronte was in the kitchen, how independent Finney was in his social world. That couldn't have happened overnight. When did her children start letting go of her hand?

"My God, Midge. Maybe you're right. I have to face that my babies are growing up."

"That's a good thing, Eve. It's a normal process. Soon you'll be free, sweetie! And if you're lucky, your children will become your friends."

"It seems too much too soon. Especially for Bronte. She's shouldering a lot of what I used to do. But I'm still her mom, not her friend."

"Maybe she wants to be your friend."

"No. That's not my role. I have to make sure my baby doesn't get hurt. She's still so young."

"Yeah, well you'd better be aware that the things she's going to start getting involved in aren't so young. Boys, sex, drugs, alcohol, driving. She'll need to talk to you and she won't if she's afraid of getting punished or lectured. Face it, Eve. She's not that young." She wiped her brow with her elbow. "And neither am I."

"But, Midge, to me, she is! Always will be. For your mom, you are still young. Speaking from the other side of the fence, it's not easy to let go of their hands."

"But you've got to, honey. You've simply got to let go or they'll never grow up. They'll feel choked—and eventually they'll resent you."

Eve stepped off the machine, balancing her weight on the sides as she balanced her thoughts. After a moment she conceded, "Maybe you're right and I need to rethink things a bit. Maybe I can find ways to be Bronte's friend." She looked over at Midge before remounting her treadmill. "And maybe, you can be your mom's."

Both women trotted in silence as the head of the machines relentlessly rose to simulate an incline. Each woman was thinking of her mother-daughter relationship. Each woman's brow furrowed and her mouth grimaced as she struggled with the uphill battle.

Doris wiped the counter clean of bread crumbs, coffee grinds and cereal in long sweeps. She washed the breakfast dishes with smooth, languorous strokes, then crisply folded the newspaper into thirds, stretched taut to close the cabinets that R.J. and Sarah left open, and bent at the waist to water the plants. Then she headed downstairs to the laundry room to start the first load of wash for the day.

She'd performed these simple chores every morning for

what seemed forever, and in the past she'd found comfort in the mindless, repeated motions that ordered her thoughts each morning as much as her house. The mother-wife's tai chi, she liked to call the routine.

Lately, however, this ritual wasn't satisfying. She was restless, feeling unfulfilled, with a sense that there was something more out there for her. A nagging isolation that had her peeking outside her kitchen window at the empty sidewalks more frequently. Especially lately. Watching Eve beginning a new life for herself was akin to that feeling of emptiness she always felt standing at a train station or an airport gate, waving goodbye to a loved one as they walked briskly away, on to some adventure, leaving her behind.

It seemed everyone was so busy now—R.J., the children. Especially in the spring. Busy, busy busy! Whereas she pretty much had nothing to do save for the same old, same old. Taking care of her home used to be enough. But now, at fifty, she wanted a little more action in her life, too. Some direction to walk briskly in, a goal to stride toward. She wanted a change that didn't involve hot flashes.

She yawned loudly as she made her way down to the basement. Goodness, she could hardly keep her eyes open. Why was she always so tired lately? And she could feel one of her "moods" settling in. They came and went at random, seemingly unconnected to any food she ate or wine she drank or any particular event. No matter what she did to try to rid herself of them—a shopping trip, a movie, a phone call to a friend—she just couldn't. Outwardly she'd laugh and smile, but inside, the blackness overwhelmed her, coloring her world gray, squeezing her heart so tight she sometimes couldn't breathe.

She reached into the clothes hamper from her bathroom

and lifted out a pair of R.J.'s dirty socks, then a pair of silk boxers. He'd taken to wearing silk more often now rather than saving them for a romantic evening. Her father would never have worn silk boxers. He was strictly a plain white cotton brief man. Anything else would have been looked on with disdain. She thought of the plain white cotton bra and waist-high underwear she was wearing under her caftan dress and suddenly felt as shapeless and old as the "granny" nickname Sarah gave the underwear. She'd feel silly in those slinky jobs she saw in the catalogues. Doris looked again at R.J.'s hunter-green silk shorts and felt ambivalence. They *were* kind of embarrassing, but she nonetheless appreciated her husband's efforts to be sexy. Maybe she should try something slinky?

She tossed the boxers in the delicate pile and pulled out one of R.J.'s shirts from the hamper. In the air she caught a whiff of a strange perfume emanating from the Egyptian cotton. Doris paused, arm arrested in midair. Slowly, she brought the shirt closer to her nose, then took one, quick sniff.

It was a strange scent—unquestionably a woman's. She threw the shirt away from her, as though it burned. Shutting her eyes, she saw the silk boxers, and his eager face when he left last night for another dinner meeting. Of course other women would be included, her heart argued. But somewhere in her brain came the whisper, "Maybe not a dinner meeting. Maybe just a dinner."

A prickly wave of heat swept through her. She swayed and grabbed the back of a nearby chair, then lowered herself into it, physically ill with the thought that R.J. could be fooling around.

Fooling around. What an archaic expression, she thought with a bitter laugh. Something her mother would say. Like *sowing his wild oats,* or *boys will be boys.* How very forgiving. Doris thought there was one good ten-cent word for it: *cheating.* Or a commandment: *adultery.* Plain and simple.

Perched on the edge of a rattan chair, Doris considered her options. What would she do if it were true? Where could she go? Why couldn't she be enough? She was a good wife, wasn't she? Didn't she entertain for him at his parties? Take an active role in community politics? Wasn't she always well dressed and respectable? What more could she be for him? What more could she do to keep him? Did he want her to be some cheap floozy? She thought again of the catalogues that flooded her mailbox and the Merry Widows advertised there. Could he want that? Could she?

So many questions and Doris felt void of answers. She only knew that, for whatever reason, biological or psychological, her husband was moving further and further away from her, spending more time away from home. It was as though his marriage to her represented to him stability, laurels to rest on, comfort and ease—all that made him feel old.

And Lord knew, he was running away from that reality most of all.

An hour later, Doris paused at the entrance of the club's restaurant, searching for familiar faces. She scowled seeing the crowded tables and the hustling waiters. Saturday afternoon brought out all the families and crowded the pool and tennis courts. Her gaze swept the floor; so many new faces. This used to be such a quiet town. R.J. was partly to blame for this population explosion. After all, he practically had a stranglehold on the new houses built in Riverton. Huge mansions were squeezed onto small, expensive lots so tight they were practically touching one another. Her own home, which she'd inherited from her parents, was enviable for many reasons, not the least of which that it was surrounded by two acres of wooded, riverfront land, the equivalent of four prime estate lots in Riverton. The land was priceless—and was in her name. She'd die before she gave in to R.J.'s relentless pleas that she divide it up and sell.

His demands had increased in number and vehemence in the past few years as land grew more scarce and pricey. She stuck out her jaw and thought of R.J.'s arrival home in the wee hours of the morning smelling of Scotch and cigars. This summer he'd purchased a silver phallic-looking sports car convertible with money that should have gone into savings, started working out at the gym, began Rogaine treatment and was planning a white-water rafting trip down the Colorado River with Bobby. Neither she nor Sarah had been invited. He'd chided her that they'd paint streaks down their chests and beat their breasts. "It's a guy thing," he'd said.

When she tried to talk to Midge about it, she'd laughed and waved it away as male menopause. "Sooner or later the old coot will come to his senses," she'd said.

Maybe, Doris thought, remembering the whiff of strange, musky perfume from his white shirt. But maybe not.

She found the Book Club members gathered around an umbrella table on the terrace. Her heart beat lighter when she saw the way their faces lit up as she approached, making her feel special and loved. Their high-pitched calls of welcome were as sweet sounding as the chirping of the birds in the nearby trees.

"There you are," exclaimed Eve. "We were afraid you wouldn't make it." Eve's blue eyes were bright with joy and her cheeks flushed from exercise. Doris felt a sudden rush of love for her; affection that was akin to pleasure rippled through her.

"When have I ever missed one of our *petites soirées?*" Her heart skipped to find a seat saved for her between Eve and Midge, a small gesture that meant so much. Across the table Gabriella's smile was as brilliant and warm as the sun overhead, and beside her, Annie, whose smile was a little more cloudy behind her sunglasses.

The menus arrived and while Doris read the specials of the day she listened to Midge, Eve and Annie discuss their workout schedules. They were laughing, making jokes and telling stories in that breezy manner only possible with the best of friends.

Doris couldn't seem to rise up from the gloomy clouds of her life, and in contrast to their sunny smiles, her spirits grew all the more gray. In her mind she berated herself for not beginning that exercise program she'd sworn she would start today. She'd really meant to. She'd promised herself after closing the novel, *Moby Dick,* late last night that tomorrow she'd begin. But she hadn't.

Doris squirmed in her chair, feeling the tightness of her blouse straining at the buttons against her full, aching breasts. The waistband of her skirt was pinching like a cinch. She felt as bloated as a whale. Irritation flared to hear these slender fit women complain about the flaws of their figures, they with bodies she'd pay a fortune for. She didn't know how she'd gained so much weight in the last five years, why it was suddenly so hard to lose it, and why lately she was always tired or aching in her joints.

How had she turned old overnight?

"I'm going to take up jogging in the park across the street," Eve declared after announcing that she wasn't renewing her membership. After the many expressions of disappointment from the group, she assured them, "It's so convenient this way and I have so little time with my new job. Besides, I prefer being outdoors to the confinement of the gym.''

Doris caught Annie's eye over the top of the menu, and in a flash of communication they both understood the real reason. Surprisingly, a shared sympathy flared in their eyes before they looked away.

"Oh, I understand," said Gabriella with a sympathetic shake of her head. "I'm leaving the club, too, when my membership ends. Since I took on more hours at the hospital I can't be bothered with gyms or workout regimes, either. I'm on my feet all day, and when I get home I've got dinner to make and the kids on my case. I can't wait to lift these puppies and collapse in front of the television after I finish the dinner dishes. Fernando loves me. He doesn't care if I lose my waistline as long as I keep my sanity.''

"And your job," quipped Midge.

Gabriella's face darkened and she looked sharply away.

Doris ran her hand along the ridge over her hips where once upon a time she had a waistline that R.J. could span his hands around.

"Ladies, ladies, ladies," chimed in Annie. "What's all this about husbands? We love the darlings, but we have to take care of number one first. We're going to live for a long time. Twenty, thirty or more years, God willing. Who wants to be sick for thirty years?"

"She's right," Gabriella added. "Nurses know this, but we're the worst. Exercise is the key.''

"It's hard to think of anything exercise doesn't help. We're crossing into a new phase, girls, but it doesn't have to be sedentary or dull. If we exercise we'll keep our bodies in shape and our minds from getting soggy." Midge raised her water goblet. "And our boobs.''

"I want mine to kiss the sun every morning," Annie said with a laugh.

"Well, good luck, sweetheart. Hope springs eternal," answered Midge.

"Don't forget the law of gravity—what goes up must come down," Eve said with hand motions.

Annie sipped from her glass smugly. "That's why God created plastic surgeons."

"Uh-uh, no way I'm going under the knife." Gabriella shook her head. She had seen too much. "This is it," she said throwing her small, rounded shoulders back and sticking out the full expanse of her chest. "Love me or leave me."

"Wrong cliché," Eve chided. "I read somewhere that the rallying call is, 'Use it or lose it.'"

"For the brains or the bod?"

"Both," answered Midge. "Use your brain or lose the brain cells. Use your muscles or watch them atrophy."

"She means *all* your muscles, ladies," Annie said in a low, deliberately sultry voice. Then with a laugh she pointed her finger at them and exclaimed, "Aha! I'll bet you're doing your Kegels right now."

Everyone laughed, blushed and sipped their wine.

"Since you brought it up," Midge said to Annie, "what's going on in the baby-making department?"

Annie frowned and reached for her wineglass. "Whoever said making a baby was fun? We arrange our lives around my body's calendar. We chart when I ovulate, we go to the doctor's office and get poked and prodded. John's having an affair with a test tube, and when I'm so-called ready, it's bim bam, I'm serviced like some ewe by the local stud. I even read in some book that if we wanted a boy we have to put cowboy boots at the foot of the bed when we do it." She leaned forward, her voice edgy. "For

twenty years I tried madly not to have a child and now
that I want one I have to try madly again. What kind of
justice is that?''

"Women always pay," replied Midge with a huff.

"I have to admit I'm glad I had mine right away,"
Gabriella said, flattening her hand against her bosom.
"Even though there were years I was exhausted and wondered if I shouldn't have had some fun first. We were so
young."

"Who knows?" replied Annie jerking one shoulder,
irked. She didn't want to hear about Gabriella's boundless
fertility at the moment. "It goes both ways. All I know is
that John and I have lost something with all this. What
happened to spontaneity? To romance?"

Eve laughed and pointed her finger at Annie. "You
asked for it. Welcome to motherhood. You'll be lucky to
get a smooch at bedtime after the baby's born."

"No, no, you've got it all wrong," Gabriella said with
her infectious laugh. "You'll be so tired at night you'll be
hoping all you get is a smooch!"

Everyone shared in another round of laughter.

Except Doris. This talk of love and motherhood was a
brutal reminder of her own sorry state of affairs. Her foul
humor redoubled. She shifted her weight and picked up
her menu in a huff. It was her own bad spirits lately that
made her so contrary, she knew. But understanding this
didn't stop her from feeling that way. Listening in stubborn
silence to the relentless, effusive chatter about diet, exercise and sex was like listening to nails scratch along a
blackboard. It made her skin crawl, and she was remaining
in her chair by sheer force of willpower. Their successes
underscored her own failure—days, weeks, months of fail-
ures.

She raised the menu and studied the dessert section with

a perverse determination. Why not? she thought grimly. She had a right to some pleasure in her life. She scanned the menu: ice cream, pie, cake... That Apple Brown Betty looked good.

"I thought you were starting up at the gym today," Midge said, dragging Doris into the conversation.

Midge's eaglelike eyes gleamed and Doris instantly realized that Midge didn't miss a trick. Midge could always tell when she was down. She might have felt grateful for the concern if she wasn't in such a mood.

"I will, I will," she said in a tone that said, *lay off.* She returned her attention to the menu.

"When?" Midge would not be put off. "You've been saying that since Christmas. Come on, Doris." She raised a corner of her lips in a wry smile. "There's more to this club than a restaurant."

It was typical of Midge to prod with stinging humor. Today, however, Doris didn't feel like laughing. She looked up and offered Midge a scorching gaze intended to wilt. Midge was no sweet flower and she'd been her friend since high school. They knew each other far too well for games of finesse. A prickly silence followed as the two women eyed each other across the table.

"She's just trying to encourage you," Gabriella said, diverting a confrontation. "She didn't mean to insult."

"Yes, I did." Midge exulted in confrontation. "Doris, I love you too much to see you suffer. It's time to start your program. Today. Come on and join us, it'll be fun. Doris," she said in a louder, sterner tone. "Put down that menu and listen to me."

"No!" Doris reared and raised her chin. "I'm sick to death of all this endless talk about exercise, aging and weight. Hot flashes and wrinkles, looking good or feeling better. Menopause. Sick of it!"

"Me, too," added Annie. "I don't believe in menopause."

"I've got news for you," Midge replied, wagging a fork in Annie's direction like a sword. "It's going to happen to you, my dear, whether you believe in it or not."

"It's going to happen to all of us," said Doris. "Who cares? I'm just plain tired of worrying about my figure. I don't care if I have the same figure I did at twenty because I'm not twenty. I'm fifty. *Fifty!* Do you hear me? I can say the word. I'm not afraid to say I'm getting old." She was breathing heavily and feeling the sweaty sweep of another hot flash. In her mind's ear she could hear her mother say, *That's right! Wake up and smell the coffee!* Yet her heart didn't buy it. Inside, she was terrified.

Their waitress approached and stood at the suddenly silent table with her pencil poised over her pad.

"What'll it be, ladies?"

Eve cleared her throat and picked up her menu. Midge and Gabriella exchanged worried glances and shrugged. Annie watched Doris quietly behind her sunglasses, her head tilted in thought.

Doris lifted the menu again with a shake that shook away all thoughts of tight waistbands, stalled exercise programs and strange perfume. A sudden voracious hunger made her want to devour everything on the menu.

"I'll start with a cup of lobster bisque," she said in a high, tight voice. "Then I'll have the bacon club sandwich. French fries on the side. Oh, yes, ketchup, please. And for dessert, hmmm…" Did she dare? Yes. "I want the Apple Brown Betty, à la mode. And coffee with cream." She lowered the menu and her gaze swept across the astonished faces of her friends, the message shining in her too bright eyes. *I dare anyone to say anything!*

She was relieved that no one did, and handed the menu

to the waitress. Yet while she sat with her hands on her ample thighs and listened to her friends' monotonous orders for various salads, grilled chicken or fish and iced tea, she cringed. There were no rallying calls now as there had been for Annie, follow-up orders with laughs and giggles for sundaes or pie. She had crossed an invisible line, broken somehow from the pack.

Doris had never felt so distant from her friends, or so alone. As she bit into mouthful after mouthful of her towering sandwich, she felt as though hers was the immense distended jaw of a large sperm whale. In her heart she knew that it wasn't her friends' fault she felt this way. They were tiptoeing around her this afternoon, aware of her mood and taking care not to offend. Yet their sympathy only fueled her anguish.

When the waitress delivered her dessert, she stared at the large square of Apple Brown Betty with vanilla ice cream melting down the sides under the hot afternoon sun. *Don't eat it,* her conscience warned. The dessert sat there, teasing and waiting, her nemesis floating in a sea of melting cream. She foresaw her own little death. Her coffin was carved from brown sugar and white flour.

The afternoon's sun glared no hotter than the four pairs of eyes around her as they sat uncomfortably and watched her devour the dessert. She was near tears as she stealthily glanced at the half-eaten portions of light foods on their plates. With her last modicum of control she set down her fork, and with a ladylike turn of her wrists, dabbed at her mouth with a thick napkin.

"Look at the time," Eve said in a choked voice, glancing at her watch. "I've got to go."

Instantly, all the other women reached for their purses, eager to leave.

Doris lowered her head to reach for her white leather

purse on the floor, and doing so, saw her middle divided into two sagging folds at the belt. Hating the sight, hating herself, her mind was swirling, round and round in a whirlpool, and she felt certain she'd soon slip beneath the murky blackness.

"Have you finished *Moby Dick* yet?" asked Gabriella, counting out her share of the bill carefully.

Doris remained silent, thinking to herself that she couldn't get the book out of her mind. It lingered and churned dangerous thoughts. R.J. was her Moby Dick. She loved him, yet she loathed him. Her thoughts pursued him. Her suspicions burned in her heart. At night and throughout the day she secretly dreamed of harpooning him, throwing the spear hard, watching it penetrate the pale flesh. Then reeling him in, tug after tug, and tethering him to the side of her boat. But of course, she couldn't tell her friends this.

"I labored through it," replied Annie, flipping down twenty dollar bills without thought. "That should cover the tip, too," she said to Gabriella, snapping her purse shut.

"I heard Melville almost lost his sanity writing it," said Midge.

"I almost lost mine reading it," quipped Annie.

They snickered and Eve asked, "By the way, whose house is the meeting at?"

"Mine," Annie said, rising in inches with more care than usual. Her hand was on her abdomen in a protective gesture that didn't slip anyone's notice. "Polish your teeth, girls," she said. "I'm serving whale skins for us to chew down." After they laughed she added, "Frankly, I now know more about whales than I ever wanted to know."

"Me, too," said Gabriella in a moan. "I'm still busy

trying to figure if ol' Moby Dick was good or bad or what?''

"And if he was good, just how good was he?" Annie said in a low voice to a chorus of groans.

Doris rose stiffly from her chair and laid her money on the table. Her face was somber and she said in a tight voice, "All you need to know is that Moby Dick is a huge, white, wrinkled, misunderstood sperm whale." She paused, then taking her purse and straightening her shoulders she said, "And I feel a sudden sympathy for him."

Eleven

"There is, I believe, in every disposition a tendency
to some particular evil, a natural defect, which not
even the best education can overcome."

"And your defect is a propensity to hate everybody."

"And yours," he replied with a smile, "is will-
fully to misunderstand them."

—Jane Austen, *Pride and Prejudice*

Eve sat in the cool of the air-conditioned office and
looked out over the dried, brown tinged lawns of the college commons. Even the shade looked hot. Although it was
only early June, already the Midwest had been hit with a
blistering heat wave. For the past week, temperatures had
hovered in the low nineties, taxing energy supplies and
breaking records. Tempers grew prickly as the relentless
glare of the sun pressed, broken only by the occasional
gathering of clouds that teased at a rainfall that never
came.

She sighed and let the shades drop, deflecting the
scorching shine of light and creating long lines of black

and white across the shadowy floors. There was nothing anyone could do but stay indoors—or escape north to cooler climates and lakes as many locals did.

Bless them, she thought, recalling her profound relief when Finney's friend invited him to their summer home in Michigan for the first two weeks of summer vacation. Monday morning she'd kissed him goodbye, feeling as though she'd been granted a reprieve from worry.

Bronte was another story. In another week she'd be enrolled in summer school. In the meantime, Doris had proved herself as good as her word by picking her up in the afternoon and driving her over to visit with Sarah and the girls at the pool. Sometimes, Bronte claimed she was too busy to see her friends or preferred to finish her book—a marked contrast from the summer before. Bronte was becoming more and more withdrawn. Eve wrung her hands, feeling that they were tied in this matter. What could she do? Bronte was fourteen, a difficult age.

At Saint Benedict's the summer term was underway and the pressure was off the office staff. Pat Crawford felt she could take a vacation, implying when she left the Friday before that it was the highest compliment to entrust her small empire to the sole care of Eve Porter. Eve smiled to herself, recollecting how she'd thanked Pat for the opportunity. Secretly she was amused. Tending to the schedules and needs of one Dr. Paul Hammond and his skeleton staff was a joy-walk compared to running a home with the dynamic Tom Porter and two teenagers. She often thought most businesses would be better run if a housewife was at the helm.

Eve pursed her lips and exhaled slowly. She gazed around the dimly lit, silent office of the English department where she sat alone during her lunch break. *Ah, Pat,* she thought to herself as she glanced at the woman's immaculate, barren desk, *if you only knew why I shivered when you announced you were going away.* The week's anxiety wasn't about how a middle-aged woman would manage running an office for the first time. It was about how she'd manage the middle-aged man, Dr. Paul Hammond.

His explosive outbursts were legendary, though she herself had never heard one. "He's a live volcano, and from time to time, he must spill out a bit of lava, that is all," Pat explained to her. During her first few weeks in the department, they'd maintained a polite distance, one too tense for indifference. One could not be indifferent about Paul Hammond. Pat was always there to act as buffer with her cheery comments, her nose in every detail and her unflagging devotion to the chairman. She positively hovered at his side. Rather like a mosquito, Eve often thought as she caught an occasional tightening of Dr. Hammond's lips or heard a subtle tone of irritation in his quick, "Yes, yes, thank you, Pat."

Pat was blissfully oblivious to these signals. Eve, however, spotted them readily. Tom and Dr. Hammond were very much alike in this way. Both men persisted in the belief that all people could read such subtleties. How she used to tease Tom that he only set himself up for disappointment! To his credit, Dr. Hammond bore the brunt of Pat's unfailing devotion with civility.

To his students, however, he was not as tolerant. Whenever a boisterous or rebellious student destroyed the English language in either speech or written form, Dr. Hammond skewered him with a piercing gaze and, using his tongue as a rapier, served the culprit up to the class in pieces. Eve found it fascinating that his students bore it almost as a compliment. Dr. Hammond was reputed to be a gifted teacher; long lines of students clamored to enter his classes each semester. It was his passion for the subject,

Eve was told, and his brilliance, that earned him the respect of teachers and colleagues alike.

It was a different passion, however, that Eve saw behind his hooded glances directed her way. An unmistakable, smoldering emotion held taut by bands of iron control that she could feel vibrate when he walked into the room. Feel it even though he wouldn't come near her, or speak to her other than the perfunctory, "Good morning, Eve," and the occasional, "Goodbye, Eve," choosing to address all his questions and comments solely to Pat.

And so, when Pat announced her vacation, Eve had thought, *So, I'm consigned to be the mosquito.*

But, of course, she couldn't let that happen. A praying mantis, perhaps. A wasp, maybe. A worker bee, oh, all right, yes. She accepted this role dutifully and had completed the routine tasks easily enough. Dealing with Dr. Hammond, however, required contact, even conversation.

She rested her head back against the wall and closed her eyes. Lord, what a week it had been! They had been alone in the office and she'd felt as though the blistering waves of heat from the outdoors had seeped in with him each time he entered the room. Her heart raced, her palms sweat and her mouth went as dry as the Sahara. She hadn't had feelings like these for a man since...she couldn't even remember. It felt wrong, illicit—at her age, especially, she told herself. But no matter, whenever she thought of Paul, the yearnings were there, tingling her spine and making her wonder throughout the day where he was and what he was doing.

He seemed equally ill at ease, all five feet ten inches of him standing stiffly by her desk, clearing his throat as he handed her reports or student schedules, barely sparing ten words at a time. She was no better, averting her gaze and accepting the papers with a curt nod of her head and a brief yet direct reply. At first she'd thought that he didn't find her worthy of more. But by the third day, she noticed the way his fingers tapped the papers on her desk, the number of times he mangled a question in her presence, his frequent glances with an aiming eye. As the week continued, he had more questions for her and lingered at her desk. His bright-blue eyes had the power to engulf. She felt like any student of his would when singled out from the hundreds by that concentrated look. It made her feel she was the only other person in the world. Between the long length of his questions and her carefully considered replies, they eventually found to their surprise that they were actually engaging in a conversation—of sorts.

By Friday morning she was not at all surprised that he didn't close his office door as was his habit. All morning, the soft classical sounds from his radio wafted through the heavy stillness of the office as they worked in their separate spaces, uniting them with an invisible ribbon of music.

Eve closed her eyes and relished the thought that someone might actually find her desirable. Not just some stranger walking past her in the street, but someone she knew, someone she saw every day, someone she found desirable herself. How very strange to feel this again—and how very lovely.

He was older than her, at least ten years, but what did that matter? There was a passion about everything he did that she found wildly exciting. What did she think would happen after a week of mildly flirtatious behavior? She scolded herself for enjoying this little game entirely too much.

She turned her attention to *Pride and Prejudice* lying in her lap. Now here was a love story worth savoring, she thought. Every word, phrase, every character in this book was a delight, even the third time around. And she and

Elizabeth Bennet had a lot in common. They both had a love-hate thing going on with a proud, devilishly handsome man.

A short while later her reading was interrupted by the opening of the door. She raised her eyes in a drowsy manner as Dr. Hammond pushed into the office. When she saw him her heart seized. His face was pale and harried, and his hair was slicked back with sweat. He always wore a suit, no matter what the weather, but today his jacket hung over his arm, exposing a broad back under a crumpled shirt, and his shirtsleeves were rolled up to the elbow. His left shoulder drooped with the weight of his overflowing leather briefcase.

He looked very much like Tom on the last day she saw him alive.

A tremor of déjà vu shot through her and she rose impulsively, the book falling from her hand. She sprang forward.

"Dr. Hammond, are you well?" She hovered an arm's length away, not touching him.

He dumped his briefcase on the floor, then poured himself a cup of cool water from the cooler and drank it thirstily.

"The electricity went out in the lecture hall," he said, his voice as low as a curse. "The lights, the air-conditioning, everything. Opened the windows but there wasn't a breath of wind to be had. It was a bloody sauna in there."

"Please, sit down, cool off. Here, give me your jacket. Let me get you some more water."

He paused, relinquishing his suit coat, registering her concern. "Thank you," he replied, eyeing her with curiosity.

She refilled his glass and he drank that down as well.

Eve was relieved to note that his color was less flushed and his breathing more steady. He had dark skin that tanned readily, like Tom's, and also like Tom, a bright rosy flush marked his prominent cheekbones. This happened whenever Tom was too hot, drank too much red wine, or they had just made love. She'd always found the high color sensual and attractive, bringing to mind the bold streaks of an Indian warrior's war paint.

Eve clasped her hands tightly before her and willed away the comparisons. But when she'd seen Paul Hammond flushed and sweaty, so like Tom on that last morning, she just thought... She abruptly turned on her heel and walked to the cooler, pouring out a cup of water for herself, holding the plastic cup with shaky hands.

"I feel much better in the air-conditioning," Dr. Hammond was saying to her. "But it wasn't so bad, really. I just can't tolerate the heat. Never could. The students managed pretty well, considering."

Eve gathered her wits and turned to face him. "Do you mean to say you didn't cancel the class?"

"Why would I do that?"

"The threat of a heatstroke, for one reason. Not just for you, but for those students."

"My job is to teach and that is what I did. I don't recall there being an addendum to my contract stipulating weather conditions."

Eve felt a flush of feminine anger rise up, born from worry. Not only about the students, but about him. There was a small drop of perspiration on his forehead that her hand was itching to wipe away.

"You kept those children in session? Today? In this heat?"

"You don't approve?" he asked, leaning back in the chair, studying her.

She walked over to her desk, tugged a tissue out of the box and handed it to him. "It's not for me to approve or disapprove."

"Ah, so you say," he replied, wiping his brow. "But I think, Mrs. Porter, that you can't help yourself. It's your nature to have strong opinions. And to speak directly and honestly. I like that about you. You don't snivel about." He crumpled the tissue and tossed it in the garbage pail. "So, which is it?"

She took her time answering, folding her arms before her. "I think," she said in a level tone, "that it takes an enormous amount of either ego or lack of concern to keep a roomful of children inside a hot cauldron on a day like today—" she paused "—no matter how brilliant or fascinating you think your lecture might be."

His eyes flashed. "I see. Well, let's skip over the comment about the quality of my lecture and stay on the topic of the students."

He seemed to be enjoying this and it pricked her vanity. "Why would you think I kept them in the lecture hall?"

"But you just said..."

"I said the electricity failed, that the room was stifling and that, nonetheless, I taught my class. You jumped to the conclusion that I forced my students to stay in a hellish classroom." He stood, picked up his suit coat and flung it over his arm. "I'm sorry to disappoint your image of me as Beelzebub, Mrs. Porter, but I brought my class out to the breezy shade of the commons where they sipped the cool drinks I purchased for them while I continued my lecture." He lifted his shoulders lightly. "If it was good enough for Socrates, I daresay it's good enough for me."

Eve felt a blush burn her cheeks and she looked down, spotting her book on the floor where it fell. "I'm sure it was a wonderful lecture, Dr. Hammond. I...well, I'm

sorry." She bent to pick up her paperback, hoping he
would have the mercy to end this scene and move on to
his office, sparing her a little dignity. But he did not. He
moved quickly to pick up her book for her. He handed the
paperback to her outstretched hand.

"What are you reading?" he asked.

"Pride and Prejudice."

"Oh."

A condescension in the tone of his reply prickled. She
knew she shouldn't say anything, that she should just say
"thank you" and let it go. But in for a penny, in for a
pound, she decided. Besides, in her mind's eye she envisioned Annie, Midge, Gabriella and Doris with their
mouths agape and their fists up and ready.

"And what does that mean?"

He raised his brows. "Just, Oh."

"You don't approve?"

"How can I not? It's a classic."

"Have you ever read it?"

He opened his mouth, then closed it with a slightly embarrassed smile and a shrug.

"Not weighty enough for a man, I suppose?"

He shook his head and wagged his finger at her, as close
to a flirtatious gesture as he'd yet made. "Oh, no, you're
not going to trap me into that one. There are any number
of books out there, Mrs. Porter, written by men and women
both that I have not read. Classics included." His smile
held enormous charm and his eyes sparkled. "Albeit, not
many."

"Then why not this one? I highly recommend it. Or—"
she paused, tilting her head in a tease "—is it that you
don't enjoy love stories?"

"Oh, but I do," he replied, warming to the debate.
"Tristan and Isolde is a favorite of mine. *War and Peace*

is a great love story, too.'' His brow rose in feigned mockery as he gathered his briefcase and headed back toward his office, ending the conversation.

''I'm curious,'' Eve called out at his back.

He paused at the door and turned his head.

''What are you reading now?''

''Now?'' He appeared surprised by the question and frowned in thought. ''Well, there are so many different things....''

''No, not for work. For pleasure.''

A sly half smile formed and he nodded in understanding. ''Dante's *Inferno*.''

Eve cringed inwardly. She'd never tackled that one, and she was convinced he was grandstanding. ''For pleasure?'' she asked, her doubt ringing clear.

He paused, then before entering his office, smiled angelically. ''Oh yes, absolutely. Reading *The Divine Comedy* is a pure, even sensual, pleasure.'' His blue eyes smoldered with conceit. ''Especially when read in the original Italian.''

Later that evening, after Bronte went to the movies with a friend, Eve ate a light dinner of vine-ripened tomatoes, cottage cheese and whole wheat toast. The evening had cooled and the soft breezes that wafted in from the open windows caressed the bare skin of her arms and the short tendrils along her neck where she'd pinned up her hair. On this balmy night her thoughts wandered to Dr. Paul Hammond. Was he reading Dante now, she wondered, imagining him pursing his full lips and rolling the musical syllables of Italian in his mouth? Did his Italian have that lovely, clipped British accent as well? She curled her tongue around the few Italian words she knew: *ciao, ar-*

rivaderci, mozzarella. Yes, Italian was musical, perhaps even sensual.

Sighing, she settled in and began reading, thinking in a smug manner how she enjoyed the rhythm and style of nineteenth century English every bit as much as he enjoyed his Italian. This was her alone time, that quiet hour after dinner with no phone, no questions, no one to bother her. She finished her book just as a slow, soft red sun lowered in the evening sky. She yawned, then stretched, as thoroughly satisfied as a sated lover. "Dr. Hammond, read what you will in Italian, but in English, you've missed a good one."

She rested her cheek against the book, thinking that the first line alone would generate a hot discussion in the Book Club. *It is a truth universally acknowledged that a single man in possession of a good fortune must be in want of a wife.* She laughed aloud, setting the book aside and collecting her dishes with her thoughts. Midge would have a field day with that one. She thought marriage was a Machiavellian scheme men devised to entrap women. Gabriella would take the moral view, no doubt, and bring up the words *sacrament* and *vows* at least twice. And Doris! If you changed the phrase to: *A single* woman *in possession of a good fortune must be in want of a* husband, they all knew it could apply to her and R.J. She licked her lips in anticipation of the hot debate on the virtues of being married.

Eve's hand stilled in the sink. She looked at her left hand in the soapy water, then rubbed the blank space between her knuckles where a gold band once sat. She'd placed that ring beside the matching one from Tom's finger in her jewelry box, to save for the children or grandchildren.

How odd, how very empty it was to think that she was no longer married.

The weekend passed as so many others. Laundry to catch up with, shopping for groceries, a little television. Eve looked forward to returning to work on Monday where she would talk to other people, one in particular. She arrived at the office early because Pat Crawford was returning from vacation and she wanted to be certain that all was in order. The heavy metal ring of keys clanged loudly in the deserted hallway as she tried one after another unsuccessfully in the lock. If she ever got inside, she swore she was going to put a red mark on the key. At last one clicked and she swung open the heavy oak door.

The office was dark and musty and each movement she made echoed like a cannon in her ears. This was the first time she'd ever been alone in the office, without people rambling in the hall. No one was likely to step inside at this hour; no student waving a schedule or form, no teacher with a request. She set her purse down on her desk, collected the mail, then walked to Dr. Hammond's office to place his share on his desk.

There was always an otherworldly aura about his office, much like the man himself. Rays of morning light poured through the gothic windows. The large desk was clean and tidy, thanks to her own efforts, but everywhere else were tilting piles of books and papers. Dr. Hammond was happiest when surrounded with chaos. "I know exactly where everything is. Don't touch a thing!" he'd ordered her.

Alone, she dared to reach out and skim her hands along the desk's smooth wood, on the shiny enamel of his large, black pen and across the papers covered with his heavy, cramped illegible script. She was ashamed to admit it but she was curious. No personal photographs sat framed on his desk, no beautiful woman smiling at him, she was pleased to note. She'd not heard that he was attached to anyone at the moment, not that it was any of her business, of course. She'd also heard that his family had money. It was an old English family with one of those old houses with countless rooms that tourists loved to visit. The kind of family that could donate a Rembrandt sketch to a museum.

Her fingers lightly grazed the crinkled leather of his chair. This simple gesture brought her a strange pleasure, as if she were somehow closer to him. Silly, of course, rather like she imagined people felt when they grabbed hold of an autograph or an article of clothing as a souvenir from someone they admired. And *admire* was probably the safest word she could allow herself to describe her feelings for him.

She looked at her watch. Pat was due any moment, and though she was fond of her, she couldn't help but wish Pat had taken another week's vacation. The quiet time alone with Dr. Hammond was over now. She wondered if he'd leave his door open this week? Would she hear the music again?

She was working at her desk when Dr. Hammond entered the office five minutes later—early for him. She tugged at the hem of her skirt and unconsciously tucked a tendril behind her ear. There was nothing extraordinary about the way he nodded his head and said his habitual, "Good morning, Eve," or in the manner he poured himself a cup of coffee, something he'd done for himself since Pat was on vacation. But this morning the air was thick between them. He seemed eager to speak to her as he stood stirring his coffee, but held curiously back.

Eve felt his presence even as she continued staring at the monitor, feeling his gaze on her, unaware of the words hammering across the screen. Suddenly she looked up, ending the impasse and catching his gaze on her.

He tugged at his ear and said rather sheepishly, "Oh, by the way, I read *Pride and Prejudice* over the weekend."

Eve blinked rapidly, thrown off guard. It was the last thing she'd expected him to say. "Oh?" she managed to reply.

"You were right. It's a wonderful book. I thank you for recommending it. Not, of course, that it hasn't been recommended umpteen times before." He smiled then, openly and without reserve. It blossomed across his face like a sunrise, altering his expression from dark to light.

"I...I'm glad," she replied simply, feeling awkward. Then, because she couldn't resist, she added, "I guess this rounds out your reading list a bit."

He seemed pleased that she would tease him and took a step closer, almost eagerly. "I should be flogged for not having read it yet, me an English professor and all that. But there you have it. Amends are made, thanks to you."

"Always happy to do my job," she said, enjoying the banter.

He looked around the room, then facing her, he tugged his ear again and said, "I have some research to do over at the Newberry Library this morning. A mountainous project, completely unorganized. I could use some help."

"Let me guess. Dante?"

His thick, dark brows gathered and his eyes sparkled with their first private joke. "No, not this time. I'm doing some research on the Romantic poets. Blake, Byron..."

"Keats, Shelley, Wordsworth," she continued for him. Her eyes flashed with excitement.

His brows rose. "So, you're interested?"

"Oh I am, very." Did he know this was her area of study in college?

"And you thought I didn't appreciate a good love story."

Her own brows rose now. "Well, *War and Peace* isn't exactly my idea of a love story.... But I am disappointed we won't be reading Dante. It seems a fair exchange."

He chuckled. "Wrong period. Maybe next time." His tone was playful.

"In Italian, I suppose?" she asked, her lips twisting into a wry grin.

"Of course!" After she laughed he added with a sincerity that took her breath away, "I'd like to share that experience with you someday." Their gazes locked for a moment and she could feel the force of the connection to her toes. Then he looked away and gathered his papers. "I catch you reading in the commons at lunch and during breaks. Once I even saw you reading while waiting for the elevator. You didn't notice I was there, you were so lost in it. And I've seen your résumé. Your background is very interesting, a degree in English literature and all those years volunteering at the Literacy Center. How wonderful that you would volunteer your time. For such a great cause. That impressed me. You must love literature very much. I do, too, you see, and that is why I wondered if perhaps, well...I hoped, rather, that you'd enjoy this project."

His words fell on her like soft rain on an arid soil. Her history was not seen by him as trivial or misguided. He applauded her choices and rewarded them with this invitation to do research in what she'd always believed to be a highbrow institution. He couldn't know what his regard meant to her now after a long, torrid season of disdain.

"The Newberry," she said in reverential tones. "I've lived in Chicago most of my life and you don't know how many times I've pressed my nose up against the window of that library and drooled, knowing what was stored behind that enormous security desk. I always thought of it as a bastion of crotchety old scholars, researchers and historians.''

''It is. Next I suppose you'll be telling me I fit right in. No, you're right,'' he said, holding up his hand to ward off her objection. ''It *was* rather elite at one time, still is to a degree. But that image is changing. You should come. There's no place quite like the Newberry. It's a grand, Romanesque building and it houses literally millions of dollars in rare collections, including one of the best collections of Renaissance literature in the world.''

Then looking up, he asked with touching sincerity, ''Will you come?''

There were a dozen reasons she could have given as to why she couldn't accompany him: Pat was returning and might resent being abandoned, there were those scholarship records to coordinate, people might talk.

There were an equal number of reasons she could give as to why she agreed to go. All sound, reasonable, respectable reasons she could look anyone in the eye and recite with a strong voice. But in the cool dark of the cab as they rode north through the city streets, she could think of only one. She wanted to be alone with him.

They didn't talk much in the cab. He seemed as uncomfortable as she in such close proximity, and she was choked by her awareness of his body. He wasn't tall as much as broad, like a great bull, and his energy seemed to suck the air out of the small space. Stealing a glance under hooded lids, she saw his hands resting on his dark suit trousers. Despite their size, they were elegant. His fingers tapped his legs with short, oval nails. The view of tanned skin at the wrist was interrupted by a flash of gold from a thin watch partially covered by the white of his starched shirt cuffs, which were snowy in contrast. She felt herself blush with the thought of those hands caressing her body, and with a short gasp, quickly looked out the window at the narrow, crowded streets of the Gold Coast.

Once they entered the elaborate triple-arched entry of the Newberry, he seemed more at ease. He had that enviable self-confidence of breeding and was obviously comfortable in the grandeur of the place. He nodded warmly in acknowledgment to the security guards, said a brief few words with a librarian ending with a pat on the back, then led her up the monumental staircase, pointing out architectural details as if it were his own home. While he seemed to grow in stature, she felt very small. It wasn't just because the ceilings were sixteen to twenty feet high, or that the mosaic tiles and marble floors were priceless, though such things always made her shrink a bit inside. What made her feel unsure were the whisperings of centuries of scholarship.

She was surrounded by an expectant silence, electric, vibrating with the thrill of the chase and the triumph of discovery. Men and women sat stooped over tables, poring through volumes or scribbling notes furiously. An elderly woman dressed entirely in black smiled as she wrote.

Paul Hammond led Eve to a small reading room he'd reserved. He was exceedingly polite and attentive, opening doors and pulling out her chair. She was aware of his nearness as they sat, elbow to elbow. He began emptying his briefcase, spilling out a mass of wrinkled, disorganized papers on the table. She could see on his angst-ridden face that he thought the mess was hopeless and she enjoyed a surge of confidence. Any mother who tackled a teenager's bedroom could tackle this mess.

"May I help?" she asked, extending her hand over the papers with a calm, quiet authority.

He looked at her a moment, then nodded and slowly smiled. He seemed to make up his mind to let her find her way, to test her abilities.

Eve cleared a space on the large wood table, mentally rolled up her sleeves, then immediately began scanning the papers, making educated decisions and organizing small, neat piles. Seeing that she was a self-starter on the scent, he nodded, clasped his hands, and muttering, "Good, good," went off in search of resource materials.

Eve worked with boundless energy that morning. She was grateful to have a task that challenged her, and attacked the research project with relish. She felt like a young girl wading out into the deep water of a vast ocean. Her chief fear was that she wouldn't be able to keep her head up in such depths; it had been so long since she'd been in school or done research at this level. She took small, careful steps. As time wore on, however, Eve felt buoyant and confident.

After a long stretch of concentration, she pushed back from the worktable and stretched. Looking up, she caught him studying her again. She felt the heat of a blush return to her cheeks and her hand shot up to her hair. "What?" she asked with a half smile.

He leaned back in his chair and smiled, never taking his eyes off her. "You were smiling while you worked."

Eve thought of the old woman she saw downstairs and her smile spread. "I was enjoying myself."

"I could tell."

"It... It's been a long time since I've worked with these materials——" She paused, then realized there was no way she could explain the many levels of connections she had made. So she simply said, "I'd forgotten how much I missed them. It's like I've been revisiting old friends."

She laughed shortly. "After weeks of filing forms in triplicate, this was food for the soul."

"You graduated from Northwestern?"

She nodded. "My parents didn't want me to go away for college." She shrugged. "I was an only child," she offered in explanation. "And you?"

"Cambridge. I am the third son and it wasn't discussed." His eyes took on a faraway look, as though he were thinking of home.

"Do you miss England?" she asked.

"Not at all!" he said, surprising her with his enthusiasm, yet she sensed anger lurking beneath the too bright smile. "I love America. Especially here in the Midwest, with the wide-open spaces and the lack of pretense. People are so real here. They speak what they mean without the need to be clever or proper. My family is very English. Very Anglican Church and society and propriety." He smiled and the devil flashed in his eyes. "When I returned home once in tennis shoes and a Cubs baseball cap, they completely gave up hope."

He stood up from the table, ending the personal conversation. "Come along, Mrs. Porter. Enough feeding the soul for one day," he said, stretching out his hand. "How about we feed our stomachs?"

They had lunch in the small park outside the library. Neither of them could face going indoors again on such a beautiful summer afternoon. The heat wave had snapped at last and they were enjoying a more typical, warm but fresh early summer afternoon. A welcome breeze rustled the bright-green leaves in the trees and scores of brightly colored annuals straightened gratefully in the shower of water from the sprinklers. Eve sat on a park bench in the shade, breathing in the sweet air, and felt a fluttering of life spark inside her heart.

Dr. Hammond bought lunch from the European deli at the corner. He came back carrying a brown bag filled with more food than they could ever eat at one sitting. Spreading white paper napkins on the bench between them, he made sandwiches of crusty *pane paisano,* fresh mozzarella, sliced tomatoes and sprigs of fresh basil.

Eve was reminded of the many impromptu picnics she and Tom had shared long ago, when he was knee-deep in his surgical residency. The hours were brutal and threatening to a young marriage. So during the summer she used to surprise him with picnic dinners on the hospital green so that they could share a few precious moments together alone. The weather was warm and breezy that summer, like it was now.

Her chest filled with air and she couldn't speak. She tore away a piece of bread and threw it to the pigeons gathering and cooing at their feet. The crumbs disappeared in a whirring of feathers and bobbing beaks.

"Are you all right, Eve?"

She looked at him, unaware that her face gave away so much of her feelings.

"I was just reminiscing…. My husband and I used to have picnics like this. A long time ago."

"Are you divorced?"

She shook her head. "Widowed," she replied, her voice barely a whisper. A shiver shot through her. It was the first time she'd used the word. It sounded cold and barren.

"I'm sorry."

"Oh, I'm doing all right. He died a year ago this month."

"Were you married long?"

"Over twenty years." His eyes widened a bit and she

nodded in confirmation. "A long time, I know. It's funny, but it doesn't seem long. In some ways it seems like we were married a short time ago, and at others, it feels like a lifetime ago." She lifted her shoulders and said more to herself, "It was a good marriage." She felt the weight of his ponderous gaze bear down on her and looked off across the park where toddlers were being pushed in swings by nannies. She didn't want to discuss Tom, especially not with him. It was too painful and far too private.

"Actually, I'm what is commonly called a widower."

"Really?" She was stunned to hear that and she felt sure her face said so.

He nodded brusquely. "I wasn't married nearly as long as you were. My wife died a long time ago. We were both quite young but, well, it was devastating all the same. I..." He waved his hand. It was clear from his troubled expression that the subject was touchy and rife with emotion. "I was an angry man for a very long time. Full of self-reproach and blame. Drank too much, did things I was sorry for." He laughed curtly, deliberately making light of it. "I was an ass. God, how emotional young men can be," he said with a disarming smile, then brightened with a quick, determined shift of emotions. Even in the afternoon's sun, his eyes rivaled the sky overhead.

"Perhaps that's why I love my students so much. At that age they're cauldrons of emotion, just stirring about, ready to bubble over. I hope to direct that passion into visions. Whatever it is that inspires them, be it literature, science, computers, I don't give a damn, as long as it focuses all that fever into something they really love—other than sex, of course. It is damn hard to direct their attention away from that venue. I don't expect them to achieve greatness in the world's eyes, but I do expect them to achieve individual excellence. It is this inner vision, however great or small it may be, that will save them in this world of change." He paused, then said as an aside, "Makes me wish I were a young man again."

"But you are young. My friend Annie says there's no such thing as age, and though my body doesn't agree with her, my heart does."

He looked at her for a long time and she could literally see the restlessness die down in his eyes. "I don't usually go on like that." He laughed and lifted his paper cup. "Can't blame it on the wine. So," he tilted his head and appraised her. She felt she came up with high marks. "It must be the company."

She felt a strange exhilaration that she'd not experienced since she was much younger, full of hopes and dreams and free to entertain the attentions of an admirer. And how interesting that he, too, had lost a mate. Could this link explain that *something* between them that went beyond mere attraction?

"I disagree that that passion is only in the young," she said. "I think it happens frequently in life, usually after some major change. For months after Tom's death I did my best to get through each day, to survive, if not for myself, for my two children. And it got better, day by day. But today—" she looked up, hoping he would understand "—working in the library, I felt like my old self again. I was filled with purpose, working on something I love."

He nodded and his eyes kindled. "Work is marvelous in the way it can redirect a life again. Tell me, did you ever consider teaching?"

She laughed lightly. "As a matter of fact, I have. It's a goal of mine. But I have to update my certification."

"You should. I'll help you. I can write a letter of recommendation. You're eligible for a tuition reduction, you know. Are you taking classes now?"

She shook her head. "I wasn't ready to sign up yet. It was enough right now just to get this job. But I think I'll take you up on that offer for next semester. My goal seems reachable now. I can tell you, it's a great relief to learn that diving back into academics isn't as difficult as I'd thought it'd be. You see, I had this worry that has nagged at me since I turned forty. That maybe it was too late for me. That my brain had somehow gone soft over the years and I couldn't compete anymore. That I'd missed the chance for learning. I know now that it was all just nonsense. There's no elitism to learning. There's only the desire."

"Mark Twain said learning was wasted on the young."

"Yessiree," she replied flippantly, chagrined at being thought of as old. "Working at the college with those kids sure makes me realize I'm not so young anymore."

"Good God, who wants to be?" He reached over to grab a bottle. "More water, old girl?"

She laughed. "Yes, thank you, Dr. Hammond."

"Paul. Please." He poured more water into her paper cup while she nibbled at her bread and cheese, aware that they'd just mentally taken another step closer.

"I was thinking," he said, screwing the top back onto the plastic bottle. "We seem to work well together, don't you think? And there's a great deal more work to be done. Could you spare some time tomorrow?"

"Oh, I think so," she replied, curling her toes in her shoes. "Paul." He caught her eye, then looked away as quickly.

"Good, good," he said before biting into his sandwich, but not before she caught the twitch of a smile at his lips.

Another shiver shot down her spine and she felt young again. Her senses were awakening after a long sleep. She would spend another day with Paul. She would go back to school and update her skills, get her teacher's certification, escape from filing and forms-in-triplicate. And someday, she would teach. It was her lifetime dream—why not fulfill it? Her life was only half over.

She glanced at Paul, who was leaning with his elbows along the back of the bench, his long legs crossed at the ankle and his bold profile tilted toward the sky. Then looking down again at her cup she saw that it wasn't half-empty—it was half-full.

On Friday afternoon of that week, Midge and Edith were walking down Walton Street on their way to a gallery where Midge was showing her work at an upcoming show. Midge was in a lather about the show, completely out of her mind with every detail of her paintings—how they should be hung, how she might word her program. It was at an upscale gallery that was extremely selective and this group show put her in more exulted company. It was both a nod of acknowledgment and a test. Of the five painters being exhibited, only one was even remotely likely to be picked up by the gallery. Opportunities like this didn't come up that often. In the past few months, she'd thrown herself into her art, focused on creating a body of work that carried her artistic statement.

Midge wanted her mother to understand how important this show was to her. Edith had begun to take an interest in her art, or at the very least, was amazed at Midge's dedication. "I never knew you were so persistent," she exclaimed, which up to that point was the greatest compliment about her art that Edith had ever offered. Edith never claimed to understand her abstract works, nor did Midge expect her to. Edith liked pretty pictures of things she could understand without squinting her eyes. But since she'd moved into the building, she refrained from calling

Midge's work "a bunch of scribbles and blotches." It was a compromise—Midge no longer referred to Edith's poodle as "that puffball."

They were taking the shortcut across Washington Park when Edith stopped short, pulling on Midge's shirtsleeve.

"Look, over there," she hissed from behind her palm. "Sitting on the park bench. Isn't that Eve Porter?"

Midge stopped and looked in the direction of her mother's index finger. A woman who looked remarkably like Eve sat side by side with a broad-shouldered man in a tan suit. They were totally engrossed in what each other was saying. Their nearness, their bent heads, the soft laughter, the manner in which the woman lightly touched the gentleman's sleeve, the way he cocked his head to catch every word, all marked them as a couple. Midge squinted, not believing this woman could be Eve.

The woman's hair was the same dark-brown, but it was styled differently. This woman's hair was short, breezy, not worn long to the shoulder. Yet, she had the same fine bone structure, the same profile....

"It can't be Eve," Midge said. "What would she be doing here? On a workday? With a man?"

"Having an affair, if you ask me," Edith said knowingly. "And she caught herself a real hunk, too. He's absolutely mouthwatering. Though a bit old for her, wouldn't you say? What is he, sixty? More my age, don't you think?" She was staring at him, twitching, like a dog on the scent.

"Good God, Mother, you're absolutely feral. Behave yourself. I wonder why she hasn't mentioned him?"

"She's keeping him all to herself. I wouldn't have thought she was that smart. Never trust the quiet ones. Come on. Let's have a little fun."

"Mother, stop!" she demanded.

It was too late. Edith was striding with the concentration of a bird-dog heading for the brush.

"Eve Porter, it is you!" Edith called out as she neared. Midge had no choice but to follow.

Eve startled when she saw Edith but she recouped quickly and smiled warmly, echoing the hello with a wave of her own. When she spotted Midge, a faint, telltale blush glowed on her cheeks and her eyes sparkled a bit too bright. It was clear she wasn't expecting anyone to discover them. Midge glanced involuntarily at the man.

He stood as the women approached. He was a bit taller than Midge, and broad. Eve was dwarfed beside him. A powerful man with a hint of eccentricity that stimulated Midge immediately. It might have been the suit and longish hair combination, or his straight-shouldered stance, or the intelligence that shone in his remarkably brilliant blue eyes, but she liked him. And her mother was practically salivating. Edith darted furtive glances his way while they made their hellos. Midge noticed he didn't jump in with his name and an offered hand, but waited, unperturbed, until Edith said with inexcusable coyness, "Aren't you going to introduce us?"

The blush on Eve's cheeks heightened a bit. "Of course, excuse me, I was just getting to it. Mrs. Edith Kirsch, Midge Kirsch, I'd like you to meet Dr. Paul Hammond, the chairman of our English department. We're working at the Newberry together. On a project. A research project, you see."

Midge had never seen Eve so unnerved. Eve was usually extremely gracious, but this afternoon she seemed positively tongue-tied. Midge, in contrast, remained aloof, nodding her head with a tight smile.

"Delighted to meet you," he said. "Eve is something of an expert on the Romantics, I was delighted to discover.

I don't know where I'd be without her." He glanced down at Eve with affection shining in his eyes.

Midge thought the comment was about as subtle as a Mack truck. She glanced at Edith. The British accent practically had her mother on her knees.

"How fortunate to be able to do research in the park," Midge said with more sarcasm than humor. Then, seeing Eve widen her eyes, she felt a flush of shame and could have bitten her tongue. "On such a lovely day," she amended unsuccessfully.

Eve's smile was brittle. "We do manage to squeeze in lunch."

"She'd work right through, but I insist. I'm a bear when I'm hungry. And since I'm the chairman, Eve obliges me." He smiled and his charm eased them past the tension.

"Well, we really have to go," Midge said, glancing at her watch. "We're headed for the Wittman Gallery, just a few blocks away. My new show is scheduled there this weekend, remember? Friday night. I have to check the wall where they'll be hanging my work. Did you receive the announcement?"

"Yes, it was beautiful. Thank you," replied Eve. Her tone was still cool.

"It was very nice meeting you, Dr. Hammond. You're more than welcome to come to the show, too. It's open to the public." She didn't expect him, but it was the polite thing to do.

"I'm looking forward to it. I've a keen interest in art and I don't know many Chicago artists. It's been a pleasure to meet you, Midge." Then, turning the force of his charm toward Edith, he nodded. "Mrs. Kirsch."

"Edith," she replied, extending her hand like a queen.

Midge took her mother's arm and practically dragged

her off. "Don't look back," she whispered, but of course Edith did, once more over her shoulder.

"Now that is someone I could fall for," she said with a throaty sigh. "Such charm. Only the British act and sound like that. And those eyes. Oh, my God, I could feast for a week just staring into those eyes." She looked up and cast her daughter a long, simmering look. "How come you never bring home anyone like that?"

"Please, Mother." Midge's voice was frigid. "Let's not start that again."

"No, I mean it. If you did a little something with your hair, wore a bit of makeup, you could attract someone like that. I wonder who gave Eve her new haircut? You'd look good in a short style like that."

When she did not reply, Edith asked with a huff, "And why were you so rude? I couldn't believe that remark about the park."

Midge frowned and held back her reply. She was ashamed of what she'd said, of how she'd behaved. How could she explain to Edith of all people that she found Paul Hammond attractive? But more than that, it irritated her no end that Eve Porter, who had been married to a dynamic, handsome, wealthy doctor, already had someone who was obviously interested in her. So soon. It was a bitter pill to swallow. Eve had only been alone for a year. While she...

She had been alone for so very, very long.

"You sly devil! What's this I hear that you're off having rendezvous in the park—with the chairman of your department no less?" Annie stood at the door of Eve's apartment with a bottle of white wine in her hand. "Let me in. I've brought fortification. This is going to take a long time."

"Who told you?" Eve said with a groan as she stepped aside and waved Annie in. There was laundry piled all over the living room sofa, the television was blaring and empty cups and candy wrappers littered the table surfaces. It was a typical Friday night.

"The word's out in the street. Film at eleven." She set down the bottle and made a beeline for the kitchen. Eve madly collected the trash and cups, then followed her in.

"Really, Eve, how unfair is this?" Annie said, driving the corkscrew into the bottle. "You tell me all the boring details of your financial life, but when it comes to your love life, zip. I'm demanding the juicy stories, dearie. Consider it my fee. You're holding back."

The cork popped out and Eve laughed, delighting in the very idea. "I do not have a love life," she argued back.

Bronte walked in at that moment. "Love life?" she asked, scowling. "Who? You, Mom?" There was no mistaking the accusation laced with horror.

"Don't listen to Annie. She's crazy," Eve hurried to reply. She turned her head to privately glare at Annie. "Where are you going tonight?" she asked Bronte.

"Just to a movie. With friends."

"Uh-huh. Just girls?"

"Yeah. Of course," she said sullenly. Eve's heart skipped, knowing Bronte's anguish that she didn't have a boyfriend yet. Eve couldn't understand why the boys weren't flocking around her daughter. On the other hand, she was relieved. It was a reprieve. "Vicki's dad is driving us. Gotta go." She paused, then asked with suspicion, "Are you going to be home tonight?"

A short laugh escaped Eve. "Gee, I don't know. Finney's spending the night at Nello's so I thought, whoopee! Time to go wild! After I finish the laundry I might really go nuts and do my nails."

"But I feel so guilty."

Annie's face hardened. "Don't."

"You don't understand..."

"No, I do. Eve..." Annie stopped herself and shook her head. "Trust me, hon. If he asks you out, go. Jump his bones. From what I hear, he's a live one. A good lay will do you good."

"You're going to make one weird mom," she teased. "Thanks, Annie. Did I tell you yet today that I love you?"

Annie's face shifted to reflect the power of her emotion. Eve's heart lurched, knowing that these were tough times for Annie and John, wishing that Annie would open up. So she leaned forward and gave Annie a big hug that told her, in no uncertain terms, she'd be there whenever.

"Okay now," Annie said, pulling back with a sniff. "Enough of this maudlin stuff. I want more details. Lots and lots of details!"

She was about to deliver the goods when the telephone rang. Reaching over she grabbed the receiver and, laughing at a face Annie made, said hello. Her smile froze when she heard Paul Hammond's voice.

"I know this is awfully short notice but I saw in the newspaper that there is a poetry reading at a coffee shop in Old Town tonight. I thought you might enjoy hearing it. If you haven't already got plans, of course."

"No, I don't have plans." She paused and twiddled at the phone cord. "Are you sure?"

He chuckled softly. It was a velvety purr. "Oh, yes, it says right here in the paper the reading is at seven-thirty at the Onion Skin."

"No, I mean, are you sure we should? You're my boss, as it were."

"Yes, so I recall. I suppose I could invite Pat Crawford to join us, but I'd really rather it was just us."

She paused again. She wanted to go, but in truth she was afraid of going out on a date again, after twenty some years. She looked up to see Annie sitting ramrod straight, staring at her, on the alert. When their eyes met, Annie mouthed, "Go, go, go!"

"If you feel uncomfortable…" he hedged.

"No. I mean, no, I don't feel uncomfortable. And yes, I'd like to go."

"I'm glad. I'll pick you up at seven. We can go for a bite to eat afterward, if you like. How do you feel about bistro food?"

"I love bistro."

When she looked up, Annie was putting her hand in a fist and hissing out a triumphant, "Yesss!"

Twelve

Che ricordarsi del tempo felice
Nella miseria.
There is no greater sorrow than to recall
a time of happiness in misery.

—Dante, *The Inferno (Canto V)*

The poetry was terrible but the company was superb. There were none of the first-date jitters or awkwardness that she'd expected. From the moment he picked her up in his red Saab to the moment he dropped her off again, they shared a seamless flow of conversation and comfortable silences, as though they'd been together for years. At the evening's end, while Eve waited for him to come around and open her car door, she marveled at this unusual ease between them and wondered if indeed they hadn't been lovers in some previous life.

It was a balmy night, moist with the fragrant air of summer. There were hoots of young male laughter coming from the park followed by the barking of dogs.

"It's becoming a hangout for high school boys," she explained, taking his arm.

"Young wolves," he said with a chuckle and pointed to the full moon overhead. "They can't help themselves."

She leaned against him with her face to the moon, relishing the feel of him beside her, her hands laced with his, and wished on the moon for happiness in her life again. They strolled to her building in silence, then stopped at the foyer door. She turned to face him.

"I had a wonderful time."

"I'm glad. So did I."

"I'd invite you up for coffee but the children..."

"No, of course. I should be getting along." He paused, then said in a rush, "I didn't get to take you out to dinner tonight as I'd planned. So I was wondering...you wouldn't want to come to my place tomorrow? I'm a fairly decent cook and I promised you that I'd read Dante in Italian. Would you?"

"Yes," she replied readily. "I'd love to."

His face relaxed and he grinned broadly. His smile lit up his face and his brilliant blue eyes shone like twin moons. Eve's breath caught, entranced, and she wondered if she'd always fall captive to the remarkable charm of his smile.

"I'll pick you up at seven."

"I'll be waiting."

There was a tense moment, thick with desire. She wondered if he would kiss her, and if she should let him if he tried. He leaned forward almost imperceptibly. She held her breath. Then, as though he'd checked his first impulse, he looked down abruptly, took her hand and placed his large hand over it.

"Good night then."

"Good night."

She watched him through the small-paned windows of the door as he walked down the sidewalk, turned, then walked out of sight. Leaning against the door, she released a long, pent-up sigh. Then, after fumbling with her key, she let herself in. She took the stairs slowly, savoring the glow of happiness she felt inside. She had been afraid to let herself feel such attraction, to let another man come close again. But now that she had, she was soaring with joy, blushing like a schoolgirl at the very thought of him.

When she pushed open her front door, she was met with a wall of hostility. Bronte was sitting in the living room and upon seeing her mother, rose to her full height, crossed her arms and scowled.

"Where were you?" Her voice rang with angry suspicion.

Eve blinked, taken aback. "I was out. I went to a poetry reading." Suddenly she felt guilty, defensive. As if she'd done something wrong. She refrained from mentioning Paul's name and turned to put her purse down on the hall table.

"With who?" Bronte asked, moving closer.

"With Dr. Hammond from school. Does it matter?" She tried to make her voice sound nonchalant but she could see from the mottled rage on Bronte's face it wasn't working. Bronte screwed up her face, signaling her unspoken disgust, then spun on her heel and stomped to her room, slamming the door behind her.

Eve leaned against the door and closed her eyes, wondering how she was going to help her daughter accept the idea of her mother dating again when she herself hadn't reconciled it.

She undressed slowly, washed her face and slid into her large, lonely bed. The curtains were not drawn and the window was open a crack, allowing the moonlight to mingle with a soft summer breeze as it filled the room and caressed her cheeks. She brought to mind every word spoken during the evening, pondered every gesture of their parting. Had it been her imagination or was he going to kiss her? Would she have kissed him back?

She brought her hand to her lips and wondered what the sensation of his lips on hers would be like. Would they be soft like Tom's? Or firm? Would they tremble in passion? During the past week the air had sizzled whenever he passed or set a piece of paper on her desk. Whenever he so much as shared the same space, her body quivered and she breathed deeply, sure that he could pick up the magnetic charge between them. Having opened the Pandora's box of possibilities, there was no closing it. Her curiosity, her senses, were aroused. Desire tingled on the surface of her skin like a prickly rash that no lotion could ease.

And he'd invited her to his home for dinner. Would he kiss her, she wondered again? Would she let him? She held her breath, heard the echo of laughter in the park—*young wolves*—then exhaled on a word. "Yes."

"Goodbye, Mother!"

From the basement where she was sorting laundry, Doris could hear Sarah's light footfall above her in the kitchen.

"Wait a minute!" she called out, dropping the dirty clothes from her hands. "I'll be right there." She hurried up the stairs to the front hall in time to catch sight of her daughter as she was opening the front door.

Sarah was a vision of summer crispness. Her small, curvaceous body was tucked into a short white tennis skirt and a crisp, freshly ironed white blouse. She was deeply tanned and athletic and wore her blond hair pulled back in a ponytail. She had the right clothes, the right look. Sarah could walk into any country club anywhere and be welcomed, Doris thought with a ripple of satisfaction. *A real corker* her father would have called his granddaughter, if he'd lived to see her grow up.

Oh, to be so young again! So fresh and perky. Doris felt a surge of maternal pride that this attractive girl was her daughter, even as she felt a sting of dejection that she, with her lumpy figure dressed in a saggy cotton dress, looked old and washed-up in comparison. Lumpy and dumpy.

"Did you eat breakfast?"

"Don't have time," Sarah replied, stuffing her nylon bag with her tennis racket and balls.

"You can't leave without a good breakfast."

"I'm not hungry."

Doris couldn't remember the last time she wasn't hungry.

A car honked in the driveway.

"Gotta go. Bye!"

"Wait, I'll cook you up some eggs. It'll only take a minute. Sarah, you're not to go without something in your stomach. How about a bagel? Sarah!" She hustled after her just in time to have the door slam in her face.

Doris closed her eyes tight against the bubbling hurt and anger, followed by a backlash of shame that she was so unceremoniously discarded by the daughter she adored. Her son had long since ignored her, but she'd hoped for more from Sarah.

She pushed back the lace from the window and peered out at the sunny day.

She saw a young girl saunter down the front walk, hips and hair swaying, toward the young man waiting in the car. He swung open the door and the girl climbed in, giving him a quick peck on the cheek, just a teasing nip. The boy's eyes smoldered and he must have said something bold because the young girl laughed coquettishly and slapped his shoulder as they roared away.

Doris let the lace slip from her hands and stood slump-shouldered in her slippers feeling suddenly very alone in a house that was meticulously clean and depressingly vacant. There were very few signs that anyone actually lived in these great front rooms filled with antiques, carpets and porcelains. How many times in the years past had she scolded the children when they tracked mud or tossed their coats on the floor? *Don't touch! Don't muss!* For what, she wondered? How sterile everything appeared now that they were grown and gone. How very silent.

Turning, she caught the reflection of a woman in the ornate Venetian mirror. This woman had pale skin and brittle, rust-colored hair streaked with a quarter inch of gray at the roots. She raised her hand to her cheek. Who was this woman? She drew back in aversion. The stranger in the mirror was the very washed-up woman Doris had sworn, back when she was Sarah's age, she would never become.

She stared at her reflection, dazed. When had she grown so old? What had happened to her skin? Over the years she'd noticed the rounding of the hips and arms, the graying at the roots, the wrinkles near the eyes. But she'd made appointments at the beauty salon, staving off the inevitable. The change was happening, however, regardless.

She smoothed out the pink cotton shift she wore more for comfort than style and thought to herself that not all women looked so dumpy at her age. Annie Blake certainly didn't. *"She looks pretty good, I'd say."* Doris's face fell. Annie was probably in court this very minute, wearing one of her expensive suits. She could see her now, hotly arguing a case and earning the admiring glances of the judge, the jury, probably even the opponents.

How regrettable that her father, a judge himself, never encouraged his daughter in her education. As far as her parents were concerned, the whole point of sending a daughter to college was to catch a good husband. And didn't she reel in a big one with R. J. Bridges, the quarterback of the Georgetown football team? They'd married immediately after R.J. graduated; it didn't matter that Doris dropped out after sophomore year. She could remember her mother's words about the matter. *"After all, dear, a marriage certificate means much more than a college degree."*

Well, what was done was done. She'd made her decision, although Midge kept urging her to go back to college. She was far too old to sit in a classroom with a bunch of children. It was too late for her. She looked back at the door and thought with grim determination, *Sarah will graduate from college.*

Thinking of her daughter again pricked the pain of her rejection. Doris turned and, with a heavy tread, climbed step after step back to her bedroom. She entered her room, then locked the door. The bedroom was dark and cool. Her drapes were still drawn and white stripes of light pushed against the shades to no avail. The disheveled bed seemed to beckon her to lie down again and shut out the disappointments with the sweet release of slumber.

She slipped from her dress, avoiding the mirror. Lying down, she stretched out her arms and legs, spreading them wide. Her skin felt delicious and decadent against the cool sheets, not the least fat or shapeless. She sighed heavily, more like a moan.

Ah yes, here in the darkness, with her eyes closed, she felt like she could be anyone she wanted. A smile curved her lips. Yes, here her imagination was free to roam without fear of censor or guilt. And she had, she'd discovered in the past few months, a very rich imagination. Exciting things happened to her here, far from the ordinariness of her life.

Here she didn't need R.J. to make her feel fulfilled. She had her mind. And that, she'd also discovered, was her most powerful sexual organ. Her hands slid along her body, relishing the silkiness of her skin that rivaled the sheets. Closing her eyes, she let her imagination go.

It was summer. She is young—sweet sixteen again. Her youthful skin is glowing like a firefly as she gracefully climbs into the sports car at the curb. She raises her lips to the adorable young man in his letter jacket....

Paul Hammond picked Eve up promptly at seven o'clock. He carried an enormous bouquet of flowers in his hand for her and a box of chocolates for the children. Finney and Bronte were beyond rude. They didn't thank him for the expensive chocolates and watched him through narrow, slitted eyes, like two man-eating cats ready to pounce.

Once outside, Eve raised her face to Paul and smiled brightly.

"Your skin is positively glowing," he said.

Her heart soared and she felt a sudden gladness to be free from her own children and their black scowls and condemnation. "I'm sorry about the children," she said as they pulled away from the curb. "They're very protective."

He turned his head, the radiance of his smile catching her off guard, and patted her hand. "I know how they feel."

She leaned back in the car then and relaxed, knowing in her heart that whatever happened that night would be all right, because of him.

His house was just as she'd imagined it might be. The

dark-brown brick Tudor was unpretentious and charming. It could have been plucked from a small village in the Cotswolds and planted right in Oakley. The sweeping, pointed gable rose high in the air. She thought it was amazing that the blue-and-gray slate didn't slide off the sharp slope that fell to just above the long row of mullion windows. There were lots of trees and neatly trimmed shrubs, creating a shady haven on the busy block.

Inside, too, the house was very much like the man. There was nothing sleek or high-tech about either. The dominant impression was of quality and comfort. This was the home of someone with educated tastes and the money to indulge himself. The rooms were small but there were lots of them and they were well proportioned. Best of all, they had interesting curves and funny little built-in bookshelves squeezed in everywhere. If she were to draw his mind in cartoon, she'd draw this house. Most amazing, however, was the carved, stone fireplace and mantel of Randolph Hearst proportions that dominated the living room. Whoever built this house had had an ego. There was room for little more than the soft cordovan red leather sofa, a few shabby chic chairs and a low, sprawling wood coffee table littered with books and magazines.

He'd obviously worked hard to prepare for the dinner. Beyond the arched entry to the dining room she spied a round table painstakingly set with heavy, thick white linen, bright-green china, old silver, thin crystal wineglasses and two tall, tapered white candles. Small white roses filled a glass bowl in the center. She released another sigh. The man certainly had style.

"Would you like a drink?"

"Yes, please." Casting him a sidelong glance, she said, "Surprise me."

He came back a moment later with a Campari and soda,

a red-colored concoction on ice with a slice of lemon. It tasted a bit bitter, a bit tart and very foreign. After a second sip she thought she could get used to it.

There were so many things she wanted to get used to tonight—like being alone with a man in his home. Her mother had always pounded into her brain that a good girl never went into a man's apartment. You'd think at forty-five she'd be past that kind of thinking but damn if that warning didn't play in her mind as she strolled through the house while Paul cooked in the kitchen. She felt all of sixteen again, tongue-tied and searching for breath mints.

"Need a refill?" he asked coming out from the kitchen, drying his hands.

She looked at her glass, surprised to find that the red drink was gone and all that was left was a chewed-up slice of lemon and a few lumps of ice. But ah, yes, her head was swimming. Through heavy eyes she saw Paul standing there in his black polo shirt, tan slacks and brown leather sandals, waiting for an answer. He looked so delicious she wanted to eat him up for supper and forget that savory aroma wafting from the kitchen. When he stepped closer, with a smile on his full lips and his eyes smoldering, she felt her insides go sloshy and her knees fill up with water so high she wasn't sure she could stand.

"No, thanks," she replied returning the glass to him. "I think I've had enough."

"You don't have to drive home."

She didn't dare analyze that statement. "What are you cooking in there?" she asked, dragging her eyes off him and directing her gaze over his shoulder. "Smells wonderful."

"I thought we'd start with some bruschetta. I have some early tomatoes, just ripening. You're in for a treat. They're—" he kissed his fingers in the Italian manner

"—*molto bene*. Then maybe a little *prosciutto e melone,* then my favorite risotto with a few grilled shrimp and vegetables—nothing too heavy. And for dessert..." He stopped short and shook his head, the devil in his eyes. "No. You need some surprises."

Slish-slosh went her insides.

"Where did you learn to cook?"

He shrugged his shoulders. "Back in the eighties I was one of the Mud Angels sent by the Newberry to help restore the historical books after the Arno overflowed. I lived in Italy for a year, then went back again to teach in Rome for four years. I go back whenever I can. I don't know which I love more, the culture or the food. Speaking of which, are we going to talk here or cook dinner? Would you like to help? I need some basil and a few more tomatoes from the garden. Could you pick me some?"

She passed through the well-stocked kitchen, where steam was rising from tall stainless steel pots. Bunches of chopped herbs, mostly basil, and chunks of fragrant cheese lay in waiting on the wooden cutting boards. As she moved out to the yard she saw that his garden was an extension of the house. The deck was decorated with terra-cotta pots filled with all kinds of herbs. How like a man, she thought, when he explained he couldn't see the point of planting anything that he couldn't eat. She had plunked flowers in every spare spot in the yard of her house. To her mind, there was never enough space for flowers. His garden, nonetheless, lured her out, and for the first time since she'd moved into the condo, she missed her old home, her garden especially.

As with everything else, Paul Hammond chose things not for design or style but simply because he liked them. And when he liked something, he obviously went overboard. All the trees were in the front; not a one cast shade on the serious garden in back. In one corner were rows of raspberries, and in the far corner a trellis of peas climbed toward the sun. But smack in the center, dominating the yard, were rows and rows of tomato plants standing as erect as soldiers in bamboo tepees and robust bushes of basil of every variety imaginable. Eve expected to see an old crone in a black dress shelling peas.

"I don't see any flowers. Not even a single marigold."

"I can buy all that," he said, as though it were obvious. "Here, taste one of these."

When she bit into the warm tomato, basil and garlic concoction spread on crisply toasted bread, the heady scent filled her cavities and she suddenly understood. She nodded, licking her lips. "It tastes like summer," she said in a moan.

"Exactly."

His smile never failed to disarm her. It was warm, sexy and full of promise. She felt the last vestige of her guard slip away with the evening sun.

Paul led her indoors to the dining room where he lit the tapered candles, pulled out her chair, then fed her a meal fit for a queen, which was precisely how he made her feel. It was a cornucopia for her senses. She couldn't remember the last time she'd felt so thoroughly seduced. Or when she'd last looked into a man's eyes over a candlelit dinner and felt she could drown in them. Or the last time she'd watched a man's hands move unconsciously in the air as he talked, or absently caught a drop of condensation on a water goblet, or fed her a plump juicy raspberry, still warm from the garden. She couldn't remember the last time she'd felt a fire of yearning for such hands on her body.

The talk was seamless, flowing from one subject to the other as they each opened up and shared and mingled their histories together. When he offered her more wine, she noticed that he didn't serve himself any. He was soft-spoken but brutally honest when she asked him why.

"I don't drink," he replied readily. "I'm an alcoholic. I gave up drinking twenty-two years ago and though I wouldn't say I'm cured—what alcoholic can ever say that?—I've got the demons under control." His words spilled out in a torrent as he got caught up in the story. "I was a hard drinker. I spent much of my youth in a drunken haze, bombed out of my mind for months on end. My father was a drinker, and a tyrant, as was my grandfather before him," he said ruefully. "I'm large like my father, I have hands like him," he said, holding them up to the candlelight. His face was dark and glowering as he fought the demons in his memory. "But I hope the comparison ends there. I can be ruthless myself, I admit. And I was. The drinking coupled with youth... Well, I was ostracized from the family until after the accident."

He sighed and plucked a strip of wax from the candle. Eve waited breathlessly for him to continue, knowing he would.

"Poor, sweet Caro. She was my drinking partner as much as my wife. We weren't married very long. We were so young and so bloody foolish. She was an actress, a damn good one, and I, well, I was middling good but I didn't really give a damn. It was an escape from the utter boredom that was my life, and, I suppose, a tweak at my father. Anyway, we were driving home from a party at the country house of a friend. She was driving. I'd passed out. The next thing I remember I woke up in hospital." He spoke slowly now, deliberately. "It doesn't matter who was driving, really. I killed her."

"Paul, you didn't."

"My drinking did. Her drinking did. Our drinking did. His, hers, ours... It's all semantics. She died and I've never touched another drop. I've spent most of my life alone since then. My body healed but there was this gaping inner wound that festered. I was angry.'' He laughed bitterly and his eyes flashed with defiance. ''God was I angry! I made not only my own life miserable but several others as well. I drove people away.'' He shrugged. ''But like most things, I mellowed in time. I like being alone now. I have my work. I love to travel. I don't need anyone, really. I don't make attachments to people easily and I have few friends.''

Paul looked up and studied her face, then reached out across the table to take her hand. She felt his heat spread up her arm to her heart.

''And now, here you are. I've been in this city for ten years and one May morning you walk into my office like a breath of spring and everything seems different. I'm suddenly lonely.''

The utter simplicity of the statement devastated her. She drew back, overwhelmed.

Misunderstanding, he released her hand and leaned far back into his chair, staring at her with an intense study. ''Why don't you ever talk about your husband?''

''It's not easy to talk about him. Especially not to you.''

''I'd like to hear about him. You obviously loved him very much.''

''Yes. Very much. But why do you want to know about him?''

''I have to in order to better know you. And I want to know everything about you, Eve Porter.''

So Eve told him, haltingly at first, then in a rambling stream of consciousness, all about her own long, happy marriage, her children and the tragedy that changed their lives. It was difficult to explain to him, a man she was attracted to, how she still loved her husband. How she always would. How, in so many ways, she still felt married.

She glanced up, sheepishly, to gauge his reaction. She expected him to be put off, to think that his attention, this divine seduction, was all for naught because she was some crazy widow with her light still burning for her dead husband.

But his expression was filled with compassion. "I've never known that kind of love," he said.

It was a bittersweet admission, difficult to make. She leaned forward and allowed him to cup her cheek and chin with his palm, to trace the contours of her lips with the tip of his thumb. She closed her eyes and sighed again, willing him to understand that she was overflowing with light. And that there was a scorching torch, raging inside her—just for him.

"I want to hold you in my arms, Eve," he said in a low voice. "I've wanted to do just that since you walked into my office. The past few weeks have been torturous. I want to hold you more than I've wanted anything for a very long time."

She took a deep breath, sensing what those words meant, hearing his request, so subtle but so clear with intent. Then she nodded her head and laid her thick napkin on the table.

They rose together but she just stood there, trapped by the chair and her memories. He came to her side and drew her out of the corner, into his arms. He held her close. She smelled basil on his shirt, felt his hand stroke her cheek. Then he moved his hands to her head and pulled slightly back.

She looked in his eyes. They were Paul's eyes, not Tom's, and for a second she felt like she was about to do something wrong, illicit. He must have sensed her hesitation because he searched her face, concern etched across his own.

"Are you sure you want to do this?" he asked.

"No," she replied honestly. "You should know that there's only been one man in my life."

He took a deep breath, then bent to kiss her forehead. "We can wait. I don't want you to feel hurried, or have any regrets."

He wrapped her in his arms again and pressed her close. She felt his arousal and it sparked her own.

Why was she being so childish? How many times in her monogamous marriage had she wondered what it would be like to make love to another man? She'd heard the jokes about size. She'd heard the ladies talk about how one man was such a good lover and how another was a loser. She'd read books in which women went round after heady round of lovemaking all through the night, mewling with pleasure. Of course she was curious, desperately so. At least to kiss another man, just to go that far, to see if another pair of lips would taste different than Tom's or feel harder, softer, wetter, drier.

Now she was free to find out—except that this cursed feeling of mindless guilt was holding her back. If she made love to this wonderful man, did she really think she would go blind or have her soul damned? The Catholic faith's chastity belt was locked tight around her mind. She should have worked these questions out when she was young, before she was married. She should have had a little more fun.

Except that she'd wanted to be pure for her husband and had married young. Even after all these years, that decision was one she'd never regretted. Her virginity was a treasure Tom had held dear.

But now? After a lifetime of being a good girl? How

unfair! She was burning inside, an inferno of desire held back by the constraints of a loony conscience. Surely only a Catholic girl would feel such guilt.

"Come along," he said, taking her hand. He led her to the sofa, then left the room for a moment, returning with a well-worn copy of *The Divine Comedy*. Settling into the cushions he brought her close to his chest. "I'll have to be content to hold you like this."

There was no hint of resentment in his tone, only humor. She felt an immediate release of tension. Grateful, she rested her head against the crisp cotton of his shirt. The familiar, delicious ease she usually felt with him returned.

"I promised you a reading of the *Inferno* and I intend to keep my promise. I wouldn't want you to think I lured you here under false pretenses."

"I've just finished reading it. In English, of course," she joked. "It wasn't as difficult as I'd imagined it would be. It was very moving. Emotional. I loved every moment of it. But the part about poor Paolo and Francesca was so cruel," she said, referring to the fifth canto where a woman named Francesca related to the traveler, Dante, how she was condemned for eternity in Hell for the unrepented sin of loving Paolo. "They fell in love and were punished for eternity."

"For adultery."

"Yes," she said softly. That was what she felt at the moment. Condemned. Burning with desire, yet fearful that making love with Paul would be a sin.

"Dante was moved by their love, moved to near death, because a love of that power was something he desired and had never experienced. A love so strong that it endured beyond death."

She knew that beneath his words he was speaking of himself and her marriage to Tom. He was probing her, and she felt the pinprick twist in her heart. Remembering how much she had loved Tom—at the very moment she was ready to love another—was a bewildering kind of misery.

"It was just plain mean of Dante to keep the two together," she continued. "Floating in a black whirlwind without hope, unable to speak."

He chuckled. "I feel like that at work, knowing you're out there somewhere but unable to take you in my arms."

She leaned farther against him, slipping off her shoes and bringing up her knees on the sofa. "Yes, me too. Our own private Inferno."

He tightened his arms around her and rested his lips beside her temple. "For me, it's a kind of Paradise. Just think. If you had not walked into my office, I'd never have known you. I'd be alone, never to have these feelings. So, in that light, perhaps for Francesca and Paolo, being together in Hell is better than being alone in Paradise."

Turning her body to rest her cheek and palm against his chest she asked, "Read the fifth canto to me? In Italian."

He reached for the book, opened it and settled her back upon his shoulder. Then in his deep, melodic voice that vibrated with emotion, he began to read.

Eve closed her eyes and listened to the foreign words roll from his tongue in terza rima. Though she didn't understand the words, she was moved by the power and cadence of the epic poem. She comprehended when Dante called to the spirit Francesca and asked her plaintively how they knew that they were in love. Francesca, grateful to tell her story, replied how one day she and Paolo were innocently reading together, as yet unaware that they were in love. During the reading their eyes met and they blushed.

Quando leggemmo il disiato riso. When reading of the

smile-long-waited-for. Then Paolo turned and kissed Francesca upon the mouth. *Tutto tremante*.

Paul stopped reading, closed the book and rested his lips on the softness of the fine hairs of her head.

They sat together in a heavy silence. Both knew that this was their story also, that at some point in the library, while fingering through ancient vellum pages and reading countless tomes, they'd looked into each others eyes, smiled, blushed and knew that they were in love.

All that remained was the kiss.

Eve reached up with trembling fingers to wrap her hand around his neck, relishing the lush feel of his soft hair tangled in her fingers. His eyes shone with the blueness and intensity of an acetylene torch. She could feel the scorching heat of it straight through to her bones.

"I warned you I could be ruthless when I want something," he said, his breath hot upon her face. "And I want you."

Parting her lips and turning just so, she pulled his head down toward her, closing her eyes, holding her breath. When his lips met her open ones at last, she knew she was lost, swirling in a black whirlwind. *Tutto tremante*. There was an intensity in his kiss, a power that she'd expected. His strong arms were like steel bands clasping her tightly to his chest. She clung to him, wanting him, wanting this.

There was no more reading, no more talk, no more doubt that night. He led her to his room where he removed her clothing with a care akin to devotion. And there upon his crisp linen sheets, she discovered that Dante was right after all. The way to Heaven is clearly marked and each of us has a chance to find it—if we want.

Thirteen

> Consider anything, only don't cry!
> —Lewis Carroll, *Through the Looking Glass*

Eve's wish on the moon had come true. She felt a happiness she didn't think possible in her life again. It was like awakening from a long slumber, feeling a bit confused and blinking at the light. The world seemed brighter somehow, more crystalline, clear and fresh. On Monday morning she dressed with extra care, gazing in the mirror trying to see herself as Paul would see her. Bronte cast suspicious glances her way under disapproving brows, but remained obstinately silent, refusing to speak to her. Finney was caught up in his own world of new friends and sports and seemed oblivious. He did, however, smile sweetly when she impulsively hugged him before going to work.

At the college, Paul was very careful not to look her way more than necessary or show favoritism, especially under Pat's watchful eye. If anything, he was more gruff than usual, but she saw through the ruse. Later in the afternoon, she managed to catch a carefully aimed smile that told her in no uncertain terms that he was aware of her and remembered every detail of their night together. Her skin tingled in anticipation. He had wanted to see her again the next night, every night this week, but she had declined. This was all going much too fast for her and she wanted the children to gradually grow accustomed to Paul. So they settled for seeing each other at lunch, either at a restaurant or for long walks in the park, and patiently awaited the long Fourth of July weekend when they would share a meal, and Paul's bed, once again.

On Tuesday morning, Annie sat waiting in Dr. Gibson's office at the university hospital. The beautiful windows were reminiscent of an earlier time of craftsmanship. John would love this old building, she thought, then felt the twinge of sorrow that always came lately when she thought of her husband. With an absentminded gesture, she rested her hand on her abdomen, tender and swollen after her last bout of heavy bleeding. It was empty, like her marriage. And perhaps it was just as well.

For the past month, she and John were just inhabiting the same space, more like roommates than husband and wife. John acted the martyr in his silence; Saint Sebastian accepting the arrows. Well, she hated martyrs. Especially when they went into a grand sulk. There was nothing saintly about his behavior. This was John's way of punishing her for her own flares of temper.

In the past, these silences could go on for days, making the air between them so thick with hostility she'd become physically sick. Then when he'd felt she'd had enough, or he couldn't stand it any longer, he'd approach her and give her the cue: "Do you want to talk about it?" And of course she would, and it would be over.

This one would not be over so easily, she knew. She'd crossed some line when she'd told him in a snit that she wanted a divorce. She hadn't meant it, and told him so, but he'd walked away, telling her she could do what she wanted. He was still walking away, refusing to talk, hiding his feelings behind the veneer of hurt pride. And now he was back and forth from Florida, slavishly directing another one of R.J.'s big deals.

The building boom there was irresistible to a man with dreams as big as R. J. Bridges's, and now John was tangled in the silken web of wealth and power. He'd been bitten by the bug of greed, and like a venom that slowly spread throughout his bloodstream, all John's own quieter dreams of craftsmanship and a simple life-style had been destroyed. Now his simpering after R.J. looked pathetic. He was not defending what was precious in himself. She fell in love with the inner toughness that he used to protect himself with, to protect her, and their nest. R.J. was threatening the nest, and John was allowing it. She hardly knew him anymore.

Annie crossed her legs and wagged her foot. Where was that doctor anyway? It was stupid for her to be here. Except that she harbored hope she and John would work it out. A baby would cement them, join their futures and return his sense of purpose. She needed a baby more than ever.

The door swung open and Dr. Gibson briskly strode into the office, carrying her medical file and several sheets of lab results. After the preliminary greetings, the doctor got right down to business.

''As far as your baby-making apparatus goes, all the tests are normal. John's sperm count is high and there's nothing wrong with you. I see no reason right now why conception shouldn't occur at some point in the future.''

Annie held back a laugh thinking, *Yeah, well how about no sex. That's a pretty good reason.*

''But—'' Dr. Gibson paused to look at the lab results ''—I still want to know why you're having such heavy periods. And this spotting in between... You can't keep losing that much blood, Annie. Your blood test shows you're still anemic. I mean ghetto level anemia, not at all usual for a woman in your health and economic level. I don't like this, not one bit."

"Oh, well," Annie replied, despondent.

Dr. Gibson folded her hands on the reports and speared Annie with one of her no-nonsense looks. "This is serious, Annie. I want you to take this to heart."

Annie felt her heart was already over full at the moment, but she nodded complacently.

Dr. Gibson continued in her methodical manner. "Your Pap smear came back unusual as well. It's probably nothing, there are plenty of abnormal Pap readings. Still, we have to check it out."

Annie sat straighter, faintly alarmed. "Check it out for what?"

"For any number of things. We'll do another Pap smear to start. And…"

Annie tensed, hearing the hedging in Dr. Gibson's voice.

"In your case, with your heavy, irregular bleeding, I also want to do a biopsy to rule out cancer."

The mere threat of the disease rocked her to the core. Suddenly, menopause didn't sound so bad. "I thought you said it was normal to have irregular bleeding at my age. That it was hormonal."

"It is, but your bleeding is excessive and causing chronic anemia. It could just be fibroids, also fairly common. A sonogram will give us a picture. Don't be alarmed. We always want to cover the bases, Annie."

Annie frowned, thinking only of more tests, more prodding and poking.

"The biopsy is done here in the office. I just need to snatch a little sample of tissue from the uterus."

Annie slunk in the chair. "Take as much as you want, Doctor. Take the whole thing if you want. I don't care."

Dr. Gibson tilted her head and studied Annie for a long moment. "You're awfully dejected this morning. That's not like you. Is anything the matter, Annie?"

Annie looked at the compassion in Dr. Gibson's lightly freckled face. In the light pouring in from the beautiful windows, her hair looked like the burnished copper pots Annie had chosen to hang in her kitchen—if the darn renovations ever got completed. So much of her life was hanging in the balance.

Annie's chest constricted. She felt like crying and spilling out how mad she was at John, how hurt.

"No," Annie replied, shaking her head, keeping her own counsel. "When do you want to do it?"

"How about now? No time like the present."

So it was that, within a quarter hour, Annie lay on the cold slab the nurses called the examining table, legs spread-eagle and feet hoisted in stirrups. She took deep breaths and stared at the countless, tiny holes in the sound-proofed ceiling. Dr. Gibson sat between her legs wielding what looked to Annie like a medieval instrument of torture. It was some long-necked, metal clamp, sort of like one of John's pliers, supersize. No matter what words of reassurances Dr. Gibson was muttering, about how there'd be a shot of local anesthetic and how it would only pinch for a moment, it looked pretty clear to Annie that that sucker was going to hurt.

And it would be cold, too—Annie just knew it.

The fans whirred in Gabriella's kitchen. Outside the humidity was rising with the temperature. It was going to be a hot one and Gabriella sorely missed her air-conditioning. The unit had broken down during that first heat wave in June and they couldn't afford to buy another one.

"It's not so bad," she told the children while they groaned about the heat and how they were the only family in town without air-conditioning. "When I was a little girl in Puerto Rico, no one in the whole village had air-conditioning. We made friends with the hot weather. We drank cool drinks, sat in the shade and went to the beach."

"At least you have air-con in the hospital," muttered her son, Freddy, not caring one whit about what she'd done in Puerto Rico.

"Would you like to trade places, eh? You go to work and let me stay home. Ha...don't I wish."

She made light of the situation, but in her heart Gabriella was worried. It had almost been a full year since Fernando was laid off and he still hadn't found another full-time job. His unemployment checks helped support them for the first several months and he was able to pick up work here and there on a part-time basis, but nothing steady. Now the checks had stopped coming and she'd had to increase her hours once again to make ends meet. This would be the first weekend she'd had to work in years. Months ago, they'd made the joint decision that he should not get off track and take a job outside of his field. The right job would come along and everything would be all right. They just had to hold on.

She believed this, she believed in her husband, but her schedule was taking its toll. She was desperately tired all the time, trying to manage both her home and her job. Fernando was growing more and more depressed, which only added to the burden. And the children, feeling the tension and the heat, were crabby and fought among themselves. More and more, Gabriella felt as if she were a firecracker being pulled at both ends. She was ready to explode.

Across town, Midge was suffering the typical mood swings of an artist before a show. During the week, while hoisting her four- and five-foot canvases, perched on ladders to hang them to her precise specifications, she was in an adrenaline rush. She worked around the clock, agonizing with worry, pushing herself to her limits, aching in every muscle, yet too wired to sleep. She imagined it was the way new mothers felt going into labor.

Susan, another artist exhibiting in the same show, laughed when Midge told her that. Susan was the most successful of the group, a teacher at the Art Institute and already represented at another gallery. She'd been around the art-scene block several times and was mildly intimidating with her swaggering confidence and boisterous voice.

"Good analogy," Susan said, wiping her cropped blond hair from her brow after hanging a six-foot canvas. She was an attractive woman, not quite as tall as Midge, with the taut, defined muscles of an athlete and pleasant features. Her eyes, a surprisingly pale-gray, shone from behind prominent cheekbones and a slightly bent nose like a ray of sunshine in the mountains. "Aren't these canvases our precious babies? Except I sure ain't no new mother. This is my umpteenth kid by that count, and they're all fucking hard to push out."

Midge grinned, liking her all the more. All week long, Susan had been generous with her supplies, helped her lift her canvases and brought her cups of coffee from the deli across the street. The art world could be lonely. There were lots of petty jealousies and behind-palm verbal swipes. It was a breath of fresh air to discover someone open and unguarded.

Midge prowled the gallery with her chin cupped in her palm. She viewed the other canvases, then walked past her own paintings again and again, studying them at every possible angle. Back and forth she walked, sensing Susan's eyes on her. There was little more to be done now; she knew she should go home. But she couldn't. She walked on air, absolutely enchanted by her own art.

Susan came closer and wrapped a friendly arm around her shoulder. Midge was surprised but didn't pull back. It was an affectionate gesture, giving and loving, and she could feel herself open up in its warmth.

"So, little mother, what do you think?" Susan asked, looking at one of Midge's large abstracts. The layered pinks resembled skin and glowed with evocative swirls and shapes.

"I feel like a mother counting toes," she said, leaning her weight against Susan's hard-boned shoulders. Susan chuckled and squeezed her shoulder. Midge felt a new undercurrent between them that was odd, but very pleasant.

Susan began stroking her back in a consoling manner. "There are ten, believe me."

"I love those canvases so much, I can't bear it. I hate to leave here."

Susan gave her back a firm pat, then she broke away, grinning sarcastically. "I should hate *you*, Midge Kirsch. I've been admiring, no, envying, your work all week. Such powerful lines, and your sense of color blows everything else here right out of the water. It's very erotic. Very O'Keeffe-ish, but not. I really like them. Very much."

Midge felt her knees weaken with a profound relief. There had been a conspiracy of silence from the other artists during the week. She had always prided herself on her confidence and self-esteem, at least where her work was concerned. Her view of the world was clear. But during the past week, her pedestal had been reduced to rubble.

"No one else has said a word," she said, speaking plainly. "You're the first. I was sure they hated it."

"Nah, the cowards. They love it but hate you because you're so much better."

"I doubt it," she chided back, enjoying the camaraderie. Then more honestly, she added, "Last night I was miserable. I went home so sure I didn't measure up. I wanted to take it all down. I agonized why I was ever enamored with my paintings." She crossed her arms and laughed. "I thought my babies were ugly."

"I feel that all the time. Don't know anyone who doesn't. Hell, I wanted to take my own stuff down last night."

"God, I hate the pressure of openings. I absolutely dreaded having to buy new clothes. My mother insisted. She has this idea that openings are still the grand fetes of the 1980s. I was so frazzled with worry about my work I let her win the battle of the clothes. How are we going to survive tonight?"

"I'll tell you what. Let's make a pact. We'll check on each other every hour on the hour. A smile, a hug, whatever. That way, if one of us freaks, we have a backup." She paused, then said with more seriousness, "We'll be there for each other."

Midge felt again that there was a subtle invitation in the comment. "It's a deal."

"How about we have dinner afterward? Some of the people are going to the Rose Bud. We can join them, but we don't have to." Susan's eyes signaled a clear interest in developing their friendship.

"I'd like to, but I may be busy. I'm expecting my friends to come by and they'll likely want to go out to dinner. You're welcome to join us."

"No, thanks. I'd feel out of place. Let me know though. You know where to find me," she said without a hint of disappointment. Midge was attracted to her open warmth and honesty, her toughness and smarts. There was no subterfuge with Susan. No backstabbing or insecurities. She was a woman at ease with herself and the world.

She was someone Midge wanted to get to know better.

Annie once believed there was no such thing as time. She took each day as it came without thought of the past or worry for the future. She was one of many of her age group who felt young, still perceived herself as powerful, her body as a temple of health—well exercised, fed healthy foods, copiously watered and pumped up with mega doses of vitamins.

On Friday morning, the third of July, however, she suddenly became aware of each day, each hour, each minute as it slipped through her fingers.

Dr. Gibson called Annie into her office, uneasy that John was out of town, unwilling to wait for his uncertain return. She wanted to see Annie as soon as possible. She was unusually reserved and her eyes reflected the worry etched in her brow.

"Annie, sometimes the tests reveal what we don't want to see. I wish I didn't have to tell you this, but the results show that you have cancer of the endometrial lining. Uterine cancer." Dr. Gibson's eyes were soft with concern, a sharp contrast to her crisp medical whites. "That would explain the heavy bleeding, the spotting and, of course, the irregular Pap smear. The good news is that uterine cancer has one of the best survival rates." She paused and pursed her lips. "The bad news is, we'll have to remove the uterus."

Annie sat still and quiet in the cushioned chair, absorbing the words like a body blow. The shock reverberated to her very foundation, cracking her identity and crumbling it like sand at her feet. Breathless and numb, she was unable to move.

"No," she blurted out, an instinctive warding off of a threat.

"Yes, Annie," Dr. Gibson replied with a sober expression. "There's no mistake. I'm sorry."

"You're sorry," she repeated.

"Normal cells grow and divide in an orderly manner," Dr. Gibson explained. "But sometimes normal cells go crazy, divide out of control and produce too much tissue that forms tumors. Some tumors are benign. They don't spread through the body. Others are malignant. Triggered by unknown factors in the genes or environment they metastasize, or spread, and destroy nearby healthy tissue and organs. Those are cancerous."

Dr. Gibson explained the process thoroughly but Annie remembered none of it. She couldn't get past the word cancer.

"We'll need to do more tests. You'll need to arrange your schedule to take time off from work." She paused to look at Annie's face, then closed the file and spoke in a gentle tone. "We can talk later about when to schedule surgery. I'd like to do it within a couple of weeks. Go home, Annie. When will John be home?"

"Not till tomorrow sometime… I'm not sure. I don't even know what hotel he's at. How's that for a lousy break?" She gave off a short, bitter laugh.

"Call a friend. And if you need me or have any more questions, call me."

Annie walked in a daze, wanting to talk to someone, not knowing what to say. If only John were home. She needed him now more than ever, but he wasn't due back until tomorrow night. He would make it home just in time for the Bridgeses' big Fourth of July party. How could he not leave his phone number? What kind of a marriage was that?

She drove home on automatic pilot, staring straight ahead and following the roads, unaware of traffic. She took the turns slowly, staying close to the curb. When she arrived in her own driveway, she applied the brake and remained in the car, unsure of what to do next. There was no one in the big house. She didn't know where to go. She'd never felt so alone and unsure.

She heard again and again the words *malignant* and *cancer* like explosions in her head. Slumping forward over the steering wheel, she put her hands over her ears and rocked. But the word echoed relentlessly inside her—cancer, cancer, cancer—a loathsome word that spread fear and shock throughout her body. Looking at her belly, she imagined thousands of the evil, horrid plague-cells multiplying inside of her. She swiped and rubbed with desperation at her midriff. All she could think was how she wanted to rip them out of her.

Get out! Get out! I'm not ready. I'm not ready, she cried to herself. Rocking was the only thing that soothed her—back and forth, back and forth.

Midge worked with Susan at the gallery until the last minute. Robert, the gallery director, chased them off at two to rest and get dressed. Even as they left, they looked over their shoulders at their paintings with concern. When she stepped inside her loft, the midafternoon sunshine was pouring in through her large windows like molten lava. The stifling air was choking and made each groggy step an effort. She barely managed to open a window, strip down and hit the bed before dozing quickly off. She was awakened some time later by the persistent ringing of the phone by her bed.

"You were asleep, weren't you?" It was Susan.

Midge blinked sleepily and stretched to see the clock. It was four o'clock already! She had to be at the gallery in an hour. "Thank God you called," she mumbled.

There was a husky chuckle. "I thought I'd better check.

I slept through an opening once and I wouldn't wish that on you.''

Midge was groggy, scratching her head. "Thanks Susan," she said, yawning loudly. "I owe you. See you at five." After hanging up she pushed aside her sweaty blanket and rose to the window, opening it wider to allow the refreshing air to flow over her body, cooling it. Music was coming from a neighbor's window. Midge closed her eyes, allowing the sweetness of the opera to slowly waken her sleep-soaked thoughts. She felt drugged, still half caught in the dream that had slipped from her memory on waking. It was odd that she woke to Susan's voice. She had the strange feeling that her dream was about her, if only she could remember. It was an erotic dream. A visit from Incubus. Her nipples tingled and there was a telltale ache in her groin. It was one of those dreams that left her feeling a strange longing for hours after waking.

She leaned her head against the window frame and felt a sigh ripple through her as she struggled with the sexual attraction she felt for Susan—the first time she'd felt such a feeling for a woman in many years.

The last time was long ago, back when she was in college. Dear Rachel. They were the closest of friends, shared everything openly and freely. Yet still, Midge had felt something was missing. They'd hugged often and held hands once or twice, but their relationship was never sexual. Their intimacy was more heartfelt than physical. After graduation they'd parted among tears and vows to write always. For years they did. They still exchanged Christmas cards and Midge knew if Rachel ever walked through the door they'd hug and pick up right where they'd left off.

In graduate school, Midge began a relationship with Tim, a jazz musician. They were friends first, lovers later. They married during the draft push of the Vietnam war. After two years the war ended and he left her for fame and fortune and a kissy-lip singer in California. After the divorce, Midge just shut down. She had a few affairs over the years, all of them with men, but none of them were fulfilling or based on anything but random sexual need. After a while, either they stopped asking or she stopped looking. A long void began and she developed a cold apathy, as though her body had died and sex of any kind was just not interesting to her.

Throughout the years, Midge's closest, most meaningful relationships had always been with women. She liked women, preferred spending time with them than with men. Yet though she'd been blessed with several deep friendships, it was her nature to remain a loner. It had been almost a decade since she'd had an intimate relationship of any kind.

Yet today, in the gallery, she'd felt a bond with Susan. Her determined warmth seeped through the cold shroud Midge wore around her heart like the spring sun that melts the blanket of snow. Once again, Midge felt there was something missing in her life. Seeing her friend, Eve, moving on with her life again, sharing intimacy again, she suddenly realized how stagnant her own life was. Watching the way Paul Hammond's large hands had wrapped around Eve's small shoulder in a tender, loving manner, she was suddenly hungry for the feel of arms around her once again.

Why not me, she anguished?

She went to the shower and stood with her palms flat against the tile as the hot water beat down upon her back. Gradually her muscles loosened as her worries, anguish and memories of the dream rolled from her body and swirled down the drain. She dressed slowly, gathering her wits and mentally girding herself for the evening ahead. She was done with the nagging worries about whether anyone would like her paintings. Now she began a distancing between herself and her work.

She thought of her friends and the image of their smiles filled the void in her heart. As her long fingers worked their way up the wide silk buttons of her blouse she wondered if Eve, Annie and Doris would joke or rave about her work? Though they were close, they never came by to see her paintings and Midge didn't expect them to. She didn't stop by to visit their children, either, except Gabriella's. They were closer friends, a unit within the unit. Like Eve and Annie, or the way Eve and Doris used to be. Clasping a large, handcrafted silver pendant around her neck, she thought of Gabriella and a smile escaped her as she wondered if Gabby would rush up to hug her in her sweet-smelling embrace? Closing her purse and shutting out the lights, she smiled, grateful that she had the Book Club in her life. They were her touchstones.

Eve stepped from the hot, scented waters of her tub where she'd just soaked with cool cucumber slices on her eyes for the past blissful thirty minutes. She'd read that cucumbers brought down the puffiness and redness from the eyes. In the past week she'd taken to reading Bronte's teen magazines with all their beauty tips and lover's advice. For that's what she felt like—a teenager again. A young girl dressing up for a date. And oh, it was so much fun! She felt a rosy glow all over just anticipating Paul's powerful arms around her again. Tom had been a wonderful lover, innovative and playful. Paul's lovemaking was different, more intense and demanding, like him. She giggled again, realizing it was true what she'd heard all those years about different lovers.

She was humming some love song, enjoying the early evening breeze on her skin, swirling with and laying out her clothes, when Finney and Bronte entered her room.

She smiled when she looked up, her heart overflowing with a warm happiness. But one look at their faces chilled the air. They approached with all the grim, solemn determination of a storm front. Eve tightened the sash of her terry robe and stood ready to clash wills.

"Hi, there. Do you two want something?" she asked, forcing cheer into her voice.

"We want to talk to you." Bronte spoke without inflection.

"What about?" In her heart Eve cringed, knowing what was coming. She glanced at Finney who slouched beside Bronte. His head was ducked and he was pinching his arm once again, something she hadn't seen him do in months. She bent her head inquisitively, searching his face for clues. Her inner alarms were ringing.

"You're going out with that man again, aren't you?" Bronte asked.

"If you mean Dr. Hammond, the answer is yes. You know that. I'm not making any secret of it."

"How could you!" she blurted out, red-faced with her fists balled at her thighs.

Bronte's outbursts were always dramatic. She had had tantrums as a child and Eve was prepared for the worst. She drew herself up with indignation and put her hands on her hips.

"How could I what? Go out with a man?"

"Yes!" Bronte shouted back, as though this admission were a confirmation of guilt.

"There's nothing wrong with that." She almost said *I'm not married* but couldn't. Not to her children.

"Yes, there is! You shouldn't go out with him. With anyone! It's not right. Daddy's only been dead for a year. It's...it's disgusting to think you're with someone else already. What's the matter? Didn't you love Dad?"

"Of course I loved him!" Eve cried out, stricken. Not

love him? The sense of injustice heaped on her by this fourteen-year-old filled her with rage. "How dare you ask me that?"

"Then how can you go out with someone else?" Tears sprang to her eyes, instantly dousing Eve's hot fury. "It makes me sick," she lashed out. "And Finney, too."

Eve, struck dumb with hurt and shock, looked at Finney for confirmation. He nodded, all humped over as if he were trying to make himself very small. While she stared at him he looked sheepishly back and forth from the floor to her. When his eyes filled with tears, Eve's own heart was near to breaking. Her boy had seemed so much better over the summer. He'd laughed again, gone out with friends, played sports. He was gradually coming out of his shell and it killed her to see him retreat into it again. She was furious at Bronte for dragging him into this battle.

"Do you feel it's wrong, Finney?" Her voice was a cracked whisper.

He nodded. "Please don't do it, Mom...you're still kinda married to Dad. I mean, to us you are. If you go out, I dunno. It's not right." He sniffed, then said, his voice full of reproach, "Don't you miss him?"

Tears sprang to her eyes as it hit her full force how much Finney missed his father. She turned to face Bronte, who stood with the same hurt and mutinous expression she'd worn when she was a two-year-old standing at her knee feeling betrayed and bereft watching the invader, Finney, nursing at her breast. Eve realized with a softening that Bronte was feeling lost and abandoned again.

"Daddy wouldn't be going out if it was you who died," Bronte added.

Eve reeled with guilt. She'd been so preoccupied with the newness of dating and falling in love again and all her renewed physical experiences that she didn't see how uprooting it was for her children to observe. She'd never meant to hurt them.

She opened her arms to them, but this time they did not come to her. That final blow broke her.

"Of course I miss him," she said, dropping her empty arms to her side. "So very much. But he's gone, and I'm lonely." For the first time since Tom died, despite all her resolutions, Eve began to cry in front of her children. She couldn't help herself, the tears just spilled over. Suddenly she felt Bronte's long arms around her shoulders, then Finney's thin ones around her waist, shuddering. Their arms encircled each other and they wept together. The memories of their father and a different time were pouring through them, uniting them. Their tears washed away all the earlier bitterness and recrimination, leaving space in their hearts for love and forgiveness.

An hour later, an exhausted Eve picked up the phone and ordered for pizza delivery. Then, taking a minute to cross the room and close the bedroom door, she dialed Paul's number. When he answered he sounded very upbeat and delighted to hear from her.

"Paul, I'm sorry. I won't be able to go out tonight."

There was a pause. "Is everything all right? The children?"

"Yes. No, everything is not all right." She caught her breath, holding back a sob.

"Eve, what's the matter? Tell me. Do you want me to come over?"

"No, please don't," she replied quickly, choking on the words. "This is all so hard to explain. Paul," she said again, determined, "I can't see you tonight. Or any other night. The children aren't ready—I'm not ready—to start seeing anyone. I shouldn't have..." She almost said *slept with you* but the words died in her throat. Still, she thought he understood because he spoke again in a somber voice.

"I didn't want to rush you, Eve. I'm sorry. I didn't think you had regrets."

"I don't. But it can't happen again. I can't see you, at least not for a while. Please, Paul, try to understand. My children need more time. They see my dating as a betrayal."

She heard a grumble over the line and knew his temper well enough to realize he was holding back a torrent of words. No doubt arguments that she'd made herself: he was not a rival, her husband was dead, her children had no right to make such demands. She had to go with her heart, however, and her heart belonged to her children. She stood her ground, unafraid to face his fury.

"Will you go to your friend's show tonight?" A simple question, though his voice was measured.

"No. I...I don't think so," she said, bringing her hand to her cheek, nonplused. She and Paul had planned to go to Midge's opening together, but in the heat of the emotions tonight, she'd forgotten about it. "The children are too upset. I need to stay with them."

"May I still meet you for lunch?"

"I think not. It would be too hard."

"Ah, I see." He paused and she could hear ragged breathing. Her decision was coming hard on him, as it was on herself. She could imagine him raking his hands through his unruly thatch of gray hair. "Well, then..." He paused. "Take all the time you need," he said with compassion. Then with sadness ringing through his self-deprecating humor he said, "I'll have to be content to be like our friend Paolo. Whirling in my black inferno, just knowing you are near...my dear Francesca."

Eve bent her head and laid the receiver beside her cheek, knowing she would be whirling in hell right beside him.

* * *

The crowd of guests at the gallery was sparse but constant. The well-heeled, those with money to buy and no personal connections to the artists, were few. They walked into the gallery dressed in suits and casual clothes, probably straight from work. There wasn't much exchange; they paced through the show making comments in low voices, then left after a quick tour. Friends and family of the artists, however, were in a celebratory mood, drinking wine, laughing, lavishing compliments and staying longer. Most of the other artists were joining in, relieved that the push was over. Midge's style was more cool. She never kissed or touched or hugged strangers but she warmly greeted with a handshake those acquaintances, fellow artists, and clients who stopped by.

Edith waltzed in with a coterie of friends near six o'clock, flushed from a full dinner served with ample bottles of wine. She was wearing a coral suit with large chunks of lapiz at the neck and ears. With her hair dyed a new tawny brown, she looked to Midge like a brightly plumed bird chirping loudly among a flock of solemn black crows. Midge only laughed and caught Susan's eye when she heard her mother's voice croon above the noisy crowd, "Look over there, girls! Those are my daughter's pictures!"

Edith preened in front of her friends and it did Midge's heart good to see her mother actually proud of something she'd done. "So, where are the girls?" she asked, looking around the room. Midge knew she was referring to the Book Club. Feeling a stab of disappointment, she merely shrugged and turned her head. Nothing escaped her mother's birdlike gaze, however. Edith pursed her lips and muttered a short, "uh-huh." For the next hour Edith lavished praise on her artwork, using words like *pretty* and *cute*, doing her best to compliment her daughter even though she didn't have the vocabulary.

"It's all right, Mother," Midge said kindly. "You don't have to like it. Abstract art isn't everyone's cup of tea."

"But I do like it! Especially that one. I don't know why, exactly, but it's sexy." She sauntered over in front of the five-foot canvas. "I see a woman lying on her back. See the way the pink goes up and down in two humps? Those are the knees. And there? Those round orbs are the breasts," she said, moving closer and stretching her hand up to move it in circles near the top of the painting. "And those dark areas are the nipples…and see those long lines up there? Those are the arms lying over her head. A woman does that when she's sated, you know. Or when she's just lying there, expectant, waiting for something. It's very womanly. Beautiful. Sensual. What's it called?"

Midge listened to her mother with an open mouth. In simple language, she'd described the painting perfectly. Edith never failed to amaze her.

"Ample Knees," she replied.

Her mother tapped her lips with her fingertip and tilted her head, squinting. "Yes, yes, exactly!"

"Thank you, Mother," Midge said sincerely, turning to face her.

Edith looked up, startled. "Whatever for, dear?"

"For caring. For coming. I'm glad you're here." She meant for more than just the show and her mother knew it.

Edith's eyes misted. Then taking a deep breath, she cast a slow, assessing gaze up and down over her daughter.

Midge involuntarily stood straighter under the power of *the look*. She was wearing a new long, black silk skirt and a creamy silk blouse that complimented her tall, slender frame. Her scarlet shawl was a find from her favorite vintage shop. In pristine condition, the satin was intricately embroidered and shone with a soft patina, setting off her salt-and-pepper hair that was swept up tonight into a loose coil. Makeup was still an anathema, but she did wear silver at the neck and ears.

When Edith finished her perusal she raised one brow, made the OK sign and winked. Midge felt her breath release in a slow sigh. Then, after an air kiss on both cheeks, Edith waved her dainty fingers goodbye and went to claim her friends. The older women were clustered together staring agog at a series of life-size male nudes. Midge watched them leave, basking in the glow of her mother's approval.

Shortly after, Paul Hammond walked in. The room seemed to swell with his presence. He had a ferocious, focused energy that drew attention and made people wonder who he was, probably mistaking him for a critic. Midge was very touched that he had actually come to her show. He looked around the room, as though searching for someone, and she caught a brief, pained expression in his remarkable blue eyes. Their eyes met and his expression immediately became impassive. He was very good at masking his emotion, she thought as she smiled in welcome. They chatted briefly, but long enough that she walked away impressed with his extensive knowledge of art. Long enough, too, to make her wonder why he never once mentioned Eve's name.

Before Hammond left, he bought *Ample Knees*.

By eight o'clock Midge knew that the Book Club wasn't coming. Her disappointment went beyond pique to real hurt that her dearest friends couldn't find the time to attend such an important occasion for her. The gallery was clearing out and most of the artists had already left for private parties or to the Rose Bud for dinner. Midge gathered her things and was about to leave when she heard Susan's voice behind her.

"Are you going out with your friends?"

She turned to face her. Susan had stopped by every hour on the hour during the show as promised. At five o'clock, just to ask, How are you doing? At six, to bring her a glass of wine and the admonition, Drink up—doctor's orders. At seven, to meet her mother. And now, at closing, she had to know that Midge's friends hadn't shown.

Midge shook her head, hating the sympathy on Susan's face. Susan didn't overreact. She appeared calm and professional in her severe style of dress. She wore plain linen pants and a black silk shirt buttoned low revealing her flat, tanned chest. On her feet she wore her inevitable flat-heeled shoes.

"I think I'll head for home," Midge said, picking up her bag.

"Don't do that," Susan said. "It's been a keyed up evening. You're all wired. You can't go home yet."

"I don't want to go to the Rose Bud. I can't stand the thought of having to endure any more of that steady talk, talk, talk. It's so boring. I've had enough of that to last me a long while."

"I thought you looked ready to bolt a few times," Susan said with a laugh. "How about we go somewhere else? I'm hungry. Do you like sushi? There's a great sushi bar just a few blocks from here. We could walk." She waited and when Midge didn't immediately reply she added, "Come on, Midge. I don't want to go alone. Be a friend."

Midge looked at her and understood unequivocally what the invitation could lead to. This was more than just the possibility of another friendship.

But, did she really want another friendship? Tonight's disappointment in the Book Club triggered a knifelike reaction that cut through the *shoulds* and *should nots* imprinted on her consciousness. Sure her friends were special to her. She loved them, and she would forgive them, she knew, in time. Yet who was she kidding? Annie, Eve, Doris, even Gabriella—they would never provide for her what was missing in her life: touch, emotional and physical closeness, true intimacy. They all had someone to love in their lives. Someone to hold them. Midge wanted to love someone, too. She wanted to be held, too. She was through with this lonely life of celibacy. She was done with being cold and alone night after night. She was tired of waiting for the phone to ring.

She looked into Susan's face. Her pale eyes gazed back, watchful, waiting, expectant. A half smile hovered on her full, sensuous mouth. More arresting, however, was her sense of physical certainty. She had a bearing and directness that was not unlike Paul Hammond's, an aura of intelligence and potency that was very attractive in both men and women.

Susan tilted her head, her eyes sparkling, and with a bright smile, she put out her hand.

Midge felt the light of that smile crack through her icy composure. She tightened her shawl around her shoulders, lifted her chin and, returning the smile, took Susan's hand.

Eve awoke the following morning feeling depressed and lonely, though she didn't know quite why. Then she remembered Paul and the confrontation with the children and it all came back to her in a disappointing rush. It was Saturday, so she didn't have to rise early and prepare breakfast for the children and dress to go to work. She could lie in bed a while longer, perhaps rise and lazily brew some coffee, even take the time to grind the beans for a richer taste. The radio clicked on automatically and she mentally flogged herself for forgetting to turn off the alarm last night. The *Star-Spangled Banner* was playing as a backdrop to the disc jockeys' mindless banter about fireworks mishaps they'd had as boys.

Eve's hand held back from turning off the radio, recalling with mild surprise that, oh yes, it was the Fourth of July. Of course she knew the date, but with all the emotion of last night, she'd put the holiday out of her mind. The Fourth—surely the children would have a hard time of it today. Eve's mind began darting from one idea to the next fending off the panic of how to handle a holiday that had always been a family affair, chiefly stewarded by Tom. This was his favorite day of the whole year, preferred even to Christmas. He spent days, weeks, in preparation.

She rose and dressed quickly, choosing blue denim shorts, a white T-shirt and, though cringing a bit, red cotton socks. For the pièce de résistance, she pulled out from her jewelry box a pair of enamel earrings of the American flag that Tom had given her years ago. It had been a long time since she wore anything so blatantly holidayish. When the children were little she liked to dress up for their sakes: red and hearts on Valentine's day, Christmas sweaters, a witch hat on Halloween. When they grew older, however, they also grew embarrassed to be seen in public with her when she wore anything that drew attention, so she ceased with the holiday getups. Slipping the flag earrings onto her ears, she thought that today they could all use a little cornball humor.

She prepared a hearty breakfast of eggs and bacon, cut up some oranges, and calling out, "Rise and shine!" roused the children for breakfast. They came tumbling out of their bedrooms like clumsy puppies, rubbing the sleep from their eyes and wondering aloud why they had to get up so early on a Saturday. Her heart skipped a beat when she saw Finney dressed only in his long, cotton boxers. His chest and arms were still so thin but his shoulders were gaining in breadth and his neck and jawline were more strongly defined. Even his hair was becoming a richer, darker brown. Her son was losing his little-boyishness. Hints of the man he would someday become were more and more evident. He was becoming a remarkably handsome young man and he resembled his father more and more each day.

"I have a wonderful idea," she announced, turning to the stove and serving breakfast onto plates. There was little response other than a few yawns and groggy gazes, but she was gratified to see that they shuffled to the table and sat obligingly without further complaint. "We haven't been to visit your father's ashes in a long time. Seeing as it's the Fourth, I thought we might do just that. Together. Then afterward we could go straight to the lakefront and spend the day at the beach. We could just lie around till dark, then watch the fireworks from the shoreline. We'll make a day of it. What do you say?"

They looked surprised by the suggestion, especially Bronte whose face, unlike Finney's, appeared more vulnerable and childlike this morning. She was an utter failure at masking her emotions and Eve witnessed a myriad of thoughts and feelings flitter across her face, most likely a war between memories of her father and her current ambivalent feelings about her mother.

"Sure," Finney said with a slight shrug, diving into his eggs. "I want to go to the cemetery and all, but I can't go to the fireworks. I'm going with Nick back to Michigan, remember? He invited me last week. A bunch of us are going. Remember? You said I could go."

"Oh, yes, I remember," she replied with a flush of disappointment. She had readily agreed last week when the invitation first came up. With Finney in Michigan, she planned on Bronte staying with Sarah which would then open up Saturday night for her to stay with Paul. It had all worked out so beautifully, she had thought. Now, of course, all those plans had changed and she'd completely forgotten about Finney's plans.

Eve turned back to her daughter. Oh please come with me, Bronte, she thought to herself. This would be exactly what the two of them needed. A little time together, mother and daughter. She'd make it a special holiday. They'd go to the lakefront festivities all day and stroll arm in arm like friends through Grant Park, eat vendor food, listen to live blues or big band music, and when the sun went down they'd join the festive crowds and make oohs and aahs at the fireworks. She'd make her little girl happy, deliriously happy.

She'd make Tom proud.

"What do you say? Will you come with me? Just the two of us?"

Bronte's face brightened with a smile and with what Eve could only perceive as a second chance.

"Yes," Bronte replied brightly. "Sounds like fun."

Eve smiled radiantly, feeling the fireworks already exploding in colors in her heart.

All Saints Cemetery was a short drive from Oakley. Nonetheless, it was a trip Eve and the children rarely took. It seemed the right thing to do today, however, especially for the children. Out of respect for Tom's memory on this, his favorite holiday, the three of them selected a bouquet of red, white and blue carnations mixed with flags and sparklers that went beyond tacky straight to ridiculous. She had a good time watching Finney and Bronte laugh and kid how their father would have gotten a kick out of it. It was good for them to keep him alive in their minds, she thought as she drove through the heavy black wrought-iron gates of the cemetery.

They strolled leisurely along the winding path that led to the mausoleum, taking turns telling a favorite memory they had of Tom and his fireworks exploits. They were laughing at Finney's account of the whistling firework that had backfired and chased Tom across the yard when Eve looked up and spotted a woman just leaving the glass entrance of the mausoleum. She was tall and attractive, with Irish pale skin lightly splattered with freckles and doelike hazel eyes. But what caught Eve's attention was her full head of remarkable red hair. Eve stopped suddenly, feeling her heart in her throat, as recognition blazed across her mind. The children, one on either side of her, stopped a step or two later, looking back at her with confusion.

The woman took a step down the entrance stairs and looked up, absently glancing their way. Then she, too, halted suddenly with a stunned expression on her face, confirming Eve's suspicion. Time seemed to stand still as the two women eyed one another, neither one of them offering the slightest move of recognition. Eve could feel her children's gazes on her, sensing a connection between the two women.

"Mom?" Bronte said, her voice hesitant.

The woman, seemingly propelled by the sound of Bronte's voice, walked quickly down the stairs and turned onto a path that went in the opposite direction.

"Who was she?" Finney wanted to know.

"I don't know exactly," Eve replied honestly, watching the slender figure in a sleek ivory summer suit with matching sandals and bag disappear around a thatch of flowering hydrangeas. Without question, that woman was the woman in the photograph she'd found in Tom's filebox. Who was she? It was all she could do not to take off running after her and demand that *she* answer Finney's question.

"A friend of your father's, I believe."

"What's she doing here?"

"Visiting Daddy, obviously," Bronte said with exasperation. But she, too, looked to her mother for confirmation, confusion and a hint of doubt in her eyes.

"Your father had lots of friends and associates," Eve said evenly, despite the uncertainty she felt in her own mind. As they proceeded, she looked down at her clothing and felt a sharp pang of embarrassment at having been seen by that woman in her ridiculous holiday ensemble.

As they stood together in silence before the square that bore Tom's name, Eve dismissed all thoughts of the nameless woman. She was insignificant at the moment. She thought instead how she never felt Tom was there among his ashes and how going to a stone mausoleum to see his name carved into a square box never brought her any solace. But it was overpowering to be there with her children, to watch them bend their heads and clasp their hands as though in prayer. These were his children. He lived on in them. They had been a family.

Tom, her heart cried out, what are you doing in there? These children need their father. Your children need you here, alive. How can you not be part of their futures?

It was expected that he, being the man, would go first. But they'd always thought death would come later, when what hair he had left was thin and white and the children were living with their own families and they were both stooped with age. He wasn't supposed to die young and vibrant with young children and a future.

Still, when they discussed such things, he'd made her promise to have his ashes placed in the cylinder of a large-shell firework so he could explode against the sky in a bright gold willow pattern and his ashes would scatter across the earth. They used to laugh that if there was a heady wind, a few ashes might fall on folks' heads and shoulders and the children could laugh and say, "Oh, that's Dad all over."

It seemed wrong for his ashes to sit in a canister in a stone mausoleum.

"I'm sorry, Tom," she whispered. "I'm doing the best that I can."

Then tapping her children's shoulders she bent to kiss their cheeks and led them out into the sunshine.

Fourteen

She turns and looks a moment in the glass,
Hardly aware of her departed lover;
Her brain allows one half-formed thought to pass:
"Well, now that's done: and I'm glad it's over."
When lovely woman stoops to folly and
Paces about her room again, alone,
She smoothes her hair with automatic hand,
And puts a record on the gramophone.

—T. S. Eliot, *The Waste Land*

Doris stood before the full-length mirror in her bedroom buttoning the long row of large wooden buttons on her red linen dress. She was complaining to R.J. for the hundredth time how thoughtless it was of them not to invite Eve Porter to their Fourth of July party.

"She's been our friend for years. I feel horrible."

"She'd just feel out of place," he replied, using that tone that implied she was being mindless and should listen to his reasoning. "Her life has changed. Face it, this isn't her circle any longer."

"Just because Tom is dead doesn't mean she is. She's

my friend and I should have invited her.'' Doris's voice
rang with misgivings, but they both knew this tirade was
but an assuaging of her conscience, that she'd already long
ago given in to her husband's will.

R.J. was angling for a huge development planned for
the River North area of Chicago. It was a major leap for
him and he had invited all the key players—politicians and
builders he needed in his pocket. He'd overseen the guest
list, the menu, even the decorations himself.

Doris did up the last button with none of the excitement
she usually felt before one their parties. She'd always
thought of herself as the consummate hostess, prided herself on this accomplishment. This time, however, she'd
been treated by R.J. little better than an assistant, just another Bridges employee.

She raised her eyes at the face she saw in the mirror,
hating it. Rather than lose weight for the party as she'd
planned, she'd put on a few more pounds. She just couldn't
seem to stop the upward slide of the scale. No amount of
makeup could disguise the doughiness of her skin. Her
once beautiful eyes seemed to have shrunk into her face.
Even her neck...

"Honey," R.J. called, approaching her.

She quickly dropped her hand from her neck and looked
up to see him advance toward her. Her eyes met his in the
mirror. She was surprised to see him not scowling, but
smiling, and in his hand was a large square jeweler's box.
She recognized the unique blue color and the thick white
ribbon and her heart jump-started with a jolt of anticipation.

"R.J., for me?"

"For you. A small token of my appreciation. You've
worked hard for this party and I didn't want you to think
I didn't notice."

Her breath sucked in, her heart flip-flopped, and all her

earlier thoughts dissipated like storm clouds after the sun came out. She mumbled unintelligible expressions of delight as she opened the box, her hands trembling. Inside she found a stunning black pearl necklace, each pearl the size of a knuckle. This was no trinket of appeasement. Tears sprang to her eyes and she reached for a tissue off her vanity lest her mascara run.

"I don't know what to say. This is so beautiful! So unexpected!"

"You don't have to say anything. I don't thank you enough, dear. You do such a good job at these things, everyone always loves you. That includes me, you know."

These verbal pearls were more precious to her than the Tahitian ones. Overwhelmed, she reached out to take his hand. Putting it against her cheek, she closed her eyes and pressed her lips against his palm. "Thank you, darling."

As he fastened the clasp around her neck she listened attentively as he told her the names of the wives he wanted her to court that evening, including little tidbits of gossip she might need to know. She watched him in the mirror, his face intent and unusually anxious. Doris thought how selfish it had been of her to only think of herself and not to realize how important this night was for him. Her gaze fell to the necklace; the pearls really were magnificent. How could she ever thank him? Perhaps, she thought, she could help him more, get involved more with his work? But the children...

Well, Bobby was in college now and Sarah wasn't a child any longer. Wasn't Bronte proving to be responsible for Eve? Yes, perhaps she should help Sarah assume more self-responsibility and give R.J. more of her time.

Her mind began racing with possibilities. She and R.J. united again! She'd make it work. She'd discuss it with him tonight. After the party. Yes, she decided, her effusive delight building her fantasy. Tonight at the party she'd sparkle; he wouldn't be able to help but notice what an asset she was to him. Then she'd quietly set aside one bottle of champagne. Then, after the guests were gone, she'd wear a pretty negligee and offer herself to him. Totally. Her time—her body...

Her toes squeezed in her shoes with excitement and hope as she forced her body to remain still. R.J. was cursing under his breath and fumbling for his "damn eyeglasses" in order to see the small clasp of the necklace. She knew he hated the indignities of growing older: the loss of hair, the dimming of eyesight, the absentmindedness. Her eyes softened with affection as she watched him slip the reading glasses on and bend over her neck. Dear man, she thought with a gush of affection, remembering the young man he once was, loving the older man he was today. This man was hers.

She sucked in her stomach and set her jaw. She would change things. She'd make herself more interesting. And tomorrow she'd begin that diet....

Annie was teetering on the edge of sanity. Any lucidity that remained as she sat in her garden waiting for John to return home had dissipated with the last wisps of daylight. John finally walked in the house just after dusk in a whirlwind, dropping luggage in the foyer, showering, changing into his dinner clothes with barely a word. He was a man on a mission. R.J. expected him at the house early for the party; there were plans to discuss, last-minute details to sort through.

Annie sat in a chair with her knees close to her chest and her arms wrapped around them, watching him pace. She was still and quiet, but inside there was an implosion of her feelings. She was being drawn inward by the density of her secret. Cancer was not news one could just blurt out. Such news required a quiet moment, the two of them seated in chairs, cups of tea in their hands and plenty of time for the right words and responses.

So telling herself that she could get through this evening, she rose and showered, slipped into a sparkly black slip dress chosen at random from the closet, and stepped into a pair of gold leather mules. She couldn't bear to fuss in the mirror tonight—what did it matter? She simply smoothed red lipstick on her lips. The brilliant color against the paleness of her skin enhanced the odd brightness in her eyes.

"John, I want to leave early tonight," she said as they were driving to the Bridges house. "I'm not feeling well. And I want to talk to you."

He turned his attention to her, scanning her face. "Sure, okay. As soon as I can get away. You look a little pale. Anything up?"

She saw immediately that he thought she might be pregnant. The realization stung and she swung her head to look out the window into the blackness. "I just want to go home early. We'll talk then."

Doris greeted them at the door in a queenly manner that was out of place, even insulting, to Annie and John. When Annie told her plainly that they'd be cutting out early, Doris looked at her with an incredulous expression. Then, turning to John, she said with insinuation that R.J. was expecting him to spend the entire evening.

"We will, don't worry, Doris," he replied quickly with a disarming smile.

Annie stood with her arms at her sides, speechless.

Doris sent her a sidelong glance of triumph.

"Do what you want, John," Annie said, furious at the tremor in her voice. "*I'm* going home early."

Before anyone could respond, R.J. stepped into the room with his usual bluster. "John!" he roared jovially. "Where

the hell have you been? Come over here and see what I've
got planned!''

John cast her a loaded glance, then turned and walked
toward R.J., all enthusiasm and smiles.

More guests arrived and Annie, stuck for the moment,
chatted rather stiffly until she could retreat somewhere and
hide. Not that it wasn't a lovely party. Doris and R.J. had
gone all out with the flowers, decorations and food. Red,
white and blue candles were cleverly positioned everywhere, creating a magical effect in the house and onto the
extended patio. The buffet table was a sumptuous feast and
champagne flowed liberally. Good lighting, good food and
good champagne—the recipe for a successful party. Yet
Annie couldn't enjoy any of it. She felt outside of it all,
an "other." It was physically painful for her to be here
tonight.

She wandered through the house, nursing her glass of
champagne. She didn't know most of these witty, chic,
well-dressed people who lit up the Bridgeses' landscape
like fireflies, nor did she want to. She had nothing against
the other guests, they all seemed perfectly pleasant in a
nondescript sort of way. While the men and women came
in all sizes and shapes, the common ground here was
status, chiefly determined by wealth. Although it would
have been considered vulgar or in bad taste to talk about
money—either her own or someone else's—in subtle ways
a person's income, connections and status were always the
first thing one learned about someone else. She could
imagine Mrs. Bennet in *Pride and Prejudice* whispering
behind her fan, "He's worth ten thousand pounds a year!"

She knew the Bridges house well, had been to many
Book Club meetings here, yet each time she visited she
couldn't help but be impressed by its size, charm and dis-
tinction. This was a home of generations of living, and the
attention to detail was all Doris. How Doris loved this

house, took pride in it, as she did in her children. John felt this way about their Frank Lloyd Wright house, too.

Why couldn't she feel attached to her own home? To her it was a nice enough place, an attractive four walls and a roof. A place to hang her hat. Yet, despite the work they'd put into it, she could leave it at any moment. Success to her wasn't about things but about the people she surrounded herself with. Success was a state of mind.

And a bankbook, she thought with a cruel realism that she was never afraid to own up to.

She eyed the door with longing. She didn't want to be here. Idle conversation felt beyond her tonight. Her brain throbbed with her diagnosis, and the fear and feelings it carried, as though it were going to burst any moment and bleed out her secret all over Doris's Oriental rug. She felt edgy, too, and anxious about the conversation she'd have with John later that night. He had to face the fact that hard, uncertain times lay ahead, that a baby wasn't going to happen. Not for them.

That thought was a heartbreaker. John had spent months hovering around her, checking her temperature and calling Dr. Gibson regularly, nagging her with questions about what they still might try. Annie couldn't stand that the whole effort was over, that her body was out of her control. She'd failed. No amount of positive thought could change that. Along with that came the onslaught of thoughts about her future—what was she working for? What was she leaving behind? The course of their future had been irrevocably changed.

She shuddered and finished her wine, dispatching to a remote corner of her mind any thought of the disease that riddled her body. She couldn't go into that dark place now. Not here. Not yet.

A few couples passed by carrying plates full of filet and salads. Annie's stomach turned. The sight and smell of food made her nauseous. Thank God this wasn't a sit-down dinner, she thought, moving to the fresh air outdoors. Then she'd be trapped twirling food around a plate between two strangers. She craned her neck to scan the milling guests. She needed to talk to someone she cared about. John apparently didn't have time for her, she thought with bitterness. Well, screw him. Where was Eve?

Annie reached for another flute of champagne, hoping the bubbles would have their usual soothing effect. She drank the liquid in gulps, ignoring the shocked expression of a white-haired woman in a long dress that looked like it had been pulled out of mothballs for one last tour of duty. She moved away, hanging on a while longer for John's sake, keeping an eye open for Eve. She hadn't seen her since the last Book Club meeting. Why was everyone so busy lately?

R.J.'s voice boomed over the crowd, calling like a carnival barker for everyone to face the river for the fireworks show. Annie moved lethargically to the edge of the patio and stood alone in the humid night with her wineglass. She sipped her drink, swatted mosquitoes and looked out with a desolate feeling as black as the darkness beyond. Somewhere out there lay the Bridgeses' large, prime piece of real estate, and beyond it a winding road, and beyond that, a dense forest preserve where mosquitoes bred and frolicked and the Des Plaines River meandered by.

John came to her side as the first firework shell burst across the sky. Against his dark-navy linen jacket, his blond hair and white, collarless shirt seemed iridescent in the moonlight.

"Hi there, stranger," he said, wrapping his arms around her, as excited as a boy. "It's going to be a great show. Just great." He whispered in her ear exactly how much it cost R.J. to purchase the show of large shells.

Annie turned her head and narrowed her eyes. John's

eyes were bright against his tan and there was no concealing his delight in the telling of the exorbitant amount. It seemed as though, in some odd way, he participated in the glory by virtue of his association with the man. *Oh, John,* she wanted to scream at him. *That's all money he's not paying you!* A shell burst like thunder and she steeled herself against the explosions in her heart, turning her head toward the sky to view a bright-red chrysanthemum pierce the darkness.

"Are you still feeling off?" he asked when the spectacular display was over. "You seem kind of down."

"I told you I didn't feel well, but that didn't seem to register. Or matter. No, no," she said, brushing away his excuse. "Never mind. Have you seen Eve?"

John shook his head but his soft blue eyes appeared troubled. "I don't think she's been invited."

Annie drew herself up. "Not invited? Eve? Why not?"

John anxiously looked over his shoulder to see who stood around them. "Shhh… R.J.'s looking for legitimate prospects tonight. This is a business dinner."

"Don't shush me! Business dinner, my ass. Look over there. Mrs. Davy. And the Lincolns. The Kochs. They're neighbors."

"They're also on the Riverton planning board. R.J. didn't want extraneous people."

She narrowed her eyes. "R.J. didn't want unimportant people." She could feel her blood boil, and once that happened, it was like a geyser spouting. "What a proud, arrogant prig! And Doris is no better. You can't tell me that if Tom Porter had left his wife well-off and she lived down the block that she wouldn't be here tonight. Screw this. Screw them. Anyone who thinks the gentry doesn't exist in America today is naive."

The subject inflamed Annie. She grew up having her nose rubbed in class difference and despised it. Just as she despised the fact that Eve hadn't been invited tonight. Had she even suspected the shun, Annie would never have come.

"How could Doris not include Eve, especially now when she needs her friends and connections more than ever? What the hell kind of a friend is that?"

She'd said this to John heatedly within earshot of Doris. He looked up with alarm, tugged at her arm and drew her aside.

"Keep your voice down," he said in a low, strangled voice. "And that's enough of that. You're getting drunk." He took her wineglass away and downed the remainder in one angry gulp.

"I'm only just getting started," she fired back. "And don't ever take a wineglass from my hand again."

"R.J. is uptight enough. I don't need to worry about you, too." He must have seen her fierce expression because he looked down and said in an appeasing tone, "What does it matter if Eve isn't here tonight?"

She opened her mouth to explain but a couple they knew approached. While John greeted them warmly, Annie looked over his shoulder and spotted Doris standing in a cluster a few feet away. She was standing as straight as a board, smiling stiffly and speaking to the mayor and his wife. Annie knew by her high color that Doris had overheard. Good, she thought.

Annie, impatient to continue her argument, shooed the couple away with a few choice, cool remarks. Then turning to John she said in a loud, deliberate voice, "I want to go home. Now."

John was furious, and grabbing her elbow, walked her to a quiet corner. His face was red and he blurted out a cuss word she'd never heard him use before.

"You had no business being rude to those people."

"Who are they anyway? They mean nothing to me."

"Now who's being a snob?"

"You deliberately misunderstood me."

"I understood you. Perfectly. Now understand this. This party isn't about you. Or Eve. Or even Doris. It's business and R.J. will have my head on a platter if I leave now."

"Ah, do as R.J. says...whatever R.J. wants.... Typical," she muttered.

"Cut it out, Annie. This is my job. I like these people. I work with them. I'm sorry if you've got it in your mind to hate everyone here. Me included. But I don't. So go if you want to. Take the keys. I really don't care. But I'm not leaving."

"I don't hate everyone," she said archly, her sarcasm ringing. "Just two people in particular."

He paused and his eyes, bright with frustration, bore into hers. "It's always about you, isn't it, Annie? What you need. What you want. For once, Annie, do something for me." Then he released her arm abruptly, almost hurting her, and stomped off, his blond hair bouncing along his neck.

So she stayed. Begrudgingly. For John's sake. But she swore she wouldn't be social for another minute. Not one more false, "Oh hello!" Not another, "I'd like you to meet...!"

The fireworks were over; the evening was winding down. John had joined the boys smoking cigars on the verandah. Women clustered, waving hands in the air as they spoke. Annie looked around, desolate, emotionally unable to scare up someone to talk to about nothing. If only she had a good book she could escape the frivolous gossip.

Well, why not escape, she thought? Perhaps no one would notice if she slipped quietly away. She scowled, firing up her resentment. Well, to hell if they did. A waiter strolled by carrying a half-empty tray of champagne flutes.

Annie hoisted two off the tray, muttering curses at John, then strolled away from the blazing lights of the house toward the welcoming, gravel-strewn trail that was seductively lit by well-placed, lily-shaped lanterns. She traveled slowly down the gently sloping hillside into the dark.

It was a lovely summer night, soft and introspective, perfect for a solitary stroll. She swung her arms wide, balancing the two flutes like dumbbells, delighting in the way the air cooled the soft underskin of her arms. In the secretive shadows, alone among the green, she felt a lightening of the oppression that gripped her at the party. She was free! The mood shift was electric and rippled through her. She swayed with drowsiness, yet her senses felt heightened. Awakened. Pulsating. The late-evening breeze was sweet with the scent of Doris's lush perennials, the pool's water and the freshly mown grass. It drowned her senses. Here and there in the distance, fireflies glowed against the purpling sky and dense foliage. In the air, the humidity hung thick like a moist tropical fog.

The long, oval pool was a good distance from the house, a secluded enclave encircled by an army of tall weeping cypress trees and countless evergreen shrubs. Walking into the hideaway in the moonlight was like entering another world. The dark surface of the swimming pool resembled a pond. The stars reflected in the water with the glitter of jewels. A soft spray of water from a fountain in its center caught in the wind and sprinkled her with its refreshing coolness, beckoning her near.

She reached the pool's edge, then bent low, tottering slightly, testing the water with her fingertips. It was warm, velvety and very, very inviting. And it seemed the fireflies were humming inside of her head now, tickling her, making her giggle. She felt light-headed and languorous as she stretched her fingers farther in the water. How utterly delightful the simple sensation of water running through fingers could be. She dribbled water down her face, along her neck, feeling it pool between her breasts. Looking out, she felt she could skim across the sheet of water on the tips of her toes. Impulsively, she kicked off her shoes far into the darkness, laughing when she heard one thud, then another, lost forever.

"Marvelous," she sighed, sticking her toes under the surface. The water felt delicious where she swirled a figure eight. It might have simply been the wine, or defiance against John and Doris and R.J. Or it might have been the impact of realizing that her time on earth might be limited and she'd better enjoy every moment. Annie felt a loosening inside and opened up to the child she once was, the girl who sang to trees and hunted for leprechauns and fairies. That child was buried deep inside but tonight, under this magical moon, she felt the girl struggling to emerge. She giggled, hiccuped and spread her arms wide in a wingspan, faceup to the moonlight, laughing.

"I am youth! I am joy! I am a little bird who has broken his egg!" she called out, reciting favorite lines from *Peter Pan*. She swirled around in a circle, then arched on her toes at the edge of the pool. Swaying, she leaned too far over the edge. Her balance was lost. She flapped her arms like a bird about to take flight, but in her heart she knew she was going down.

"Doris, have you seen Annie?"

Doris, seated at a card table with friends, swung her head to gaze up toward the familiar voice. John's expression was part worry, part annoyance. Her lips pursed, remembering Annie's strident demand that she be taken home. Annie's words about Eve had burned Doris deep, shamed her because they scorched away all her rationalizations to R.J. Annie Blake was right. She didn't invite her dear friend Eve and it was indefensible. Annie Blake had character. And that was more credit than she gave herself at the moment, though she'd never admit it to Annie.

"Did she go home?" she asked.

John's face tightened. "I hope not."

"I'm sorry, John," she replied curtly. "I haven't seen her in quite a while." Her gaze shifted to search outside the family room to the patio where a few guests milled about. The big guns had left already. Only a few close friends and stragglers remained. Suspicion flared, and she suddenly narrowed her search. Her gaze picked off the pink, drowsy faces with more urgency. She turned to face John again.

"Have you seen R.J.?"

Their eyes met. In that moment's communication, they both sensed trouble.

"Well, she's probably somewhere outside," John said in a rush. He was eager to move on. "I'll just go take a look."

"Yes, do that," Doris replied, distracted. After he went outdoors, Doris stood and went to the window to again scan the grounds: her perennial beds, her herb garden, her greenhouse, her play area filled with swing sets and climbing equipment no child had used in a decade. Out there were acres of meticulously landscaped and maintained grounds that had won awards in the past when gardening was her hobby. A few guests mingled along the fringes of the patio, one or two strolled to inspect her greenhouse, but nowhere in her sites did she spot her husband.

Back at the card table she heard a swell of laughter. Robanna Scott, the mayor's wife, was telling fortunes with Tarot cards. "Here is the Belladonna, the lady of situations," she was saying with dramatic flair. When Doris returned to the table, Robanna turned another card. It was the Hanged Man. "Fear death by water," she said.

Doris felt a sudden chill. The other three women leaned forward in their seats, while Doris slipped out the door.

Annie hit the water with a loud splash. She sputtered, found her feet, then, catching her balance, leaned back and laughed loudly. The young girl she once was slipped out to splash and kick unselfconsciously in the pool.

She wanted some fun again in her life! She wanted understanding. Like a child, she wanted something else, too, but couldn't put a name to it. It was elusive, just out of her reach. She only knew that if she didn't laugh, she'd cry.

Her dress clung like a second skin, constricting her. Looking around she felt safe in the deep isolation of the pool and the tall privacy hedge. No one else was here. An impulse triggered. Why the hell not? She tugged sloppily at the dress, slipping underwater a few times, until she was free of it. Then with a tremendous whoosh, she tossed all seven hundred dollars worth of ruined fabric into the wind with a casual laugh.

Yes! This was how life was meant to be experienced, she sang in her mind. Exultant. Raw and free. Natural. Not bound by calendars and thermometers, court dates and drywall. She delighted in the cool ripples cascading through her thighs and swirling around buoyant breasts.

"Ah, Mama and Daddy, I am your child after all," she said aloud, remembering the many nights she'd watched, appalled, while her hippie parents skinny-dipped in the pond.

She arched her back and floated, feeling the cool night air kiss her nipples, then swinging her arms, she stroked back, back through her memories.

Mama and Daddy...Drs. Henry and Lydia Blake. Her pot-smoking, free-living parents were Jungian therapists in the sixties, then later hooked up with Gestalt, then grad-

ually moved into Orthomolecular. In the mid-seventies
they founded a group therapy home—*don't call it a com-
mune!*—for troubled teens. These kids had all sorts of
problems that fell under the era's wastebasket diagnosis of
schizophrenia. No insurance covered their stay at Mill
House in Oregon, and the stay was never brief or cheap.

Mill House—home sweet home. Annie still cringed after
all these years. Mill House was a rambling farmhouse on
a crooked stone foundation overflowing with hemp rugs,
garage sale furniture, macramé and bizarre teens. They ate
what they grew in their immense garden—a strictly veg-
etarian menu—and what they didn't grow they bought at
the local co-op. Annie never knew what fast food was until
she came to Chicago. For her, meals consisted of various
kinds of beans, lentil soup, soy products, whole grains and
sprouts on everything, all taken with fistfuls of vitamins.
She could never rid her olfactory memories of the stale
smell of cigarette smoke, peculiar body odor and farts that
were pervasive throughout the house.

Nor could she remember one heartfelt conversation with
her parents; it was all psychobabble. They weren't bad
people, Annie knew now, they were just bad parents. Drs.
Henry and Lydia Blake placed their focus on their troubled
kids, and in the shuffle, they never realized that their own
child was growing up neglected and angry. One would
think that in this warm, supportive environment Annie
would have acquired throngs of new brothers and sisters
and thrived.

Life was rarely that easy. As troubled as these pam-
pered, wealthy teenagers were, most were never so sick
they didn't let her know—in ways only adolescents
could—that as the daughter of the therapists, she was considered "the help." While other children her age were
watching *Lost in Space* and *The Brady Bunch* on television, she was living *Lost in Life* and *The Crazy Bunch*.

It all came to an ugly head at the age of thirteen, a time when her body was blossoming and her insecurities were raging along with her hormones. One surly, acne-ridden, mean-spirited seventeen-year-old boy trapped her in the bathroom and placed his hands on her small breasts and the small, smooth mound between her legs, molesting her. He probably would have raped her if it hadn't been the only bathroom on the floor and someone else had to use it. She ran crying into her parents' office, spilling out her story in half sentences and fits of tears. When she demanded that he be kicked out of the home, they'd refused. They used all sorts of the psychotherapists' phrases she heard all the time, *He was acting out, he was hypomanic, of course the behavior was inappropriate but*... They argued that the boy wasn't well and needed their understanding and help. They assured her he was feeling very remorseful. They promised they would increase the dosage of vitamins and medication.

All she heard was that no one was defending her. No one cared how *she* felt, or whether *she* was safe. Even as a child she could cut through the lies to the cold truth: the boy was rich, his family paid good money for him to live at Mill House. In a white, blinding fury Annie had stuffed what clothes would fit into her backpack and stolen money from petty cash. Without a backward glance, she rode a Greyhound bus from Oregon to Illinois, straight to the west side of Chicago where a return address on an old Christmas card led her to her grandparents.

It had been a turning point in her life. She never went back; rarely communicated with her parents despite their many heartfelt letters. She could never forgive them for not putting their own child's needs over strangers'. Even after all these years, Annie couldn't face them. Last she heard they were taking in boarders, still seeing a few patients and living on a shoestring. She'd left that carefree, dreamer of a girl behind in Oregon as well, having figured out that kid was a loser destined for a painful life.

Annie reached the length of the pool, then flipping over, breaststroked her way back to the shallow end. The wine was swirling in her brain with the power and danger of a whirlpool. Common sense told her to get out of the water and back on dry land. No novice to the ups and downs of artificial stimulants, Annie obeyed. She rose from the pool, her long hair slicked against the sides of her face and shoulders and her pink nipples hard and erect, like a ripe Venus from the seas.

Or so R. J. Bridges thought.

From the corner of his eye he'd watched Annie Blake swipe a couple of flutes of champagne and head all by herself for the pool. Typical, he thought with an admiring chuckle. He'd been watching Annie Blake all evening, as was his custom. He found her different from most of the women he knew. A maverick. Bright, insolent, refreshing, with a tongue that could lash out unexpectedly. He'd always dreamed of feeling that pink, pointed tongue lash out on him—between his lips, his neck, trailing down to where he wanted her tongue the most. His business was finished for the night, so he'd grabbed a flute of champagne and followed her down. He was feeling pretty cocky. He'd all but nailed down the deal.

And the River North project wasn't the only thing he wanted to nail tonight.

Annie slicked the dripping hair from her face and immediately hunted for a towel. The pool area was dimly lit by the moon overhead but she could see enough to figure out that Sarah Bridges had had a party here earlier and that the teenagers hadn't bothered to pick up. Bowls of salsa and dip sat on the table beside platters of soggy chips and pretzels. Apparently they were too lazy to pick up their towels, either—a slip she was grateful for. Annie scuttled directly over to grab one. She wrapped the long towel around herself and tucked it in like a sarong.

Feeling decent, she sauntered around the beautiful, blue-tiled pool in search of her dress and shoes. Where was John, she wondered? He'd love this. He could skim across a pool with his long back arched like a porpoise. He'd been a competitive swimmer all through college; the butterfly was his specialty. She'd always appreciated the long, lean, sinewy lines of a swimmer's body. The memory of their recent fight lowered her shoulders and her mood. The sorrow physically hurt.

A scuffling noise sounded near the lounge chairs. Annie crouched, tightening her towel. "John?" she called out.

There was no answer. She stood still, listening to the night sounds. All was quiet save for the song of crickets and the backbeat of music from the house. She walked to the lounge chairs, calling out "Who's there?" but no one replied.

It must have been an animal, she thought, feeling the evening breeze raise the hairs on her arms and neck. A cat, or maybe a dog? Whatever, it was gone now. She felt so tired the droplets of water seemed to weigh her down. She slunk into a strappy lounge chair and stretched out her long legs. The hell with John and his party, she thought, yawning. Right now, she felt like closing her eyes and...

"Is this seat taken?"

She bolted up, grasping the arms of the chair.

"Sorry," R.J. said with a chuckle. "Didn't mean to scare you."

"What are you doing here?"

"I live here."

"Well, go on back to your party," she said, leaning back again and closing her eyes. "I'm taking a nap." She pried open one eye and said suspiciously, "How long have you been here?"

"Not long."

She sniffed, adjusting her towel higher. "Just long enough, I'll bet. Do you always creep up on ladies?"

"Depends on the lady."

He was smiling, not lecherously, more like someone enjoying the game of cat and mouse. He was a big man, tall, broad-shouldered, tan, with that sexiness in an older man who stays fit. He wore his confidence well.

"May I sit down?"

"What if I said no?"

He tilted his head and his gaze swept her body with an audacity she found oddly scintillating.

"I'd say that, considering this is my property, you have *cojones*."

She raised her brow. "And I'd say, given what you undoubtedly just saw a moment ago, you know that I don't. So let's not pretend you're not a voyeur."

"Ha! Let's not pretend you're not an exhibitionist."

"I prefer to call myself a free spirit," she said, but her half smile gave her away. "Go ahead, take a seat if you want. As you said, it's your place. Only, are you sure you want to sit by lowly little ol' me? I'm not a player."

He lowered himself into the chair, choosing to sit upright with his arms resting on his knees. Again, she felt his gaze creep slowly up and down her body. Instinctively, she tugged the top of the towel.

"You could be."

"Look, R.J., I don't know what you might be thinking but..."

He widened his eyes with innocence. "What? What did you think I meant? I'm talking about John's career. He has such potential. He could climb higher, especially with your support."

She remained silent a moment, considering. His expression was friendly, that of a good, concerned boss. A neighbor, a friend. Someone sincerely interested in her husband's welfare. Annie's lips twisted. He was good. He almost had her believing him.

"He could climb a lot higher with a decent salary," she said dryly. "And benefits. Hell, why not be really decent and throw in a pension plan?"

R.J. guffawed and she felt his hand on her kneecap, then felt him pat it. It was a seemingly careless gesture, one a friend might make while laughing. One moment it was on the skin, the next it wasn't. Very smoothly done. He talked on as though nothing had happened, about the grand projects he planned for himself and John, schemes that would make them all rich.

She leaned back in the sultry night air and listened to the cicadas chirp as a background to his grandstanding. Another time, another place, another age, she might have found R.J. attractive. Powerful men had an aura that was an aphrodisiac for her. Tall, short, fat, thin, balding or as hairy as a gorilla, it didn't matter. It was the power—and the brains that often went along with it—that was the ultimate turn-on for her. Perhaps because such men were her heroes growing up. Men with drive, brains, ambition, wealth. These were men she went after.

Men so unlike her father. Men so unlike John.

She felt again the tingling sensation of R.J.'s hand grazing her thigh. She looked up sharply. He was still talking but the fire in his eyes, the tone of his voice, all spoke clearly of his interest. Did he think she was naive? Another glance told her that his interest was rising.

Annie's catlike eyes glistened in the dark as she contemplated how to play with this very large mouse. Why she even bothered she wasn't sure. Was it because she was angry at John? At Doris? Was it simply because it was dangerous? Reckless? For it was. She knew how easy it would be to escalate the game—a feathery touch of her fingers on his palm, a knowing glance, a lift of the knee allowing his hand to slide along her soft, inner thigh.

From the corner of her eye she caught a movement off to the right. A tall man stood in the shadows. A wisp of blond hair caught the moonlight. *John.* Her body tensed as her senses heightened, knowing he was watching. She lay still, watching him, no longer listening to R.J., hearing only the pounding of her heart. Her finger twitched at her side. How long John stood there she couldn't know, but the thought that he hung back and watched while another man's hand grazed his wife's thigh made her heart shrivel. Just how long would he watch? What would it take for him to step out of the darkness and finally confront his boss?

She told herself she was blameless. That she was only sitting there, but something in her made her want to test him. She had to know. She listened while R.J. droned on, and waited. Sure enough, his palm came to her thigh again, just above the knee. And as she'd predicted, this time it rested longer, testing. Annie fought the urge to slap the hand away. Instead, she lay as still as a cat, holding her breath, watching the shadows.

R.J. murmured something about how beautiful she looked in the moonlight. She dragged her attention back to his face and met his gaze, at first gauging the serious-ness of his intentions, then challenging him. She knew she had crossed some line between them, throwing everything up for grabs. His pupils quivered, his nostrils flared, and she saw in his expression a certain conceit of his own appeal. He didn't know that this was a deliberate move, that he was merely a pawn on the board.

As he lowered his face toward hers, she looked point-blank into his eyes, her hands-off message clear. Then she pushed him away. Darting a glance in the darkness, she saw John still standing, watching. R.J., thinking she was being coy, or not caring about anything but his own desire, moved toward her again.

He surprised her by moving quickly and grabbing hold of her shoulders with his meaty hands. With a jerk, he drew her up to his lips. She tasted brandy and cigars and squirmed, but his grip was as taut as iron. His fingers dug into her shoulders, hurting her. He continued the assault, pressing his lips hard against hers with a brutality that was all about male ego and showing her who was in charge of this situation. When he thrust his tongue into her mouth, she gagged and pushed harder against his chest, angry now.

"Cut it out," she growled against his lips, pushing hard with flat palms against his chest.

He pulled back at last with a feral gleam in his eye. Annie reached up and wiped her mouth with the back of her hand. Her gaze darted over his shoulder to the darkness of the shrubs.

She saw John turn his head and walk away from them, back up the slope.

The pain was raw in Annie's chest. Her cheeks burned and she exhaled in a hot, scorching whoosh. He was walking away!

Suddenly she was thirteen again, feeling the same shame and hurt she had the day her parents turned away from her, disbelief in their eyes, even when she'd showed them the ugly purple-and-black bruises forming on her arms. Like then, she didn't know whether to shout obscenities or crumple and weep.

R.J. misunderstood her silence. He leaned forward and playfully tugged at the corner of her towel. Hardly aware, she lifted her gaze to peer into his eyes, which were pale and rheumy with drink. As though from far away she heard

him say again how beautiful she was, that he wanted to
see her breasts again, that they could move to the cabana
He placed one hand upon her belly and made small circula
motions.

For one moment Annie considered going with him. He
heart ranted against the coward who was her husband
Here was a real man. What kind of man was John? He'd
abandoned her. She wanted to punish John. She would
show him! Her heart beat heavily with the battle of loving
John—of hating John.

Overhead a bat swerved in the violet light. Behind he
the wind rattled the leaves. What did it matter, she won
dered, feeling defeat engulf her as her mood plummeted
There was nothing left for her. Her bones felt dry and
brittle, ready for the grave. What did it matter, she though
again? She was dead already.

R.J. rose to his feet in a swoop. Then taking her hand
he pulled her up beside him, close to his chest.

"The cabana is right over there," he said bending close
his sour breath hot on her ear. "We don't have much
time."

Annie hung back, weaving, feeling sick inside. Wha
was she doing? It *did* matter. She looked at the tall, mid
dle-aged man before her and saw that he wasn't just any
man. He was R. J. Bridges—Doris's husband, John's boss
This wasn't just about her and John. It was about Doris
and R.J., too. This wasn't just about sex. It involved peo
ple. John's words echoed in her mind: *It's always about
you, Annie.* Yes, it *is* about me, John, she thought to her
self. Ultimately, the decision was hers to live with. R.J
may be a rat, but he was Doris's rat.

Revulsion shook her and she reared, whacking away
R.J.'s fat, sweaty palm from her arm. "Keep your hands
off of me," she said, stepping back.

R.J.'s face flushed but he recouped quickly. "That's

what I like about you, Annie," he said with a nervous laugh. "You're sassy. Tough."

"Try married." She tightened her towel.

"I am, too," he said with an urbane shrug. "Listen, Annie, nothing happened. We both had a little too much to drink, that's all. Let's leave it at that."

"I'm a lawyer, R.J., not a judge. Save the defense for Doris." She turned and walked away in a blaze of anger and shame.

Behind the pool house, amid a cluster of rhododendron that had grown thick with age, Doris stood in the shadows and watched Annie Blake swoop down, scoop up her dress and shoes, then head for the gravel path toward the house. Her long legs took coltish strides and her slim hips swayed beneath the thick terry cloth towel.

Doris clutched a broad waxy leaf and watched from deep in the shadows as R.J. sat back in the lounge chair, mopped his face with his palm, lifted his long legs and pulled out a cigarette. A flame lit the air, then the cigarette tip glowed red in the blackness. He smoked as he stared out at the night, frowning, inhaling deeply. Her husband raked his hair with his hands and sighed heavily.

With frustration, she wondered? With relief? Did he care whether his own wife found out that he'd made a move on her friend?

Doris's breath was shallow and it felt as though her blood was draining from her face, down her body, straight into the soil. She couldn't move. She could no longer run away, rooted as she was by the reality of what she'd tried to ignore for years.

Forty minutes later Annie paid the cabdriver, then raced in her bare feet across the expanse of lush green lawn into

her house, pushing open the front door so hard it banged
against the wall.

"John!" she screamed in the front foyer. Her fury was
bubbling in her veins like lava about to erupt. She dropped
her purse and the plastic bag that contained her ruined
dress and shoes, and pounded through the halls, shouting
John's name over and over.

She found him in the kitchen dressed in his white work
overalls taping drywall. At this late hour he was working
calmly, steadily, easing out his anger as he applied tape in
smooth, even strokes. He kept his back to her.

Annie would not be ignored. "You left me there!" she
shouted at him. "I had no money, no dry clothes, and you
just left me there!"

John's arm paused in the air for a second, then he continued working.

Annie felt her stomach twist, her throat constrict and her
heart break. She trembled with hurt and shame and fury.
After all that had happened that night, all the errors made
on both their parts, he wouldn't even turn around and face
her.

She swallowed hard and said in a low, shaky voice, "So
you're going to be the martyr, huh? It's all my fault. It's
the silent treatment again."

He kept working but said in a controlled voice, "We'd
better not talk now. We'll both say things we'll regret."

His calm was like oil on a flame. "I don't care! At least
we'll be talking. I'm sick of your pussyfooting around
fights. For months we've been seething, making swipes. I
hate that. I want to fight! To get it all out. Come on, damn
you, turn around." She approached him, tripping over the
tarp on the floor and falling against his shoulder.

His muscled shoulders tensed as she tumbled against
him. He went still, his hand clenched white on the roll of
tape against the wall over his head. She could see his face

turn pale with anger and the bitter control he was exercising not to turn around.

"You're drunk, Annie."

She hated the superiority in his voice. "Not drunk enough," she retorted, eager to get a rise from him. "Not as drunk as I want to be." She shoved his shoulder, this time on purpose. "Damn it, John, at least when I'm drunk I talk. Turn around and look me in the eye. Stop hiding behind that wall you're building."

He wouldn't.

"You stubborn, arrogant prig! Why did you walk away?" She cut to the chase.

He dropped his arm and looked at her over his shoulder. His gaze swept her and he noticed that she was standing in her muddy bare feet, her hair was straight and stringy, and she was wearing an oversize man's raincoat buttoned up to her neck. She saw the second his concern flashed to anger.

"It was clear you'd already made your decision."

Her chin stuck out. "Oh? And what decision did I make?"

"To cheat."

Her breath exhaled on a curse. "That's what you think was happening? That I was fooling around with that asshole R. J. Bridges?"

He spun around, throwing the roll of tape across the floor. "I was there."

"I know you were! I saw you. Just standing there in the dark, watching. That's why I played that game. To see what you'd do. But you just stood there!" She heard the pain in her own voice, felt the tears burn in her eyes. "You didn't fight for me. Defend me..."

"There was nothing to fight for. Nothing to defend."

She almost doubled over from the blow of his words, delivered in a razor sharp tone that cut deep. All her hurt

and doubt coursed through her, making her heart pump
hard, stealing her breath. Her brain echoed the words
Nothing to fight for. Nothing to defend.

He didn't love her enough to fight for her? His own
wife? No one had ever defended her—not as a child, not
as a woman.

She turned her head, hiding her face. She couldn't let
him know how he'd just injured her. To tell him now, in
the heat of battle, was to expose her vulnerable underbelly.
A street urchin like herself knew better than that.

"Nothing to defend?" she cried, facing him with mean
desperation. "How about your manhood? What kind of
man would just watch while another man made a pass at
his wife?"

John's face was tight with matched fury. "What kind
of a woman would accept a pass from her husband's
boss?"

"I didn't!"

"He kissed you, Annie. I call that a pass."

"He did that, not me. Okay, it was wrong. I didn't mean
for that to happen. I just wanted to see if you'd stand up
to R.J." Her finger jabbed the air between them. "And
you didn't! You didn't do squat!"

"What?" he shot back, lunging forward, his face in
hers. His long hands formed fists at his thighs. "Would
you feel better if I'd hit him? If I'd hit you?"

"Yes!" she shouted back, her eyes gleaming with challenge. "Yes! I want to see you do *something*. Be a man!"

John lurched closer like a prizefighter, breathing heavily,
his eyes rimmed red, his mouth a thin line of determination. Suddenly he brought back his fist.

Annie raised her arm to fend off the blow.

With a violent swing John turned his shoulder and
slammed his fist into the drywall.

Annie ducked, yelped and covered her face.

She remained huddled for a moment, clenched, waiting, listening. All was silent. When she opened her eyes, she saw John leaning forward in exhaustion, his forehead resting against the wall, and a line of tears carving through the white dust on his cheek. His knuckles were bloodied.

She gulped deep breaths of air, feeling suddenly sober, sick and drained of all emotion. She wanted only for the anger to be over.

"I'll get you some ice," she said.

"Leave me alone."

"I want to."

It seemed her feet were made of lead as she walked in automaton fashion to the freezer, kicking up the fine white dust as she went. Her hands trembled while she loaded cubes of ice into a towel, wrapped them up, then brought it to John. He was sitting on a kitchen chair. His long blond hair fell limp over his drooping shoulders.

She knew he was withdrawing. He'd be ashamed of his anger, embarrassed that he'd been so physical. But she wanted him to know that she was glad of it. Glad to know that his feelings for her were strong. She wanted to hold him now, to bring him out of himself, to kiss him, to make it all better now that the anger was spent.

"John, I'm sorry. About everything. I was wrong to play that game with R.J. Wrong to push you..."

"Don't, Annie." His voice was as cold as the ice in her hands. "I don't want to hear it."

She halted clumsily, her hand still in midair. She wanted to talk to him, to clear the air, but when she tried again to touch him, he backed off, raising his bloodied hand to ward her off as though her touch would contaminate him.

"I've got to get out of here. Get some air."

"Don't go," she said, deadly serious. How many times had she advised her clients never to leave in the middle of a fight. "We need to talk. There's so much more we need

to talk about. You don't know, John. Please. We're not
done yet."

He rose in a swoop and, grabbing his keys off the
kitchen counter, made his way over the tools and debris
to the back door. There he stopped and spoke in a dead
tired voice.

"Maybe we are, Annie. Maybe we are."

Doris lay in her four-poster bed, the embroidered sheets
and down blanket tucked high up over her breasts, right
to her double chin. The gray light of the television flashed
in the darkness. She remembered a conversation she'd had
once with her mother, on this very bed, long ago when
this was still her parents' bedroom. Bobby was still a tod-
dler and she was pregnant with Sarah. At that time, she
suspected R.J. was having an affair. She'd gone running
to her mother in tears, threatening a divorce.

How calm and accepting her mother had been of the
possibility of infidelity. She had settled Doris beside her
on the bed, held her hand, and in her lighthearted manner
made Doris feel naive that such a thing as a "fling" should
upset her. She recalled her mother's words vividly.

"My darling, does he beat you? Does he abuse your
son? No! Is he a good provider? Yes! Does he love you?
Yes! Oh, don't be silly, Doris, of course he does. In his
way. We can't all expect romance and flowers, my dear,
but we can expect respect." Her mother had patted her
cheek. "Successful men have these...needs. It has something to do with their egos, pressures of the job. Oh, who
knows," she'd said, waving her hand in the air. "And who
cares? You have this nice life. A nice home, car, your
children, and a bit of spending money." She'd patted
Doris's hand. "Sometimes it's best for a wife to look the
other way."

Doris focused again on the four-poster bed—her bed

now. *You made your bed, now sleep in it,* her mother had told her.

Doris lay in the bland gray light and fondled the string of black pearls still around her neck. Twenty-five pearls, one for each year they'd been married. A quarter of a century with Robert James Bridges. She'd been patient; she'd looked the other way always believing that, by this point in their marriage, he would have sown his wild oats. These should have been their golden years together, with the hurt far behind.

She rolled the pearls in her fingers, considering, registering the soft, waxy feel. Twenty-five pearls. Worth quite a bit. Certainly nothing to toss away lightly. Closing her fingers tightly over the pearls she weighed her decision. Suddenly her fingers tightened around them. Grimacing, she gave a firm, fierce tug. The clasp broke, sending the necklace collapsing into her fist. She raised her palm and looked dispassionately at the broken string, then leaned over and allowed the pearls to slide through her fingers onto the bedside table.

When R.J. stepped into the room a short while later she didn't bother to look up but her body tensed involuntarily under the blanket. The sound of his shuffling in the dim lighting as he changed from his dinner clothes into pajamas seemed deafening.

"Hey, what happened to the necklace?" he asked, his gruff voice reflecting shock and dismay.

From the corner of her eye she saw him standing, stooped over her bedside table. His belly hung a bit over the waistband of his pajamas and in his hands he held the black pearls.

"The clasp is all broken," he added, screwing up his eyes.

"Yes," she replied, deliberately keeping her eyes on the television.

"How the..." He looked up at her, his eyes narrowing in suspicion. "Are you okay?"

She closed her eyes. "Why wouldn't I be?"

"No reason," he replied quickly. "You just seem..." He shook his head, then set the pearls back onto the vanity. "Well, I can repair it."

Doris raised her eyes for the first time and affixed her gaze on her husband. He appeared to her neither as handsome, nor as dear, as he had just a few hours earlier.

"Can you?" she asked without a trace of emotion. She saw a shadow of puzzlement flicker across his face, and in his eyes, a flash of worry. Doris turned her head and returned to her black-and-white movie.

In a dull voice, she replied, "I'm not sure that it *can* be repaired."

The night passed in excruciating slowness. Annie drank more, hoping to deaden the pain that would not be doused. And the fear. Yes, that was worse. John had not yet returned. She lay her forehead against the cool of the table. Retracing each phase of the horrible evening, she examined with the discipline of a lawyer her actions and reactions. Yes, she'd acted irresponsibly. No, she should never have gone to the pool. She was sorry about what happened there, wished she could take it all back.

But always there came the nagging voice that said, What about John? Didn't he have a duty to her as well? Wasn't he partly to blame? Back and forth, back and forth. Yet beneath the rationalizations lurked a haze of guilt she couldn't escape. She was wrong and felt the need to make amends.

A little after 3:00 a.m. she heard a shuffling at the door and rose from her chair with a start, clumsily knocking over the chair in her haste to open the door.

"John! Where have you—"

Her breath hitched, choking her words. Standing under the dim light was Doris. She was wearing her nightgown under a navy windbreaker. And though she was dressed for sleep, Annie saw in the flashing of her eyes that she was ready for battle.

"May I come in?"

Annie wanted to say no, to tell her to go home, that she was already battle weary. But she stepped aside and held the door open, groaning inwardly as Doris passed, her shoulders erect with righteous fury. She closed the door and faced her, wary.

"It's a bit late for a social call," Annie said. "Is everything okay?"

"No, everything is not okay," replied Doris briskly. She was clasping and unclasping her hands, visibly shaking.

Annie blinked heavily, trying to marshal her woozy thoughts. "If it's about my falling in the pool, I'm sorry. I lost my balance and went right in."

"Don't be ridiculous. Of course that's not what this is about!" Her facade of control was crumbling.

Annie wearily mopped her face with her palm, knowing a major confrontation was blowing in. "Look, I'm tired. Believe me when I tell you I've had a hell of a day. If it's all right with you, let's table this till tomorrow."

"No, it's not all right with me!" Doris shouted back, all pretense of a social call shattered. "I came here to tell you a few things and you're going to listen."

Annie crossed her arms in an unconscious, protective gesture. "So spit it out, Doris."

"How could you, Annie?" she cried.

Annie went cold and the wine in her stomach threatened to shoot forth like a geyser. "What are you talking about?"

"I was in the garden. I saw you and R.J."

"Aw, damn it," she moaned, shaking her head. She was

certain now this was going to be a showdown. At the stroke of twelve, one of them, if not both, would be left bleeding. "Nothing happened, Doris. Nothing at all. R.J. just had a little too much to drink. He got a bit carried away. You know him."

Doris swiped at her eyes and regained her control. "Yes, I do. And I know you."

"What's that supposed to mean?"

"You think you're so superior. You like to play games, Annie Blake, and tonight it was with my husband. I resent that deeply."

"You don't know what you're talking about, Doris."

"You have no idea, do you? Well, I'm here to tell you that playing with fire is dangerous. You can get burned. And not just you, but me, your husband, even R.J."

"Okay, you've told me. Will you go now?"

"You're just like so many women I know who indulge themselves in a seemingly harmless flirtation. A brief letter or a phone call. Maybe a snuggle while the tennis instructor teaches a serve. A wiggle and a kiss. Little do you know that these sparks can flare up out of control, destroying everything in their path." Her eyes raked Annie with accusation. "Turning good marriages to ash."

"And weren't you playing, too?" Annie shot back. "You were hiding in the bushes. Spying. What kind of sick game is that? God, I hate sneaks."

"I came looking for you. John was worried."

"You could have called out. I wish you had! A good ol' blowout would've been better than this sneaking around. Hide-and-seek. Well, you found out all right. The whole sordid mess. Talk about games. What I want to know is, what was the prize? As far as I can tell, there were no winners, only losers. Everyone was hurt."

"And it's all your fault! You didn't stop to think of who

you were hurting, Annie. That's so typical of you. Act first, think later. To me, that's the height of selfishness.''

Annie sputtered, she was so angry. Livid. It was so unfair of Doris to blame it all on her rather than her own husband. ''Doris, stop pretending to me and to yourself. I hate to be the one to tell you this, but I didn't go after your husband. He came down to the pool after me. He put the make on me.''

''You lured him!''

''Wake up, Doris! Everyone but you knows R. J. Bridges chases anything in a skirt.''

Doris looked away, stricken.

Annie blew out a sigh and shook her head with regret. ''I'm sorry, Doris. That wasn't the right way to tell you. But I'm glad you know. Sometimes a friend doesn't cover up the truth, no matter how tough it is to hear.''

''You're not my friend,'' she said, her voice low.

Annie's heart skipped a beat, registering another hurt. ''No, I don't suppose I am,'' she replied in a sad voice. ''I tried to be, but you wouldn't let it happen. The point is, I still think of you as a friend and I swear I would never go after a friend's husband. Hell, I don't go after anyone. I'm married too, you know. And I happen to love the creep.''

Doris placed her palms to her face and began to cry. Deep heaving sobs shook her shoulders while a low muffled wail echoed in the kitchen. Her copper-shiny hair fell forward to mop the tears.

Annie stepped closer to place a comforting hand on her shoulder and was relieved Doris didn't shake it away. She waited until Doris's breathing was less ragged.

''Have you ever thought about leaving him?'' she asked gently.

Doris nodded her head. ''Yes. But I can't imagine ever divorcing R.J. He's my life.''

"Well, maybe he shouldn't be."

Doris drew herself up, collecting her wits as she wiped her eyes. "You don't understand," she said with cold dismissal. "It's just not done. Not by women like me. It's not the way we were raised."

Annie's voice softened with pity. "Don't I? Doris, I've got a practice full of good, upstanding women who've gotten the shaft. It ain't pretty. Women who've given up the best years of their lives living by the rules of that social code you're referring to, waiting on these jerks hand and foot. And then get dumped for a younger model. That's when they come to me. Good ol' Annie's door is always open. They're stuck without an income, without skills and a coupl'a kids in tow who are also angry and hurt and afraid to admit they love their father. And you know what? I love it when these women finally get angry. Really pissed. I feed it, use it to help them throw off that 'poor me' attitude and get started on building new lives for themselves."

Doris took a deep breath. "You imply I have no life."

Annie leaned against the door, unspeakably weary. "No, of course not. I don't mean for you to change everything, or to go out and get a job. That's not the answer. It's about cultivating your own interests, Doris. Not getting stuck in your own house staring at the walls with all the time in the world and not a clue what to do with that time. So many women give, give, give until they have nothing left. Then one day they wake up, look in the mirror and don't know their own reflection."

Doris shivered, her face frozen in thought. When she spoke again, her voice was quiet, without a trace of the earlier venom. "And what about you, Annie? With your high-powered law practice and self-centered life-style, are you happy?"

Annie was taken aback. She looked down at her hands and shook her head. "Touché, Doris."

"It's late. I should go." She gave a short laugh. "I can't imagine why I came in the first place. I snuck out of bed. Isn't that pathetic? R.J. doesn't even know I'm gone."

Annie opened the door. "Oh, don't forget this." She walked across the room to grab the raincoat hanging off a chair and returned it to Doris. "Your maid lent it to me."

Doris held R.J.'s coat away from her body as if it were contaminated. "Throw it away. Burn it. I don't care."

"Okay," Annie said, taking it back, wishing she could burn away all memory of this horrible evening.

Before leaving, Doris hesitated, and with a puzzled expression on her tired face asked, "I'm thinking about the woman you described earlier. The woman who can leave her husband. You make her sound so empowered and successful. But she sounds vindictive, too. And angry. If that's the kind of woman you want me to become..." She shook her head and tears sprang again to her eyes. "No," Doris continued, struggling to control her voice. "That's not my idea of being a woman. I think the answer lies somewhere in between. I don't know. I'm not sure of anything right now. I'm just very tired."

They didn't hug or kiss or even smile. Their eyes met, they nodded in brief acknowledgment, and Doris left.

Annie closed the door and leaned against it. She had no strength left. She felt as though she'd been cut into little pieces and fed to the ravens. With an automatic gesture she smoothed the hair from her face, ending with her palms at her eyes. She still hadn't told John about the cancer. It was too late now. She wouldn't want him to come back to her out of pity.

How had things reached such a low, she cried as she paced the house? She walked through room after room without purpose, turning her head from left to right as she counted the number of projects that still had to be done. There was so much junk and clutter everywhere. Not a damn room was finished. Suddenly she hated the house, hated that they'd spent two years patching and painting, planning and dreaming, spending so much of their free time and money on this project—and all for naught. It was just a place, not a home. This was not the dwelling of a family. No milestones were reached under this roof. This huge, architectural elephant was nothing but a mausoleum, as silent as the tomb.

She stood in the middle of the long, spreading living room with its distinctive low ceilings and small, green-and-red stained-glass windows. Suddenly the gloomy darkness and the eerie silence frightened her. The air felt thick and her heart began pounding erratically. She couldn't get enough air in her lungs.

Panting, she heard Dr. Gibson's words play again in her brain. *Sometimes tests reveal what we don't want to see.*

Oh God, she was crying. She'd thought she'd forgotten how. John, where are you? She didn't want to be alone in this tomb. She didn't want to be sick. She didn't want to die. It was too quiet in this house, she thought in a panic. Clutching at her breast she hurried to the stereo system and clicked on a CD. She leaned against the table, bent over, taking deep breaths while she waited for the system to begin playing.

When the velvety voice of Otis Redding filled the air she slumped to the floor and lay on her back. At last she could breathe normally again. She knew this voice. His music transported her away from her current fears back to a time when she was younger and happier. Pressing her hands against her abdomen, she clung to Otis's words like a lifeline. *Try a little tenderness.*

Fifteen

Weeping comes in the evening but
Joy comes in the morning.

—King David, *Psalm 29*

The telephone's ringing startled Eve from a deep sleep. Phone calls in the middle of the night were only bad business, she thought as her heart pounded. Her mind fumbled, sweeping away cobwebs to recall where her children were: Bronte was asleep in bed. Finney... Oh my God, Finney was in Michigan. Her baby...

"Hello?" she gasped, her mouth dry.

"Eve it's me, Annie. Did I wake you up?"

Eve was so relieved she almost wept. "God, Annie, do you know what time it is?"

"No, I'm sorry. What time is it?"

"I dunno. But trust me, it's late." She cleared her throat and rubbed her eyes while her heart rate returned to normal. It sounded like Annie had been drinking. Her words were slurred. "What's the matter? Is everything okay?"

"Nooo..." she wailed.

Eve sat up, wide awake. Annie never cried. "Are you all right?"

"I'm a mess. I'm a creep. A dirty rotten scoundrel." She hiccuped.

Eve rubbed her eyes, gathering her wits. Annie was obviously drunk. "Where's John?"

"I dunno. He's not home yet."

Eve stretched out to reach for the alarm clock. It was four in the morning. "Not home? Where can he be?"

"I don't know. We were at a party. We had a fight. He left, sort of. I dunno."

"Are you alone?"

"Yes." Her voice was mournful, overflowing with grief.

"Open the front door, sweetheart. I'm on my way."

Fifteen minutes later Eve was climbing the stone steps to Annie's house. The front door was wide-open, only the screen door kept the insects at bay. Eve opened the door, stuck her head in and called Annie's name. There was no answer. With her heart pounding, she raced through the house, pushing open doors and tripping over the heavy tools and cardboard boxes littering every room. "Annie!"

"I'm out here." The voice came wafting in the window, seemingly from the backyard.

The grass was dry under her shoes and in the shifting moonlight, the yard appeared vacant. The only movement came from the shadows of branches and leaves across the broad expanse of green. It was creepy outside, alone, in the middle of the night. "Where are you?" Eve called, feeling her throat close up.

"In here."

Eve followed the voice to a clump of overgrown lilac bushes in a corner of the yard. Bending at the waist, she spied through the tunnel of branches a figure in a white, cotton nightgown sitting Indian-style on the dirt, camouflaged behind the green leaves. Eve sighed, then got down on hands and knees and navigated her way around clumps of branches and saplings that scraped through the thin cotton of her own short nightgown. "You're really getting weird on me, Blake," she said as she drew near. "If there's poison ivy in here, I'll never speak to you again."

"Hey," Annie said as Eve settled beside her. She was leaning back, perusing Eve's nightgown worn under a sweater. "If I'da known I was gonna have so many visitors in pajamas tonight I'da had a slumber party."

"Why?" Eve replied, slapping soil from her palm. It was clear from Annie's low slurring and her weaving that she was loaded. Annie could be a belligerent drunk so Eve immediately tried to placate her until she could figure out how to cajole her back into the house. "Who else was here?"

"Doris."

"Doris? Here? In her pajamas?"

"Yep. She came to give me what-for. And you know what? She done good. Right between the eyes. I'm a shell of my former self."

Eve narrowed her eyes. Annie always hid her hurt with humor. "Care to tell me about it?"

"It's..." She paused and Eve could hear her frustration, a clamping down on words before spoken. "Never mind." She reached out for the wine bottle.

Eve arrested her hand, gently holding it. "Hold off, Annie. I think you've had enough."

"Who asked you?" Annie said gruffly, pushing away Eve's hand. "I don't want you, or John, or anyone telling me what I can or can't drink. Got that?"

Eve swallowed down her anger, reminding herself that this was Annie's drunkenness talking.

"If it's about Doris's party, don't worry. You're not spilling the beans. I already know about it. She called earlier tonight to apologize for not inviting me."

"Huh? Well, whaddya know." Annie shook her head in wide swings, then looked back at Eve with her brow furrowed. Her voice changed, became solicitous. "So how are you? Are you hurt?"

Eve sighed wearily. "Sure, I guess I was. At first. Not anymore. I've known Doris and R.J. for a long time and even though she gives the appearance of being in control and bossy, she kowtows to him all the time. He has no loyalties at all, except to money. Tom and I always knew that about him, which was why Tom couldn't stand being in the same room with him. The friendship was always between Doris and me. And now, well, even that's changing. We don't have so much in common anymore."

"Well, I hafta hand it to her for calling you up. That took a lotta courage. She must really care about you."

Eve was silent.

"Anyway…" There was a long pause.

"What's the matter, Annie?"

In a low, broken voice, Annie told Eve what had happened in the Bridgeses' garden, the fight with John, and the odd confrontation with Doris.

"My poor Annie. I'm speechless," Eve said with a gentle laugh that came from release, not humor. "You got it from all corners, kiddo. Annie, Annie, Annie, you get yourself in the weirdest predicaments."

"I know. It's a curse."

"It's just you, Annie. You take risks. Speak your mind."

"You bet," she said with punch, but her voice didn't carry any conviction.

"You and Doris will work things out."

"Yeah, maybe. But John… I never saw him so cold. Well, he can just go out and drive all night, see if I care."

"You shouldn't have tested him that way."

"I'm glad I did. When he turned away, just walked off, I thought—" her face tightened into a grimace "—*you wimp.* I lost all respect for him." Her voice hitched and she became weepy. "He didn't do anything. He just left me there. Do you know how that made me feel?"

It was frightening for Eve to see Annie like this. Annie was her rock. To see her crumble shook the terra firma of Eve's own world. She wanted to slap John silly—and R.J., too. But she was wary of where Annie's thoughts were headed. John loved Annie, she knew it. And Annie, John. It wouldn't help either him or Annie if she took sides right now.

"Maybe he didn't see it as a pass," she said, playing devil's advocate. "After all, it was R.J., it was late, you were talking..."

"It was R.J.! That's my point! Not only is R.J. his boss but he's supposedly his friend too. The big pal. Shit, I can't count the number of times we sat at dinner with him and R.J. dom...minated the table. The li'l king. John can run circles around R.J. But he never says a damn thing. He just sits there like the goody schoolboy and smiles." She cursed under her breath then said in a sorry tone, "Maybe I shouldn't have told Doris about R.J."

Eve felt her heart skip. "Tell Doris what?"

Annie appeared haunted. "About R.J. You know, about the women."

"Oh, Annie," Eve replied softly, covering her eyes and shaking her head. "Poor Doris."

"But he is!" Annie said, raising her chin defensively.

"But you shouldn't have told her."

"Come on...let's be real. I'd say she figured it out for herself tonight. Hiding in the bushes. What's with the bushes? Shit, everyone else was playing in the bushes tonight, I figured why not me? I wanna play too. It's kinda nice in here, whatchya think? Kinda like a secret fort." Her face drooped in sorrow as she looked off toward the house. "So many secrets... I don't wanna be in that house."

Eve let out a long sigh, still thinking of Doris. "How could she not know?"

"You might ask how can she stay?"

Eve closed her mouth, understanding Doris's position perfectly. She knew Annie's strength was also her weakness. She was quick to make decisions and form opinions. While that might be good for business, it wasn't always good for relationships.

"Nothing is black-and-white," Eve replied. "There are a lot of good, solid marriages that work because two people try hard to make it work. Divorce isn't always the answer."

"Of course not. I know that. But it kills me to watch women like Doris get hurt. Those are the easy targets, Eve. The good girls. The sweet ones who trust. Dream that it'll last forever, but live like it'll end next week. That's my new credo."

"What kind of a cynical attitude is that? I worry for you, Annie. Lots of marriages work because each member tries to make the other person's life better. It may sound old-fashioned and trite, but fidelity and monogamy exist. And for the right reasons, too. Love, romance, trust."

"Like yours, I suppose?"

There was a bitterness, almost an accusation, in the statement that set Eve's teeth on edge. Alcohol had a way of bringing out truths that sobriety kept muffled. Especially ugly truths.

"Yes," she said, archly. "Like mine."

"Don't be so sure of yourself all the time, Eve. Sometimes you get a little preachy."

Eve was stunned. "Just what are you saying?"

"You're turning your marriage to Tom into some holy perfect..." She waved her hand, grasping for words. In her drunken state, she was having a hard time. "...thing. Tom wasn't any saint, you know. He was just human. You forget, I was there. You were having a few problems when he died. You just happen to forget that now. Well, don't forget it. Move on.''

Annie's eyes were blazing with indignation, matching the fury sparked in Eve.

"The day that I listen to a drunk tell me the value of my husband, or my marriage…"

"A shrine," Annie blurted out, pointing her finger in the air. "That's the word I was thinking of. You think of your marriage as a goddamn shrine. Well, it isn't! It's a boulder tied around your neck, pulling you under. And I'm gonna save you."

"You don't know what you're talking about." She moved to her hands and knees, ready to crawl back out. She'd had it. "I don't need you to save me."

"There was someone else, Eve," Annie blurted out.

Eve felt as if someone had just thrown ice down her back. "That's it. I'm leaving." She began crawling out fast, to escape, ignoring Annie's cries that she stop. Stepping out from the bushes, she scrambled to her feet and stumbled across the lawn, stubbing her toe on some blunt metal thing in the grass. She let out a yelp and grabbed her toe as tears of rage and pain sprang to her eyes. From behind her she could hear Annie running up.

"I'm sorry, Eve," she said, clutching her arm in a panic. "I didn't mean it. Never mind what I said."

Eve shrugged off Eve's hands. "Go to bed, Annie."

"Don't go, Eve. Please. Not yet. I'm sorry. I don't want to go back inside alone. Oh…hold on," she groaned, covering her mouth. "I think I'm going to be sick."

"Lord…" Eve instinctively turned to help. As Annie took deep breaths and spit, Eve stroked her back, crooning, "That's okay, you're okay now." She was amazed at how thin Annie had become, startled that she hadn't noticed before.

"I feel better," Annie said with a groan, holding her stomach. The fight was gone, leaving her face pale and drawn.

"Well, you look like hell. Come on, let's get you to bed."

"I don't want to go in there." She balked and Eve worried if she was getting paranoid.

"Annie, you're just drunk. We have to get you to bed."

"No, you don't understand. It's like a tomb in there. That's why I came out here. To get some fresh air. Please don't leave me in there alone." Her eyes were wide with fear and she clutched Eve's arm again. "Please."

"Okay, I won't. Shhh, I won't go. Come on, sweetie. We'll go inside together. I'll get you some water and aspirin. Don't scrunch your nose, it's your own recipe. You taught it to me. You'll feel better in the morning."

With their arms linked, she guided Annie back toward her home. As they walked, Annie leaned against Eve and said in a faraway voice, "I'm not that drunk, Eve. I'm just sad...so sad."

Once inside, Annie stubbornly refused to sleep in her own bed so Eve settled her onto the big, upholstered sofa in the living room with a few pillows and blankets. She made her way quickly into the kitchen, carefully stepped around the litter of tools and drywall dust, and poured water in a tumbler, then found aspirin in the cabinet over the sink. She returned to find a brooding, seemingly more sober Annie staring into the darkness. She accepted the water and aspirin like a good patient, swallowing the pills down with noisy gulps. When she was through, she brought her knees up to her chest and tucked the sheet around her ankles.

"I shouldn't have said that about Tom," she said. "I'm sorry it came out like that."

Eve felt an icy cold spread from where the wet earth

seeped through her gown. The chill spread up her limbs and throughout her body, numbing her inside and out.

"I found this photograph of a woman," Eve began in a low voice, "stuck in among Tom's personal things. I wondered who she was, but forgot about it. Today, I saw the woman again at the mausoleum when I went with the children to visit Tom's grave. I froze when I saw her. I knew I'd seen her somewhere before, and then driving home, it clicked where."

"The redhead."

Eve shuddered. "Yes. Was she the..." She felt the words choke her.

Annie sighed heavily. She spoke slowly, as though each word had to be dragged from her mouth. "As your lawyer, I should have told you a long time ago. As your friend, I couldn't. It's better you know the truth now." She placed her hand on Eve's leg, patted it, then registering Eve's rigid, silent stance, tucked her arms back around her own legs.

"I only found out myself," she continued in a measured manner, "because there were bills I had to pay from the estate—a hotel in Washington D.C., a florist, that kind of thing. I did a little tracing. It didn't take much. I found out about a woman, a doctor on staff." She paused, glancing briefly at Eve. "It didn't go on too long, if that means anything. It only just started about six months before he died."

"My God," Eve said, feeling a first sharp stab of Tom's betrayal.

"She was at the funeral. Did you see her?"

"She was at the funeral?" Eve felt like a fool. "And she brought flowers to his grave.... Well, the bitch must have really loved him." She felt as cold as she knew she sounded. "This is so much worse. I wish it was some sordid affair. You know, just sex. I wouldn't care so much

about that. But to think Tom might have loved someon
else.''

"Just because this woman loved Tom doesn't mean th
he loved her. Eve, I'm telling you, Tom loved you. You.

"I don't know that I can believe that, or that I care rig
now. I feel nothing. Empty."

"Me, too, honey. Totally."

Annie stuck out her tongue and jabbed a finger towa
her throat with such a comic expression that Eve just ha
to laugh.

"You're so stupid," she joked, feeling the sudde
giddy relief that came with dumb humor.

After a short laugh Annie replied, "Boy, *am* I…. The
I was, awake in the middle of the night, sitting in th
bushes, asking myself, What have I done with my life
What am I supposed to be doing? Remember how I use
to say there's no such thing as age? Well, there is. Age
real and life is short. It's foolhardy to deny it. We gro
up, our bodies grow frail, death is coming. There's s
much I want to do! There's a whole world out there
haven't seen, people I haven't met and who haven't know
me. God, there are a million books I want to read. I don
want to sleep, Eve. I want to be awake. This is my life–
I want to live it."

Eve listened with her eyes wide. She heard Annie
words—*this is my life*—and felt the shackles she'd wor
for a lifetime break free. What was she doing? She love
her children, but she also loved Paul. This was her lif
She couldn't let her children dictate how she lived it. Tha
wasn't healthy for her or for them. She was the parent an
they were young adults. They didn't need to know abo
their father's indiscretions but they did need to understan
their mother's choices. She would help them to accept th
new reality that, though she would always be their mothe
she was also a single, independent woman.

"It's time for me to go home." Eve was suddenly tired beyond endurance. She needed to get Annie in bed, then be alone, to digest what she'd learned about Tom. She needed time to think things through.

"Don't go."

Irritation flared. She wanted to go home to her own bed, to her own pillow. "Come on, Annie. We've had all the secrets we can handle for one night. Besides, I can't stay all night. Bronte's at home."

"Yes, you can. I've got lots of room and Bronte's a big girl. We'll have a sleepover. Girls' night out."

"Annie, what's the matter? This isn't like you."

"What is me? I don't know anymore."

Eve stilled and narrowed her eyes. "Okay, Blake. What aren't you telling me?"

"Nothing." Then with a haunted expression she said, "Everything." She paused. "If I tell you something, you have to swear that you won't tell anyone."

"All right. Sure, I promise." The weight of her consent dragged her into the cushions. She settled down on the couch beside Annie, keenly aware of Annie's utter seriousness. She expected her to say she was getting a divorce.

"I have cancer."

Her breath exhaled in a whoosh. "What?" Instantly her fatigue cleared and she moved closer to hold Annie's hand.

"I found out yesterday. It's uterine cancer. That explains the bleeding." She snorted. "Who'd have guessed? I thought cancer only happened to the other person."

"I'm so sorry, Annie," Eve replied, fumbling for words. "So shocked." Of course Annie didn't want to be alone tonight. In a flash, the drinking, the paranoia, the behavior, were all understood. But why was she alone? A fury flared up against John. "How could John fight with you tonight? Why isn't he here with you?"

"He doesn't know. I didn't have time to tell him. Eve, you have to promise me you won't tell him."

"Of course I promise. But you have to, as soon as he gets home."

Annie turned her head away, not making the promise. Not knowing when, or if, John would come home.

"I'm tired," she said, leaning back against the cushions. Outside the window, dawn was just piercing the blackness. "Stay with me a little longer, Eve. It's almost morning. I'll be myself then." She closed her eyes, holding Eve's hand. "Just till morning."

Eve stayed until after the sun came up and filled the room with gray morning light. She stayed until Annie had fallen into a deep, troubled sleep, whimpering softly like a child. Eve's heart ached for her friend as she tucked the blankets over her shoulder, knowing that Annie tucked the hurts deeper inside. Smoothing back her hair, she kissed her forehead, thinking as she did how fragile Annie seemed while she slept. This was a side she rarely showed anyone. It occurred to Eve that it must be very hard to always be the strong one, the tough one with all the answers. Who did you go to to let your hair down? Perhaps that was why Annie liked to drink. Her poor, dear Annie.

And poor Doris... In her heart, Eve thought Doris had always known about R.J. on some level, just as she had known about Tom. Why was it so hard for some women to confront the possibility of their husband's infidelity? Everyone wasn't like Annie, ready to pick up and go. Some women would gnash their teeth and maybe cry to a mother, a sister, a friend, but then put up a false front and let the suspicion slide into oblivion. Was the truth too much of a threat? Or was it because they knew, deep in their hearts, that even if the suspicion were true, they wouldn't leave?

Would she have left Tom?

With the question nagging in her mind, she closed Annie's front door, locking it behind her. Stepping out into the morning air, she saw that clouds were gathering from the northwest, a sure sign of rain. The dry leaves clattered on the branch like clicking fingers. They could use a good, hard, cleansing rain. The earth was parched.

Eve drove home and parked the car, lucky to have found her spot left unoccupied. The wind was picking up and trees rattled their dry leaves. She slipped inside her apartment, locking the door behind her with a sigh of relief. Her cozy home was quiet and still, welcoming and safe. Bronte was sound asleep. She kissed her daughter's forehead, relishing the sweet smell of her skin and hair. Then she tiptoed down the hall, slipping off her sweater and sliding back into the comfort of her own bed, just as thunder rolled in and rain splattered her windows.

Her body cried out for sleep but her mind was racing, as though charged by the bolts of light flashing outside. She punched her pillow, shifted several times on the mattress but it was no use. Her mind was not going to allow her rest until she analyzed the truth about Tom. Her consciousness was not permitting her to tuck it under a rock. Annie's words had torched a fuse of memories as bright and dazzling as fireworks—vibrant red, vivid blue and whistling white memories all with long sparkling plumes and thunderous percussion. The memory of Tom was blazing across her mind and she was compelled to look up and wonder at it, even as she smelled the sulfur.

Tom. Every year he'd store up a hoard of fireworks like a miser, then bring them all out on the Fourth and blow them off in the backyard, laughing and running away like a naughty schoolboy when the police cruiser eased by. Tom Porter, her husband, her lover, her betrayer. He suddenly seemed so alive in her mind. Oh, Tom…

She rose and walked to the closet, her heart aching for him. Opening it, she pulled out his white terry cloth robe. She'd given away most of his clothes to charity, saving only his personal items for the children—gold cuff links and onyx tuxedo shirt buttons for Finney, his watch and gold pen for Bronte. Eve only wanted the robe for herself. She slipped her arms into the robe and wrapped it tight, hugging herself. If she closed her eyes and pressed her cheek and nose against the terry cloth, she could smell his scent and imagine that he was here with her, that his arms were around her. And she didn't feel so alone.

It wasn't that weird, really. Sort of like giving a child her favorite toy at bedtime, or a dog his master's shoe. Eve didn't allow herself to play this charade often. There were other oddities she confessed to no one, like the way she never sat in his seat at the table, or slept on his side of the bed. Small signs that her grieving was not yet over. But on nights like tonight, when the memories were close, she needed to suspend belief, to fool herself any way she could, in order to find a little comfort.

She returned to bed still wrapped in Tom's robe and lay quietly, staring up at the ceiling. In the shadows she saw a younger Tom and Eve, when their love was fresh and strong, when they'd vowed that they'd be different from a history of lovers who allowed their love to grow old and tired with their bodies.

Her memory of the night he proposed marriage was as fresh in her mind as though it had happened yesterday. They were lying in his bed, more a thin foam mattress on a wood platform, in his dingy, cramped apartment in Old Town. Tom had put her head on his shoulder after they'd made love. He was so thin then that his collarbone protruded hard against her cheek. If she closed her eyes she could still feel his long, tapered fingers as they stroked her moist hair from her face.

"I can't promise you anything more than I have right now," he'd said. "But I offer you my love and my future, if that is enough."

Knowing that he was just beginning medical school, that he didn't have two dimes to rub together, she still said yes. It was enough, more than enough, had always been enough. The money that came later, the bigger houses, the better, faster cars, the designer clothes—all those *things* were meaningless.

Hot tears flowed down her cheeks. Why hadn't she stopped to remember that when he was alive? Remembered the thin young man with bony shoulders who loved the stars, who shared lengthy, intense debates over whether there was a God or an afterlife, who had so many dreams.

When did the dreams vanish? When did the quiet talk before sleep cease? The minutia of every day, the demands of others on their time, the petty irritations bred by familiarity—these were the enemies. Oh, how she'd be nettled by the way he scratched behind his ears every morning when he rose from bed, or how every night he left his underwear on the floor, or how he answered "uh-huh" when he wasn't really listening. He must have found her habits irritating, too, because he often rolled his eyes or walked away from her. Why didn't we try to find a common ground of interest again, she agonized?

Now she was left only to regret having lost the opportunity to find that young man again in the middle-aged one, the dreamer she'd fallen in love with. Did Tom miss the young, impassioned Eve he fell in love with? Is that why he searched for those qualities in someone else? Why, Tom? Why?

The past seemed more real to her than the present. What was that line from Faulkner? *The past isn't dead. It isn't even past.*

Well, Faulkner was wrong. The past was dead and

burned to ashes. She had to accept that reality or condemn herself to the fate of an Indian princess who threw herself on her husband's funeral pyre. Just as she had to accept that Tom wasn't perfect and neither was their marriage perfect. Annie was right. As long as she held them up as a shrine she would never be free to move on. But seeing Tom's imperfections made him more human. She couldn't say now how she might have handled the truth when he was alive, although she wanted to think that if he had returned home from San Diego, they would have somehow worked things out. She wanted to believe that if she'd stayed with him it would have been because she loved him, not because it was easier. She would never know for sure. But she did know, lying here alone in her bed, that she was a different person now. She was stronger, more independent.

She lay while the storm moved on, till the rays of sun slipped through the curtains and pierced the gloomy, cold darkness, chasing off the tears like a ghost at first light. She hugged the robe close, smelled his scent still lingering in the fiber. She knew on some level that he was close. She felt it very strongly. He was here with her, and he was at peace. And he loved her. She felt that, too.

"I forgive you, Tom," she said aloud, meaning it, believing she was heard. "And I loved you. I truly loved you."

Sixteen

Mrs. Pontellier was beginning to realize her position in the universe as a human being, and to recognize her relation as an individual to the world within and about her.

—Kate Chopin, *The Awakening*

Doris woke early, despite the scant amount of sleep. R.J. hadn't noticed that she'd slipped away from their bed last night, nor that she'd returned an hour later, her feet damp and cold. He'd slept right through it, snoring up a cacophony of sound along with the rolling thunder. While he was in the shower, she lay still, listening to the sound of the old pipes and his vigorous movements as he joyfully prepared for another day on the job. No holiday for him. The dinner had gone well and he was charged. She could still see the sparkle in his eye as he told her he was leaving for a business trip this morning, something that had suddenly come up.

How convenient for him, she thought dryly as her gaze swept across the intricate baroque pattern of the room's yellow wallpaper. Her bedroom drapes were still drawn.

Hot, white stripes of light pushed against the shades, to no
avail. The bedroom was dark and cool, welcoming.

As soon as R.J. left the bedroom for the kitchen she
rose, slipped from her nightgown while avoiding the mirror, and entered the bathroom. Hot steam billowed and
fogged the windows. She saw herself reflected in the glass
as a ghostly shadow. Annie's words came back to her.
*Women look in the mirror and don't recognize their own
reflections.*

She moved across the slippery tiles like an old boxer
heading for the locker room after a lost match. She turned
on the water faucet for the tub, making it so hot it would
hurt; she wanted to feel scorching clean of whatever foul-
ness was oozing from her pores this morning. She could
smell last night's mendacity clinging to her skin.

Lifeless described her limp manner as she soaked in the
tub. The sound of dripping water from the faucet made her
sleepy, but outside the room the thumping of her husband's
footfall in the bedroom, banging closet doors and slamming drawers intruded on her peace. R.J. had a heavy
tread, hard on the heel. Occasionally the footfall would
stop outside the bathroom door and pause. She lay still
then, her muscles going taut, thinking, *Go away, go away.*
The steps did eventually move away again. Then came the
sound of a suitcase hitting the floor, followed by another
stop at the bathroom door.

"What are you doing in there for so long? Are you okay
in there?"

She opened her mouth then closed it. She couldn't answer him.

The door handle jiggled. "Open the door." It was a
command. When she didn't answer he jiggled the handle
again, pounding once. "Open this door, or I'll break it
down."

"Go away, R.J., to wherever you're going," she called back. "I don't want to open the door and I won't."

There was a pause and then he said in a harsh voice tinged with relief, "You're acting like some prima donna. You only think of yourself, you know that? You lie around all day doing God knows what, while I'm out there earning a living. I'd hate to think what'd happen to you on your own. You sure as hell couldn't earn enough to take hour-long baths. Or gossip with your ding-a-ling friends. I take good care of you. You've got a pretty good life here. You should appreciate it."

Doris stewed in the tub, her toes and fists clenched, her jaw stuck out and her lips mouthing retorts she did not give voice to. *It's my money that built your business in the first place. Money my daddy gave to me, not you. It's all your fault that I'm so unhappy. You and your women friends. You haven't touched me in months. I don't feel like a woman anymore.*

"So, you're not going to open up that door? All right. Well, as far as I'm concerned, you can just stew in that tub for as long as you like. Enjoy yourself. I'm going out to do my job. I just hope you come to your senses by the time I get back tomorrow night. And when I do, I'd like dinner on the table...if it's not too much to ask as head of this household."

Doris writhed in the tub, determined not to answer him. She waited until she heard the footsteps walk away into the hall, then the creak of the front door and the slam when it closed.

He's gone, she thought with inexpressible relief. Everyone was gone: R.J., Bobby, Sarah. She was alone again in this large house she'd spent her lifetime in. There was only herself and the yellow wallpaper. She could hear her mother's voice in her mind's ear: *Face the facts, Doris. You're fifty years old and still living in your parents'*

*house. You're still being told what to do, how to behave.
When are you going to grow up?*

She raised her palm from the water and looked at her
wrinkled, prunelike fingertips. She remembered when she
was young, looking at these same puckered fingertips and
marveling that she could look so old on the outside and
still be so young on the inside.

That was how she felt now. Old on the outside but still
so very young inside!

She rose from the tub and wrapped a large yellow bath
towel around herself. With the corner she wiped off the
steam and droplets of water from the mirror over the sink.
Doris took a good long look at the face in the mirror. She
saw a woman with puffy pale-blue eyes with lids as thin
as tissue, washed-out peachy-colored hair, and skin that
was pale and lifeless. But this time she didn't turn away
in disgust. She looked harder, deeper, into the same eyes
that she'd looked into all of her life, trying to find the child
in the reflection.

What she saw was her face, the way she looked right
now. This face belonged to a fifty-year-old woman named
Doris Bridges. Doris looked hard at the face and decided
that she couldn't let this woman die before getting to know
her.

Her first thought was to get out of the room. The next
was to get out of the house. She couldn't pack fast enough.
R.J. wasn't the only one who could just pack up and leave.
She threw a few essentials into a suitcase, then sat at her
desk with dripping hair, smoothed out a piece of her best
stationery and wrote a note to Sarah.

Her daughter would feel shock followed by indignation.
How dare her mom just up and leave? Now *she* would
have to cook and clean house. Doris smiled. Not that she
did, really. There was a maid, a lawn service and a telephone. It would be good for her daughter to grow up and

assume a little responsibility—like Bronte. Or, she thought with a chuckle, she could dump it all on R.J. It would be interesting to see which Sarah did. Nonetheless, maternal habit kicked in and she wrote Sarah a long list describing what was where, who to call for this and that, and how often to feed the fish.

She wrote a note to Bobby as well, but she doubted her departure would make much of a dent in his life. He was living in his own world, a college man now, meeting with friends. Doris licked and sealed the envelope thinking that was as it should be.

The next letter was for R.J. Her pen stilled over the paper. How could she write to him all that she felt at the moment? Should she tell him she knew of his affairs? But she wasn't leaving because of the other women. Not really. She was only thinking of one woman now—herself. Or should she mention how angry she was at him for not touching her, for neglecting her body and her soul for so long she'd almost died? But could she blame him? Hadn't she neglected herself more?

She tapped the pen against her lips, trying to put together the right words to tell him she wasn't running away from anything, except perhaps the yellow wallpaper. She'd been locked inside this house of rules and memories for so long she had stopped growing. In so many ways she was still the little girl who'd lived here with her parents, the same blushing bride she had been when she'd married R.J. His opinions were hers. His beliefs dominated hers. And wasn't she strongest when she preached his ideas to others? She'd been a regular pillar of the community. But underneath the coifed and polished shell she was empty. A wax figure. She'd given her *self* to her husband. To her children.

And now, R.J. had moved on and the children had grown up and they knew that she was nothing but a parrot

to their father's words. They looked away when she tried
to make a serious point. Or when they listened, it was with
a patient look followed by a wry, pathetic smile.

Doris looked at the sheet of steel-blue stationery and
heard R.J.'s voice again, the rattling of the door handle
and his incessant demand that she open the door. Putting
the pen to paper, Doris wrote: "Dear R.J. I opened the
door. Doris."

Doris drove directly to their lake house in Michigan.
The roads were crowded with wagons and vans packed
with camping gear, coolers and kids as city dwellers
headed north for vacation. For fifty years she'd traveled
this same route, sometimes in the back seat, sometimes in
the front. There were shiny new gas stations and food bars
where once upon a time there had been only a few diners
and wide-open fields of crops.

When she turned off the interstate onto the rural roads,
however, the landscape remained much the same as in her
childhood. Rolling hills were lined with rows of concord
grapes still green on the vine, large-scale nurseries overflowing with stock, and rickety farm stands leaning by the
roadside. She stopped at one to pick up lettuce, berries and
a bouquet of brilliant flowers—reds, blues and yellows—
for her table.

Back on the road she remembered riding in the back
seat of her mom's Buick with her brother, Bill, counting
the out-of-state license plates, each vying for the dollar
promised by Dad for the most sighted. Bill usually won.
She always suspected he cheated but it didn't matter. It
was only on vacation that he played games with her and
he always bought her Charleston Chews, Bit O' Honey,
Pay Day candy bars and Lik·A·Stix with the winnings anyway. Sarah and Bobby had played that same game on their
journeys north as well, but oddly, she couldn't remember

those days as clearly as those of her own childhood. Mom and Dad, Grandma Alison and Grandpa Jack, Uncle Hugo and Aunt Deb... Their faces were real, almost tangible today.

She arrived at the lake house in good time, stopping only once more for milk, eggs, bread and butter. Pulling up on the gravel drive behind the cottage, she turned off the engine, and resting her head on her arm over the steering wheel, sighed deeply. She felt that she had traveled not so far in miles as in years. The memories were still rolling inside her, careening up and down, around dangerous corners and slippery slopes. She felt the wheels still turning in her veins.

Opening the door she stepped out into the fresh air of a Michigan summer's afternoon, eager to escape from the relentless clamor in her head.

Summer was ripe. There was a heaviness in the humid air that soaked her clothes and went straight to her bones, weighing them down. She stood in the driveway a moment, ears cocked, nose high in the air. The scent of barbecue mingled with honeysuckle. Motorboats churned out on the lake beyond the wall of trees, children shouted with glee, and a dog chained to an old sycamore tree was barking.

Nothing ever changed here. She was deeply grateful; she felt secure.

Ordinarily when she arrived she took note of all that needed doing. The screen on the porch door was torn, her impatiens were wilted and desperate for water, a trail of ants marched single file to the base of the cottage. She saw all this and felt the familiar pinpricks of conscience to get the work done, to do her wifely duty. Today, however, she didn't want to. If she hadn't come up on the spur of the moment, she reasoned, those ants would be getting their dinner uninterrupted, the mosquitoes would continue to slip in through the tear free-as-you-please, and her flowers just might die. Life would go on without her. She was not indispensable. And rather than finding that depressing, she felt it was freeing, like dispensing with an old, heavy coat that she'd never really liked all that much anyway.

Over the porch door was a tacky metal sign that looked like a license plate and read: Leave Your Troubles At the Door. Her father had found it at some roadside stand when she was a little girl and bought it, claiming that it was perfect for the cottage. Her mother had laughed and patted his arm, and Doris had always suspected it was some private joke between them. The sign stayed up there getting rustier every year and before they entered her Dad would always say, "Okay everyone! Leave your troubles at the door!" R.J. had wanted to get rid of the sign, calling it an embarrassment, but Doris couldn't bear to part with it. In time, her kids said the magic words as well.

"Leave your troubles at the door," she said aloud, then picking up her baggage, walked inside.

She wrinkled her nose and sniffed. The house had that stale, closed-up scent of dank upholstery, dusty corners and cold ashes. After bringing in her groceries, she immediately walked to the windows facing the lake and opened them wide. Out there, down the slope, the lake glistened wet and wavy in the sun. She knew it was cool and refreshing just by looking at it.

If she were with the children, she'd have to begin right away putting fresh linens on the beds, scouring the sinks and toilets, vacuuming up the armies of dead bugs at the windowsills and cooking a meal for the hungry crew. Organize, clean, accommodate. As the mother, she'd feel compelled to make this house a comfortable home for her family. She didn't begrudge the role. Not at all! For years she'd gloried in making her family happy.

But things had changed, and she had to come to grips

with this fact. The children were older; they didn't need her. She didn't have to tend house now. She realized this with an amazement that was as welcome as it was unexpected. Looking around at the cottage she smiled, realizing with a secret delight: *Why, this house has been sitting here empty—just waiting for me!*

John returned home late the morning after the party, still dressed in the same overalls. He paused at the door, looking at Annie on the sofa. Then, without a word of explanation as to where he had spent the night, he went straight into the bedroom, walking with the kind of rigidity that implied he was a superior being for his ability to restrain his anger. Annie lay quietly waiting on the sofa while he showered and clumped around in the bedroom. A short while later he returned to stand at the end of the sofa carrying a suitcase in his hand. He set it down on the floor, then straightened in the manner of a grand announcement.

"I'm going to Florida," he said matter-of-factly. "I'll be there for a week. At the end of that time, I'll call and we'll see if I should come back home." His face was solemn and impassive, but she didn't miss the deep circles under his eyes or the brittle quality to his stance.

Annie only looked back at him, returning the same impassive expression. She thought that he was surprised by her reaction. It was out of character for her not to jump up, and with her usual straightforwardness, demand an explanation or coerce him one way or the other to talk or fight. She didn't want to do any of those things, however. She didn't have the energy. She had rather hoped that he would ask his usual, *Do you want to talk?* Then she would say *yes*. Then, if her fantasy were allowed to continue, they would lie together on the sofa all day while she told him that she had cancer and that she needed him and loved him and then he would tell her how much he loved her, too.

But this wasn't a fantasy, this was real, and he wasn't saying any of that.

So she only replied, "Okay."

He stared at her a moment longer, his face losing color, then he bent to pick up the suitcase and walked out of the house.

Hours later, Annie sat motionless on a garden chair in the darkness staring into the black. She was free-falling without a parachute. Isolated. She wasn't going for alcohol. She wasn't calling a friend. She wasn't expecting a knight to come along on a white horse and rescue her. She had no more expectations from life. Her cup was empty; she had no more tears.

It was an unusually cool evening for July, she thought, feeling detached, as though she were already separate from the earth and climate. Autumnally cool. A brisk breeze rustled the leaves of the trees. The night was whispering. Annie closed her eyes and listened. It was a beautiful sound—very peaceful.

Why did she never come outside to listen to the trees talk, she wondered? Or follow the movement of a storm in the sky, or smell honeysuckle on a summer's breeze? How did she get so busy that she lost touch with nature?

Her parents had always found time. They used to dance with her in the rain or laugh while they all jumped in puddles and muddied their toes on a hot, humid summer afternoon. In the fall they hiked in the mountains, holding hands, smelling the earth's ripeness and witnessing the vibrant golds, reds and oranges of nature's palette. In winter, Mom bundled her up in woolens so they could stand in the backyard, lift their heads and catch snowflakes on their tongues. And in the spring Dad told her that her finger was exactly the right size to poke holes into his freshly tilled soil for seeds in the garden.

Those were happy times, she remembered with a bittersweet twinge. It was so easy to find fault with her parents, to blame them, to cast them from her life and forget the one big truth: they loved her.

She had decided long ago that she didn't need them. She rejected them in her struggle for control. She'd thought with control came safety, that nothing bad could happen to her. She lived indoors, in a climate-controlled environment. She passed day after day totally unaffected by the mercurial weather out of doors or the turn of seasons outside her window. How naive she was, she realized too late. Nature marched on.

To everything there is a season. A time to be born, a time to die...

A car door slammed in the driveway. Annie cocked her head and listened intently. She heard footsteps up the front walk, then the squeaky hinge of the front door. A suitcase hit the floor, followed by the jingle of keys.

John was home.

Her body tensed. She brought one knee up close to her chest, wrapping her arms around it tight, but remained sitting on the back porch, listening. She followed the sound of his footfall as he paced through the house. He did not call her name, but she knew he was looking for her, so she waited, crouched on the chair.

When he stood behind her at the screen door she could hardly breathe, couldn't find the air. He knew she was out here, just as he knew she was aware of him standing at the door—two shadows in the night.

Make your move, she cried inside. She wanted boldness now. Wanted him to take her in his arms, speak his mind, kiss her and make it all better. She didn't want to be the one to make the first move, to once again be the strong one. She was tired, afraid. She was the little girl she'd just remembered and wanted to be taken care of. Just once.

The silence lengthened as he waited and she worried he would play the poor puppy needing a pat on the head. Let good ol' Annie burst the bubble with a hearty laugh, a good joke or some rousing sex. *Not this time, John,* she thought, clenching her fists. *I'm not that strong.* If he wanted to make things better, it had to come from him.

"Do you want to talk?"

He gave the cue, except his voice sounded like the rustling of the leaves. She was supposed to say yes now. Words and emotions seemed to rise up in her throat to form a knot she couldn't push out. There was too much in there to say. Annie opened her mouth but nothing came out.

She felt adrift when she heard him turn and walk away. She lowered her head to her kneecap. Her shoulders shook as she silently wept in the blackness.

Suddenly she heard a pounding of heels on the floor. The back door flung open again, banging against the brick, then slamming shut behind him. John rounded her chair and stood before her. He looked distraught, his blond hair tousled, his cheeks unshaven, resolve carved into his long face. Their eyes finally met and she was blinded by the love she saw in that brilliant blue. Her insides ached just looking at him.

"I won't do this anymore," he shouted. "I don't care if you don't want to talk. You were right, Annie. These silences are no good for us. We need to talk, and we need to talk now. No more silences between us. No more games."

Annie felt overwhelmed. When she didn't move or respond, he grabbed hold of her shoulders, hurting her, pulling her to her feet and holding her at arm's length.

"Look at me, damn it."

She dragged her eyes up. Through the blur of tears she

was amazed to see tears in his eyes as well. The blue pierced through the water, stunning in their beauty.

"I'm dying here, Annie," he said, his voice raspy with emotion. "Can't you see? I'm so angry, so hurt, I don't know whether to scream at you or just walk out that door and never turn back. I tried that, but I can't do it. Damn you, I can't. I love you."

"John..."

He released her, sighed and rubbed his forehead hard with his clenched fist.

"You think I let you down, that I didn't love you enough, that I wasn't man enough to fight R.J. over you. Don't you know how that's killing me? I don't give a damn about R. J. Bridges. It's *you* I care about. How do you think I felt when I saw R.J.'s hand on your thigh? I wasn't mad at him, I was mad at *you*. For letting it happen. For allowing it to happen. Aw, come on, Annie, you're nobody's fool. You don't let things just happen to you. You're always in control."

"I...I'm not. John, I'm not."

"Yes, you are," he shot back, angry. Then after a strangled pause he added, "And I let you be. I used to think that's what made us such a great couple. You were left brain and I was right. Tough cop, nice cop. Abbott and Costello. But it doesn't always work that way, does it?"

She shook her head and looked at her feet, confused.

"Hey, look," he said, misinterpreting her silence. "It worked for a while. Maybe it's time to break up the act. If that's what you want, I'll go along with it. Don't get me wrong, this isn't about my not fighting for something. My pulling some caveman act might work in movies but not in real life. At least not for me. That's not who I am." He paused and took a deep breath, furrowing his brow. "I've given this a lot of thought the past few hours. Tortuous thought." He grit his teeth and said in a low voice laced with accusation, "You made me question my manhood."

Annie's breath froze in her chest. "I'm sorry, John. I shouldn't have said that. I shouldn't have done so many things. Please forgive me."

Hearing her words, his lips tightened and she thought he might break down. But he pulled himself together, putting his hands on his hips and speaking deliberately.

"The way I see it, a man isn't someone who wields a club, Annie. A man sticks by his principles. A man defends his honor and that of his family. A man doesn't just take care of his own, he cares for them. There's a difference. I've gone through that scene in the garden a million times and what I saw was my wife playing a dangerous game, taking a chance with what I treasured most in the world—our marriage. What does that leave me to defend?

"I'm done with R.J.," he said with a swipe of his hand. "That's a separate issue, between him and me. But this—" he jabbed his finger at the ground "—is between you and me, Annie. Two adults. I shouldn't have walked away from you that night. Or this afternoon. I'm sorry. I'm telling you I won't walk away again. I want to make this marriage work. I'll fight for it. And I'll go to counseling, 'cause baby, we need help. I'm also telling you that if you don't want it to work, then I'm not going to hang in here and fight for crumbs. That's not my idea of being a man. I'm perfectly capable of leaving and getting by without you. But I won't like it. I love you, Annie."

She shrank within herself and felt very small, a gust of wind could blow her away.

"Hold me, John."

Suddenly his arms were around her. She smelled John's skin, his hair. She felt the scrape of his beard against her cheek, the calluses on his fingers as he wiped the tears from her face, the dry chap of his lips as he kissed her forehead, her mouth.

She kissed him as if her life depended on it, because it did. She needed him more than he needed her. She never knew she could just let go and he'd catch her. Now that she did, she was no longer afraid. Wasn't that what marriage was all about?

He bent to lift her in his arms, cradling her, and carried her into the house, into their bedroom, onto their bed.

"Yes, yes, yes," she whimpered, her lips against his neck. She tasted the saltiness of her tears against his skin. She needed him to make love to her now, to feel all of his skin on her, around her, in her.

Their bodies clung to each other tenaciously, neither wanting to lose touch with the other, not even for as long as it took to fumble with buttons and zippers and clasps, to slip fabric from their bodies. Their desire was fueled by need. Her only thought was to physically join with him. *Flesh of my flesh, bone of my bone.* She'd never understood those words so fully. His hands roamed her body, and his lips devoured her hungrily as she raked his back and stroked his hair. When at long last she welcomed him in her body, she arched back, opened her lips and released the cry that was strangled in her throat. She cried out in joy and sorrow, in pleasure and in pain. What bliss to simply let go, to float somewhere in space and time without a worry or care, trusting she would open her eyes and be in his arms.

Because in his arms, her body was not diseased or old or dying. In John's arms, her body was beautiful, ageless and alive. In John's arms, she was safe.

When the sweet sighs subsided and she lay wrapped in the warm, safe cocoon of his arms she heard him chuckle softly and felt his arms tighten around her. He nuzzled against her ear. She smiled and nestled deeper.

"Maybe we made a baby tonight," he whispered.

She heard the hope in his voice and physically felt the pain, jerking in reflex.

"Annie, what's the matter?" He rose up on his elbow to peer down at her face, his blond brows knitted. "Annie?" he repeated more firmly.

She turned on their mattress and looked into his face. He wasn't asking her to shield him or protect him. His arms were open; he was there to catch her. Taking his hands and holding them tight, she spoke in a voice that she hoped conveyed all she felt for him.

"John, there won't be any babies." She paused, took a deep breath, then leaped. "I have cancer."

Several days later, Midge called the Book Club together for an emergency meeting at Vivaldi's, their favorite trattoria in town. When they arrived, she'd already ordered a grilled-vegetables-and-goat-cheese appetizer and a bottle of Merlot, knowing they were on their lunch breaks and time was short. Midge had put her disappointment in the group not coming to her show behind her in wake of her concern for Doris. This was a crisis and demanded a calm, caring attitude and clarity.

"Doris left for her cottage in Michigan," she said giving them a loaded glance. "And she went alone."

After that bullet lodged, Eve looked at Annie, then asked, "Just like that? Without the kids?"

"That's not like her," Annie agreed. "I didn't think she had it in her."

"You'd be surprised," said Midge, rushing to her defense. "Doris can be a tough lady."

"Sure, about school budgets and community taxes. But leave R.J.? He says, 'Kick,' and she says, 'How high?'"

Midge leveled her with a glance. "What is it between you two lately?" Midge asked in a concerned voice.

Annie slipped her sunglasses back on and said evenly, "It's something we're working out."

"It's between them," Eve interjected, signaling with her eyes to Midge that she should let it drop.

"It's some kind of competition," Gabriella said knowingly. "Doris has strong opinions and so do you, and you're not afraid to blare them out."

"Why should I be?"

"No reason. Except before you joined the group, some of us were." She stopped, startled by the surprised looks on their faces. "Why are you all looking at me like that? Come on, admit it."

"I never was," Midge said with a huff, shaking her head.

"A little bit," Gabriella nudged. "Doris was the queen bee of the group. And we let her be."

"Well, maybe it's lonely up there on the pedestal. Always having to be perfect." Eve leaned back in the chair and offered Annie a wry smile.

"She probably just wants a little time for herself," Gabriella said. "Nothing to be alarmed about."

"I don't know," Midge said, tapping her fingertips together. "I don't like that she's just gone off. Especially since she's depressed."

"Depressed for months now, I'd say," Gabriella added, nodding.

Eve sat up, her eyes wide. "Depressed? Who, Doris? I didn't see it. I guess I was too caught up in my own problems to notice. What did you pick up on?"

Midge, Annie and Gabriella looked back at her with incredulity shining in their eyes.

"Didn't you notice how much weight she's gained?" asked Midge.

"And how tired she always is?" added Gabriella. "Every time I call lately she says she's been napping. And she never dresses up anymore or puts on makeup, unless she absolutely has to. She used to be such a classy dresser."

"Hel-lo," Midge said, shaking her head. "It's time for Vitamin P."

"I thought she was just angry because of R.J," Eve said slowly, taking it in. "Anger and depression are two different things."

"Yes, but they're a volatile combination," Midge replied soberly.

"Dangerous," added Annie.

"So, you all thought Doris was depressed?" Eve asked again. When they nodded, she pressed on, "Did anyone confront her with it?"

Midge frowned and looked away, irritated. "I'm not sure it's always a good thing to confront friends."

"But sometimes we need to be prodded," replied Eve. "Remember how I was after Tom died? I didn't have a clue how seriously depressed I was but Annie shook me up, made me see that I was wallowing." She met Annie's eyes again. This time, Annie did not look away. "She made me laugh, and that made me stronger. That and the honesty. That's what friends are for. To be there when we need them most."

Midge snorted and grabbed for her wineglass. Gabriella turned her head inquisitively but Midge didn't reply.

Annie, who was being uncharacteristically silent, sat up and spoke in a low voice. "I confronted Doris."

There was a gasp of surprise from Midge and Gabriella.

"What did you say to her?" asked Midge accusingly.

Annie looked at her hands. "I told her that R.J. chased women."

"Oh, my God," Gabriella muttered behind her palm. "You didn't."

Midge sat staring at Annie with a silent fury.

"You have to hear the whole story," Eve said, then looked at Annie for the explanation. With a reluctant sigh, Annie skimmed over the whole tale, hitting only the salient points. She didn't think anyone needed to know the details of the pool.

"How'd she take it? You don't think she'll do anything stupid?" Gabriella's brown eyes were as wide as they were round.

"No, no..." Annie replied, but her brows furrowed. "She was pretty cool."

"Damn, we would be reading *The Awakening* now," Gabriella muttered. "Real smart, us picking a book where the woman goes off by herself and commits suicide in the ocean." She paused and chewed her lip. "Does Doris swim?"

"Don't be silly," Annie snapped, removing the sunglasses. "I hardly think that one character's walking into the ocean will influence Doris in a life-and-death decision. God, I like to think we have more backbone than that."

"Books can really influence us," Gabriella argued back. "Especially when we're down."

"She's actually doing the right thing instinctively," Midge said slowly. "To go off on her own for a while. But if she starts hitting some dark inner chords she won't have anyone up there to support her."

"Should we go up?" asked Eve. "To check on her?"

"I don't think she'd welcome the intrusion," Midge replied. "She'd resent it. Doris isn't one to share her troubles or complain. Besides, I just received this letter telling me she went to the house and—isn't this just like Doris—to inform me that she wouldn't be able to make our next

Book Club meeting. It sounds to me like she's thinking clearly.''

"Well, we can't just sit here and do nothing," Eve replied.

"I say we send her some flowers, books and tapes just to let her know we love her and miss her," said Gabriella. "You know, to keep the door open. I don't like her being alone up there or feeling cut off."

"That's a great idea," Eve said. "And we should all send cards. Lots of cards, so she doesn't lose touch with us. She won't likely be talking to R.J., and her children are even less likely to call and check on her."

"We'll call her at the next Book Club meeting, too. We'll let the phone ring and ring till she can't stand it any longer and she'll have to pick up. We'll let her know that we're only excusing her just this once. After all," Midge said dryly, "isn't Doris the one who's always saying 'No one misses a Book Club meeting'?"

A late July humidity settled over the small lakeside community. The day had been quiet and still under the haze of heat. Children who had to be dragged from the lake an hour earlier, now sat quietly inside and played board games or watched television. Sunset brought little relief from the heat. The silence only deepened with the purpling sky.

Doris stood at the window and looked out, thinking that it was an odd night, pensive, as though the stage were set for mischief and magic. The moon hung full and robust over the glistening lake like a golden goddess overlooking her kingdom.

Doris felt the gravitational pull of the moon as surely as if she were the tide. The crickets sang their trilling song, "Come out! Come out!" Doris felt her cells come alive within her as she stared, motionless, at the iridescent, cheery faces of the impatiens gleaming in the twilight against the lush foliage. She thought to herself that she could just stand here and watch as she'd always done—or heed the invitation and go out and dance.

Suddenly she felt eight years old again, felt the exuberance of ripping off shoes and socks and tearing off for the water with an inner tube under her arm. Why not? She couldn't wait to get outside, to shake off her worries and problems and jump into the lake.

Twilight made the long climb down the rickety wooden stairs from the cottage to the lake risky. Pausing on a step, holding fast to the railing, she looked out to see small yellow lights flicker around the lake, one last powerful motorboat dragging a skier for a final spin around and one old, single-engine motorboat with a lone fisherman and his rods heading out toward the setting sun. A quiet peace was lowering over the lake like the lid of a summer pail, closing up for the day. *Time to go home,* the mother in her called out.

But Doris didn't want to go inside. She wanted to go into the glistening water. Sticking out her chin like a belligerent child, she traveled down the slope, step by step. Goldenrod clustered by the sugar maple, the canoe had overturned and was filled with brackish water and the sand along her beach needed refilling. But she didn't care. Out there the water lapped against the metal dock, rocking it against the pilings, inviting her in.

She stood at the water's edge with her toes sampling the water. The lake was as warm as a bath. She wrapped her arms around herself and inhaled gulps of fresh air, opening herself up and airing out her stale cavity from the stench of disappointment and disillusionment. Her mind emptied. She had no great thoughts or insights, no quotes from books or wise words counseled her. She was enveloped in the scented night air deepening around her, in the gentle sound of water against the shore, and by the feel of soft, muddy sand between her toes. Before her was a ribbon of moonlight stretched out across the black water like a shimmering, golden road, beckoning her to follow to a new adventure.

Doris stepped into the water, toward the light. The lake wrapped around her ankles. She moved farther out, her fingers unbuttoning her dress, then her bra, stepping out from her panties. The garments slipped from her body, drifted then sank beneath the black. She relished the feel of the warm water swirling between, around and in her, so free, as she reached one arm out, then another, stroking in its silky embrace. Just her and the water. Ahead the sky met the water seamlessly and the lights twinkled in the water. It was like swimming in diamonds. She smiled, felt her heart expand to take in the horizon and was filled with a yearning to mingle with the lights, to stay there forever. Nowhere to go, nothing to leave behind. Just to be. Floating in peaceful solitude with the stars.

A familiar wheedling whisper in her mind said, "Just let go. Go on, don't look back." Doris shivered, suddenly cold. She blinked, then looked over her shoulder. The lights of her own little cottage flickered far off in the distance.

She'd swum out too far, she thought with a surge of panic. She'd not be able to make it back home. A fear of death struck deep, freezing her. Dog-paddling, she jerked left, then right, looking at the circle of lights around her, realizing that she'd traveled squarely to the middle of the lake.

Doris looked at the shore and picked out the one light from the many that was her own. The light of her family cottage was small but it shone bright and clear, as it had for years for her children, her friends, her mother and father and her husband. She felt calmed and determined.

Doris turned in the murky water and changed direction. Her arms were tired, her heart pounding, but she stretched her arms forward, one after the other, kicking her legs, reaching for home. The trip back was arduous. Waves splashed against her cheek. She coughed back mouthfuls of water but pushed on, toward the one small light of her very own cottage. She struggled but made it back to the skimpy, muddy shoreline of home.

Doris's legs and arms felt like lead as she pushed a little farther up the shore and collapsed upon the soft grass. For some time she was aware only of her breathing and the blades of grass poking her bare skin, of the rich, pungent scent of earth at her nostrils, of the chorus of crickets in the trees and of the single mosquito that hummed a high song around her head. She felt oddly comforted, unconcerned with her nakedness, as though she were wrapped by the night, cradled by Mother Earth. She wasn't afraid of the dark, or the bugs, or the mysteries that hid in the mud. Rather, she felt as though her veins had escaped from her pores and burrowed deep into the soil, connecting, rooting her to the ground. She couldn't move. Closing her eyes, Doris slept deeply.

When she awoke some time later the night was chill and intensely quiet and the stars shone cold overhead. Doris's knees were near her chest and her hands were small fists at her breasts. She was shivering. She rose and found her beach towel a few yards away, then, with the light of the moon and stars to guide her, as they've guided a millennium of weary travelers before her, Doris found her way back up the hill to the warmth of her own bed.

Dawn broke to a brilliant morning. The birds sang loudly outside her window, insisting that she rise and meet the new day. When Doris finally rose, she stretched long and yawned noisily before catching sight of her reflection

in the mirror. This time, she did not turn away. Doris
looked long and hard at her body—at the breasts that had
nursed two children, the stretch marks that scarred her pale
flesh, the soft contours of waist, hips and thighs. She allowed her hands to travel across the length of muscle and
bone. This was *her* body, the vessel that had taken her on
an odyssey of experiences. It wasn't weak or ugly. It was
strong and beautiful. Resilient. Enduring. It simply was
what it was, and this morning, Doris made friends with it.

As much as she would have liked to remain naked and
free, she didn't think it fair to shock—or heavens,
frighten!—the neighboring children. Yet she didn't want
to wear anything tight, or restraining, or that made her feel
fat. So she dug through the closet that was jam-packed
with old clothing from years gone by, and pulled out a
flowing bright-raspberry-colored, crushed-cotton skirt and
banana-yellow top. She'd purchased these in Jamaica years
back on her honeymoon and had never worn them. They
were of the one-size-fits-all variety, thank God. She liked
the way the gauzy skirt swirled around her legs and her
nipples rubbed against the thin cotton top, almost as if she
were wearing nothing at all. Looking in the mirror, she
thought she looked like some wild, enormous hybrid fruit
from the tropics, then laughed, because Gabriella would
think she looked fabulous.

Ravenously hungry, she prowled the kitchen but didn't
reach for the croissants, as was her habit. She had a craving
for fresh fruit and water—lots and lots of water. It was as
though the remnants of a black poison had to be flushed
out. After breakfast she wandered about the house, feeling
all jittery inside. The cottage felt too confining. She needed
to remain outdoors. So she took a long walk around the
lake, watered the impatiens and emptied the hull of the
canoe. After picking berries, she picnicked on those and

nore fruit under the immense sugar maple by the lake that he used to climb as a child.

That tree had the best limbs, she thought again, lying n her back in the soft grass. She locked her hands beneath er head and dreamily marveled at the way the light fil-ered through the leaves as though through tissue paper, hanging the hues of green. Doris curled her toes, wishing he could climb up to those treasures beckoning lazily in summer's breeze, pick one, and bring it back to hold ear her chest. As a child she used to sit up among the eaves for hours, just looking out at the lake and the cot-ages, dreaming, feeling as if she were a queen, or in a paceship, or even just a kid lucky enough to be high up n the best climbing tree in the world.

Too bad she'd never had a tree house. She used to pester er dad every summer to build her a house in this very ree, but he never had the interest. Then for years she'd egged R.J. to build one for their children. But he never ad the time. She sighed and frowned, checking out the road expanse of parallel limbs that crisscrossed at just the ght places to support a floor. It was a shame no one had ver built her a tree house.

Then a new thought took seed in her mind. It rooted, prouted, grew stronger, then blossomed in a wide, ear-to-ar grin on her face.

"Where was that hammer?"

Two weeks later in Oakley, Fernando was standing in ne doorway of his home, shuffling his children out the oor. "Gabriella! We're going out for pizza, now," he alled. "Then I'll take the kids for a movie. We'll stay out s long as we can. Don't worry, we'll be quiet when we ome back in." He gave her a chaste kiss on the forehead. 'Have a good time with the Book Club."

"Yeah, Mom," her two youngest children echoed as

they were hustled out the door. ''Have fun with you friends.''

Gabriella ran her hands through her hair, relieved to se them shove off. She had so much to do before the Boo Club arrived and had been screaming at the family like witch. The meetings were only at her house twice a yea and when the girls came over, Fernando always took th children out because the meetings could get a little rowd Freddy and Elena loved the Book Club because wheneve the ladies came to their house it meant treats for them.

She stood at the door and waved as she watched h family load into the gold Saturn and pull away from th curb. A brisk wind was picking up in short gusts, shakin the long limbs of the canopy of trees that lined the street They scratched at the low-lying clouds. She smelled rai in the air, could feel it in the coolness of the wind cuttin through the thick veil of humidity.

Nights like these always reminded her of her childhoo in Puerto Rico. The rains would come and stay for month, making music on the tin roof. They'd stay in th house with Mami and eat warm soup. Their house had onl two rooms with an electric lightbulb hanging in the middl

She turned and looked at her own sturdy, three-bedroo frame house with a wide, welcoming front porch, a ne kitchen, two bathrooms and outlets in every room. Eve though compared to the elegance of Doris's house, h house was a small and uninspired little bungalow, in th small mountain town she came from her house would b a mansion.

But *virgencita*, it would take a miracle for her to get th place in shape in time for the Book Club! She'd been stuc doing overtime with a hysterical patient at the women' health center, tonight of all nights, and now had to scram ble before her friends arrived.

Gabriella rushed indoors and began plowing through th

narrow hall like a Mack truck at full speed. With her left hand she commandeered the roaring, wheezing vacuum, with her right hand she was dusting anything she passed. She'd never make it, she thought, crashing the edge of the vacuum against the dining room table legs. Sweat formed on her upper lip as her frustration grew. They'd moved here sixteen years ago with one child and still lived here today with four. Four kids and a husband, all of them home all day, and not one got off his or her keister to do anything to help.

Everything looked so…shabby! The fabric on the sofa and chairs was frayed, the lace at the windows was yellowed. Her mind spun as she wondered why she hadn't tried to clean last night? The answer was simple—she was too tired after a day on her feet. Annie and Midge always had clutter at their places, but it was *artistic* mess—tools and canvases and paint. Works in progress. Not a pigsty, with clothes hanging from chairs, dirty dishes on tables and magazines, toys and mail lying everywhere.

She straightened, one hand on her aching back, sniffing the air. Something was burning…. *"Madre de Dios,"* she cried, flicking off the vacuum and running to the kitchen. The oven was belching gray smoke. Her appetizers! Those spicy Cajun meatballs she'd spent an hour and a half last night mixing and forming into little balls were going up in smoke. Opening the oven, waving away the blackened smoke, her heart fell when she saw what looked like two dozen black lumps of coal on the cookie sheet.

The front doorbell rang. Her face blanched and all hope vanished.

"Gabriella? Yoo-hoo, anybody home? Gabby? What's all that smoke?" It was Eve and Annie.

Gabriella hurried from the kitchen with her long hair flying, flapping a towel in the air like a wild woman.

"Open the front door! I've got to clear out that smok
Hurry."

Eve cracked open the door but Gabby barreled past h
pushing it wide and propping a rocking chair from th
porch against it. "Leave it open. I don't care if the da
bugs get in. The smoke is everywhere," she wailed.

"What were these poor little darlings?" asked Annie
she looked down at the twenty-four black crisps on th
cookie sheet.

Gabriella's face fell. "They were supposed to be cu
little Cajun meatballs, to go with the Louisiana setting
Her face crumpled and she started sniffing. "I'm so f
behind, I...I just forgot about them. Now look at them
she wailed plaintively. "Look at my house! The vacuum
out, there's junk all over the place. My kitchen's a mes
And look at that! Elena didn't even bother to pick up h
cotton balls after she did her nails. No one does anythi
to help me. I live with pigs. I can't keep up. I'm fed
with them!"

"You just live with teenagers, Gabby," Eve said wi
a laugh, patting her back. "Finney drops his clothes
the floor right next to the hamper. Hopeless."

Midge walked into the house through the open do
waving her hands through the smoke. "What's going
in here? A barbecue?"

"A disaster," Gabriella replied, walking forward to h
Midge.

"*Pobrecita,*" Midge replied with humor, patting h
gently. "At least you didn't burn down your house."

"Don't take it so seriously," Eve said, eager to disp
the sorrow that seemed so out of place on Gabriella's fac

"This is a new low," Gabriella said, breaking dow
She sniffed and wiped her eyes. The words flowed out li
water from a dam. "Things are really piling up for r
right now. Fernando's still out of a job and the money

tight. I can't take on any more hours than I already have and I'm so tired all the time I just want to lie down and cry.''

Midge stepped closer, her eyes soft with concern. ''If you were in trouble, or needed help, you should have just called.''

''You're always the first to help us,'' added Eve.

''I didn't want to tell you because, you know—'' she tore at the tissue ''—it would embarrass my husband. So I just kept going as though nothing was the matter. I wanted to cancel tonight, but couldn't face disappointing you all. I thought I could handle it. Instead I drove myself crazy and ruined everything.''

''You didn't ruin anything. We're here together, we have our books. That's all we need,'' said Eve.

''But I have nothing good to serve you.''

''Gabby, we wouldn't care if you served a bag of chips as long as we got together. You don't have to knock yourself out for us.''

''As long as you've got wine, sweetie, who cares?'' said Annie.

''It's always Muenster cheese on Ritz crackers at my house,'' Midge said without apology. ''So Gabby, I hope you see that you have absolutely no hope at all of convincing us that we should be upset with you because you feel you've failed Hostess 101.''

''You know how it is when you want everything to be perfect for your friends? What's that saying? *At twenty you dress for men. At forty you dress for women.* Is that true or what? And look at me.'' Gabriella was still wearing torn sweatpants and a soiled Bulls basketball T-shirt. ''What does this say about me?''

''That you're a busy mom,'' Eve replied lightly as they shooed her upstairs to change clothes.

''Don't you dare come back down until you're sweet

smelling and gorgeous,'' Midge called after her. Then, after Gabriella was out of earshot, Midge muttered, ''Ladies, is this the time to tell you there's nothing I hate more than housecleaning?''

But she did her part, helping Annie and Eve finish the vacuuming, toss out the trash, wash up the dishes and give the infamous meatballs a salute and a send-off down the disposal. They found a box of crackers and a bag of tortilla chips in the pantry and in the fridge, a wedge of cheddar cheese and salsa. Midge opened a bottle of red wine while Annie started a pot of coffee.

Upstairs, Gabriella felt the return of her equilibrium. She wasn't sure what had happened down there. In fact, she felt a little bit embarrassed, but whatever, it worked. Support was all she really needed right now, to know that she wasn't alone. Juggling her job, plus her husband's emotional mood swings, had proved too much. She'd been too proud to tell anyone. She thought she was so competent she could handle it all.

Well, she wasn't. She had to remember that. And wasn't it nice to know that she could ask for help?

When she came back downstairs in her clean clothes, she paused at the bottom step and allowed a wide smile to carve deep into her cheeks. Her friends were sitting around the coffee table, relaxed and chatting amiably. Everything seemed to be running smoothly and her home looked beautiful. Perfect. It wasn't *House Beautiful*, but she had never wanted that. Her home was a reflection of her own tastes, not those of someone she'd hired. The cherry-red upholstery on the sofa, the beautiful mosaic coffee table from Puerto Rico, the gilt-framed Lord's Prayer signed by Pope John Paul II over the fireplace—each of these was a part of her.

''You guys are the best,'' she said, coming into the room and sitting next to Midge.

Midge leaned back into the cushions while her friends chatted. Eve was graceful as always dressed in a light-blue gingham summer dress that skirted around her ankles. Annie appeared more subdued than usual, curled up like a sleek, sleepy cat in an enormous, cushioned chair. Her clothes were baggy and soft and she wore little or no makeup at all, which made her fair skin appear all the more pale. Gabriella had changed into her signature bright colors and her magnificent, long black hair fell loose down her back like some unicorn's mane. She seemed relaxed again and was busy cutting up slices of cheese and setting them atop crackers while she talked.

Midge's emotions had come a long way in the three weeks since her opening at the gallery. After the show she'd considered dropping out of the club, or at the very least to be frosty and let them know in blunt words how hurt she'd been that no one had showed up. Wasn't she always there for them when they fought with their husbands, or talked about their kids? And that was fine. But she wasn't married and she didn't have all those hallmarks. Sometimes it seemed that she was always the one giving.

Then she'd received Doris's letter, and heard about the trouble that had exploded at her party and sent Doris and Annie spiraling. Eve had telephoned to apologize for missing the show. After they had talked awhile, Midge understood, even agreed with, her decision to stay home with her children. And tonight, seeing Gabriella at her wit's end, Midge was left to wonder how she could have been so blind herself not to see her dear friend reach the end of her rope. Most of all, yesterday Annie had confided to her that she had cancer. In that moment Midge's own problems seemed petty and insignificant.

Friendships were easy when life was going smoothly. What was hard was to be there for your friend when life got rough and the friendship was neither easy nor fun. The challenge was to forgive the friend when she failed. She'd heard that a person should count herself blessed to have even one true friend in her life. She had four: Gabriella, Eve, Annie and Doris.

The thought of Doris reminded her of the letter she'd received only this morning.

"I received another letter from Doris," she announced. Immediately the others quieted and leaned forward with comments on how relieved they were to hear from her.

"I brought it along so I could read parts of it to you," Midge continued, pulling the letter from her leather bag along with a pair of tortoiseshell reading glasses. "It's so unlike her. Tell me what you think."

She spread open the three-page letter filled with tiny script and slipped her glasses on. Scanning it, Midge explained, "She starts with asking how I am, etcetera etcetera.... She tells how she made a quick decision to go to the cottage, how she'd never done anything like this before." Midge raised her eyes and they all shared a worried look. "Apparently she wrote R.J. and the children letters, too, and asked them not to call or come up."

"You mean all this time she's cut herself off even from her family?" asked Eve, frowning with concern.

"Yes. Completely," she replied, eyes on the letter. "Ah, here we are." Midge shifted in her seat, cleared her throat and read.

"I needed to get away from R.J. for a while. And even from the children. Far away from the isolation I've been living in. I know you think it strange that I escape isolation by going to deeper isolation. But I'm not! That's the surprise. You see, up here I'm with myself in a way I never was before. Don't laugh, but I'm always singing that song we liked so much in chorus in high school, 'Getting to Know You.' It makes me feel happy somehow.

"Because I'm getting to know me. It's been quite a month. Sometimes I'm a sad, silly little girl, pouting and crying and kicking my heels. Other times I'm very weary and ancient and can do little more than lie on the deck and let the insects feast. I have no distractions so daily I face all the characters that run around inside me. I hear my mother and father a lot. They're so judgmental all the time, so very critical. But their voices are getting quieter and quieter. I don't seem to care so much whether they'd approve anymore, and I mean that in a good way. They're gone now, and this is my life.

"And, of course, I hear R.J. and the children in my mind, too. When I want to skinny-dip in the lake—yes I do!—I sometimes hear the children's horrified voices in my head, 'Oh, Mother, how could you embarrass me like that!' Or R.J.'s, 'What kind of an example are you setting?' I laugh now thinking how angry he'd be with me! Tra la!

"I'm not crazy. Really, Midge. I'm okay. I hope you'll understand most of all. Sign me up for a few of those self-exploration sessions you're always trying to get me to join. I'll do it with you when I come back. I promise. Whenever that is. I can't come home yet. There are still so many voices, so overbearing, that I can't make sense of them all. It's like they're festering inside my body, hovering, stealing bits of me. Poisoning me.

"But I won't be like poor Emma. I'm determined to exorcise them, one way or another. I can't go on listening to everyone else because that only makes me feel weak and insignificant. And angry. Oh, Midge, I am so weary of being angry.

"So please give my apologies to the Book Club. I

won't be at the next meeting, either. Or perhaps not
even the meeting after that. I don't know when I'll
be returning, so please don't plan on me. I don't want
anyone to plan on me for anything right now. I need
to take care of myself.

"Someone told me once about women who give
and give, and find they have nothing left. I was angry
at her at the time. I thought she was selfish. But in
the past few weeks I've come to know that she was
right. So for now I need to give to myself. And I hope
later, I can give to others again.

                                        Love, Doris"

There was a long silence that no one knew how to fill.
Annie rose and excused herself, dashing off to the bathroom. Midge began to rise after her but Eve held on to
her arm and gently shook her head.

"Leave her alone for a moment. She'll be okay."

Midge sighed, uncomfortable with that, but agreed and
settled back in the chair. "That party was only the tip of
the iceberg for Doris, I'm telling you."

"I'm sure it was," replied Eve.

They picked at their food as they picked apart the letter,
searching for clues. By the time Annie returned to the
group, composed but with eyes rimmed red, they had
started discussing this month's selection, *The Awakening.*

"We're just beginning," said Midge when Annie sat
down. "You didn't miss anything. Basically we've agreed
that both Doris and the heroine have rotten husbands."

"Hold on, *you* said that," countered Gabriella. It was
no secret that Midge never could stand R.J., and that the
feeling was mutual.

"That's where the comparison ends," Eve argued back.
"Edna Pontillier, our heroine, didn't enjoy motherhood.
But Doris treasured every moment of it. I think that's p

of the problem. Her kids are growing up and leaving home."

"There might be more comparisons," Annie said, twiddling the stem of her wineglass. "In Edna's day and age, she had no choice other than to conform to the rigid social code. Divorce wasn't an option. In her mind, I'm not sure it was so different for Doris."

"Come on, it's not the same at all," complained Gabriella. "Edna committed suicide because she couldn't have her lover. Just like Madame Bovary and Anna Karenina. That really made me mad."

"No, no, no!" Eve cried. "You're all missing the point of the novel. Edna had an awakening on the island. Her senses, her desires, her sense of self all came alive that summer. She could never be the same after that happened. I believe that all women have these epiphanies throughout their lives. At puberty there's a first awakening when we see ourselves as individual, sexual beings. Then somewhere in our early twenties there's another when we get a sense of ourselves as a woman. Then there's that panic at forty when we think we're running out of time and click into high gear. But somewhere between forty-five and fifty-five we have another true awakening, every bit as powerful as the one at adolescence. Our children are grown, we've enjoyed some success in our lives, and we're looking for something else now to fulfill ourselves."

"And our outer beauty is fading, too," Gabriella said. "God, I hate it...I keep working at it but I'm beginning to think the upkeep isn't as important anymore."

"Perhaps because we're not so eager to please or to impress others as we once were," said Midge. "It's like being adolescents all over again, only this time we don't care if everyone likes the way we look or the clothes we wear. Or even if people like us at all. That nasty competition is over. I see this as a time to be who we've always seen ourselves as being, deep in our hearts. The advice-giving wise woman or the heel-kicking rebel.''

Eve nodded. "That's exactly what I mean. That's what I took from the book.''

"Well, I'll never understand how some women can drink poison or throw themselves in front of trains or walk into oceans because of a man.'' Midge crossed her arms and legs in a huff of disgust.

"You know, I hate to say it—'' Gabriella was sitting at the edge of her chair "—but am I the only one thinking that Doris is up there all depressed and alone, thinking she lost her lover, too?''

There was a sudden silence.

"Maybe we should call Doris,'' Gabriella said. "Now.''

"Yes,'' echoed Eve. "Just to let her know we're thinking of her.''

This suggestion was met with a chorus of agreement and a rippling of relief. Gabriella brought the portable phone into the living room and they all circled close while Midge dialed the number. It rang five times, but finally Doris picked up.

"Hello, girlfriend,'' Midge called into the phone, her dark eyes flashing in Morse code to the group. "We're at the Book Club meeting and we miss you. What are you doing up there all alone?''

Eve, Gabriella and Annie all sat on the edges of their chairs, eyes bright, their hands clenched tight over their knees. They called out "Hi, sweetie!'' "Miss you, Doris!'' "I love you!''

They couldn't hear what Doris was saying to Midge, but they could eke out from Midge's responses that she was okay, that she just wanted time for herself for a change, that she didn't know exactly how long she was going to stay but she'd know when it was time to come home. Tha they shouldn't worry about her, but she was glad that they did.

Midge said to all of them, "Doris says she loves you. But she needs to love herself right now."

The power of that statement zinged right to the marrow. No matter that in the Book Club meeting they were discussing poor tragic heroines Edna Pontillier, Emma Bovary or Anna Karenina. Tragic characters, true, but they were fiction. In real life, they had Doris! Who'd have thought that proud, conservative, romantic Doris Bridges would break the mold and become Diana the huntress, hunting down herself. If Doris could do it, then they could, too. They were ready for their own awakenings, damn it!

The women of the Book Club raised their glasses high into the air. Midge put the receiver in the center of the close circle as they all brought their heads close.

"You go, girl!" they shouted.

After they hung up, they danced and laughed, then settled down and tore apart the book line by line. They couldn't know that in a small cottage in Michigan, Doris sat in a low chair with her feet up on the deck, wrapped in a red-and-black checked flannel blanket, with a glass of herbal tea in her hand, looking out at the moon's golden pathway across the lake. Tears of happiness flowed freely down her cheeks while in her head the chorus of her dearest friends' support danced in her head. Even far away, she knew she wasn't alone. She mattered to the Book Club.

She leaned back in her chair and stared at the moon. It hung in the sky beside her, a silent but steady presence—inspiring, enlightening, timeless, changing. Sometimes fat, sometimes thin, sometimes glowing. Sometimes those blotches were right there on the surface for the world to see. Some nights the moon dominated the sky, other nights it slipped quietly through veils of clouds. Sometimes it was mysterious, other times it was exposed, scarred with the

prints of men's heavy boots. Tonight the moon seemed
be smiling with her, keeping her company with a glow th
seemed to radiate from within. It filled her with its gold
light.

The moon had to be a woman, Doris decided. Raisi
her glass, she toasted her new friend and called out, "Y
Go, Girl!"

Seventeen

> To everything there is a season,
> and a time to every purpose under heaven.
> A time to be born, and a time to die.
>
> *—The Bible*

The mint-and-white-colored hospital gown made Annie's skin appear even more sallow than when she had walked in that morning.

"You'd think they'd have some pretty bright colors, wouldn't you?" Annie said, plucking with a grimace at the thin fabric. "For all the money they spend, they should hire a color consultant. How smart do you have to be to figure out green and sick is a bad combination? I'd look like shit in one of these on a good day, but right before surgery? Can I sue? I'm sure there's some psychological trauma I'm going through just looking in the mirror."

Eve laughed and reached out for Annie's hand. "You look beautiful, kiddo," she lied. "But then, you always do to me."

Annie squeezed her hand and her facade slipped away like a mask removed.

"It's going to be fine," Eve said, mustering encouragement. "The doctor said there's every sign that they'll get all the cancer out with the uterus."

Annie nodded, then glanced over at the wall clock and swallowed hard. Surgery was scheduled in an hour and her tension was mounting by the second. "This is the pits, waiting here. Why do they have clocks in here, anyway? They should at least be cuckoo clocks, just to make sure we all don't forget to pay attention to how long we're waiting." All at once her expression changed to reflect her fear. "I've never had surgery."

"It's nothing I'd go in for if I didn't have to, but believe me, once you get the gas, you don't remember a thing. It's in and out, no pun intended. The worst part is getting over the anesthesia, but we'll all be there when you wake up and you can yell at us."

"I won't yell, if you just promise to be there."

It was hard seeing Annie lying in a hospital bed with her hair limp, her face gaunt, looking like a bag of bones in that pitiful hospital gown. Such a switch from the vibrant, stylish Annie she knew and loved. This Annie was so vulnerable.

"Sure, I'll be there," she said, patting her hand. "And so will John. He's been great, hasn't he? Always by your side."

"I know. I never knew he could be so strong. He watches everything like a hawk. Brings my vitamins and medication in on schedule, consults with my doctors, feeds me organic meals, and he's on a first-name basis with the homeopath at the health food store. Where is the bully?"

"Out talking to the nurses. I'm not swearing by it, but I thought I saw candy pass hands."

"Such a schmoozer." She shrugged her thin shoulders "I guess he really loves me."

"You sound so surprised!"

"I am," she said, rubbing the gold band on her long fingers. "I never thought of myself as lovable."

"You're either crazy or just plain stupid then. We all love you."

Two pink stains blossomed on Annie's white cheeks. Eve never thought she'd live to see the day.

"Did you talk to Doris for me? Tell her that I was sorry? I mean…" She paused, then forced swagger into her voice. "I wouldn't want to die unforgiven."

"Yes," Eve replied seriously.

"What did you tell her?"

"Everything."

"So," Annie said, her long, slender fingers tapping the bedsheet. "What did she say?"

"Not much, actually," Eve replied. Then with her mouth twitching she said, "She was too busy crying."

Annie chortled quietly. "Typical," she said, pleasure shining in her eyes. Then changing her tone, she tapped Eve's fingers playfully. "How'd it go with the prof? Are you back together? If I die before you tell me, I'll haunt you, I swear to God."

"Don't even say that."

"Well, then?"

"We talked, and I introduced him to the children. Bronte cooked dinner, if you can believe that. I think things will work out but I don't want to go too fast. And Paul, well, I think he does. He's so definite. He tells me he loves me."

"You really are a marriage magnet."

"Whoa, we're not anywhere near that yet. Besides, the last thing I want to do is get married. I've worked too hard to get this far. I'm not willing to give up my independence."

"And you don't have to. But promise me you won't go around telling a lot of women that you're turning down a hot prospect like Paul Hammond. I'd hate to find you murdered in your sleep. Trust me on this one.''

Eve laughed as John walked in the door with a nurse and the doctor behind him. They had that business smile plastered on their faces.

''Annie, I'm letting you go to sleep now and when you wake up we'll laugh and talk and you can tell me what else I should do.'' She bent over to kiss Annie's tense cheek. ''I need you, sweetie. I love you,'' she whispered in her ear.

Annie and Eve squeezed hands and shared a gaze that transcended words.

''Okay, guys,'' Annie said, looking up at the medical team, swiping the tears from her eyes with the backs of her palms. Her voice was rollicking. ''Let's get this thing over with.'' She abruptly turned her head so she wouldn't have to see what the nurse was doing with the veins in her arm.

''By the way, Doc,'' she asked the young medical student scribbling into her chart at her side, ''do you know how to make a hormone?''

John groaned. Eve rolled her eyes and slipped through the door. But the student shook his head, taking her question seriously. Annie just loved gullible guys.

''Don't pay her!''

When Doris walked into the waiting room several hours later, Eve, Midge and Gabriella gasped in unison, then ran forward to wrap her in their arms. They hugged and kissed and gathered reassurance from their circle of friends.

Then they took notice of how much Doris had changed in the past six weeks.

''You look positively svelte!'' Gabriella exclaimed, noting the weight Doris had lost and the tan of her skin, and most of all, the gleam in her eye once again. She was not svelte, really, but healthy and glowing. She looked like a woman from the country in her long denim skirt, blue-cotton blouse and thick-knitted, jewel-toned shawl. "I hate you!"

Midge narrowed her eyes and checked out Doris's body. "So, Bridges, just how many pounds did you lose?"

"I haven't a clue," Doris said blithely. "There isn't a scale at the cottage and frankly, I don't want to know. I'm not thinking about calories or fat grams. I never want to go on another diet. I eat healthy foods when I'm hungry, stop when I'm full and swim and walk every day. It's called healthy living, girls. To tell you the truth, I never tried to lose weight. It just happened. I'm more concerned about my health than my looks right now. And what's going on inside my head."

"Speaking of your head—" Midge smirked, but her eyes were glowing with approval "—I noticed the outside's a little different."

Doris's hand went to her hair. She had colored it a flattering soft white, a marked change from the strawberry-blond color. "I got tired of dying it. I thought if I colored it once more, just to get the red out, then my own hair could grow back in on its own. And the fact is, that color is mostly gray."

"But why stop coloring it?" asked Gabriella. She was horrified at the very concept of her own hair going gray. "Why would anyone want to go gray?"

"I don't want that fake color on my head in the same way I don't want artificial fibers on my body. You might think I'm crazy, but when I first arrived at the cottage I felt that I had some black poison in me, oozing out of my pores, even out of the follicles of my hair. I drank lots and lots of water, swam every day and ate so much fruit and fiber I pumped ship for days. Now I feel clean inside. And empty, too, like a big old steamer trunk waiting to be filled.

But I'm going to be very choosy about what I fill the space with this time.''

''So you don't want anything artificial?'' Midge was fascinated, drawn in. As an art therapist, this was right up her alley.

''Right. It's not hard once you're committed.''

Gabriella studied her hair intently, tapping her full lips. She was having a hard time getting past the no-dye issue. ''It's weird. I mean, white is for old ladies, sure. I'm thinking Barbara Bush here. But your skin looks pinker and it kinda makes your eyes more blue. Sexy.'' She broke into a grin despite herself. ''I can't believe I'm saying this, but I like it. On you, that is.''

''So do I,'' agreed Eve.

Doris beamed. ''I was afraid that I was turning old overnight,'' she admitted. ''But in fact, it was happening in bits and pieces for years, only I denied it. I was so angry all the time. I didn't really even know what I was angry about. And the anger made everything worse. To tell you the truth, now I don't worry about getting old anymore. All those gray roots were signals that I was ignoring, along with other physical changes. What was I afraid of? It's just my body, my hair. I'm going to spend another twenty to thirty years in this vessel so I better start taking good care of it. And oddly enough, since I've started, I like my body with all its imperfections—even the gray. I accept them all as part of me. And that makes me feel strong, and maybe not young but youthful. Anyway—'' her brow rose in a saucy manner ''—this is me and the gray stays.''

''What does R.J. say?'' Midge's voice was testing.

''I didn't ask him and I don't care.''

This was met by ooohs, laughs and pats on the back.

''Don't get too excited. I'm not sure he'd notice anyway.''

''But that's another issue,'' Eve said, her eyes still admiring the straight-shouldered stance of Doris, her glowing skin and her bright-eyed awareness. Doris hadn't lost weight as much as the puffy pastiness. Most beautiful of all was her buoyant confidence. She was more like the Doris Eve had met years ago when she'd first moved to Riverton, the Doris who had knocked at her back door with a cherry pie and a pot of coffee, with young Sarah peeking behind her skirt.

"How about inside the head?" Midge probed.

"Fine," she replied brusquely, revealing a bit of the tight-lipped Doris they remembered. "I'm still working on it, but I'm okay. We can talk about all that later." Then changing tone she asked, "What's going on with Annie? Have we heard anything yet?"

"No," Eve replied, suddenly somber. "They've been in there for about an hour. We're just waiting for word."

"I'm so sorry for her," Doris said. "And to think we were worried about menopause and getting old. We should be happy we *are* getting old."

"Makes you think."

"I wish I'd known earlier," Doris said with a frown. "Things might have been different between us."

"Hey, they still can be," Midge offered. "She'll be out of there in a little while."

"I can try," Doris replied softly. "I want to."

"Well you made a good start by coming here today," Eve said. "Coming all this way."

"Of course I came. But, to tell you the truth, I almost didn't. When I heard from you, I got scared. The news burst my little nest of security there at the cottage. I didn't want to call or come home, as if I'd be contaminated by the news. Out of sight, out of mind."

"I think we all felt that to some extent," Eve said. "It's threatening. The thought that one of us actually got cancer...and Annie of all people. She exercises, eats right. If someone like her can get it, what does that say for us?''

"Well, don't go thinking you should give up fighting," Gabriella muttered, giving them all the warning gaze. "I hope you're all getting your mammograms and doing all that self-screening stuff. I'm not up to going through this again.''

"Yes, Mother," Eve said, wrapping an arm around her shoulder.

"How's Annie taking it?"

"You know Annie. She meets everything head-on, fists in the ready." Eve walked to a row of chairs and sat down, suddenly very weary. "But I'm worried. This is going to come hard on her later on. She hasn't really dealt with the fact that she's not going to have any children.''

"She was so determined."

"Yes...Annie is used to going out and getting what she wants.''

"But life isn't like that," Gabriella said, taking a chair beside Eve.

Eve nodded and cupped her chin in her palm. "I depended on her for so long for advice and strength. Now it's my turn to pay her back. Poor Annie. For her this is like hitting a wall. Splat. And on top of that is the threat that the cancer will reoccur. It hangs over her head like a dagger.''

"She's a survivor." Gabriella patted Eve's hand.

"She's going to go through depression and anxiety in the next few months," Midge replied, moving closer.

"We'll all be there to help her," Gabriella said gently

The mood lowered again. The women sat quietly together in a long row of chairs. Eve thought glumly that whoever chose the colors for the hospital gowns also chose the dreadful colors on the walls. The room was depressing not a window anywhere. It even felt germy.

"I was thinking," Eve said, breaking the silence. "Maybe we should pick a book for the next meeting that will be inspiring to her. Something that will point our discussion in the right direction."

"Good idea," Midge said. "Any suggestions?"

They tossed around the titles of a few bestsellers, books about women friends, memoirs of survivors, and a few classics and biographies. All of them made do but none of them seemed quite right.

"We need something with real impact, wisdom and comfort," said Gabriella scooting forward in her chair.

"How about the Bible?" Midge said as a wisecrack.

There was a thought-filled silence.

Eve tilted her head.

Doris pursed her lips.

"Oh, no," Midge said, shaking her head.

"Why not?" asked Gabriella, sitting up.

"What? The whole thing?" Midge was appalled.

"We could." Eve found the concept intriguing. "I have to confess, I've never read the Bible through. Have you? Most of what I know from the Bible I heard Sunday morning from the pulpit. It might be quite a journey."

"We're turning into a Bible group now?" asked Midge.

They all laughed lightly but it was clear which way the vote was swaying.

"We don't have to read the whole thing. We could break it up somehow. I'm sure we could get lots of advice from our pastor or the Divinity School," said Doris.

"I'd like to read the whole thing, cover to cover. We've done that with other books. Remember the *Odyssey*? And we went for weeks and weeks doing the *Artist's Way*. This could be a special project." Gabriella was sitting at the edge of her chair, lobbying hard.

"I think it's a good idea," pushed Eve. "Hey, it's a bedrock of our culture. Great literature is derived from it.

And then there are the psalms. Hard to find anything more beautiful.''

"You've got to admit it's different," added Gabriella. Then pulling out her date calendar she said, "We don't have any books chosen for the fall. The calendar is free." She looked up, smug. "It's perfect."

"And it's timely," added Doris. "It may take a long time, but so what? Maybe it wouldn't be a bad thing for all of us, not just Annie. I say, let's do it."

Midge leaned back in the chair and clasped her hands across her belly. She was never herded into anything but even Midge could see the decision was already made. There was nothing left for her to do but join in. She shrugged, and with a lopsided smile said, "Just don't tell my mother. I'll never hear the end of it. She'll be lighting candles and saying novenas, claiming a miracle has happened."

Eve sighed and leaned back into her chair, too. "Now all we have to do is convince Annie. She's not exactly spiritual."

"After today she will be," Gabriella said with a knowing eye.

Doris nodded and crossed her arms across her chest. "After this, I think we all will."

Two hours after Annie was wheeled into the operating room, the door to the waiting room opened and John and Dr. Gibson walked in. The Book Club all rose to their feet.

John looked shell-shocked. "The cancer went a little farther than we'd hoped." He looked to Dr. Gibson for confirmation.

"The tumor invaded the uterine wall," she said, in a professional, dispassionate voice. "We removed the uterus, both tubes, the ovaries and the pelvic nodes. Unfortunately, radiation will be required. But she made i through beautifully." She paused then and offered a warm smile that encompassed all of them. "You know, a potent weapon in battling cancer is a strong support network. I'm sure Annie will do well with friends like you."

After Dr. Gibson and John left for the recovery room, the four women wound their arms around each other and cried with relief, openly and without shame. They had all faced mortality with Annie. Each of them knew that in the scheme of things, they were next in line to cross that bridge. But today, Doris, Eve, Midge and Gabriella all felt like survivors.

Later that afternoon, Doris entered the colonial redbrick house that had, for fifty years, been her home. She walked serenely through the same, sunlit rooms she'd skipped through as a child. As she looked at the familiar furnishings, she felt an ancient energy sizzle in her veins, as though another self was rising from the ashes.

Her mind began creating a to-do list in its customary efficient manner as she walked from room to room. The windows would have to be washed, dust was building up under the cabinets in the living room—evidence of a missing mistress to watch over things. In the kitchen she prowled through the cabinets and the fridge, making up a grocery list to add or replace food that had been consumed in her month's absence. She was amused to find several low-fat, low-cal items among the instant meal selections. It was obvious Sarah was doing the shopping.

Still, she had to hand it to her daughter. She'd grown up quite a bit in her absence. Their long conversations on the telephone had gradually shifted from endless wailing and complaining to conversations that revealed bits of themselves. Sarah wasn't looking for her mother to solve problems or step-and-fetch it as much as she was looking for a role model. Doris felt that now, for the first time in many years, her daughter was looking at her, if only through one squinted eye.

Doris went to the library, sat down at her desk and began writing out long lists and copious notes of all that had to be done. While she wrote, her hand reached out to take hold of the phone. Her first call was to her maid. Would she consider adding a few days to her schedule? At least through the fall? Next she called the lawn service to relay instructions for the fall cleanup, then the cleaners to pick up the dozen or so items she'd collected from the children's closets to get them ready for the new school year, and the milkman to cut back the order after Bobby returned to college. Twenty-five minutes passed quickly. She realized with horror that this was only the top of the list. It would take days to complete and she hadn't even begun shopping for fall clothes for the children and...

Her mind shut down when she saw R.J. standing in the doorway, looking at her with an expression of surprise mingled with a mocking *I told you so*. She felt her back stiffen as she set down her pen and calmly folded her hands upon the table. She'd wondered—worried—what she would feel when she saw her husband again. In the past month her hatred for him had ceased. Unfortunately, so had her love and respect. Looking at him now, ruddy-cheeked and fit in his golf attire, leaning with a cocky insolence against the door frame, she was amazed at how very little she felt for him at all.

"So, you're back," he said.

She waited to reply, half expecting him to ask for his dinner on the table.

"It's about time," he added huffily, straightening and crossing his arms. He looked down at her from his height like a general about to mount a charge, or perhaps a judge considering the punishment.

Doris remained silent. She tilted her head and stared at

his heightening color. A month earlier she might have fluttered about him, trying to appease him, to please him. Or cried... Thank heavens that sniveling creature had gone, she thought to herself. She relaxed her hands and recalled her beloved cottage, her mornings spent sitting alone on the deck watching the sunrise. And the freedom there of not having to accommodate the constant neediness of one husband and two children while neglecting her own.

Doris looked down and saw the piles of lists and notations she'd created, the dozens of projects that would tie her time up for days. She laughed shortly, quietly, at her own folly. How easy it was to slip back into a mold, to always do what was expected.

She looked back into R.J.'s angry eyes. Bobby Jr. had those same eyes and that same fierce expression when she had told her twenty-year-old son that she would not be available to pack his suitcase for college.

"It's good you're back," R.J. was saying. "The place is falling apart without you. We need you."

Not *we missed you,* or *we love you.* But *we need you.*

"But I'm not back, as you put it."

"Wha—what do you mean?" His face was thunderous. "You don't think I'm going to allow you to just waltz out of here again, do you?"

Rather than cringe, Doris watched the performance and had to struggle to keep from laughing.

"It doesn't matter to me in the least what you will or will not allow," she said crisply.

"We'll just see about that."

"Sit down, R.J. We might as well have this conversation here and now. And close the door, please."

R.J. appeared stunned, like a bullet had whizzed by his head and he didn't know whether to duck or run. He closed the door, then gathering his bluster, strode across the room and sat in his favorite wing chair, crossing one leg over the other in his usual manner.

"What's this we have to talk about?"

She looked up and said calmly, "I won't be coming back, R.J. Not in the way you might expect. I will stay for a few days to visit my friend Annie in the hospital, and to help the children organize for school. I intend to give them cash and send them out to the malls to fend for themselves. Before you sputter and rage, I should tell you now that my plans are set. Bobby and Sarah and I have already discussed this. Frankly, Sarah is thrilled to not have me breathing down her neck all the time." She smiled briefly at the recollection of her heart-to-heart with Sarah the night before as they lay stretched out on her bed, chatting as they had not in years.

R.J. was listening in silence, studying her as though seeing her for the first time this morning. She felt his gaze sweep over her with a thoroughness she hadn't experienced in years.

"You look good," he said magnanimously, as though he'd just awarded her the highest compliment. "You lost some weight? And your hair. I don't know, you look different."

"I am different, R.J." Doris refused to allow herself any flush of pleasure at his compliment.

He settled back into the chair, creating an aura of comfort, perhaps even of intimacy. "Maybe your little vacation did you some good, after all. I guess we needed a little separation, a little time to miss each other. Things just weren't the same without you here. I mean, I guess I just didn't appreciate all that you do around here and maybe I took you for granted. Oh, Sarah did a pretty good job at organizing the meals and shopping, and the maid kept things pretty clean. But no one can do things quite the way you can. You have a special touch. I guess I don't tell you that enough.''

"R.J., what's my name?"

He seemed startled by the question. "What?"

"My name. You never call me by my name. Really, I can't recall a single time in the past several years when you've called me by my name. Someone once said that the sweetest sound in any language is the sound of your own name. I believe that is true because I have longed to hear my name on your lips."

"Doris, I…"

She held up her hand in an arresting gesture and shook her head. "Please, R.J., not now. It's too late."

His mouth shut and his face grew impassive, even cold. She imagined this was the face he used at meetings when he wanted to close the deal. "It's too late? For what? What does that mean?"

"It means, R.J., that our marriage is over." Despite herself, she felt a ripple of pleasure at the sight of his stunned expression. "I've already been to see my lawyers and I've been informed that I have more than enough evidence of adultery to establish cause. I suggest you find a divorce lawyer of your own because I intend to initiate proceedings at the earliest date possible. Also, I've contacted a real estate agent and I've put the house on the market. I intend to divide the property into four lots and sell them individually." Her eyes sparkled with triumph.

He rose and came forward toward the desk, his face mottled. "You can't do that."

"Oh yes, I can," she replied. "And I have. The house and the property is in my name. As is half your business." She gathered her lists neatly into a pile, then tossed them into the wastebasket. She was intensely aware that R.J. stood on the other side of the desk, breathing like a locomotive, watching her every move. She rose to a stand, smoothed out her skirt, then tugged at her cuffs.

"You have until the end of September to vacate the house. I'm going back to the cottage and I want you gone when I return. Now then—" She gathered her hands together in front of her and smiled politely. She might have been smiling at a salesman for all the warmth it conveyed. "I think that's everything that needs to be said between us, don't you?"

R.J. stood speechless, but his face reflected both shock and defeat. Doris felt no triumph but as she turned and walked from the room, she held her head high and her shoulders straight. With each step toward the exit she felt the same courage and strength of decision within her that she had experienced in the middle of Glenn Lake when she turned around and paddled back to shore, stroke by stroke, rather than sink beneath the murky waters. When she left the room, she smiled with relief, feeling free of R.J.'s gaze upon her.

Another school year was beginning. The vacationers had all returned home and the traffic in Oakley had doubled in volume. Mothers everywhere were packing lunches again, buying socks and underwear, paying school fees, and sighing in utter relief while they waved farewell to their little, and not so little darlings as they headed off to their first day of school.

Bronte and Finney were more nervous than usual, which was to be expected on the first day at a new school. Sarah Bridges and Bronte had made peace again after a summer's estrangement and had spent the previous week shopping together for school clothes and supplies. Finney had hidden his anxiety about entering a new school and making new friends with his anxiety over whether or not he'd make the football team. He'd been in football camp all of

August and poured his every waking moment into practice and mental preparation.

Eve, too, was a new student. She'd registered at last for night classes at Saint Benedict's to update her teaching certification. Bronte and Finney supported her decision and had promised their support at home while she tried to balance work, home and school. And her love life. Once the children's own lives took shape again, her relationship with Paul Hammond was no longer the monumental, life-threatening issue that they had perceived it to be over the summer when they were lonely, unhappy and without goals of their own.

She smiled as she parked her car in a space right in front of her building. Perhaps her luck was changing, she thought, yanking up the brake and patting the wheel of her old Volvo affectionately. Faithful old beast, she thought. It had to make it through one more year before she could apply for a teaching job and buy a new car.

When Eve arrived home, the scent of basil and garlic lingered in the hall. Her mouth watered and her stomach growled, envying her neighbor's dinner. She opened her door, then dropped her purse on the floor, kicked off her pumps and dragged herself to the living room. There, she paused and leaned against the door frame while a smile played across her face. She watched the scene before her with the same pleasure she would watch a scene from a favorite movie.

Bronte was sitting on the green velvet sofa with Sarah, wrapping shiny new schoolbooks with thick brown paper. The two girls were laughing, commenting on the new kids at school. On the floor, Finney was playing video games with two boys she didn't recognize, no doubt new friends from his new school. It was an everyday scene witnessed by mothers throughout the country: children at home goofing around after school.

Eve relished the ordinariness of the scene. For her, the ordinary was welcome. Her life had been a quixotic drama in the past year and a half. Bronte and Finney had new friends—that was a huge step. They were smiling—even bigger.

Eve took a deep breath, saving the image in her mind. "Hi, kids!"

"Oh, hi, Mom," Bronte said when she spotted her at the door. There were no signals of distress or anger, only a free-flowing smile and genuine pleasure at seeing her. "How's Annie? Is she okay?"

"She came through just fine," she replied. "I'm exhausted, though."

Bronte stood and came over, then surprised her by giving her a heartfelt hug, woman to woman. Eve clung tight, grateful.

"Well, we were worrying about you, too, Mom. You look real tired. Did you eat anything? I made pesto for dinner."

Eve looked at her daughter with wonder, realizing those tantalizing, homey smells from the hall had come from her own kitchen. How had she ever managed to raise such a girl as this? This was a woman she wanted as her friend.

"You're an angel of mercy. So, tell me, how was school?"

Bronte's face lit up and she rushed into a long monologue about the new year at her new high school. She flowed from one topic to another but all Eve heard was a musical backdrop to the vision of Bronte's face, animated, alive with curiosity and excitement again after a long year of apathy and sadness. When Bronte finished, Eve reached out and hugged her again.

"Why'd you do that?"

"No reason. Just because I love you."

Bronte blushed but rather than spurn her, she smiled.

Finney turned around and waved, acknowledging her presence.

"Hey, tiger," Eve called out. "So....?"

His dark-brown eyes, so much like Tom's, sparkled with news. "I made the team."

"Oh? You just made the team?" piped in Bronte, looking as proud as a mother. "He's first string."

Finney had always been a natural athlete but he was also naturally modest. He never would have boasted that fact but she could tell he was pleased because a streak of red bloomed over his cheekbones and he looked so much like his father at that moment she felt choked.

"I'm so proud of you," she said. Then, because she wanted to keep Tom alive in the minds and hearts of his children she said, "Your father would have been so proud of you, too."

Finney's face pinched. He nodded curtly, then caught her eye. On a corny, emotional impulse she opened her arms and was delighted that he rose with fluid grace, stepped into them and allowed her to give him the briefest of kisses. She played fair, relinquishing him quickly. Then sighing, she leaned against the arm of the sofa, overcome with love for him. He was her own, sweet Finney again. Always the loner, he had gone quietly off to lick his wounds over his father's death, hibernating in his cave. Now he had emerged again, a young man. Ah, the resilience of youth.

He turned and moved on to the kitchen. His new friends were tripping over themselves to catch Finney's attention, to bask in his glow.

Bronte turned her attention back to her friend, as well, and their project. Within moments, Eve was invisible in her own home. She marveled at how she could seemingly float unobserved from one room to the next while her children's lives spun around her in their separate orbits. And wasn't that how nature intended it to be?

Eighteen

New Beginnings

Glenn Lake, Michigan
September 12, 1998

Dear Book Club,

The equinox is approaching! The swallows have
already departed. The leaves are dry on the limb and
trimmed with gilt. The little nut squirrels are plump,
busily gathering provisions for the long winter ahead.

Come to my cottage for the next Book Club meeting!

We'll eat savory meals and take end-of-summer
dips in the lake. We'll dance and sing and roast
marshmallows around a campfire while we tell our
own stories.

Please come! We'll be like those gray squirrels
and swish our bushy tails and gather our harvest under a full moon. We shall feast, I promise!

Love, Doris

A trumpeting coming from the north heralded the Book Club as they packed suitcases and coolers crammed with food and wine into Eve's wagon. Midge pointed to the piercing-blue sky and called, "Look! Look!"

Eve, Annie and Gabriella stopped what they were doing to watch in an awed silence the formation of geese pass in an undulating skein on their way to points south. The long-necked birds were calling out the alert to all who listened that a cold wind was coming, not far behind.

No one spoke as the geese's calls grew faint and the birds became specks in the distant sky. Another season was past. Time flew by. The summer had ended. They'd had so many plans! Their hearts replied, *Too soon! Too soon!* as they strained to catch the last glimpse of wing and the echo of the call.

Annie broke the introspective mood with a slap on the roof of the car and called, "Let's go, girls! Time's a-wastin'. We're bucking the system and heading north!"

The festive mood was tugged back as they turned their eyes from the sky to smile at each other with an unspoken understanding. Chatting happily, they loaded up the car. They also brought with them all their dreams and sorrows, a few problems and the odd collection of funny stories that they'd stored in their hearts like a scrapbook. Just maybe they'd be brave enough to share these, too.

None of them knew quite what to expect from this girls' weekend, but as they took their seats and buckled their seat belts, they felt like wild geese in formation, flying wing to wing, migrating to a place of refuge.

They talked nonstop as they pushed past the tentacles of the city, off the highway, then onto two-lane country roads. Rolling down their windows they welcomed the sunshine on their faces and smelled the sweet scent of green. Signs of fall were more evident here than in the city. Cornstalks stood dry and brittle, plucked clean of their harvest. Fields of bright-yellow sunflowers that once smiled at the sun now drooped their heads, their season done. Everywhere were signs that the summer was over and harvest time was upon them.

The sun, however, was in a mischievous mood, playing tricks with the weather. The sky was cerulean, the weather unseasonably warm and dry. "Indian summer!" Eve exclaimed.

After two hours they turned off the main road onto a dirt one that twisted its way through a shady tunnel made by the leaves of maples and poplars and elms that bordered it, sometimes too closely. Occasionally the car rolled over a large, cragged root that had stretched onto the road to act as a speed bump.

Eve slowed to a crawl. They passed a few small, tilting cottages built generations before, made one more turn, then spied the quaint, tidy hamlet of cottages and a few large houses that encircled Glenn Lake. Though no one said it, they all felt as though they were leaving their old world with all its problems and urgencies behind and entering a new, peaceful one. A Brigadoon of their own making.

Doris stood at the end of the short driveway before her white cottage wearing a long, plum-colored cotton dress and a broad-rimmed straw hat encircled with bright silk flowers. She was waving her hands over her head in welcome as they pulled up. Eve gave three short honks. Annie leaned out of her window and called out, "Here comes the gaggle of geese!"

It had been nearly a month since their reunion in the hospital but when they hugged and kissed cheeks they all exclaimed how it seemed like only yesterday. The little white cottage gleamed with a fresh coat of paint. Doris's cheery impatiens and bright-yellow marigolds were at their peak, thriving in their fertile oasis by the front door. They were a sharp contrast to the dry, brittle grass, yellowed milkweed and spurts of thistle that grew tough and sparse between rocks near the slope.

Everyone—except Annie, who was forbidden to lift any-thing—lugged suitcases and coolers from the back of the wagon along with the treasures they couldn't resist pur-chasing from farm stands en route. Doris's mouth fell open when she saw the bags of late-season vegetables, a bushel of apples, bunches of grapes and pots of hearty mums.

"You'll have to bring food home," Doris said, wagging her finger. "I've been cooking all week!" She led them along the flagstone walkway from the stark rear of the house to the open, cheery front that faced the lake.

"Don't worry," Annie said behind her, holding the arm-ful of dried flowers she was allowed to carry. "I'm starved and will eat all the leftovers." Everyone was glad to hear this, worried as they were over her scrawny frame. The radiation had brought her down to mere bones and her gorgeous hair had thinned and was cut short, resembling the dry hay they'd passed in the fields. But everyone was careful not to mention it, choosing instead to echo her words about being starved.

"Leave your troubles at the door!" Doris called out as she opened the front door, pointing to the overhead sign. The women loved the dented, rusted sign instantly and promptly obeyed, laughing loudly, bursting into the first of many stories that would be told that weekend.

Eve relished the joy bubbling in the house, feeling a bit overcome. She wrapped her arms around herself and qui-etly walked around the large, sunny front room of the cot-tage. She adored the comfortable, mismatched sofas tossed with several bright colorful pillows, the game table in the corner and the huge stone fireplace that separated the living room from the kitchen. At the front of the cottage was a large expanse of sparkling glass that opened to a broad wooden deck perched high on a slope overlooking Glenn

Lake. Three Adirondack chairs and a hammock faced the
lake. Every surface was spotlessly clean, the lace at the
windows was crisp white, fresh flowers had been gathered
and placed in vases and she could smell a hot lunch in the
oven.

Doris's touch was everywhere and Eve was instantly
relieved by the obvious signs of her friend's healthy mind-
set. Eve had heard about Doris's cottage for years but had
never been able to come up in the past. With a busy husband and two children's summer schedules, it had never
worked out. She hoped this was the first visit of many in
the future, a first step to rekindle their friendship, to re-
connect after this year of transitions.

"Everyone, pick a number from the hat for a room as-
signment," Doris called out. "It's luck of the draw. We're
doubling up tonight so I hope no one snores!"

After they finished the first of the many feasts Doris
would cook them, they changed into their swimsuits. Sated
and serene, they meandered down the long flight of
wooden stairs and across the wobbly dock to spread out
on towels and bask in the sun. Women being women, they
checked each other out in their suits. Doris wore a funky,
navy, dotted Swiss tank suit that she claimed she'd pulled
out of an old trunk at the cottage.

"Very retro chic, don't you think?" asked Doris.

Midge swore she saw Doris's mother in that suit back
in the sixties, which set them all howling.

"There's no escaping our mothers," Midge said with a
shake of her head and a hearty laugh, but there wasn't a
hint of maliciousness.

Gabriella wore a brightly colored Hawaiian floral one-
piece. Midge and Annie wore plain black one-pieces. Annie grumbled that because of her scar, her bikini days were
over, so Eve wore one in her honor. There was no sucking

in of the stomachs or worrying if their thighs were too fat
or their butts too broad.

"Those days are over," Midge officially declared, to
which they all murmured, "Thank God!"

Doris passed around straw hats and suntan lotion as they
verbally passed around games of trivia. "What's your favorite movie?" "When was your first kiss?" Silly games,
but the playing acted as a subtle tool to weave them tighter
together. As they lay massaged by the warm rays of the
sun, they relaxed and shared hitherto unknown minutia
about themselves and their lives—those little, revealing details only best friends know. And in the telling, each felt
reacquainted with herself as well.

When Eve, Midge and Gabriella went into the lake for
a swim, Doris stayed behind with Annie. Annie lay against
a beach chair, half drowsing in the sun under an enormous
straw hat that spread shade over her shoulders.

"I'm so glad you came," Doris began, her tone indicating that she wanted a personal moment with Annie,
away from the others. She poured water, keeping her hands
busy. "I wasn't sure you'd be able to, so soon after surgery. Or even if you'd want to. How are you feeling? The
stairs weren't too much for you?"

Annie shook her head and pried open an eye. "No, I'm
fine, really," she replied in a lazy drawl. "I get tired
quicker and there's still tenderness, of course, but the doctor wants me up and around. As long as I don't overdo.
And with John at home and Gabriella here, there's no
chance of that happening." She chuckled and smiled
warmly. "And Doris, I really wanted to come."

Doris laughed lightly, relieved that the old tenseness between them was gone and they'd made it through their
first solo session since that infamous Fourth of July. Doris
knew that she herself had changed, but so had Annie. She
wasn't subdued, exactly, but Doris thought she was more

reserved, not quite so quick to mouth out an opinion or a wisecrack. They talked comfortably awhile, then slipped into an equally comfortable silence, just friends sitting side by side listening to the shrieks and calls of the swimmers cavorting in the lake. When the others sputtered and splashed back to shore, the two reached out to briefly touch each other's hand in mute acknowledgment.

The lake was quiet. Most of the houses had been closed up for the summer and those few hearty souls who remained year long had grown bored with summer and were busy indoors. The first blush of fall was visible in the palette of color encircling the lake: the reds of maples, the yellows of poplars, the blending of orange, ocher and rose from the varying shrubs.

The air cooled sharply as the afternoon waned on and the sun lowered, another sure sign of fall. Steam rose from the warm lake, foglike, and from somewhere they could smell the familiar pungent smoke of leaves being burned. Climbing from the lake, the three women wrapped themselves up in towels still warm from the sun, and all of them gathered their sundries and returned to the cottage at a leisurely pace to change into jeans, sweaters and warm socks. Someone mentioned how she felt like they were at camp, heading back to their cabins.

On their pillows they found invitations to a tea party. They were hand-painted with scenes from *Alice in Wonderland*, only in this version the Dormouse, the White Rabbit and the Mad Hatter were all women. With each invitation came a long, multicolored twine necklace attached to a playing card, each one a different ace. They were instructed to wear the necklaces and follow the directions to the party.

"Step outside the front door," read Eve aloud. Gabriella, Annie and Midge clustered around her. "Walk six paces east, then look up."

"Look up? Those directions sound like they're from Wonderland," said Gabriella, eyes round as teacups.

"Curiouser and curiouser," Eve exclaimed, delighted, as she slipped the twine necklace and the ace of diamonds over her head and took off on the adventure.

"I hope Doris hasn't been eating too many wild mushrooms up here," Annie joked as she followed, noticing with a perverse pleasure that she got the ace of hearts and not the ace of spades. "It's been a long time since I took that kind of trip."

Midge and Gabriella started singing "White Rabbit" from Jefferson Airplane as they took up the rear.

At the end of six paces they came to an enormous, ancient maple tree with limbs that stretched far into the sky and over the lake. A ladder perched against the broad trunk led to a sprawling tree house made of fresh cut lumber. Doris peeked out from a small window lined with blue gingham curtains.

"Curtains," muttered Midge with affection. "Only Doris!"

"Come on up!" she called, then made a face and pointed to the wooden sign nailed over the doorway. Printed in bold, childlike letters were the words: No Boys Allowed.

"Is it safe?" Gabriella asked, scrunching her lips with doubt. Midge and Eve looked up with equal consternation written on their faces.

"Oh, don't be such babies," Annie chided them, reaching for the ladder.

"Annie, are you sure?"

"Sure I'm sure." Annie's face was flushed with pleasure and her old spark was back in her eyes. "Doris, what a! This is so cool. A tree house! I always wanted a tree use when I was a kid."

"So did I," called back Doris, stretching out a hand to guide Annie safely in. "I built this one myself."

"No kidding?" Annie's eyes gleamed with respect. "Good for you!"

Doris's chest rose with pride.

As Eve climbed rung after rung she felt a light-head-edness, as though she were going deeper and deeper into the rabbit hole. Up and down were all mixed up here beyond the looking glass. She felt Doris's firm grip on her arm as she guided her inside the tree house. Crawling in on all fours, she cautiously tested the wood's firmness and checked out the nails and supports. It was a charming and secure fort, built squarely on a broad base of mighty limbs. Even the planks of wood at the ceiling were lovingly painted sky-blue with fluffy white clouds. She smiled and joined the others sitting Indian-style, knee to knee, around the snowy white linen tablecloth.

It was a tea party they'd never forget. Doris served fragrant Darjeeling tea in dainty china teacups, tiny water-cress and cream cheese sandwiches, and flaky, buttery scones dotted with currants. They continued on with their stories, beginning with amusing vignettes of their children then gradually moving on to the tales of their own childhood. By the time the tea leaves lay cold in empty cups the stories grew more ribald as they traveled back to those earlier days, acting more like children than they did as children. They laughed so hard they clutched their sides and tears pooled in their eyes as they confessed secrets they swore they'd never reveal. The first adolescence, they all agreed, was mere fodder for this glorious second one.

Their past, present and future blended together in the stories. They talked on and on as they moved from the tree house to the cottage to eat dinner, then talked some more as they put on warm jackets and bug spray and headed back down to the lakeside. They carried with them bottles of wine, a pack of matches and a bag of marshmallows. And more stories. It was as if they'd all been bottled up like vintage champagne just waiting for someone to uncork them and allow the bubbles to erupt.

The night fell around them, thick and heavy as a blanket. Overhead the stars shone with a brilliance only seen in the country. As Doris lit the prepared logs in a circle of large white rocks, Eve began singing old songs. Knowing the words, the others joined in, flirting with harmony and leaning on each other's shoulders. The sun, swimming, laughter, wine and countless stories played together in their minds until their thoughts were as filmy as the Milky Way. At last their stories wound down, fully played out, the finale punctuated by wide-mouthed yawns. They sat in a chummy peace around the campfire while their drowsy comments seemed to float in the air.

"Thank you, Doris, for this wonderful day," Eve said.

"And for all you've done," added Gabriella. "You thought of everything."

"It's been such a short time but I feel so refreshed," Midge said on a sigh. "Like I've been up here for weeks."

"It's the mental distance," Doris said. "A separation from the everyday. I needed a lot more time than all of you to rid myself of the Furies, but I did, and my mind is my own again."

"Let's do this every year," Gabriella suggested suddenly, leaning forward into the light of the fire to stick a marshmallow on the end of her stick. "Doris, I hereby volunteer your adorable cottage!"

"I'd love that," Doris replied. "I was hoping you'd all feel that way. This can be our first annual equinox Book Club meeting. We won't read a book. We'll just tell our own private stories."

"Those are the best, anyway."

"As long as they have happy endings."

"Maybe not always happy, but satisfying."

"Yeah, that's good enough in real life."

"I don't want to go home tomorrow."

"Careful. Retreats can be dangerous. You never want to go back to the real world," Doris said wistfully. "But sooner or later winter comes with all that snow and ice and it gets pretty lonely cut off from the outside."

"Sounds like you've given this some thought," Midge said in a gentle voice.

"I have," Doris replied in kind. "I've spent a long summer up here. That's a lot of time to spend alone. I don't want to be alone anymore. I miss my children. My life." She paused. "I've decided to divorce R.J."

"Are you sure?" Annie asked after the initial rush of comments of surprise.

"Yes, as sure as I can be of anything in life. I'm no the same person I was when I left, I know that. I don' know what to expect, how things will be. When I sit an think about it I only get apprehensive and edgy and that' no help. So I'm going to pack up the cottage and go bacl home. When I get there I'll just have to take it one day a a time."

"So will we all," Eve said. "I'm not the same perso I was when Tom was alive, or than I was early this summe when I moved into my condo and got a job. And I won be the same person next year when we meet around th campfire. My story will change, and so will yours. We' just go on changing, making a new set of choices, the living them out. That's what life is anyway, just a lor string of choices."

"Well, I certainly hope we all keep evolving," Midg said. "Consider the alternative."

Doris moved toward the fire to stoke the embers. Spar shot into the air like fireflies.

"Let's all tell one more story," she said, settling ba

in her chair. "Of a sort. Tomorrow we're all going home. Summer is over and I'm wondering… What are you all going to do when you get home? What are your plans? Now that my babies are grown, I've got time to think about what I want to do with the rest of my life. I'm going back to school. I never graduated from college and I always felt bad about that. So I figured that was a good start."

"Good for you," Eve exclaimed, understanding that particular awakening fully.

"My mother is staying in Chicago permanently," Midge announced with a sigh of resignation. "But she's not the same woman I grew up with. She's more frail. I think she needs me now more than I need her and that, ladies, is a strange set of affairs for us. In fact, I think we've both mellowed."

"Well, I've got some good news," announced Gabriella. "Fernando is going for a final interview at a job he really wants. I've got my fingers, legs, arms and eyes crossed and I've lit every candle at Ascension Church. If he gets it, and he thinks he will, I'm going to cut back my hours. Spend more time with my family. I want my kitchen back!"

After the commiserating chuckles there was a heavy silence. Everyone was waiting for Annie to speak. She took her time, but when she did, her voice was soft yet steady.

"I suppose now's as good a time as any to tell you," she began. She poked a stick in the fire, staring at the flames. "Everything is up in the air right now. I didn't mention it to you, Doris, but John has left R.J.'s firm. He's looking at firms all around the country now…but we both know it will be hard for me to leave Chicago. Not only because of my law practice, but you guys are the only real family I have. It will be really hard for me not to have you nearby, especially now." Emotion shook her voice so she paused to regain control. Her face settled and she tossed the stick into the fire with a jaunty flip of her wrist.

"Once I get the all-clear from Dr. Gibson, I'm taking an extended leave from work and John's taking me on the road. He's really psyched. Every day he buys me something new for the trip. When he brings it home, his eyes are lit up like a cub scout. I've got polar fleece everything and space-age liners so my fingers and tootsies don't get cold, my own Swiss Army knife with more gadgets than I know what to do with, and a first-aid kit that makes my makeup bag look huge. He goes nuts for all those little navigational and camping tools, the teenier the better. He fondles this state-of-the-art pocket-size radio like it's a woman." She snorted and shook her head. "It's neat to see him so excited again. We're just gonna head west, see the sites, stop when we want to, take loads of pictures like all the other tourists and…" She raked her hair back from her head and shrugged. "I want to see my parents," she said in a brutally honest tone. Then, as if flicking on a safety switch she added, "But if we come back chanting mantras and wearing beads, don't be surprised!"

With renewed enthusiasm the women began offering suggestions for Annie's trip. No one needed to discuss the uncertainties of a cancer survival because it was already understood between them. Only time would tell.

Doris glanced over her shoulder to see Eve sitting pensive and still in her chair, her small hands tucked between her knees, staring up at the Milky Way. Of all of them Eve could lapse into isolation the easiest. She'd unknowingly drift as far from the group as the stars overhead.

"Eve, what about you?" asked Doris, gently calling her back. "What are your plans when you return home?"

Eve blinked and lowered her gaze to face Doris. Doubt streaked across her features as swiftly as a falling star. The rest of the women hushed, curious to hear her answer.

She was silent a moment, then said, "I was just thinking about that. I don't have any, not really. I've had so many changes in my life, I don't think I want to make any more plans quite yet. I'm hoping for a little status quo."

"But Eve, change is a part of life," Midge said. "It's as inevitable as the changing of seasons. And," she added, striving for levity, "the changing of our bodies."

"I have an idea," Gabriella suggested with a lilt in her voice. Reaching into her pocket, she pulled out a small spiral pad of paper and said, "It's a game we used to play as children. I think it would be good for us right now. Everyone has to write down one wish for themselves on a piece of paper. Come on, Midge," she whined when Midge rolled her eyes. "Stop being such a curmudgeon. You'll enjoy it."

She ripped pieces of paper off and handed one to each woman. As the pen went around the circle, the women thought in silence, taking the game to heart. When everyone had written their wish on the paper, Gabriella told them to crumple the paper into a ball.

"Now you make the wish in your mind. Then you toss the paper ball into the fire, like this." Gabriella closed her eyes and leaned nearer the fire. Her long dark hair blended with the night like a veil and her face glowed over the red kindling flames. As she silently made her wish, her lips moved and her brow creased in fervent thought. They all leaned near, sucked into the heightened suspense of the moment.

"Look at us," Midge murmured sotto voce. "We're like a coven of witches bent over the fire chanting a spell."

"I like to think of us as wise women," Eve countered with a smirk.

Gabriella's lips twitched but she stayed in character. Opening her eyes, she tossed the tiny ball into the fire with dramatic flair.

The paper caught flame instantly and curled, sending sparks into the air. They all leaned back with a collective sigh.

"See? Isn't that fun? Now, who's next?" Gabriella asked.

One by one they tossed their paper balls into the fire and watched their wishes rise to the heavens as small sparks of flame.

Eve's glance moved from one face to the next. Her friends encircled the fire, each face flushed with heat and hope. Such was the nature of wishes and dreams, she thought to herself. A wish upon a star, a penny tossed into a fountain, the chasing of a rainbow—all such wishes were small acts of faith that anything was possible.

Suddenly the fire crackled and the log's center exploded with a ripping crash, sending a plume of countless fiery sparks into the black sky. Everyone leaned back and gasped, "Oooh," as they watched the impressive shower of scarlet rise high to mingle with stars.

Eve's face tingled and her heart raced as she stared with amazement at the glowing fire. That had to be a sign! On her slip of paper she'd wished for Tom to somehow guide her in her next step. She'd asked for some sign—and he'd sent one. Eve brought her palms to her warm cheeks and felt her heart rise up in thanks. Her journey from that fateful day last June to this moment was still ongoing. Tom had left her alone so suddenly. It had taken all this time and the help of her friends and good books, for her to reconcile that. And yet, her soul couldn't rest until she said goodbye to her husband.

Eve had a plan. She knew what it was she had to do when she went home.

It was a frigid November night. The stars shone crisp like ice shards in the sky. In the distance, mighty Lal

Michigan roared and crashed like a velvety fist against the breakwater of granite boulders. Everyone could feel the icy spray against their cheeks as they curled collars around their necks and faced the water. The trees lining the park had finished their season of green and celebration and had long since dropped their autumn finery. They stood, stripped and bare, in somber gray—an honor guard for this requiem.

Eve spotted the orange flare wave from some eight-hundred feet farther down Lake Michigan's shore, a signal that everyone should come together. An anticipatory hush settled over them. The time was drawing near. They gathered close to form a tight circle on the grassy slope near the beach. Everyone was here tonight: Annie and John, Midge, Susan and Edith, Gabriella, Fernando, and her four children, Doris and Bobby Jr. Sarah and Bronte stood together, arms linked.

She stood flanked by the two men in her life. Finney, on her left, stood as tall as she. On her right was Paul, a silent sentinel keeping a respectful distance. She wanted him here tonight, for her.

Suddenly the silence was rent with a percussive *whomp*. Eve felt her throat tighten as she followed the silent ascent of a faint orange glow shooting skyward. There followed the burst of a symmetric flower, a sphere of sparkling stars that shot out across the northern sky. The glowing gold spray changed to delicate streamers that draped to the ground in the shape of a weeping willow.

Tears flowed down her cheeks as she observed the wondrous twinkling of gold dust that seemed to hang in the sky forever, knowing that Tom's ashes were now mingling with the stars.

She felt Finney's arms tighten around her waist, saw his face illuminated in the glow of the firework, a face so like his father's. Bronte came to her side to join them, wrapping her long arms around both of them, locking them together as a family while Tom's ashes sprinkled down into the welcoming water of the lake.

"Goodbye, Tom," Eve said at last, knowing in her heart that she was heard.

Then she wiped her eyes, kissed her children's cheeks, called out to her friends, and taking Paul's hand, headed for home.

Epilogue

All stories come to an end. That moment when we sigh
and close the book, perhaps sit back in our chair and rest
our palm over the cover, is met with quixotic emotions.
On the one hand, we're satisfied if the author successfully
tied up loose ends, turned a memorable phrase and rewarded the hero's moral choice with his heart's desire. Yet
we're also saddened that the adventure is over.

Sometimes when we see that we only have a few pages
left we slow down, savoring each word, staving off the
inevitable. The characters we've come to know and love
are no longer part of our lives. This can leave us with a
certain longing. Perhaps we'll open the book again and
skim through it, searching out favorite passages to kindle
again those powerful emotions. But the passion is never
stirred quite as strong the second time around.

So it is with life. We rush through the days that we're
given, eager to engage in the conflicts and passions, to
push through and conquer and see how it all ends. When
suddenly the end is in sight, we're surprised. We stall,
frantically savoring each moment. The sun shines brighter,
the smiles appear more tender and we listen for words of

love with an urgency that would be poignant if it were not so heartbreaking.

So it was with me after Tom's death. In retrospect, I look at myself and my friends and I think that some of us are offered early warnings. The death of a loved one, a serious illness, the struggle of a marriage, or the despair of loneliness—as tragic as these events are, they serve to box us in as clearly as any clever plot structure, forcing us to make a choice.

I choose to live. Each day to the hilt. I want to hug my children close, kiss my lover passionately, attack my work, relish my books, and laugh heartily or blubber like a baby with my friends.

Isn't life grand?

THE BOOK CLUB

MARY ALICE MONROE

Topics
for
Discussion

1. The books, poems and verses selected for each chapter were chosen by Monroe to structure the novel around the "Book Club" theme. How does the selected book or poem at the chapter heading influence the action within the chapter? How does this structure affect the novel as a whole?

2. In Chapter 16, the women offer several reasons why they think Doris might be depressed. Are they accurate? How well does the reader know Doris by this point? Have you recognized these symptoms in women you know?

3. Midge states to the club, *"I'm not sure it's always a good thing to confront friends."* She is referring to honesty, yet Midge *is* indirectly confrontational with barbs and humor. Discuss various forms of confrontation between the friends in this book.

4. Women are traditionally acknowledged to be skilled in making and sustaining relationships. How do the relationships between the women of the club affect their individual relationships with husbands, children, loved ones?

5. Gabriella states in Chapter 16 that *"Books can really influence us."* Throughout the novel, the books the women read in the club influence them. Cite examples. Do you find this to be true in your life? After Annie's surgery, the group wants to choose a book to help Annie through her upcoming struggles. How can books promote growth and healing? What do you think of the club's desire to read and discuss the Bible?

6. *"She heard the calling in her heart, in her soul, in every fiber of her being."* This describes Eve in Chapter 9. What is the calling Eve hears? How does it compare to the calling Buck hears in Jack London's novel *The Call of the Wild*?

7. *"When lovely woman stoops to folly and... Paces about her room again, alone,"* How does this line from "The Waste Land" describe Annie and her behavior at the Bridges' party and the aftermath? Doris? What lessons did they eventually learn from these "follies"?

8. Annie tells Doris in Chapter 14, *"So many women give, give, until they have nothing left. Then one day they wake up and look in the mirror and don't know their own reflection."* Later in the book, Doris remembers this statement and looks into the mirror (Chapter 16). Describe her reaction to her own reflection at this important turning point. Doris refers to this statement again in her letter to the book club (Chapter 18). How has the character grown and evolved in the time between these references?

9. *"Weeping comes in the evening, but joy comes in the morning,"* refers to the epiphany Eve experiences in Chapter 15 when she realizes truths about herself, her husband, and their marriage. What were these truths? How is this a turning point for the character Eve? Discuss the observation: *"Now she was left to regret having lost the opportunity to find that young man again in the middle-aged one, the dreamer she'd fallen in love with."* Do you think this is a common observation for women who have been married for many years?

10. In Chapter 16, Eve states, *"I believe that all women have these little epiphanies all throughout their lives."* Do you agree and if so, discuss what these epiphanies are. At what points do you believe women experience them? If not, why not?

11. In Chapter 16, Doris is alone with "the yellow wallpaper." Later, she feels that *"she wasn't running away from anything,*

except perhaps the yellow wallpaper." This refers to a short story written in 1892, *The Yellow Wall-Paper* by Charlotte Perkins Gilman. This story powerfully traces a woman's descent into madness. How can a woman's home become a prison rather than a sanctuary? Doris believes: *"she was left alone polishing furniture in this formidable, huge, empty house. Without a room of her own."* Compare and contrast Doris's mood and thoughts in the cottage versus her large home in the city.

12. Three heroines from classic novels are discussed by the book club in Chapter 16: Emma from *Madame Bovary*, Anna from *Anna Karenina*, and Edna from *The Awakening*. What tragic ending did these three women share? Discuss the similarities and disparities between their situations and the choices each of them made. How did the social and moral conventions of their time period influence their choices? Might their choices have been different had these women lived in the twenty-first century? Consider Doris's choice in the lake in light of this discussion.

13. Mothers and daughters are a continuing thread in this novel. Compare and contrast the relationships between Eve and Bronte, then Midge and Edith.

14. In the Epilogue, Eve states how tragedies *"serve to box us in as clearly as any clever plot structure, forcing us to make a choice."* At the climax a character reveals her true self. Trace and discuss how each of the women in the club were forced to make a choice. Did you agree with their choice? What did Annie's choice by the poolside reveal about her character?

15. The characters we care most about are often those we most identify with. Which character did you identify with? In the novel, the characters were not only good and loving, but at times, spiteful and angry. How did the characters' flaws bring them to life as much as their goodness?

16. How did Midge feel she was different from the other women of the group? At a turning point, Midge recognized her need for intimacy in her life. Discuss this term, "intimacy" and how it applies to her choice.

17. This novel is a story of women facing change: in their looks, in their health, in their relationships, in their goals and dreams and in their self-perceptions. How have some of the characters moved from dependence, accommodation and denial to independence, original thought and acceptance? Do you think this is a natural evolution that comes with age or not? Discuss the evolution of Eve, Doris, Annie, Midge and Gabriella from the first chapter, "End of Story" to the last, "New Beginnings," and why Eve claims, *"there is no resolution."*